The One

MARIA REALF

A division of HarperCollins*Publishers*
www.harpercollins.co.uk

Harper*Impulse* an imprint of
HarperCollins*Publishers*
The News Building
1 London Bridge Street
London SE1 9GF

www.harpercollins.co.uk

This paperback edition 2018

1

First published in Great Britain by HarperCollins*Publishers* 2018

A catalogue record for this book
is available from the British Library

ISBN:9780008278960

Set in Birka by Palimpsest Book Production Limited,
Falkirk, Stirlingshire

Printed and bound by CPI Group (UK) Ltd, Croydon CR0 4YY

MIX
Paper from
responsible sources
FSC™ C007454

This book is produced from independently certified FSC™ paper
to ensure responsible forest management.

For more information visit: www.harpercollins.co.uk/green

The One

nce graduating with a degree in multi-media journalism,
aria Realf has worked on a staff or freelance basis for
any of the UK's best-known magazines, including *The*
ail on Sunday's *YOU Magazine, Cosmopolitan,*
osmopolitan Bride, Fabulous, Marie Claire, Now and *You*
Your Wedding. In her spare time, Maria is also an
-round movie obsessive, theatre lover and karaoke enthu-
st.

@MariaRealf
www.facebook.com/mariarealf
vw.mariarealf.com

For Rob, my love,
Zac, my treasure,
And Stephen, my hero

1

13 weeks to go . . .

Finally, I've found The One! Lizzie Sparkes gazed at the full-length mirror in the changing room, hardly daring to believe that it was her own reflection staring back. The Grecian gown was perfect, with tiny beads twinkling along the asymmetric strap, and a delicate train skimming the carpet as though it was practising for the Oscars. It wasn't too tight, it wasn't scratchy and it didn't make her look like a human doily. The only downside was the eye-wateringly expensive price, but she had decided to overlook that part. *It'll be worth it when Josh sees me walking down the aisle*, she reassured herself, a lump rising in her throat. *I look almost . . . beautiful.*

She was afraid to step out from the safety of the cubicle, in case the look on her mum's face – or Megan's – betrayed the fact that they didn't feel the same. They were both polite when it came to watching her try on wedding gowns, and had patiently sat through some 30 or so now, but she knew them well enough to read the signs. When her mum wasn't keen on a dress, she blinked

1

three or four times in quick succession, while Megan pulled a weird half-smile that made her look as though she'd had a dodgy facelift. It was a total giveaway, every time.

Lizzie drew a deep breath and swept back the purple velvet curtain. She took a slow step out into the centre of the boutique, her dark hair swishing loosely behind her like a glossy veil. 'W-O-W,' said Megan.

Her mum promptly burst into tears, which was a more confusing reaction.

'Mum? Don't you like it?'

There was a long pause while Lynda Sparkes rummaged through her overcrowded handbag, before pulling out a crumpled tissue and nearly poking herself in her right eye. 'Oh, Elizabeth,' she sniffed, mascara smudging into her crows' feet. 'You look like a movie star.'

Yep, this is definitely The One . . .

The store manager tottered over in her nude skyscraper heels, clearly anticipating a hefty commission. 'That dress looks *amazing* on you,' she gushed. 'It fits so well, you'd hardly need any alterations. We could maybe just take it up an inch or two.' She bent down and folded the hem with her hands by way of demonstration, though it didn't seem to make a great deal of difference. 'What do you think?'

'I'll take it.' The words popped out of Lizzie's mouth before she had a chance to peek again at the price tag.

'Excellent!' The manager clapped her manicured hands

loudly and two blonde minions, one tall and one tiny, raced over. 'Let's open some champagne, please, for Ms . . .'

'Sparkes. Soon to be Cooper.'

'Of course. I assume we're all having some bubbly?'

'You assume right,' said Megan. She was not the kind of girl to turn down champagne at any hour, especially if it was on the house.

'Marvellous.' Moments later the two blondes reappeared, one bearing a tray of glasses and the other carrying a bottle of fizz. The manager made an elaborate show of popping the cork and pouring it out with a flourish. 'Well, congratulations!'

'Thank you,' smiled Lizzie, edging away from the drinks so as not to spill anything down the pristine white silk. After six long months of searching, she was still in shock that she had found the dress of her dreams. Everyone kept telling her that she would know the right one when she saw it, but she'd been starting to suspect that might be a bridal myth. Last week she'd had a nightmare that she arrived at the wedding in a gown made from loo roll, which began to unravel in front of all their guests. She'd woken up covered in sweat and couldn't get back to sleep, but Josh thought it was hilarious when she relayed the story the next morning. 'Don't worry, I'll still marry you if you turn up in Andrex,' he joked. 'And think how much money we'd save . . .'

It was easy for him to laugh, of course; he'd chosen his suit after just two shopping trips and looked like a male model in it, the slimline cut complementing his lean, athletic build. 'You're not supposed to upstage the bride,' she'd only half-joked when he tried it on, feeling the pressure to pick an equally special outfit increase tenfold. It was a huge relief to have finally found something so perfect.

'I can't believe you're getting married!' squealed Megan, the bubbliness of the champers already kicking in. 'And in that *fabulous* dress.' She glanced over at Mrs Sparkes, who had finally managed to stop sobbing long enough to take a sip of her drink. 'Mrs S, we're really going to have to get you some waterproof eye make-up.'

'Oh, I don't think I can manage anything else today, love. I'm completely shopped out.'

'Fair enough, but you'll want some for the wedding. I'll see what I can find at work.' Megan was a journalist for a popular style website, and was sent so many samples that her bathroom was starting to resemble the cosmetics hall at Harrods. The retail worth of her monthly beauty booty was probably twice her modest salary.

She turned her attention back to her friend. 'You'll need to start thinking about bridal make-up too, Lizzie – plus there's hair, underwear, shoes, not to mention my bridesmaid's outfit . . .'

'I think I'd better get out of this dress first,' said Lizzie. 'Can you give me a hand, Meg?'

'Sure, no problem. As long as I don't have to help you to the loo on the day.'

Just then Megan's mobile squawked like a melodramatic

duck, and they both burst out laughing. 'What on earth is that?' asked Lizzie.

'It's my new email alert,' grinned Megan, reaching for her phone. 'It quacks me up.'

'Oh, please stop. I swear your jokes are getting worse.' She waited for the witty riposte, but suddenly realised her friend was no longer smiling. In fact, all the colour had flooded from her face, leaving her skin whiter than the row of wedding dresses behind her. 'Megan? What's wrong?'

The sound of her name seemed to snap Megan out of her trance, and she shook her curly blonde bob. 'Nothing. It's not important. Now, where were we?' She put on her most lopsided smile, and Lizzie knew she was lying.

'You were about to stop being weird and tell me what's going on. Is everything OK?'

'Yes, everything's fine. I'll fill you in later.'

'Please fill me in now. You're starting to freak me out.'

Megan looked around nervously, as if hoping someone might interrupt this awkward exchange, but Mrs Sparkes was deep in conversation with the manager, waffling on about her own 1980s bridal gown.

'*Megan!* What's going on?'

'Alright, I'll tell you, but promise you won't stress out, OK?'

'Stress out about what?'

There was an uncomfortable pause. 'Alex is back.'

It took all of Lizzie's willpower not to vomit down the front of her dazzling new dress.

Lizzie tried to unlock the front door, her hand trembling so much she could barely insert the key. Megan's words replayed on a loop in her mind: *Alex is back.* For years, she had wanted to hear that more than anything in the world, but as a decade had ticked by she'd slowly swept aside the shards of her old life, carefully filing all thoughts of him away in the archives of her past.

What the hell is he doing here?

He had been in such a dark place the last time she'd seen him. She wondered what he would look like now; whether she would recognise him if they passed one another on the street. Perhaps he had gained weight or gone prematurely grey; maybe his casually cool wardrobe had been replaced by corporate suits or skin-tight gym gear. *I'd know those eyes, though*, she thought, momentarily closing her own. *I'd know them anywhere.*

She finally managed to wrestle open the door, stepping quietly into the snug Surrey home that she and Josh had moved into six months ago. Her lips moved on autopilot to shout a loving greeting, but today her tongue felt as paralysed as her brain, unable to process the million questions those three little words had unleashed. She decided to head upstairs for the sanctuary of the bathroom, where she could take a moment to compose herself – or at least throw up the butterflies swirling around in her gut. But before she could creep past the bedroom, a strong pair of arms bundled her up from behind.

'Trying to sneak past me, eh?' said Josh. 'And without even a kiss, too . . .'

Lizzie turned round and looked into his teasing brown eyes, her composure melting under the warmth of his unsuspecting smile. Confusion hit her like a right hook.

'I . . . um . . . I'm not feeling so great,' she said, taking a step back.

'Was it the tacos?' She shook her head. 'Now you mention it, you do look a bit pale. Come here.' He wrapped her tightly in a hug, stroking her hair rhythmically with his right hand. His skin smelled fresh, like mint shower gel, and she buried her face in his Diesel sweater, hoping to avoid further eye contact for a moment longer.

Half of her wanted to tell him the truth – the whole truth – but she didn't exactly know where to start. They had not talked much about her ex before: it was a painful can of worms she had sealed tightly shut, and Josh seemed to have the good sense not to prise it open. He knew there had been someone else – maybe even heard the name muttered by old friends – but until now Alex was merely the whispered ghost of a boyfriend past.

'Do you think it's all this rushing around for the wedding?' Josh unwittingly gave her an escape route, and she took it.

'Maybe. I am feeling a bit stressed.' She pulled back and rubbed her eyes. 'There's still so much to sort out with the flowers and invitations and everything. I think my Bridezilla hormones must be kicking in.'

Josh looked relieved. 'Freddie said that might happen.' His annoying best mate had only been married for nine months, but now acted like he was the world's leading authority on weddings. 'Maybe you need a bit of a break, like a spa weekend or something? I could do some invites, if you like.'

His concern only made her feel worse. *Just calm down*, she told herself. *Alex being back doesn't change anything. It's going to be fine.*

'I'm OK,' she said slowly. 'I was having a funny five minutes, that's all.' She forced a thin smile. 'But, actually, it would be great if you could help with the invites. Thank you.' Wedding admin wasn't exactly Josh's forte, as she'd found out when it came to sending the save-the-date cards, so she appreciated the offer.

'No problem.' He kissed her gently on the tip of her nose. 'Just let me know if there's anything else I can do.'

She ran her fingers through his sandy hair, which was looking adorably ruffled. 'Well, there is one thing while you're here . . .'

'Go on.'

'Kiss me.'

He took her in his arms and grinned. 'Honestly, woman, I thought you'd never ask . . .'

2

2 October 2002

Without warning, the bedroom door flew open and Megan flounced in, forcing Lizzie to look up from her well-thumbed copy of *Wuthering Heights*. 'Here's a thought,' Lizzie suggested affectionately. 'Perhaps you could learn to knock. I could have been naked or anything.'

'Like I haven't seen that before.'

'Yeah, well, you should probably knock before entering the bathroom as well.'

'Whatever . . .' Megan tossed her hair, making her sparkly top shimmer like something out of a pop video. 'I just wanted to tell you that I've had a great idea for this evening! Dominic's asked me to this karaoke night at Ignition and he's bringing his housemate, so I thought you could join us. Cab's coming in 45 minutes.' She beamed as though she'd just extended an invite to an all-expenses-paid cruise around the Caribbean.

Lizzie's heart plummeted. *Karaoke? You've got to be kidding.* She stretched out on the blue and white striped bedspread and faked a large yawn. 'I'm not really in the mood for another double date, Meg. No offence, but you know they never work out.'

'They haven't been that bad,' said Megan, looking insulted. 'Nathan seemed nice.'

'He's about 5ft 7.'

'And? So's Tom Cruise.'

'Which is fine for you. But I'm 5ft 10, in case you hadn't noticed. Without heels!'

'Well, Eric was tall,' she huffed.

'True, but I'm pretty sure Eric's gay.'

'What makes you think that?'

'He gave his phone number to our waiter!'

'Really? I don't remember.' Megan could conveniently forget anything if it didn't further her current plans. 'Anyway, this one will be different. You'll see.'

'I don't know . . .' Lizzie hesitated. 'I was kind of looking forward to just chilling out tonight.'

'Why? There'll be loads of time for that when you're old!' Megan strutted over to the beech Argos wardrobe and started rummaging around inside. 'You've got some gorgeous stuff in here, Lizzie,' she said, rifling her way along the rail. 'What's the point of buying dresses unless you bother to show them off? You can stay in and read tomorrow – it's not like Heathcliff's going anywhere.'

Just then there was a noise from upstairs, and the sound of Tom Jones singing *Sex Bomb* began to echo around the landing. Lizzie immediately knew what that track meant: their other housemate, a cheeky Welshman called

Gareth, had a hot date in his room, and any hope of a quiet night had now gone out of the window. A triumphant smile flickered across Megan's face.

'Fine, I'll get ready,' Lizzie grumbled, rolling off the bed and plugging in her hair straighteners. 'But you're going to owe me big time.'

Facing the wonky mirror in the bar's dimly lit loos, Lizzie applied a slick of lip balm and frowned at her reflection. Two tired brown eyes glared back at her in annoyance. She could have bet a month's rent before leaving the house that she wouldn't fancy Dominic's flatmate, and her instincts had been spot on. Though admittedly he wasn't the worst-looking guy Megan had ever tried to set her up with, he was clearly a complete sexist, and when he'd started on the subject of women's sport she'd had to make her excuses and escape to the ladies.

Give it one more hour out there and then you can leave, she promised herself. *Hopefully by then Gareth will have stopped his Sexbombathon, and you'll be able to go to bed in peace.*

She slipped the balm into the pocket of her vintage red tea dress, a total bargain she'd snapped up at Oxfam, then smoothed her hair and strode out of the door – smack bang into a barman carrying a tray full of drinks. Lizzie watched in horror as glasses came crashing down around them, spilling their contents everywhere in torturously slow motion. A lone Bacardi Breezer just managed to stay on the tray, wobbling defiantly from side to side like a skittle.

'I'm so sorry,' she winced, wondering why she'd ever agreed to leave her cosy bedroom. Her left arm felt cold and sticky. 'I . . . I didn't see you there.'

'Evidently,' he growled, surveying the front of his soaked black T-shirt.

'Are you alright? I'll pay for the drinks.' A surreptitious check of her dress revealed that he had borne the brunt of the spillage, which was both unfair and a big relief.

He set down the tray, glanced straight at her for a second, then surprised her with a wry smile. 'Don't worry about it,' he said, his voice low and smoky. 'There's no point crying over . . . well, two pints, a Hooch and what I think might have been a Malibu and Coke.' He sniffed the top of his T-shirt. 'Yep . . . coconut.'

Despite her mortification, Lizzie found herself laughing. 'If it's any consolation, I've always liked coconut. But I still feel terrible.'

'Don't. It's an occupational hazard.'

'What, spilled drinks or clumsy girls?'

'Both, I guess. Are you OK?'

'Yes – well, apart from my rubbish eyesight, obviously. I swear I'm not as drunk as you must think.'

He smiled again, and Lizzie noticed that he was quietly attractive, with unruly dark hair that flopped into striking blue-grey eyes, and a jawline scattered with stubble; not the pretentious, landscaped kind, but the sort that suggested he had better things to do than shave every morning. He was tall – she guessed around 6ft – with broad shoulders, and his damp T-shirt clung just tightly enough that she could tell he was in good shape. She was beginning to stare now, she knew, but she couldn't quite bring herself to look away.

In the end, he moved first, gesturing to the broken glass on the floor: 'Well, I suppose I'd better sort this lot out before someone loses a toe.'

'Yes, of course.' She paused. 'I really am sorry.'

'You said that already,' he teased. 'Maybe we'll bump into each other again sometime.' And with that he disappeared into a room behind the bar.

Realising that she hadn't even caught his name, Lizzie was surprised by the sudden surge of disappointment inside – but not half as surprised as when the karaoke compere made his next announcement: 'Alright, now I'm looking for Lizzie Sparkes . . . Lizzie Sparkes, please come up.' Lizzie looked round frantically, hoping by freak coincidence that someone else might share the same moniker, but then she spotted Megan and the boys howling with laughter.

'Oh, *there* you are, Lizzie,' shouted Megan, singling her out with an exaggerated pointing gesture. 'You're on.'

Lizzie tried frantically to get the attention of the chubby compere, wanting to let him know that it was all a stupid joke, but he interpreted her frenzied waving as a sign that she was coming and began to queue up the mysterious backing track. Blind panic set in. *What have they picked?*

The contents of her CD collection flashed before her eyes. *Britney Spears? Sugababes? S Club 7?* There was only one thing for it: she would have to go up there and put a stop to this confusion.

Taking a deep breath, she jostled her way up to the makeshift stage, a blush creeping across both cheeks. 'Look, I'm sorry, I think there's been a mistake . . .' she said to the host, but her voice was lost over the opening bars of the music as he thrust a microphone into her hand. Lizzie froze as she recognised the intro. It was *Tragedy*, a guilty pleasure she enjoyed playing on her Steps *Gold* CD – maybe a little too loudly if Megan had noticed – but would never dream of performing in the shower, let alone in public. The three cocktails she'd consumed earlier churned uneasily in her stomach.

Shit, shit, shit. I'm actually going to have to go through with this. The opening lines popped up on the ancient monitor in a garish shade of neon green, as if to further highlight her public humiliation.

Megan's going to meet with some kind of tragedy when we get home, that's for sure.

Mumbling along to the first verse, Lizzie tried to keep in time with the loud audio, her voice quivering almost as much as her legs. In desperation, she held out the microphone to the audience, encouraging her fellow students to sing along for the catchy chorus.

To her amazement, they did.

Seconds later Megan jumped up on stage beside her,

tucking a straw behind one ear like a headset mic and belting out the rest of the lyrics. A group of girls near the front stood to perform the Steps dance routine in perfect unison, as though they'd been rehearsing for precisely such an occasion.

Just when Lizzie was starting to think that this karaoke business wasn't all bad, the song came to an end and the audience went wild. 'Good work, ladies,' said the compere. 'Well, who's brave enough to come up and follow that? Looks like it's going to be Tony, taking us back to the 80s . . .'

'That was amazing!' said Megan, sauntering off stage with rock-star swagger. 'I didn't know you had it in you.'

'I didn't exactly have much choice,' replied Lizzie, not sure whether to hug her or slug her.

'Don't be mad. It was meant to be a joke. I never thought for a minute you'd actually get up there! I'd have stuck you in for two songs if I'd known you were going to bring the bloody house down.'

Lizzie smiled in spite of herself, still buzzing from the adrenaline. 'I guess it was kind of fun, wasn't it?'

'Steady on, Kylie.' Megan stopped and sniffed. 'Can you smell coconut?'

'I think that might be me. I knocked a tray of drinks everywhere just before you put me in for *Pop Idol*.'

'Oh, so you've really outdone yourself tonight, then?' They both cracked up and Lizzie realised she'd already forgiven her friend, though she wasn't exactly sure when.

'Yes, I have. So the next round's definitely on you.'

Suddenly Lizzie felt a tap on her shoulder, and spun around to face the enigmatic barman from earlier. *Damn, please say he didn't just see me making a fool of myself . . .* She could feel the hot blush seeping back, hoping the redness wouldn't be visible beneath the bar's crappy lighting.

He began to clap. 'I'm impressed. You didn't say you were going to sing.'

'I didn't know I was going to sing. My housemate stitched me up.' She motioned to Megan, who raised a quizzical eyebrow as she backed away, no doubt already planning a full interrogation as to the identity of this mystery man. 'I've never done anything like that before.'

'Well, the crowd certainly seemed to enjoy it.'

'Yeah, I suspect the alcohol might have had a lot to do with that.' She wished she were better at accepting compliments from attractive guys.

'So what do you do when you're not pursuing your pop career?' He leaned in to make himself heard as the karaoke kicked off again, and Lizzie could detect the subtle scent of leather, still imbued with a splash of coconut. The rest of the room blurred into the background.

'I'm at uni, studying English. Second year,' she shouted over the tinny backing track. Trying to chat in noisy bars was always tricky, but she wasn't ready to give up on this conversation just yet.

'How are you finding it?'

'Good,' she replied. 'Most of the time, anyway. How long have you worked here?'

'Only about six months.' He moved closer, his lips almost touching her ear. His breath felt warm against her cheek. 'I'm a student, too.'

'Doing what?'

'Scientology. With contemporary dance.'

'Very funny.'

'Oh, alright.' He gave an exaggerated sigh. 'Hospitality.'

'So you work here for experience?'

He laughed. 'Not really, more to pay the bills.' Lizzie immediately wished she hadn't sounded quite so naive.

Just then a bloke with a hairy beer belly protruding from his shirt interrupted their conversation. 'Hey, mate, could we get the same again over here?'

'Be right with you.' He smiled apologetically. 'Guess I've got to go. Maybe I'll see you around sometime?'

'Maybe you could see me at the weekend,' said Lizzie, surprised by the confident words spilling from her mouth. *Did I just ask him out?*

'Sounds great. I'm free Sunday. I'll give you my number.' He pulled a pen from his jeans and jotted the digits down on the back of a peeling coaster. 'I'm Alex, by the way. Alex Jackson.' He held out his right hand.

'I'm Lizzie,' she whispered, a faint current coursing through her fingers as she pressed her palm to his. 'Sparkes.'

3

12 weeks to go . . .

'*How* much?' Lizzie asked incredulously, fishing around in her wallet for more cash as the sales girl on the ticket desk drummed her long nails. 'What does that include?'

'That's just the admission fee,' the girl replied politely, taking Lizzie's notes and handing back a few loose coins in change. 'Everything else can be paid for inside the wedding fair.' She slid two fancy white tickets across the counter.

'What are these made from, real brides?' Lizzie grumbled. The two women behind coughed impatiently. 'Oh, alright, we're going,' she said, as Josh led her away from the queue by the elbow.

Stepping through the main entrance, Lizzie was struck by the sheer scale of the hall before them, which was filled with a seemingly endless succession of stalls: fairytale dresses floating on rails, chocolate fountains dripping with temptation, sweet bars bursting with candies of every colour, and travel agents barely visible behind huge piles of honeymoon brochures. The air hummed with the sound of thousands of brides and their entourages, all chattering loudly in chorus. It was an utterly surreal experience, as though one of her wedding magazines had sprung to life on steroids. She wasn't sure whether to dive in or bolt for the emergency exit.

'Remind me why we're here again?' she asked Josh. She had nearly passed out with shock that morning when he suggested they go along, and curiosity had compelled her to agree. She knew several of her friends had to bribe their fiancés with sexual favours just to get them within 50ft of a wedding fair.

'Well, I know you were worried there was still lots to do, so I thought we could come here and cross off a bunch of jobs in one go.' He reached for her hand, weaving his warm fingers through hers. 'Then you can relax and just look forward to it.'

'Ah, OK . . . makes sense, I guess.' Lizzie tried hard to shake a disloyal seed of suspicion. *Why's he acting like Mr Wedding all of a sudden?* Up until last week, Josh had shown zero interest in the finer details of the planning process. Sure, he was happy to get involved with the fun jobs, like booking the DJ and choosing a cake. But the moment she mentioned anything else – such as paying deposits or ordering stationery – he normally glazed over and went into lockdown. Then, since her little wobble at home last weekend, he kept asking if she was OK and if there were any jobs that needed doing. It wasn't that she was complaining, really – she was grateful he was making an effort – but his sudden attentiveness was strangely disconcerting, like he'd been invaded by obliging aliens.

To be fair, it didn't help that she seemed to have a defective bridal gene: she still couldn't tell the difference between cream and ivory, she didn't give a toss whether the chair bows were organza or satin, and something about those beady-eyed cake toppers was really starting to creep her out. Deep down, she had never pictured herself having the big, traditional wedding, but lately it seemed to be snowballing of its own accord. Back when she was with Alex, she used to imagine them tying the knot in a small, intimate ceremony, or eloping spontaneously up to Gretna Green. She wondered what he would say if he could see her now, knee deep in place cards and confetti.

'So what should we do first?' asked Josh.

'I don't mind,' replied Lizzie, stepping to one side to avoid being spritzed in the face by a woman brandishing bespoke fragrances. 'What do you think?'

'Maybe flower arrangements?'

What did you do with my fiancé? Lizzie figured he must be keen to get that one crossed off the list so he could spend more time with the stag reps and car-hire companies. She had already told him that they would struggle to afford an Aston Martin, but she knew his James Bond dream would die hard.

'Alright,' she said.

Josh held on to her hand as they made their way across

the huge hall, squeezing past gaggles of shrieking girls and pushy mothers. Watching him stride confidently through the crowd, Lizzie noticed that he attracted admiring glances from several women, including one trying on a wedding gown who really ought to know better. *Window shop all you want*, she thought, *but I'm the one who's marrying him.* She felt a fresh rush of adrenaline. The events of last weekend might have thrown her momentarily, but now things were getting back on track. *Who cares what Alex does? I've got Josh.* This time, she had fallen for someone who would always be there – for better or worse.

They continued to head for the kaleidoscope of blooms in the far corner, encountering eager reps promoting stag and hen packages, glamorous ladies ladling out skincare samples, magicians performing card tricks, and even designers flogging ushers' outfits for pets. 'Can we get one of these for Freddie?' Lizzie joked, picking up a sparkly dog collar and leash. 'Then Megan could keep him under control . . .'

'It's Megan I think we should be more worried about,' laughed Josh. 'Anyway, perhaps you should stick that back. I don't want the woman to think we're shoplifting.'

'Are you trying to say I look dodgy?'

'Never,' he said with a smile.

Finally, they came to the floral section, which was as overwhelming as it was colourful. Lizzie had assumed you simply chose your favourite stems and got a florist to arrange them prettily in posh vases, but now she could

21

see that the options were endless: birdcages bursting with lush green foliage, centrepieces in oversized cocktail glasses, even topiary trimmed like hearts and bells.

'Let's keep this simple,' she whispered to Josh, nudging him away from a man displaying a combination of gerberas, sparklers and citrus fruits who was frantically beckoning them over. 'We don't need anything edible.'

He grinned. 'How about flammable?'

'I'm thinking . . . nope.'

'Spoilsport. What about over there?' He gestured towards a white-haired woman in a powder-blue suit, surrounded by subtle yet stunning arrangements in tall crystal vases. Blush pinks and soft mauves mingled with creamy neutrals, looking as though they'd just been freshly plucked from a country garden.

Bingo.

The florist caught her gaze and waited for them to come closer. 'Hello,' she said warmly, extending her right hand. It was soft and crêpey, though her grip was surprisingly firm. 'I'm Peggy Bloom. How are you today?'

Lizzie wondered if that was her real name or a clever marketing gimmick. 'We're good, thanks,' she replied. 'Just on the lookout for some wedding inspiration. I love what you've done here.'

'Thank you. When's your big day?'

'Just under three months away, actually.' Her heart began to beat faster, ticking rhythmically like a clock. *The final countdown* . . . The hit 80s anthem suddenly began playing in her head, and she realised she hadn't caught Peggy's last question. 'Sorry, could you say that again?'

'Is it a church or civil ceremony?'

'Church.'

'What kind of look are you going for?'

'Nothing too fussy,' said Lizzie. 'Just something romantic and elegant.'

'Do you have any particular flowers in mind?'

'Yeah, cauliflowers,' said Josh. Lizzie laughed out loud and tried to pretend it was a tickly cough.

'I'm sorry?' Peggy looked puzzled.

'We're open to suggestions,' said Lizzie, steering the conversation back on course. 'But I was thinking maybe lilies.'

'Really?' Josh seemed surprised. 'They always remind me of funerals. How about roses?'

She gave him a bemused glance, trying to figure out if he was being serious. *The aliens must be back again.* 'Don't you think they're a little, you know . . . clichéd?'

'Not really, but I'm hardly the best person to ask.' He held up his hands in mock surrender. 'Look Lizzie, if you love lilies, have the lilies. Far be it for me to deny my beautiful bride.' She suspected that his attempt at feigning interest in flowers was already wearing thin. He snuck a sideways glance in the direction of the stag section.

She decided to cut him some slack. 'Look, why don't you go off and have a look round while I run through our options with Peggy? I'll come and find you when we're finished.'

'Really?' Josh looked unsure, as though he might be snared in some kind of wedding trap.

'Honestly, it's fine. I won't be long. Go sort out your stag do or something.'

'Well, if you think I should . . .'

'I do,' she nodded.

'OK, then – just give me a call when you're done. Nice to meet you, Peggy . . .' He bounded off before he'd barely finished his sentence, his bright blue T-shirt disappearing into the crowd. Josh's cheerful exuberance was one of the first things she had noticed about him, and probably explained why he was one of the most popular teachers at his school. That, and his cheeky sense of humour. The pupils knew a big kid when they saw one.

Lizzie turned her attention back to the florist. 'Right, so lilies are out, roses are out . . . any other ideas?'

'Why are they out?' asked Peggy.

'Yeah, I know he said he didn't care, but I can't exactly order lilies now knowing he doesn't like them. After all, it's his wedding too.'

'Ah, but flowers are a little like marriage,' said the florist sagely. 'Sometimes the secret lies in the compromise.'

'Sorry?'

'Picture this: you walk down the aisle carrying a bouquet of pure white Calla lilies. Maybe eight or ten stems, very tasteful. At the front are two beautiful displays, with

Oriental lilies nestled among Vendela and Sweet Avalanche roses. Then, for your reception, we could do miniature versions for the tables. It'd be like the best of both worlds.'

Lizzie could have kissed her. 'That sounds perfect,' she said. 'How much would something like that cost?'

'How many tables are you having?'

Hmmm, something else we still haven't sorted . . .

'I'm not totally sure yet. Probably about ten.'

'OK, no problem. If you fill out this sheet with your contact details, I can go away and put a quote together. We can always fine tune it later.'

'Great, thanks,' said Lizzie. She scribbled her details down on the form and passed it back.

'Gosh, that's a pretty ring.' Lizzie held out her hand so Peggy could see it more clearly, the square-cut diamond winking under the artificial lights. She had not expected Josh to choose something quite so showy, but it was undeniably dazzling, with two smaller diamonds in the platinum band flanking the main attraction. 'You're a lucky girl, dear. I'll be in touch soon.'

Lizzie smiled to herself as she ambled off, reminiscing about the day Josh proposed. They'd spent a brilliant afternoon over in Notting Hill, pottering around the vibrant stalls of Portobello Market before catching *Spectre* at the cinema. They'd cosied up on the back row, munching sweets and missing more of the film than they saw as they kissed like teenagers.

Afterwards, Josh drove her back to her flat in Shepherd's

Bush and looked at her intently. 'Are you coming in?' she asked, wondering why she suddenly felt nervous.

'I can't right now,' he said. 'I wish I could, but I promised Freddie I'd go round to his to watch the game. Wanna come?'

'No thanks. You know I'm not really into football.' *Or Freddie.*

'Yeah, I figured. But I'll ring you later, OK?'

True to his word, he called at 10.30pm, just as she was about to get ready for bed. 'Hey,' he said, a faint crackle on the line. 'How was your night?'

'Fine. Quiet one. Megan's out and I thought I'd have a go at some writing.'

'What for?'

'Just for fun. I actually had an idea for a short story.'

'Uh-huh,' he said distractedly. 'So did you miss me?'

'Of course. You're very missable.'

'Maybe we need to come up with a plan so that we miss each other less.'

'What do you mean?' She paused. 'You practically live here anyway.'

'I know,' he said. 'But I was thinking we . . .' She strained to hear what he was saying, but just then the front door buzzer went off and made her jump. *Aaaargh.* She hated that thing. It always felt like someone had taken a tiny drill to her brain.

'Hold that thought,' she said. 'Meg's forgotten her keys again. I'll be back in five secs.'

Throwing the phone onto the bed, she rushed to open the door – only to find Josh on his knees carrying a huge bouquet of roses and a blindingly shiny sparkler.

'So as I was saying, I've been thinking . . . Elizabeth Sparkes, will you marry me?'

Lizzie was still lost in her romantic reverie when a lady transporting a four-tier cake almost ploughed straight into her: a fate not entirely unappetising, but best avoided all the same. *I've got to stay focused.* In some ways it felt like an eternity since Josh proposed, and yet the past few months had gathered a momentum of their own, hurtling towards the marital finish line. For every task they managed to cross off the to-do list, another two sprang up to take its place.

First thing I need to do is find a fiancé in this haystack.

She pulled her mobile from her pocket and hit the speed dial. Josh didn't pick up. He probably couldn't hear his phone in the noisy hall, what with the giggling and the squealing and the super-jolly sales people. To her right, a string quartet struck up as if to really put the boot in. Lizzie sighed and shoved her phone back in her jeans. *Guess I'll have to go and hunt for him instead.*

She strolled over to the nearest row of stands, but Josh was nowhere to be seen. Behind one table, a gangly lad with raging spots glared at her like she'd just walked into the men's toilets. 'Can I help you? This is the *stag* zone,' he said, gesturing to a poster of two bikini-clad girls on a quad bike, which hardly seemed like the most practical racing attire.

'Oh, I'm sorry, I was looking for the hen section,' she said sweetly. 'Though I could use a second opinion . . . Do you think I should go for the pole-dancing party or the mud-wrestling weekend?'

As his jaw dropped, she turned and walked off in the opposite direction, hoping Josh hadn't wandered too far. After passing a caricaturist, a cellist and a woman dressed in medieval costume (she didn't stop to ask why), she finally spotted him emerging from what looked like a taxi.

'Lizzie! Lizzie! Hey, you've got to see this.' He pulled her inside and onto his lap, shutting off the outside world with a slam of the door. She could feel his belt buckle digging into her back, so she shuffled sideways into the space beside him. 'It looks like a normal cab, but really it's a photo booth in disguise!'

'Is this part of your Bond man-crush?'

His laughter reverberated around the shiny interior. 'I was thinking we could have it at the reception,' he said. 'Guests can pose for photos, then they get a copy to take home and we get one as a souvenir. We can get everyone to sign them instead of a boring old guest book. And . . .' he rummaged around in a box of props on the floor, 'you haven't seen the best bit yet.' He donned a pair of red heart-shaped glasses, and placed a sailor's hat on her head. 'What do you think? You on board?'

Lizzie couldn't help but smile. *It's very . . . Josh.* 'I don't know,' she said diplomatically. 'I mean, it's cool and everything, but do we need it? We've already booked the photographer.'

'Nah, this is totally different. We've got to do it!'

'Why? Because the wedding will be doomed unless we all don fancy dress?'

'Because it'll be a laugh. Go on . . .' He wiggled his eyebrows mischievously. 'Sometimes you've got to live dangerously.'

His words stung unexpectedly, as though she'd been jabbed again by his buckle. It had been more than ten years since anyone had said that to her, but suddenly she could remember it like it was yesterday. She rubbed the faint line on the inside of her wrist, as though that might somehow erase the memory.

'You OK?' asked Josh, for the hundredth time that week.

'Yeah, sorry, I was just thinking about something. So you really like the taxi, huh?'

'Not as much as I like you,' he said, cranking up the charm. 'But I do think it'd be great.'

'How much?' She could feel herself relenting. After all, she had spent months trying to persuade him to have more input into the wedding, so it seemed mean to veto the first thing he'd asked for. And besides, it *did* look kind of fun.

'Normally it'd be £500, but if we sign up today there's 20 per cent off.'

'Can we afford it?'

'Yeah, I think so. Especially if we don't hire the Aston Martin.'

'Are you sure?' Lizzie was happy to forgo the fancy car, but she knew that was a major sacrifice for Josh.

'Yeah, we'll find some other way of getting there. Or you'll have to haul your arse on the bus . . .'

She slapped his arm playfully. 'Hey, this bride doesn't do buses!'

'Fair enough. Maybe they'd let you hitch a ride in the photo booth?'

'Stop it!' Lizzie was giggling so hard now that her eyes began to water.

'Well, there's no need to cry about it,' said Josh. He stared ahead at the high-tech screen. 'Do you want to try it out?'

'I guess we should.'

'OK, when I press the button do happy face, sad face, poker face and scary face.'

'Ooh, I like it when you're bossy.'

'Hey, do you want this to look good or not?'

She adjusted his oversized glasses, kissed his cheek and hit the flashing button.

'I don't think there's much chance of that,' she said.

4

6 October 2002

Lizzie took another sip of wine as she read the coffee-stained dessert menu. She was almost too full to think about a third course, but she was having such a good time with Alex that she didn't want their date to come to an early end. *Maybe I could squeeze in a scoop of gelato,* she persuaded herself. *Possibly even two.*

Before she could make up her mind, a sticky dough ball came flying through the air and landed on the red and white checked tablecloth with a thud. She looked around the Italian restaurant, and noticed two small boys laughing hysterically in the corner. 'Will you two *stop it?*' hissed their mortified mother from across the table. 'Sit down and behave yourselves!' She looked over at Lizzie and waved both hands apologetically. 'I'm so sorry, really I am. I don't know what's got into them today.' She glared back at the boys, who were now pulling faces at one another. 'When their dad hears about this they're going to be in *big* trouble.'

'It's OK. No harm done,' smiled Lizzie. She turned back

to face Alex and they both burst out laughing. 'Are we still getting dessert?'

'Only if we can get it before those little terrors,' he joked. 'Otherwise we might end up covered in chocolate next.'

Lizzie tried hard not to visualise that thought, but for a split second her mind went off on a dirty tangent. Alex was looking even fitter tonight than she remembered, dressed down in a pair of faded jeans and a grey T-shirt, with a well-worn leather jacket strewn over the back of his chair. He was different from her usual clean-cut type, but there was something about him that she found intriguing, more than any of the lads she had briefly dated before.

The cheerful manager came over to take their order. 'What will you like?' he asked in loud broken English, the words resonating almost musically around them. 'You have one of my *speciale* desserts?'

'I'm pretty full,' said Lizzie, patting the front of her cream fine-knit dress. 'But I think I can manage some lemon gelato.'

'*Molto bene*,' he replied. 'We have the saying, like there are two stomachs: one for the main and one for the dessert. Always little room for dessert.'

'Quite right, too,' said Alex. 'In that case, I'll have the tiramisu, thanks.' The manager nodded approvingly and hurried off in the direction of the kitchen.

Alex turned his attention back to Lizzie. 'So, where were we?'

'You were telling me about your adventures.'

The One

Though they were in the same year at university, Alex was 18 months older, and had spent his gap year in Australia taking part in all kinds of adrenaline-inducing activities. He'd been bungee-jumping in Cairns, climbed the Sydney Harbour Bridge and gone sky-diving in Melbourne. Lizzie found his stories both fascinating and terrifying. She literally couldn't think of anything worse than jumping out of planes. In fact, she hated even boarding the things ever since a particularly bumpy flight resulted in her barfing halfway across the Atlantic. She had forced herself to get on an aircraft a couple of times since, but could never fully relax, her heart thumping and her palms sweating before it had even taken off.

'Yeah, that was a fun year. So, where's the best place you've been?'

'Oh, I . . . I'm not much of a traveller.'

Alex looked surprised. 'You don't want to visit other countries?'

'No, I'd love to visit other countries, but . . . I'm not exactly a big fan of flying.' *Ha. That's putting it mildly.*

'Like a phobia?'

Lizzie hesitated. She had never told anyone besides her family and Megan the full extent of the problem before, and she wasn't sure if it was something she should confess to a globetrotting boy she really liked. But there was a quiet self-assuredness about Alex that made her want to trust him.

'Yeah,' she confided eventually. 'I guess you could call it a phobia.'

'Have you always had it?'

'No,' she sighed. 'When I was about 15, we hit some terrible turbulence on the way to Florida and I spent half the flight throwing up. My parents saw the funny side – my dad still calls that plane the "chunder-wonder". But I think it put me off for life.'

'That must be tough,' he said, nodding sympathetically.

'It's not the end of the world,' she said, trying to shake off his pity. 'There are plenty of other things I enjoy.'

'Like what?'

'Loads of things . . . writing. Reading. Swimming. Not all at the same time.' Alex laughed, giving her an adrenaline rush of her own. 'Oh, and I'm totally addicted to *The West Wing*. Have you seen it?'

'No, but I heard it's good.'

'It's better than good. Aaron Sorkin is like some sort of writing genius.'

Alex smiled. 'I'll have to check it out. What sort of writing do you do?'

Lizzie confessed she'd been trying her hand at fiction, but her efforts so far just made her want to cringe. 'You'll get past that,' he said. 'You've just got to keep putting words on the page. They'll make their own sense, eventually.'

Now it was Lizzie's turn to look surprised. 'You write?'

'Not really – not like books or anything. But I taught myself to play the guitar a while back, and now I'm trying to come up with some of my own stuff. I could spend all day doing that.'

Lizzie was intrigued. 'Don't take this the wrong way, but why study hospitality if your passion's music?'

Alex leaned forward, his eyes lighting up. 'Because what I really want to do, one day, is open my own bar,' he explained. 'Book some bands, host some cool gigs, be my own boss. That's the real dream, I guess.'

'So you don't want to be a rock star, then?'

'Nah, I wouldn't last five minutes being famous,' he said. 'I'd hate the whole circus that goes with it. But that's OK. It's never been about playing at Wembley. I just wanted to learn the guitar, see what happens . . .' He trailed off as a waitress returned with their desserts and plonked them down on the table. 'So anyway, what about you?'

What about me? It was hard to focus while he was looking at her so intensely. His eyes were distractingly sexy. She dipped her spoon into the soft gelato. 'Sorry, what?'

'What do you want to do when you leave here? Write novels?'

Lizzie laughed. 'Well, that would be amazing, but it's not as simple as that. The odds of me getting published are pretty slim.'

'Why?' asked Alex. He took a bite of his tiramisu. 'You've got as much chance as anyone else.'

She'd never thought of it like that before. 'Maybe,' she said. 'But if that doesn't happen, there are still some other options I'd like to explore. I could go into journalism, or advertising, or—'

Just then she was interrupted by a shrill cry, which rang out across the restaurant like an alarm.

'TOMMY!'

She whipped her head around to see the mother of the two boys on her feet, frantically slapping the taller one on his back. His hands were clutching tightly at his neck, and his face was beginning to turn blue.

'Somebody help me!' she screamed. 'He's choking – my baby's choking!'

Alex pushed back his chair, leapt to his feet and ran over. He tried to give the boy five firm back blows between his shoulder blades, but the child continued to gasp for air, his eyes beginning to bulge from their sockets. 'Is there a doctor here?' shouted Alex. Lizzie looked around the room, her stomach lurching violently. None of the other diners replied, but simply stared on in horror.

'Please, somebody do something!' yelled the mother, gesturing to the manager, who had turned a sickly shade of green. 'Call 999!'

There's no way an ambulance is going to make it in time. What's the drill for choking? Lizzie jumped up and ran across to Alex, racking her brain to try to remember the advice she'd been taught for children. She'd done a basic first-aid course while training for her lifeguard qualification, but administering help to a plastic dummy in a leisure centre and trying to do it on a writhing, petrified boy suddenly seemed like two entirely different prospects. Her heart was beating so fast she could barely breathe herself.

'Let me see,' she said, opening the boy's twitching mouth to see if she could spot the obstruction. *Nothing*. The terror in his tiny eyes was unmistakable.

His mother was standing right next to her, wailing uncontrollably. 'Please help him!' she cried. 'I don't know what to do!'

'I need some room,' said Lizzie, moving behind the lad. She bent him slightly forwards and used the heel of her hand to slap him five more times between the shoulder blades. He made an awful rasping sound, his hands never leaving his throat, but whatever was stuck stubbornly refused to budge.

Shit.

Instinct kicked in and she threw her arms around Tommy's small waist, forming a fist with one hand above his belly button, and wrapping her other hand over the top. Then she pulled sharply upwards and inwards, the child's squidgy flesh feeling much softer against her hands than the Resusci Anne she had practised on.

One.

She could feel the boy squirming against her. *Try again!*

Two.

She gave another thrust, desperately hoping that she was doing it right. *Come on, come on, come on, come on . . .*

Three.

The boy made an unnerving noise that sounded like retching, and a half-chewed piece of dough ball shot out of his mouth and across the table. He inhaled loudly, sucking in air in noisy gulps, then burst into frightened tears. His mum rushed forwards and wrapped her arms around him, tears streaming down her face too. 'Oh Tommy, I've got you. I've got you. You're going to be OK. Mummy's here.'

The diners burst into a spontaneous round of applause, and Lizzie began to tremble. She couldn't bear to think what might have happened if that hadn't worked.

'Hey, are you alright?' Alex was peering at her closely with those piercing eyes. 'That was unbelievable. How did you know what to do?'

'I, er . . . I . . .'

'You know you just saved that child's life, right?' His voice was a mixture of shock and awe.

Before Lizzie could speak, Tommy's mother rushed over and hugged her tightly. 'Thank you so much,' she sobbed, her chest heaving. 'You're an angel. If you hadn't been there . . .' She couldn't finish that sentence. 'I want to do something to thank you both. If there's anything at all that you'd like, anything you need . . .' She pulled her purse from the back pocket of her jeans, her hands shaking.

'Oh no, you don't have to do that,' protested Lizzie. 'I'm just glad that he's alright.' The other diners were still gawping, which was making her feel more uncomfortable by the minute.

'Well, at least let me buy your dinner,' said the mother. Her face was all red and blotchy, make-up streaked across her cheeks.

'That won't be necessary,' said Alex kindly but firmly, his eyes hardly leaving Lizzie's face. 'I would like to buy this amazing woman dinner.'

Just then the manager came over, the colour slowly trickling back into his face. 'What you did was incredible,' he said, pumping her hand vigorously. 'Dinner is on the house! Pliss. Anything you want.'

Lizzie looked at Alex. He was still staring at her like she'd just walked on the moon. She nodded at the manger. 'OK, that's very kind of you. Thank you.'

'Can I get you some more wine, Miss?'

She glanced back at their table where her glass and half-eaten dessert remained in situ, as if she'd simply stepped away to visit the ladies. The thought of consuming any more food or drink right now made her feel queasy.

'Actually, I don't think I could manage anything else,' she said. 'Thanks for the offer, though.'

Alex took her arm, his grip firm and strong. 'Are you OK?'

'I'm fine, but I could do with a bit of fresh air.' She hesitated. 'Do you think we could go somewhere else for a bit?'

'Anything for the heroine of the hour,' said Alex, grabbing his leather jacket from the back of his chair and retrieving her wallet. 'Let's get you out of here.'

Lizzie felt her sandals sink into Cliffstowe beach, enjoying the sensation of the cool grains tickling her toes. In the distance, the Dorset coastline was flecked with the lights from local houses, illuminating the night sky like tiny stars. A solitary seagull squawked overhead while waves crashed in the background, compiling nature's own soundtrack.

'How are you feeling now?' asked Alex, as they set off along the shore.

'Better, thanks,' she said, inhaling that distinctive seaside scent as the wind tugged at her hair. The truth was she was feeling pretty strange: scared and relieved and alive all at once. It was as if she had stepped into the lion's den and emerged the other side, exhilarated but also aware of how badly wrong things could have gone.

'OK, good.' His face relaxed a little. 'That was way too much drama for a first date.'

'I know.' She exhaled loudly, shuddering at the memory. 'It's certainly not one we'll forget.'

'No, I guess not . . .' His deep voice drifted off over the waves, and she could tell he was still shaken up, too. 'You know, I really thought we were going to lose that kid for a minute there. I was smacking his back, and nothing was happening, and all I could see was that look on his mum's face.'

'Yeah, I know what you mean. I was totally starting to freak out.'

'But you didn't.' He turned his head towards her, his eyes finding hers. 'You kept calm and you saved him. How'd you learn to do that?'

'I worked as a lifeguard the past two summers,' Lizzie

said. 'I had to do a first-aid course as part of the training. I have to admit, though, I wasn't really expecting to have to use it. The pool's only about a metre deep.'

'Lifeguard, eh?' Alex smiled.

'Yes, but don't get too excited. We don't run around dressed like we're on *Baywatch*. We have to wear some pretty unflattering orange shorts.'

'I bet you pull it off,' he said.

Lizzie blushed and looked away, squinting at the darkening stretch of shore ahead. 'Are you sure we can get back to yours this way?' she asked.

'Of course – I do it all the time,' he replied, suddenly catching the inference of what he'd just said. 'Not usually with company,' he corrected himself. 'But I prefer to go this way when the tide's out. It helps me think.'

'About what?' asked Lizzie. She had been thinking about him non-stop since Wednesday, trying to work out how he'd got inside her head in a way that none of Megan's blind dates ever had.

'I don't know,' he said. 'Nothing . . . everything. Sometimes I just like to get away from it all for a while.'

As they continued their walk, she stole a sideways glance at his profile in the moonlight, admiring his strong jaw and untamed hair. Just the nearness of him made her feel both excited and nervous. She couldn't put her finger on it, but he had a worldly confidence that belied his age; she, on the other hand, had been living a pretty sheltered existence for the past 19 years, and had only slept with three guys ever, if those clumsy fumbles could technically count. She wasn't planning to fall into bed with him tonight, but she was glad she'd worn her favourite undies, just in case.

'What's on your mind?' he said.

'Er, nothing really. I was just thinking that this evening's gone fast.'

'I know. It wasn't exactly the date I had in mind, though. So I'm hoping you'll let me take you out for another one?'

Her pulse began to race. 'Yeah, I'd really like that.'

Just then the autumn breeze wrapped itself around her again, causing her to shiver. It had been a surprisingly sunny day, but the temperature had suddenly dropped and she was starting to feel chilly. She felt a light splash of rain land on her arm and wished that she'd bothered to bring a coat.

'Are you getting cold?' Alex asked. 'Here, take my jacket.' He shrugged his arms free from the sleeves and wrapped it around her shoulders, pulling her closer as he did so. She felt his thumb brush against the back of her neck, almost imperceptibly, but it was enough to stop her in her tracks. Every inch of her began to buzz with electricity.

'Alex . . .'

He fixed those incredible slate eyes on hers, studying her face as though he might be tested on it later. Slowly, he ran one hand through her windswept hair, tucking several runaway strands behind her ear, his fingertips warm against her cool skin. Lizzie could barely breathe, afraid to even exhale in case it shattered the moment.

Just then an almighty rumble broke the spell, as the sky began to spew raindrops with surprising force. 'We're going to get soaked,' yelled Alex. 'Come on, let's get back to mine.' He grabbed her hand and they raced along the shore, running fast and free, not knowing what would happen when they finally stopped.

After minutes that felt like hours, he veered off to the right. 'It's just through here,' he promised, leading the way along a dimly lit path.

Lizzie followed him up a flight of stony steps and watched as he opened a side door, the rain still pounding overhead like the beat of her heart.

5

11 weeks to go . . .

Irresistible. Sizzling. Orgasmic? Lizzie stared at her computer screen, trying to concentrate on the words floating around in front of her. She was writing a press release about a new cookbook by a top TV chef – the kind of project she usually enjoyed as PR manager for a small publishing house – but today her mind kept wandering mid-recipe, scuttling off to flowers and first dances and whether or not they ought to have favours on the tables.

'Can I get you a coffee?' interrupted Phoebe, the new marketing assistant, who had only joined six weeks ago and was still in that phase of sucking up to everybody. She seemed a nice enough girl, but she was a bundle of nervous energy, rushing all over the place and swivelling around on her chair every time she sat back down. It was knackering just watching her.

'No, thanks,' said Lizzie. 'I think I'm alright for the moment.'

'How about tea, then? Or some water? It's good to stay hydrated in the office.'

'Actually, Phoebe, I'd love a drink,' piped up Naomi, who ran the company's website. Blunt, ballsy and prone to bouts of swearing, she was by far Lizzie's favourite person on the entire team, even if she did insist on having the radio turned up distractingly loud while she worked.

'Of course!' The youngster scurried over to the next desk, looking thrilled to be making herself useful. 'What can I get you? Tea? Coffee?'

'Do we have any fruit smoothies?' asked Naomi sweetly. 'Maybe banana and mango? Or some mixed berries? I'm doing a juice cleanse at the moment, you see.'

Really? If she was, it was the first Lizzie had heard of it, and Naomi didn't usually keep much to herself.

'Oh, er . . .' Phoebe's smile faltered. 'I'm not sure we've got anything like that in the kitchen.' Then she perked back up again. 'Ooh, the café round the corner might have some, though. Do you want me to run down and see?'

'Would you mind? Thanks so much.' Naomi reached into her wallet and pulled out a crumpled tenner. 'I'd prefer freshly blended anyway. Why don't you grab yourself one, too, if you're going to the trouble of walking round there?'

Phoebe beamed, like she'd just been tasked with an important assignment for the Queen. 'That's really nice of you. I'll be back as soon as possible.'

'No rush, take your time,' said Naomi, watching her go as she trotted off towards the lifts, her auburn hair swinging like a shiny conker.

'I didn't know you were into juicing now,' said Lizzie. 'How long's that been going on?'

'Since about five minutes ago. She's doing my head in this morning, all that flapping about. I reckon it'll buy us a good ten minutes of peace.'

'You're mean!' smiled Lizzie. 'She's harmless. Remember what it's like when you start a new job and just want to impress people?'

'Not really,' said Naomi drily. She liked to give the impression that she couldn't care less what anyone thought, but Lizzie knew there was a sensitive core beneath her spiky exterior. 'Anyway, it's alright for you. Don't you have some sort of extended holiday coming up?'

'If you're referring to my honeymoon, then yes – yes I do.' Lizzie couldn't even try to hide the huge grin that broke out across her face.

'Where are you going?'

'Not sure yet.' That was another thing they still had to finalise, largely because they couldn't agree on a destination. Josh wanted to go somewhere far-flung and exotic, but Lizzie wasn't sure if she could cope with a long flight. Even just the thought of it made her palms grow clammy. 'We're still deciding.'

'How long are you off for?'

'With the wedding as well? Nearly three weeks.'

'Lucky cow.' Naomi shook her head enviously. 'I'd marry psycho Mel for three weeks away.' Mel was Naomi's on-off girlfriend. It was easy to keep track of their relationship

status, because whenever it was off she always prefixed
Mel's name with 'evil' or 'psycho'.

'Sorry,' Lizzie smiled. 'I'll miss you, if it helps.'

'Yeah, well . . . you'd better bring me back something
really good. And some duty-free fags.'

'I'm not getting you those. I thought you were meant
to be quitting?'

Naomi pulled a face. 'Whatever,' she said, cranking up
her radio another few decibels. 'Anyway, stop distracting
me with all this talk about holidays. I need to upload this
before Her Perkiness gets back.'

'Fine by me.' Lizzie glanced over at the laminated
calendar on the beige wall to her right, counting with
glee that there were only 51 working days to go before
she could escape. She was desperate for a proper break.
While other brides-to-be seemed to enjoy every second
of wedding planning, Lizzie was finding the whole thing
so stressful that she'd started waking up at 3am, her
mind whirring so loudly she was sure it would disturb
Josh.

'Do you think it's got anything to do with . . . you know
who?' Megan had asked last week, when Lizzie complained
that she was having trouble sleeping.

'What, Alex? What makes you say that?'

'Well, you seemed kind of upset when I mentioned it
at the dress shop.' Megan pursed her lips. 'I know you said
you don't care, but I just wanted to check you were OK
about all that.'

'About what? That he upped and left? Or that he's back right before my wedding?'

'Ah,' said Megan, looking uncomfortable. 'Do you wish I hadn't told you?'

'No, I'm glad you did,' sighed Lizzie. 'I'm sorry. I didn't mean to snap. I guess I'm still a little freaked out. I just wasn't expecting him to come home after this long.'

'Look, I get it. I was pretty shocked myself when I heard. And I'm not the one who was madly in love with him.'

'I'm not sure I was *madly* in love with him . . .' replied Lizzie. Even as she started to protest, she knew it was a lie. 'I mean, I thought I was at the time – but if our relationship was so great it wouldn't have ended that badly, would it?' She could still feel the hurt in her bones, all these years later, like a fracture that had never fully healed. *Don't think about it*, she told herself. *Josh would never leave you like that.*

'Guess not. I was worried about you back then. You were in a right state.'

'Don't remind me.' The first few months after Alex disappeared had been, without doubt, the most miserable of Lizzie's life. After the tears and the anger and the guilt subsided, all that was left was a strange nothingness, which in many ways was worse. It had taken the best part of two years for her to feel halfway human again. 'I must have been a nightmare to live with. I'm so embarrassed.'

'Stop beating yourself up,' said Megan. 'That was a rough time, especially after what happened with—'

The One

'Please, let's not go there,' said Lizzie. She wasn't ready for a maudlin trip down memory lane, not even with the one person whose turbulent relationship with Alex almost rivalled her own. During university, he'd become one of Megan's closest friends, the surrogate big brother she'd always wanted. But when it all came crashing down – with Lizzie's heart among the wreckage – he'd been rebranded as public enemy number one.

By now, news of his return had prompted much gossip among their old crowd, but Lizzie still didn't know why he was back in the country, or for how long. She found herself wondering whether everything was alright with his family, the not-quite-in-laws she'd once been so fond of.

I hope they're OK. As if they haven't been through enough already.

Her musings were cut short by the portly man from the post room, who thrust a huge bouquet of flowers under her nose. 'Special delivery for you, Miss Sparkes,' he said, his short fingers gripping the stems tightly.

'Thanks, Bob. I didn't know you cared,' she joked. The arrangement was amazing: large white lilies mixed with yellow tulips and orange gerberas, the citrus shades standing out against the foliage like miniature suns. Their fresh scent reminded her of the displays from the wedding fair.

'Well, you know you're still my favourite, miss. But I think someone might be trying to steal you from me.'

'Nah,' she said with a smile. 'That'll never happen.'

Bob gave her a wink and set off for the rest of his rounds. 'See you later, kiddo.'

Lizzie admired the bouquet again, which was almost bigger than her head. *It's so sweet of Josh to do this*, she thought, *especially when I've been kind of moody lately. I'll have to make it up to him.*

'Nice blooms,' said Naomi, nosily. 'What's he gone and done now?'

'He hasn't done anything,' laughed Lizzie. 'People can send flowers for other reasons, you know.' Noticing that there was a card attached with twirly yellow ribbon, she ripped open the envelope, eager to read the romantic message inside. Instead, it simply said: Lizzie, I'm in town. Please can we talk? Alex x

A burst of adrenaline shot through her body. *Has he been here?* She looked around the office furtively, as if half expecting him to pop out from behind the photocopier, but nothing seemed out of the ordinary. Glancing back down, she saw that underneath the message was a sprawled mobile number, the last two digits of which were smudged. Lizzie dropped the card and leapt from her chair, chasing after Bob like a champion sprinter.

'Bob! BOB! Where exactly did these come from?'

He spun around to face her, looking puzzled. 'A bloke just dropped them off not long ago. I brought them straight up. Why?'

'What did he look like?'

'Hard to say, miss – tall, about your age. Nice chap. Could have been a courier, I suppose. Is something wrong?'

Lizzie ran past him down the corridor, almost knocking over Phoebe as she returned with the drinks, and hammered on the lift button as though her life depended on it. 'Come on!' she yelled, causing the mousy intern on her right to jump. The lift was being stubborn now, its green arrow flashing upwards in defiance.

She would have to take the fire exit.

Her heels clacked against the cheap lino as she raced down the dingy stairs, her palms sweating so much that she struggled to grip the chipped banister. Finally, after four hellishly long storeys, she burst through the door and out into the cobbled side street.

'Alex!'

A startled pigeon flew past her, but otherwise the alley was deserted. She strode round the corner to the main entrance, half hoping that he would be waiting; half afraid of what would happen if he was.

'Alex, are you there?'

Only the whistle of the wind came back at her, and she knew that once again he had slipped away without saying a word.

After sending a quick text to request an emergency summit, Lizzie rushed straight round to Megan's flat after work, which proved easier said than done with a giant bouquet on the Tube. Not only did she have to squeeze into the crowded carriage, but the bald man standing beside her seemed to have severe hayfever, and proceeded to sneeze in her direction all the way to Shepherd's Bush.

'Need . . . wine . . . now,' she gasped, as the front door finally swung open.

'What's going on?' said Megan. She peered at the huge arrangement. 'You look like you've raided the Chelsea Flower Show. Are these for me?'

'They are now. Alex sent them.'

'What the fu . . . ?'

'I know,' Lizzie interrupted. 'Have you got wine?'

Megan stared at her, highlighting the sheer stupidity of the question. 'Red, white or rosé?'

'I don't mind, as long as you make mine a large.'

'Coming right up. Then you have to tell me *everything*.' She eyed the flowers again. 'I suppose we'd better get these in water, if they even fit through the hallway.'

Lizzie stepped inside the bijoux apartment, noticing that it was pretty tidy these days, or at least a lot better than when the two of them moved in after uni. 'The old place is looking good,' she murmured, her mind still boggling from the afternoon's events.

'Thanks,' replied Megan. 'Lily's a neat freak, so she's been spring cleaning again.' Megan's cousin, a leggy model, had been renting the other bedroom since Lizzie moved in with Josh. The girl had a wardrobe to die for and was hardly ever around, so most of the time the deal suited Megan perfectly. 'Sit down and make yourself comfy,' she continued, taking the flowers through to the compact kitchen. 'I'll be with you in a sec. Wine is on the way!'

Lizzie collapsed into the soft, threadbare couch, now tastefully adorned with a scattering of gold cushions. A few seconds later, Megan returned with a bottle of Pinot Grigio and two glasses, and settled down beside her. 'Right, have some of this and start from the beginning,' she said, pouring a couple of sizeable servings. 'When did the flowers turn up?'

'Today.'

'What, at home? Did Josh see?' Her voice began to climb higher and higher.

'No, at work. But obviously I can't take them home. Not that I'd want to,' Lizzie added hastily. She took a large gulp of Pinot, hoping the cool wine would soothe her frazzled nerves.

'Did you talk to him?'

'Who, Josh?'

'No, Alex!' Megan was dangerously close to soprano territory now.

'No.' Lizzie tried to adopt a nonchalant expression, omitting to mention that she had nearly set a new land-speed record trying to sprint down the fire exit.

'Then how do you know they're from him?'

'Because he left a note.'

Megan's eyes widened. 'Saying?'

Lizzie put down her glass, retrieved the card from her purse and handed it over. Megan's mouth flapped about like a fish deprived of water. 'But . . . what . . .' she paused. 'He's got some balls.'

'I know.'

'As if you'd want to talk to him!'

'Exactly.' Lizzie picked up her wine and necked another large mouthful. Megan sipped hers more slowly, looking deep in thought.

'I wonder how he knew where you'd be,' she mused.

'What?'

'Well, if he sent flowers to your office, how did he find out where you work?' She wrinkled her nose suspiciously.

'I've no idea. Maybe someone told him, or he looked me up online or something. You're the one who's always telling me you can find anything on the internet.'

Megan mulled this over for a moment. 'It's possible, I guess. But he doesn't seem too into the whole social media thing. He's not even on Facebook! My 90-year-old gran's on there poking people, no problem. But Alex? Nothing.'

'You tried to look him up?' Now it was Lizzie's turn to be surprised.

'Only when I heard he was back. I was just going to check out his pictures, do a bit of harmless reconnaissance.' She narrowed her eyes. 'Don't tell me you've never tried to do that?'

Lizzie ducked her gaze. 'Maybe once or twice,' she muttered. Not that she'd ever found anything. Alex was very good at going under the radar. In another life, he'd have made an excellent secret agent.

'If you say so,' scoffed Megan. 'Anyway, you're missing the point. The important thing is what you do next.'

'What do you mean?'

'Please tell me you didn't phone him already?'

'Course not,' Lizzie spluttered. 'I can't read the number anyway. The last two digits are smudged.'

Megan peered at the card, then threw it down on the coffee table. 'I think it's a 6 and a 0. Might be an 8. Not that it matters, though. You definitely shouldn't call.'

'I won't.'

'In that case, I think we should get rid of it,' she said. 'Just so you don't feel tempted to ring him later. You know, once we've polished off the Pinot.' She set down her drink and went into the kitchen, returning with a large ashtray and a box of matches. 'Here, we can set fire to it. It'll be like it never existed.'

Like Alex for the past ten years, you mean.

'You don't need to mess around with all that, Megan.' Lizzie shuffled uneasily in her seat.

'Well, you can't keep it! What if Josh sees it? How dodgy would that look?'

'Why would he see it? I was going to bin it.'

'Good. Because I'd hate to see you screw things up with Josh for that bastard.' Despite their long-term friendship – or perhaps because of it – Megan still hadn't learned to keep her opinions to herself.

'Don't say that.'

'Why not?'

Lizzie didn't have a good answer. It wasn't like she hadn't called him that – and worse – since the split. But somehow it sounded different coming from Megan.

'Never mind. I should probably talk to Josh about all this though, right? Maybe tell him what happened with me and Alex?' Not that she had much of an explanation. She still didn't understand how two people could swiftly go from being inseparable to being continents apart.

'What? Noooooo!' Megan looked horrified. 'That's a terrible idea.'

'Why? I'm sure he won't mind. It was a million years ago.'

'Yeah, I can hear that conversation now: "Hi darling, how was your day? Oh, by the way, the love of my life just waltzed back into town." He'll be thrilled about that.'

'Alex isn't the love of my life,' said Lizzie, her head starting to throb from the strain of it all.

'But still, it doesn't exactly sound great, does it? And then poor Josh is going to spend the next couple of months worrying that you're going to call off the wedding.'

'Why would I call off the wedding?'

'I'm not saying you would. I'm just saying that I don't think now's a good time to dump all of this on your fiancé.' She raised one perfectly plucked eyebrow. 'Look, at the end of the day, what he doesn't know won't hurt him.'

I hope not, thought Lizzie. *I really hope not.* 'So what do you think I should do?'

Megan picked up the card. 'I think we should destroy the evidence right now.'

'You've been watching too much *CSI: Miami* again.'

'I'm serious. Unless you're having second thoughts about phoning . . .' She shook her head disapprovingly.

'Fine, you win. Let's just get rid of it.'

Lizzie watched as her friend scraped the safety match against the coarse surface of the box, the sound grating like nails down a blackboard. The tip sprang to life, its golden head gently kissing the corner of the card, engulfing it in a sunset-coloured glow before it burned out with exhaustion and everything turned black.

Megan was right. There could be no going back.

6

6 October 2002

Lizzie stepped into the dark cottage, scattering a trail of watery drops as she took off Alex's jacket, her hands struggling to grip the slippery leather. Her wet hair clung to her neck and shoulders, the rain trickling down her back and tickling her skin.

As her eyes slowly adjusted to the lack of light, she could just about glimpse Alex in the shadows, but then he switched on a table lamp, infusing the living room with a soft glow. The place wasn't big, but what it lacked in size it made up for in character, with its exposed brick walls and dark wooden beams. It was not your typical student digs, but then she was beginning to realise that he was not your typical student.

'You must be drenched,' he said, kicking off his shoes with a thud. 'That really came out of nowhere.' His hair had been slicked back by the rain, but a few rogue strands fell forward and she wanted to brush them from his face. She did not move first, though, thrown by the wet and the cold and the sudden realisation that her dress had become almost see-through. *Do I look a total mess?* Alex had wanted to kiss her on the beach, of that she was sure, but the rain had extinguished the moment and now she felt self-conscious.

'I'm OK.'

He took the dripping jacket from her. 'Here, let me get you a towel,' he said, disappearing for a second before surfacing with a large white one. She wrapped it tightly around herself, feeling the warmth flood back into her body, then bent down to remove her sodden sandals. 'I'll see if I can find you something to change into,' he offered, striding towards what she assumed must be his bedroom.

He did not close the door fully behind him, and she couldn't help but watch through the gap as he peeled off his T-shirt, revealing a muscular back. As he reached into his wardrobe, she could make out a jagged scar to the right of his torso, silvery and faded but noticeable nonetheless. *I know nothing about this guy*, she thought suddenly, and yet she wanted to find out more. She pretended to concentrate on towel-drying her hair while she kept one eye firmly fixed in his direction.

He threw on a black jumper and returned brandishing two large shirts in white and blue. 'I don't have much that'll fit you, sorry. But you're welcome to wear one of these. You can change in my room, if you like.'

'Sure, thanks.' She draped the towel over the back of a chair and took the white one from him, her heartbeat accelerating as she closed the bedroom door. Wriggling out of her drenched dress and into the crisp cotton shirt, its length barely skimming her thighs, Lizzie felt almost as exposed as she had a few minutes earlier. Not wanting to seem tarty, she fastened the buttons right to the top, but then that felt stuffy, so she undid the top two. She wished that her boobs were a size or two larger so she could really work the curvaceous angle.

Checking her reflection in the wardrobe mirror, she realised that her eyeliner was running halfway down her right cheek. As she scanned the room for tissues, she noted with relief that it was simple but clean, with a double bed covered in navy linen. The matt-white walls were peppered with posters of music icons – Kurt Cobain, Jimi Hendrix, John Lennon – which were starting to look a little frayed around the edges. There was no sign of food-encrusted plates, like the ones she had to rescue from Gareth's room, or mounds of dirty student laundry; instead there was just a small pile of magazines and textbooks, a guitar leant lovingly in the corner and a corkboard dotted with photographs.

She leaned in. The same faces cropped up in multiple snaps, including a middle-aged couple who she guessed must be his parents, a guy who looked a lot like Alex and a pretty blonde shaped like a swimwear model. Lizzie peered more closely at her and felt a pang in the pit of her stomach. *I hope that's a relative*, she thought, trying to avert her eyes from the blonde's ample cleavage.

She couldn't spot any tissues, though, and in the end

she had to settle for a lick of saliva on her little finger. Before their date, she had spent over an hour perfecting her outfit and make-up, yet now she was stripped of both. *Not the best look, but it'll have to do.* She ran a hand through her damp hair, gave the shirt a final inspection and stepped back into the lounge.

Alex had lit a fire and was pouring two glasses of white wine. He passed one to her then sat down on the crinkled brown leather couch, which was barely big enough for two. Lizzie sank into the adjacent armchair, curling her legs up beside her.

'This place is beautiful,' she said, hoping her breezy voice wouldn't betray her nerves. 'How long have you been here?'

'Actually, I've been coming here since I was small,' he said. 'It used to belong to my grandparents, and when they died my mum couldn't bear to sell it. Too many memories. I think she's hoping to bring her own grandkids here someday.'

'I can totally see why.' She took a sip of her drink. 'I wish I'd had grandparents to go and visit.'

Alex leaned forward. 'You didn't see any of them?'

'Not really. My dad's parents were killed in a car crash before I came along, and my mum's both died before I turned five, so I don't remember them much. And I never actually met my real grandparents.' She stopped, realising she hadn't told him the full story. 'I was adopted when I was a baby.'

She waited for him to get that look people got when she told them; that awkward not-sure-what-to-say-now kind of look. But he didn't. He just looked interested.

'Are you in touch with your birth family?'

'No, never.' She shrugged her shoulders. 'Mum offered to help me track them down last year when I turned 18. But, honestly, I don't think I want to any more. As far as I'm concerned, my mum and dad are my real family.'

For a while, during her early teens, she had thought about her birth parents obsessively: what they looked like, where they might be living, whether they lay awake at night and wished they hadn't given her away. Above all, there was this overriding sense of loss, as though she'd misplaced something but couldn't remember what. Still, her adopted parents had always made her feel so loved that she refused to regret going to them. It could only have been a trade up, and she couldn't bear to hurt their feelings by searching for two strangers simply because they shared some DNA.

'I understand,' he said, raising his glass to his lips. 'They sound like great people.'

'They are.' She shifted her weight slightly. 'What about you? What's your family like?'

'Can't complain, I guess. There's me, the folks, my twin Connor and my sister Andi.'

'Oh, you have a twin? That must be so cool!'

'Mostly. He has his moments.'

'Do you see them much?'

'As much as I can. They're up near Windsor – close enough to visit but not so close they can turn up uninvited.'

'Sounds perfect.' She smiled. 'So you live here by yourself?'

'Yeah. I thought about renting out the spare room once, but I kind of like having my own space.' He looked around the cosy cottage. 'At least this way I can mess around on my guitar without disturbing anyone.'

'Will you play something for me?'

He seemed surprised. 'Like what?'

'I don't mind. Anything.'

'Oh, I don't play in front of other people. Trust me, it's for your own good.'

She put her glass on the wooden floor. 'Hey, I sang in front of you this week, remember? Not to mention half the uni.'

'True,' he smiled. 'But perhaps we should leave the music to the pros for one night.' He gestured to a tall, teetering pile of CDs in the corner, which resembled the Leaning Tower of Pisa. 'I must have something you like. Though I'm pretty sure there's no Steps.'

She extracted herself from the chair to inspect his collection, discreetly tugging down the shirt to what she hoped was a respectable length. 'Alright, let's have a look. Coldplay, Train – love them – Foo Fighters, Roxette . . .' She paused. 'Really?'

'What's wrong with Roxette?'

'Nothing. I like Roxette. I just didn't think they'd be your thing.'

'What can I say? I've got eclectic taste. There might even be an S Club single lurking in there somewhere, you know.'

She continued to rifle through the mountain of discs, not quite sure what she was searching for. 'Travis . . . The Ramones . . . ah, Oasis.' She pulled the CD slowly from the precarious pile, hoping it wouldn't topple like a giant game of Jenga.

'Which track?' he said. 'Choose wisely.'

'You'll see.' She took the disc out of its plastic casing and switched on his stereo, feeding the flash of silver into the hungry slot. The familiar opening of *Wonderwall* echoed over the speakers.

'This is my all-time favourite song, you know,' said Alex quietly, setting down his wine glass.

She held out a hand. 'Then dance with me.'

'What? You can't dance to this.'

'You don't sing, you don't dance . . .' she teased. 'What do you do?'

As if to answer her question, he rose slowly, strode across the room and kissed her with an intensity that made her knees buckle. She had been kissed before (by 12 different boys, in fact, if you counted those drunken snogs in Fresher's Week), but this was the kiss to obliterate all others.

She gave into it completely, running her hand through his rain-soaked hair and down to his broad shoulders. He wrapped his strong arms around her back, pulling her in so deeply that she could hardly breathe; his lips were warm, with a faint taste of wine that was intoxicating, his stubble brushing against her skin.

'Do you want to stay here tonight?' he whispered.

His question caught her off-guard and she pulled back slightly. She had never done anything like this before – 'Make 'em wait until at least the third date,' Megan always said – and the sensible thing to do would be to slow down. She knew that if she didn't leave in the next 30 seconds, she was going to lose a piece of her heart that could never be reclaimed.

Looking into her eyes, he gently undid three buttons on her shirt and traced the outline of her lacy bra with his finger. She did not want to leave: not now, not ever.

'Yes,' she murmured, pressing her lips hard against his, her hands finding the taut abs beneath his jumper. He did not say another word as he lifted her off the floor and swept her into the bedroom.

This time, he did close the door.

7

10 weeks to go . . .

As the DJ on the radio teed up yet another 80s power ballad, Lizzie glanced at the plastic clock on the office wall. It seemed to have been stuck at 5.05pm for the past ten minutes. *How is that even possible?* She hid a yawn behind her coffee cup. Josh had kept her up half the night fidgeting, convinced his recent sniffles were spiralling into full-blown flu. He'd called in sick today and stayed at home, curled up on the couch with the remote control for company, while she'd had to trek into town amid freak summer storms, cursing commuters who nearly decapitated her with their umbrellas.

She hadn't been sleeping well for weeks, really, which was partly due to wedding stress but mainly Alex's fault. The questions she was afraid to ask out loud ran through her mind at night: *Why is he here? What does he want with me?* She wished that he had never come back, so she could be kept awake by guest lists and seating charts like normal brides.

Her eyelids felt heavy, and she allowed herself to rest them for one peaceful moment.

'Elizabeth? Elizabeth! Are you with us?' The shrill voice of her boss, an imposing woman by the name of Ella Derville, jolted her back to attention. Tall and wiry, Ella always wore her hair in an immaculate topknot, which was slicked back so tightly it made her skin look eerily stretched. She had the eyes of a hawk and the stealth of a ninja. 'I do hope we're not overworking you?'

'No! I mean, er . . . sorry. Thought I had an eyelash in there. Did you need me?' Deep down, Lizzie had a quiet respect for the publishing director (though she knew that Naomi secretly called her Cruella de Vil), but right now she could tell that the woman was in no mood for pleasantries.

'Yes, I want to review your campaign strategy before next week's meeting,' she said, peering down her nose. She paused expectantly just as the chorus of *Don't Stop Believin'* rang out in the background. Ella swivelled her long neck in Naomi's direction. 'Will someone turn that radio off? I am *trying* to have a conversation here.'

Naomi begrudgingly did as she was told, plunging the office into an ominous silence. The rest of the team tried to pretend that they were busy, shuffling papers or playing with their staplers, but Lizzie knew they were hanging on to Ella's every word. Perky Phoebe wheeled her chair a fraction closer to the action.

'Where was I?' said Ella brusquely. 'Oh yes. I need that plan.'

What plan? The semi-permanent knot in Lizzie's

stomach tightened another notch. 'Er, I'm actually working on quite a few things at the moment,' she said in what she hoped was her most polite, super-efficient voice. 'Could you remind me which project you were referring to?'

'The new yoga book.'

Aaaargh. It would have to be the one I've not started. 'I'm just finishing that off,' she said, not quite making eye contact. 'I'll move it to the top of my in-tray and have it with you by noon tomorrow.'

'It was supposed to be on my desk yesterday!'

Lizzie didn't know what to say, but it didn't make much difference; the woman was on a roll now, her disapproval rushing forth like an unstoppable tidal wave. Naomi got up and walked behind her to the water cooler, rolling her eyes as she went.

'And then there was that press release for the travel guide, which was so full of typos I had to re-do it myself. It's not up to your usual standard at all. Is something the matter?' She placed one hand on the desk and leaned in. 'Because if there's a problem, you know, perhaps you should talk to me.'

Lizzie couldn't imagine anything more excruciating than telling the boss about her complicated private life. 'I'm really sorry,' she whispered, her mouth drying up. 'I've just been under quite a lot of pressure lately. I'll make sure this doesn't happen again, I promise.'

'Please do.' Ella stood up sharply, pulling herself to her full height. 'We've got a busy month ahead.' And with that she slinked off, no doubt preparing to pounce on some other poor unsuspecting underling.

Lizzie was mortified. A rush of heat surged up her neck and spread contagiously across her face. She had been working for the company for more than four years and had always considered herself an exemplary employee. Now she was suddenly being cast as the office slacker. *I've really got to get my act together – before I get my P45.* She looked around at her colleagues in stunned disbelief, but most of them refused to meet her eyes. Naomi gave an embarrassed shrug and trudged back to her seat.

Seconds later, an email alert pinged up in Lizzie's inbox.

Hey, Sleeping Beauty! Cheer up. If you can stay awake for another 15 minutes, let's get out of here and have one for the road. I'm buying.

N x

Lizzie glanced out of the window, where the sky looked grey and miserable. Another storm cloud rumbled overhead.

Sure, why not? she replied. Assuming I'm not fired first . . .

Naomi jostled her way through the after-work crowd, plonking a tray down on the wonky table. 'Fuck me, this place is getting pricey,' she said, offloading two glasses of house white and a small bowl of dry roasted peanuts. 'Since when did nuts cost nearly a fiver? It used to be alright in here.'

Lizzie glanced around the dingy pub, which looked about 100 years old, and tried to envisage a time when it was ever alright in there. 'That's London for you,' she said. 'You sure you don't want some cash?'

'Oh, don't worry about it,' said Naomi. 'I'll get this lot. You get the next one.'

'OK, thanks. It might have to be next week, though. Josh isn't well today so I thought I'd go back and make him a decent dinner.'

'Well, aren't you a regular Nigella?' teased Naomi. 'I wish there was someone at home to cook for me. I'm sick to death of ready meals.'

'So, how are things at home these days?' Lizzie asked tactfully. She took a large swig of wine and immediately wished she hadn't. It tasted like vinegar and needed another hour in the fridge.

'Not great.' Naomi ran a hand through her platinum blonde hair and shuffled uneasily on the rickety stool. 'I think evil Mel might be seeing other people.'

'What makes you say that?'

'She keeps posting selfies with all these other girls.'

'Maybe they're friends?' said Lizzie helpfully.

'Yeah, right.'

'Did it occur to you that maybe she's posting them to make you jealous?'

'No,' she said glumly. 'Anyway, it doesn't matter. I'm not sure I want to date someone who knows that many hot women. It's not good for my ego.'

'Now you're being ridiculous. You hardly fell out of the ugly tree.' It was the truth. Naomi looked like an urban rock chick, with her short, choppy bob and edgy dress sense. Even Megan thought that she had style, and she never said that about anybody.

'Anyway, let's not talk about that psycho,' said Naomi. 'How's the wedding stuff coming along?'

'Fine, I guess.' She took a smaller mouthful of the warm wine and tried not to pull a face.

'Well, don't sound too enthusiastic . . .'

Lizzie debated whether to tell her about the whole Alex saga, but decided against it. She didn't really have time right now, plus she knew from experience that Naomi could be a bit indiscreet when she had a few drinks in her – and she didn't want her getting smashed at the wedding and recounting the tale to other guests.

'No, it's all good. I've just had a lot on my plate this month.'

Naomi nodded. 'I noticed. What was all that about earlier?' She leaned in curiously, and Lizzie wondered if this was the real reason she'd offered to take her out and buy the drinks. *Either she's feeling sorry for me or she's fishing for gossip.* She didn't know which was worse.

'It's nothing. I've been juggling several projects and I forgot to submit something on time. Then Ella went a bit . . . you know. Like she does.'

'Batshit?' Naomi popped a handful of peanuts into her mouth and washed them down with wine.

'More like . . . disappointed. But I get where she's coming from. It was my fault.'

'Oh, don't do that,' she groaned.

'Do what?'

'Act all reasonable about it. How many times have you handed in something late since you started here?'

'Hardly ever. Why?'

'Well, she needs to give you a break. Everyone knows you've got the wedding coming up. You're bound to be a little preoccupied.'

'It's not just that,' said Lizzie quietly. 'I'm not really sure my heart's in it any more.'

'In what? The wedding?' Naomi looked shocked.

'No! I meant PR.' She had never confessed that to anyone before, and if she'd thought it through properly, Naomi wouldn't have been her first pick to keep a secret. But it felt good to finally admit it.

'Oh, right.' She leaned in closer, beckoning Lizzie to do the same. 'If I tell you something, can you keep your mouth shut?'

'Of course,' she replied. *Better than you, I'd imagine . . .*

'OK.' She tapped her hands on top of the table to mimic a drum roll. 'I've decided to quit!'

'Smoking?'

'No! Don't start that again. Work.'

'What? Are you serious?' Lizzie almost fell off her seat. 'When?'

'I'm going to wait three more months, just to make sure I've saved up enough. But if everything goes to plan, I'll hand in my notice while you're on your honeymoon. That's assuming I don't explode first. Everyone's on my case this week.'

'Then what?'

'Then I'm going to set up my own web business. It'll just be me to start with, but at least I'll be the boss!'

Lizzie toyed with the rim of her glass. 'Won't that be a big pay cut?'

'Ha, now you sound like my mum. That'll be the first thing she says.' Naomi reached for another handful of peanuts. 'I don't think it'll be so bad. I've been saving up for a while and my old roommate reckons she can put some work my way.' She threw a nut in the air and caught it in her mouth. 'Anyway, my mind's made up.'

'Whoa. This is huge.' Lizzie was quiet for a second, allowing the news to sink in. She was going to miss Naomi horribly, but she admired her guts. *Maybe it's time I moved on, too.* She'd only meant to take the job for a couple of years before writing a book of her own, but now her five-year work anniversary was creeping up fast, and she was becoming part of the office furniture. 'Don't get me wrong, though; I think it's amazing. I'd love to do my own thing.'

'Like what?'

She hesitated. 'Don't laugh, but I'd really like to write a novel.'

'Why would I laugh? You'd be a great writer!'

'Really?'

'Definitely. You should totally do it.' She grinned. 'You only live once, right?'

Lizzie was tempted. *Naomi's got a point. If I never give it a go, I'm always going to sit there wondering, aren't I?*

'Let me think about it for a while. I need to talk it over with Josh.'

'You should tell him tonight!' Lizzie had never seen her friend so excited.

'Maybe,' she smiled. 'Depends what kind of mood he's in when I get back. He's a terrible patient.' Josh was normally so active that he couldn't cope when he was laid low. 'That reminds me, I should probably head off soon and pick up some stuff for dinner. It'll take me a while to get home.'

'Not so fast,' said Naomi. 'Let's have a toast before we go.'

'To what?'

Naomi looked thoughtful. 'To taking the plunge,' she said with a cheeky grin. 'And to your future bestseller, of course.'

'I like the sound of that,' said Lizzie, raising her glass. 'Cheers.'

'Cheers,' said Naomi, clinking hers against it. 'Oh, and there's one thing you have to promise me before you go.'

Lizzie was curious. 'Go on . . .'

'When you're a famous writer, can I run your website?'

Lizzie hurried up the front path, desperate to set down the two carrier bags that were digging painfully into her left palm. One had a large split in the side and was threatening to burst open at any second, spilling its contents every-where. *Just . . . one . . . more . . . minute.* She opened the door with her other hand and squeezed into the hall, promptly tripping over Josh's mud-caked trainers in the process. The bag gave way and two tins of chopped tomatoes tumbled out, almost landing on her toes.

Aaaargh.

She bundled up the food as best she could and lugged it towards the kitchen. The sound of the fridge door being slammed made her jump.

'Josh, I'm going to make spag bol tonight. You hungry?'

A figure stepped out from the shadow of the kitchen doorway into the hall. 'Hey, Lizzie, got any more beers?' said Freddie. 'I can't find any.' He had, however, managed to find the tortilla chips that she'd been saving for movie night with Megan. He fished one out with his stubby fingers, overloaded it with salsa and licked it. Then he double-dipped it back into the jar, before crunching it loudly between his big teeth. *Gross.* Lizzie tried not to gag and pointed him in the direction of the bottom cupboard.

'There's usually a few more in there. They won't be cold, though.'

'Shame. Never mind.' He shuffled back into the kitchen and shoved the half-eaten salsa in the fridge. *As if we'd want it now!* Then he bent down, his ill-fitting jeans giving her a view she'd rather not have seen, and retrieved two cans of lager.

'Got any bitter?'

'No, I don't think so.' *What do I look like, a pub?*

'OK, then, we'll take a couple of these . . .' It didn't seem to occur to him to ask if she might like a drink.

'Want some pork scratchings with that?' she asked sarcastically.

'No thanks, I'm alright,' said Freddie.

That's debatable.

She changed the subject. 'How's Josh feeling now?'

'You what?' Freddie blinked gormlessly.

'He wasn't feeling well today. He called in sick.'

'Oh. Dunno. He didn't mention it.'

Probably because he couldn't get a word in edgeways. Freddie liked the sound of his own voice way too much, though most of the time he didn't say anything worth listening to. Whenever he and Josh met up, it was like they were sucked back to their sixth-form days, where they'd bonded over sport and beer and immature banter – which, to be honest, was pretty much still the glue that kept their friendship together. Lizzie had started to dread him showing up at their place, and would have stayed out with Naomi if she'd known he was coming over. Still, at least she could send him home afterwards. She pitied his new wife Fran, who was stuck with him for good.

She followed him through to the lounge, where Josh was looking decidedly more lively, shouting at the footballers on the TV. The only sign of his illness was the trail of used tissues scattered on the sofa beside him.

'Hi, gorgeous. Freddie's here,' he said, stating the obvious.

'Yes, we were just chatting,' she said. 'How are you feeling now?' When she'd left for work that morning, Josh made out that he was practically dying, blowing his nose loudly and speaking with a rasp that could have impressed Darth Vader.

'Much better, thanks. It seemed to shift once I got up.'

'That's good.' She gave him a big smile. 'Don't suppose you managed to write a few invites then, by any chance?'

'What?' He forced a cough. 'No, I mean I'm on the mend, but I'm obviously not 100 per cent yet.'

Obviously.

'Alright. Well, I guess we could do them on Saturday.'

'That was never a foul,' interrupted Freddie, oblivious to the fact that another conversation was taking place. 'Did you see that? Unbelievable.'

'Er, no, I didn't,' said Josh. 'Rewind a minute and we'll watch it again.'

'The ref's a twat,' said Freddie.

'Takes one to know one,' Lizzie muttered under her breath.

Josh turned his attention back to her. 'Sorry, hon, what were you saying?'

'I was just saying we need to sort the invites. But it can wait till the weekend.'

'Oh. Does it have to be this weekend?'

She was starting to lose patience now. 'Well, it has to be soon. It's not like your Christmas cards, Josh – you can't send them out the week before. People need a bit of notice, you know.'

'Isn't that what those other things were for?'

'What? No, they were just save-the-dates. They don't give any of the details.' She took a deep breath and tried again. 'Could you please help me out for a couple of hours on Saturday? It's not exactly my idea of fun either, but it won't take long if we do it together.'

Josh looked sheepish. 'The thing is, we've managed to get a couple of tickets for the match now,' he mumbled.

'It's a big game,' chipped in Freddie.

They're all big bloody games. 'How about Sunday?'

'Sunday's the kids' tournament, remember? I'm ref for that one.'

'The referee's a wanker,' chanted Freddie, pointing at Josh.

Lizzie wanted to throw a cushion at both their heads. 'Let's talk about this later,' she sighed.

'Alright,' said Josh. He gave her his widest don't-be-mad-at-me eyes. 'I'll make it up to you. Maybe I can do a few this week after work instead?'

'OK. Are you hungry?'

'I'm famished,' said Freddie. 'What time's dinner?'

I take it you're staying, then? 'About half an hour.'

'Oh.' Freddie turned his attention back to the telly and whacked the volume up. 'What the hell is he *doing*? I've seen parked cars go quicker than that . . .'

Lizzie couldn't listen to them any more. She went back

into the kitchen and began to prepare the food, taking her frustration out on the mince as she jabbed at it with a wooden spoon. No one had ever told her that planning a wedding would feel like this much hard work. The bridal magazines made it all sound so glamorous and fabulous.

Her mind drifted back to the relaxed wedding she'd once dreamed of, without any of the fuss. She couldn't help wondering how different things might have been if she'd been doing all this with Alex. It suddenly occurred to her that maybe he was already married, or engaged, planning an elaborate extravaganza of his own elsewhere with some spreadsheet-wielding fiancée. It wasn't a vision she could easily picture, or perhaps she just didn't want to. Still, she was pretty sure he'd have hated a big, conventional bash.

She threw a tin of chopped tomatoes into the pan and squished them forcefully against the sides. Alex's return had wound her up in a way she hadn't expected. *He couldn't have picked a worse time, could he? Like he was waiting for me to be happy again, just so he could come back and spoil it.* The more she thought about it, the more she began to burn with anger. *Who does he think he is?* The heat from the hob made her temperature surge even higher, until she felt she was at boiling point.

For a split second, she wished she could run away, just as Alex had done all those years ago. Quit her job. Leave town. Tell Freddie where to stick it on her way out. The thought was incredibly tempting, but even as she savoured it, she knew she was kidding herself. That sort of thing only happened in trashy soaps and Hollywood movies, not suburban Surrey.

Besides, I do love Josh. I'd miss him a lot.

'Hey Lizzie, can you grab us a couple more cans, please?' Freddie yelled from the front room. She gave the mince a violent stir.

Him, not so much.

8

25 December 2002

Lizzie reached under the Christmas tree and retrieved an envelope with her name on it in swirly black biro. The spruce was huge – almost touching the ceiling – and haphazardly strewn with decorations, from fairy lights to tinsel to chocolates. It was a far cry from the small artificial version at her parents' house, with its tasteful red and silver baubles and solitary star. This one was uninhibited, unashamed and beautiful. She decided then and there that if she and Alex had a family of their own someday, they would have a tree just like this one, in all its delightful disarray.

Opening the envelope carefully, she extracted a card and two crisp £10 book vouchers. 'Oh, thank you,' she said, smiling at Alex's parents. 'I know exactly what I'm going to get with this. There are a couple of new novels I've been dying to read.'

'I'm sorry it's not more exciting,' said his mum Pamela, a slim woman in her late 40s with a mass of bottle-blonde hair and kind blue eyes. 'Alex told us you were into books, but we didn't know what you'd got already.'

'No really, it's brilliant.' Vouchers were better than cash because they had to be spent on something readable, rather than getting frittered away on something boring like the looming electricity bill.

'I do like a good bookshop, don't you?' his mum continued. 'More than that online jungle . . .'

'I think you mean Amazon, Mum,' Alex interrupted, trying not to laugh. He caught Lizzie's eye and she had to bite her lip to stifle her giggles.

'Right, who's next?' said Alex's dad, his voice booming around the homely living room. Frank Jackson had a hearing impairment that always made him seem as if he was shouting. Lizzie had found it pretty daunting at first, but now she was starting to get used to it, like watching TV with the volume turned up too loud.

'I am!' said Andi, a bubbly 18-year-old who Lizzie had immediately recognised with relief as the pretty blonde from his corkboard. Her real name was Andrea, but Alex said no one had called her that for years. She reached for a parcel and gouged at the wrapping paper with her crimson talons. Inside was a pair of expensive-looking hair straighteners. 'Yes! You got the right ones. Thanks, Mum! You too, Dad.'

'Don't thank us – thank Santa,' came the deafening reply.

'Oh Dad, you know you can stop that now.'

Just then, Alex's brother trudged downstairs in tracksuit bottoms and a crumpled white T-shirt, his hair ruffled and his eyes barely open. Though they weren't identical twins, he looked even more like Alex in the flesh, with the same muscular build and strong features. From a distance it could have been hard to tell them apart, bar the series of distinctive Sanskrit tattoos running down his right arm. Today, however, he also seemed a little worse for wear, resembling a picture of prehistoric man.

'Afternoon, Connor,' said Mr Jackson. 'Glad you could join us.'

'Yeah, sorry, Dad. Turned into a bit of a heavy session last night. I was only planning to stop by for one.' He yawned loudly, not bothering to cover his mouth. 'Could you give me a lift into town later to fetch the bike? I had to leave it there.' Lizzie still hadn't seen the famous bike, but she knew from Alex it was his brother's pride and joy, a Honda Fireblade he had spent two years saving up for while working at the local gym.

'Well, not really. I promised your mother I'd give her a hand with the food.'

'I'll run you down in a bit,' said Alex. 'But I've got a couple more presents to give first.' He held out his hand to Lizzie. 'They're upstairs.'

'I bet they are,' grinned Connor cheekily.

'Eeeew,' groaned Andi. 'No sex jokes in front of the olds, please.'

'Less of the old, missy,' yelled Mr Jackson. Lizzie guessed he was joking, but it was hard to tell at that volume. She absorbed the banter between them like a Christmas pudding soaking up brandy, enjoying the warmth of their comfortable familiarity. It was the first time she had ever spent Christmas away from home, and while she was looking forward to getting to know Alex's relatives better, she'd had a niggling fear that she might feel like the odd one out. But she needn't have worried: they had all gone out of their way to put her at ease, especially Mrs Jackson, who had even filled a small stocking with fruit and chocolate coins, just like Lizzie had told Alex her own mum used to do.

She followed him out into the hall – almost stumbling over the family's sausage dog, Jagger, who was busily trying to bite the head off a plush Christmas toy – and up to his old room, with its moody blue walls and single bed. There hadn't been space for her in there, so she was staying in the chintzy spare room down the hall, which reminded her a little of her great-aunt June's house.

They sat on his bed, and Alex reached underneath and retrieved two presents: one small and square, the other longer. 'These are for you,' he said simply, and Lizzie wondered whether he had spent as long shopping for her as she had for him, not sure how extravagant to be with those tricky first Christmas gifts. She had placed hers under the tree for him to open that morning: the first was a chunky charcoal-coloured jumper that matched his eyes, which he was now wearing; the second was the new Badly Drawn Boy CD, but the main surprise was a customised leather guitar strap with Alex's initials embossed on it, which he had been chuffed to bits with.

'Does it matter which one I open first?'

'Do the bigger one first.'

She peeled off the wrapping paper, not sure what to expect, and pulled out a rectangular box. Inside, buried beneath layers of white tissue paper, was a beautiful A5 notebook in soft pink leather. On the first sheet was written:

For words on pages. Alex xxx

'I . . . I . . . don't know what to say,' she whispered. 'I love it.'

'Good.' His eyes met hers. 'Because I love you.' The words that had been hovering unspoken for weeks were finally released into the wild.

The room began to spin before Lizzie's eyes as she tried to absorb the news, feeling warm and dizzy and ecstatic all at once. She threw both arms around his neck and kissed him fiercely. 'I'm totally in love with you, too, in case you hadn't guessed.'

'Well, in that case, I think you can open the second surprise.'

She smiled. 'Would you have taken it back if I hadn't said anything?'

'I don't know. Luckily for you it was the right answer.'

Lizzie began to open the smaller parcel, her hands still shaking from his sudden declaration. The wrapping paper fell away to reveal a small, hard box bearing a fancy gold-embossed logo. *A ring? No, don't be daft – it's only been three months. Would I say yes, though, if it was?*

She opened it slowly and gasped. Softly nestled on a red velvet cushion was a delicate silver heart pendant, the most stunning piece of jewellery she'd ever seen in real life.

'Turn it over.' She gently lifted it out of the box and read the inscription on the back: *Forever*.

'It's beautiful,' she beamed, holding it up against her top. Alex leaned behind her and fastened the clasp, his fingers brushing the nape of her neck.

'I was going to put both our names on, but it would have taken the engraver all day,' he laughed. 'And been really tiny.'

'No, it's just right,' she said, turning her face back to his. 'They're both perfect. The best presents anyone has ever given me.' Alex looked pleased with himself, and she knew what a gamble this must have been. *Good job I didn't buy him those novelty headphones.*

He gestured to the notebook. 'Now you can get started on that bestseller.'

'Maybe not right this second . . .' She kissed him again.

'Alright then, maybe after lunch. Did I tell you my mum makes a mean Christmas feast?'

It was 3pm in the afternoon and the Jacksons were all well fed, the scent of the succulent turkey still lingering throughout the house. Alex's mum had dished up a banquet of epic proportions: juicy meat with a herby stuffing, crispy golden roast potatoes, sausages wrapped with sticky pancetta, slivers of colourful carrot and perfectly cooked

brussels sprouts, all followed by Christmas pud with lashings of brandy butter. Everyone dived in for seconds, and
it took all of Lizzie's willpower not to go back for more
than that. She was glad she hadn't now, though; the waist-
band on her skirt wasn't expanding anywhere near as easily
as her stomach.

'Right, I think it's time for some games,' said Mr Jackson,
who was well on his way to a merry Christmas, having
necked four glasses of wine over dinner. 'What do we want
to start with? That one with the humming?'

'Definitely no humming,' said Connor. 'You lot couldn't
carry a tune if it came with handles.'

'How about charades?'

'Oh, yes, I love charades,' piped up Mrs Jackson, still
wearing her paper party hat. 'Shall we split into teams?'

Alex raised his eyebrows. 'I don't think Lizzie is used to
Christmas charades, Mum. Maybe we could just chill out
after lunch and watch telly?'

'No, I'm intrigued,' said Lizzie. 'Sounds like it's a bit of
a Christmas tradition.'

'Yes, it is,' smiled Mrs Jackson. 'And we'll have nice even
teams with you here for a change. Shall we say me and
Dad, Andi and Connor, and Alex with Lizzie?'

'No way, I'm not going with Connor again,' said Andi.
'Last year he called me his Andicap just because he was
too thick to get my clues.'

'You do know *Bugsy Malone* isn't an insect, right?'
Connor looked amused.

'Yes, but nothing rhymes with *Bugsy* so I was trying to break it down, you ignorant—.'

'Oh yeah, we're definitely going to have to split you two up,' said Alex.

'Why don't I go with Lizzie?' suggested Andi. 'I could use some help outside this limited gene pool.'

'Fine with me,' said Connor. 'I'll go with big bro.' There was actually only a 13-minute age gap between him and Alex, though it was starting to feel like more to Lizzie. 'We'll kick your arses!'

'You'll look like arses,' Andi shot back. Lizzie wasn't quite sure what she'd let herself in for, but she figured it had to beat watching *The Snowman* for the millionth time.

Mr Jackson poured himself another large glass of wine and sank down into the sofa next to his wife.

'Let the games begin!' he said, even more loudly than usual.

Nearly two hours, three games and umpteen rounds later, Connor and Alex emerged victorious, whooping loudly and slapping one another on the back. Lizzie was fascinated by their boisterous banter. Christmas at her house was a much more sedate affair, with her parents settling down quietly post-lunch to watch the Queen's speech, or perhaps the *EastEnders* special if they were feeling really indulgent. She felt a momentary pang of guilt about leaving them alone today, even though she and Alex had been to visit them in Twickenham last weekend. She had already tried to call home once, but the line had been engaged, and she hadn't yet had a spare minute to try again.

'Hey, do you think you could give me a lift into town to get my bike now?' Connor asked Alex.

'Sure,' he replied. 'Lizzie, do you want to come, too?'

'Yeah, go on then.'

'So, you two really are joined at the hip, huh?' said Connor, grabbing his bike keys from the hall table. 'What happens when one of you needs the toilet?'

'Whatever,' said Alex. 'Just because you can't get a girl friend.'

'Correction: don't *want* a girlfriend,' grinned Connor. 'In case you hadn't noticed, I'm far too much of a catch to be tied down to any one woman.' He winked at Lizzie. 'Of course, if you ever get bored with bro here, you know you can always come on a bike ride with a real man.'

'Only if one steals the Honda,' said Alex, punching him playfully on the arm.

Connor clipped him back. 'You're just jealous. It's way better than your crappy old banger.'

'Yeah, keep telling yourself that while you're walking into town to get your bike.'

'Ooh, someone's touchy today. Is it the wrong time of the month or what?'

'Piss off, Connor.'

As they sparred back and forth, joking and jostling, Lizzie could barely keep up.

'Do they always go at each other like that?' she asked

Mrs Jackson later over a cup of tea in the kitchen, the aroma of turkey still lingering in the air. Jagger was yelping excitedly in the corner, happily ripping used wrapping paper into shreds.

'Yes, ever since they were small,' she said, dunking a ginger biscuit into a fancy mug marking the Queen's Golden Jubilee. 'It's funny – the two of them used to fight like you wouldn't believe, but if another kid ever tried to pick on one of them . . . well, then all hell used to break loose.'

'Really?' Lizzie glanced out of the window to where the brothers were tinkering with Connor's bike in the floodlit garden. She still couldn't get over the striking resemblance between them.

'Oh yes. I remember once, back when they were in school, this bully down the road – Sean, I think his name was – stole Connor's skateboard. And wouldn't you know, Alex went down there to try to get it back, even though this kid was twice his size.'

'What happened?'

'Sean refused to hand it over, so Alex kicked him right in the shin. Gave him a big old bruise, he did! I made him apologise, of course – we've never encouraged the boys to use violence. But sure enough, the next morning, that skateboard was back in our front garden. I think the kid even cleaned it.'

Lizzie tried to imagine what it would have been like to have siblings who stuck up for you no matter what. Her mum and dad had always been protective, but it wasn't the same as having your own personal backup squad on standby. She sometimes wondered if her birth parents had ever had any more children: an extended family tucked away somewhere who probably didn't even know she existed.

'I kind of wish I'd had a brother – you know, to look out for me like that.' She wasn't sure why her parents had never adopted again. It used to make her feel guilty growing up; sometimes she worried that she might have put them off. When she was 13, she plucked up the courage to ask why they'd not wanted a bigger family, and her mum said it was because they could never love another child as much as they loved her. She still didn't know if that was the whole story, but it had made her feel a little less lonely.

'Yeah, they're my double act, alright. I feel sorry for poor Andi sometimes, having to put up with all the testosterone in the house. It'll be good for her having you around.' She polished off her biscuit. 'Do you have any sisters?'

'No, it's just me and my parents. Actually, that reminds me, would it be OK to try calling them again?'

'Sure, sweetie, go right ahead. You can take the cordless phone up to your room if you like.'

'Thanks.'

Heading for the cream carpeted stairs, Lizzie dialled her parents' landline and waited for one of them to pick up. 'Hello, Sparkes residence,' answered her mum after five rings, using what Lizzie knew was her poshest telephone voice.

'Hi Mum, it's only me,' said Lizzie. 'Happy Christmas. How's it going?'

'Oh, Elizabeth, hi! Yes, we're fine here. Dad and I went to the pub for lunch with Auntie Carole and now we've all come back for a few mince pies.' There was a mumble in the background. 'What's that, Carole? No, it's our Elizabeth.' She paused. 'Carole sends her love.'

'Same to her.' She pushed open the guest room door and sat down on the faded floral duvet. 'Sounds like you're having a fun day, then?'

'Yes, we are. So you don't have to worry about us.' Her voice dropped to a whisper. 'Although I think your father could have used some help with his Christmas shopping. I asked him for some hot tongs and he got me a pair of salad tongs.'

'He didn't?'

'He did! I hope he's kept the receipt.' She chuckled. 'So, how's Christmas with Alex?'

'Yeah, great. His family are nice – I can't wait for you to meet them.'

'Get any good presents?'

'Loads. Alex got me a proper writer's notebook and a silver necklace.'

'A necklace, eh? Sounds like a keeper. Perhaps he can have a quiet word with your father next year.'

'Is Dad around now?' She could just about make out

the opening strains of the *EastEnders* Christmas special starting up.

'He was, but he's gone and locked himself in the bathroom. Probably too much turkey.'

'That's gross!'

'It certainly is. And you're not the one who still has to live with him.'

'Too much information, Mum!' Lizzie coughed.

'Sorry.'

'Well, tell him I called, won't you?'

'Will do. Say hello to that handsome young man of yours. I'm going to have a sit down and watch the telly.'

'OK.' She hugged the phone closer to her ear. 'I miss you.'

'I miss you too, love.' The crack in her voice would have been imperceptible to anyone but Lizzie. 'Merry Christmas.'

'Merry Christmas, Mum.'

9

9 weeks to go . . .

Lizzie took a sip of coffee and smiled at her mum over the kitchen table. They had spent the past two hours slipping gold-trimmed invitations into satiny envelopes, addressing each one carefully with their neatest writing. She was grateful not only for the helping hand while Josh was at the football, but also for the chance to spend a quiet morning together. In the whirlwind of the wedding prep she hadn't seen as much of her parents as she normally liked.

'Only a couple more to go now, love,' said her mum. 'We'll be finished in no time.'

'Thanks for this,' said Lizzie. 'You've done a brilliant job.'

'Oh, you don't need to thank me, Elizabeth. I still can't believe our little girl's getting married! Your dad hasn't stopped telling people, you know. Last week the poor postman couldn't get away for half an hour. And you should have heard him on the phone to Auntie Carole.'

'I hope he's not too upset we can't invite his work lot. I did feel bad about that, but there's just so many of them.'

The first draft of the guest list had been over 200 names long, with both sets of parents hoping to include every known acquaintance under the sun. Lizzie and Josh had been forced to slash the numbers right down – no easy feat, but crucial given the cost per head. In the end, they'd restricted it to close friends, family and a few of her mother's 'must-haves', trimming the total to 100 for the day and another 25 for the evening.

'No, he understands. I haven't seen him this excited in years. He keeps leaving notes for his speech all over the damn kitchen. It's driving me round the bend!'

'Well, that's good. Not that he's getting on your nerves, I mean, but that he's looking forward to it.'

'Oh, yes, we're all looking forward to it. It's going to be so much better than Judy's daughter's wedding. Terrible canapés.' Lizzie remembered that for her mum and her badminton friends, social events were another form of competitive sport. 'But enough about us, how are you feeling?' She looked her daughter up and down. 'You seem to have lost weight. You're not doing one of those faddy diets, are you?'

'No, I'm not,' said Lizzie.

'Because you know what I think of those . . .'

'Mum, I'm not! Really. I think it's just all the rushing around for the wedding. It's been a bit stressful lately.'

Her mother shook her head. 'You youngsters, you get yourselves worked up over everything. What's there to be stressed about? You should be bursting with excitement.'

Lizzie took a deep breath, wondering whether to confide in her about Alex's recent return. Like Megan, her mum had been a huge support when he left, and would hopefully dish out some sensible advice. *Or maybe I'd just freak her out, too? She knows he broke my heart.*

The confession hovered on her lips for a second, before she swilled it down with another swig of coffee. It was probably best to tell as few people as possible. *Besides, it's not like I called him. Better to just keep quiet.*

'Of course I'm excited. It's going to be amazing.' She slid another invite into its envelope and sealed it with a flourish. 'You only get one wedding day, right?'

'Well, look at Joan Collins,' her mum replied. 'But yes, I'm sure you and Josh will just have the one. Unless you decide to renew your vows – your father and I have been thinking about that, you know.'

'Really?'

'Maybe. All this wedding fever has got us in the mood. Perhaps we'll elope somewhere sunny, do it in style.'

'There's always Las Vegas.'

'Oh, I'm not sure about that. You know what your dad's like – he'd be turning up in an Elvis suit or something.' She winced at the thought. 'But it would be good to get away, maybe take that second honeymoon . . .'

Lizzie wasn't sure whether the prospect of her parents on honeymoon was endearing or disgusting, but she admired the way they still seemed loved-up after more than 30 years of marriage. 'Mum . . .' she mused tentatively, 'how did you know Dad was The One when you met him?'

'Gosh, I never really thought about it, love. The first few times I met him, I didn't notice him all that much, if I'm honest.'

'What, even though he lived down the road?'

'Well, it wasn't like he was next door. We never really got chatting properly until that day my car broke down. And even then it took a while for him to grow on me.'

'But when were you absolutely sure? Like, 100 per cent?'

'I don't know. There wasn't just one moment.'

Lizzie was disappointed, realising that her mum wasn't about to impart some magical formula for marital bliss. 'So over time, you just knew?'

'I guess so. Why all the questions?' She patted her daughter's hand. 'Are you feeling a bit weird about the wedding?'

'No! Not really. Maybe a little.' Lizzie coughed nervously. 'Is that normal? Do you think there's something wrong with me?'

'Oh darling, I think there'd be something wrong with you if you didn't feel like that,' her mum reassured her. 'Marriage is a big commitment, and you're bound to get a little outbreak of cold feet from time to time. It happens to most people, believe me.'

'Even you?'

'Oh yes, I was a mess the week before! But it's nothing to worry about. You love Josh, don't you?'

'Yes. Josh is great.'

'Well, then, it'll all work out fine – you'll see. I remember when they opened the door to the church on our wedding day, and I saw your father standing at the other end of the aisle, I just knew that there was no one else I'd rather marry. And now look: I'm still stuck with the daft git.'

Lizzie patted her mum's hand. She always knew how to make her feel better. 'Thanks. If Josh and I are half as happy as you two, we'll be lucky.'

'When's he getting back?'

'Not for a few hours. They'll probably go for a drink after the football.'

'Well, maybe the two of you should go out and do something nice tonight. We've done really well with these invites.'

'Yeah, that sounds like a good idea.' Just then Lizzie's mobile rang, and Megan's name flashed up on the screen. 'Hi, Meg. Can I call you back in a bit? I've got Mum here at the moment.'

'OK,' said Megan. 'Tell her I said hi.'

'Megan says hi.'

'HI THERE,' her mum shouted loudly in the direction of the phone. She kissed Lizzie on the cheek. 'Look, don't hang up on my account, love. I was about to leave anyway.'

'But I thought . . .'

'You girls have a good chat. I'd better be getting back.' She picked up her bulky handbag. 'Now remember, don't get yourself all worked up worrying. I'll give you a call in the week. And I can see myself out.'

'Are you sure?'

'Yes, yes . . .' Her mum gave a cheery wave. 'BYE MEGAN,' she yelled as she made her way towards the door.

'Er, bye, Mrs S,' said Megan.

'No, it's me again now,' said Lizzie.

'This is way too confusing for a Saturday. My hangover's not up to it.' Megan sounded tired and a little croaky.

'Heavy night?'

'Yeah, kind of. I went to this launch event with work. I wasn't going to stay that late, but there was a nail bar and a candy bar and a free bar, and it all got a bit messy.'

'Sounds like it. Any cute guys there?'

'At a beauty do? Oh, please. The only guy I saw all night was the doorman.' She groaned melodramatically. 'I think I might have to get back online.' Megan had been totally addicted to dating apps until the last guy she went out with started sending her snapshots of his manhood. To her work email.

'Really? I thought those photos had put you off for life.'

'I think I was just unlucky there.'

'I'll say . . .'

Megan giggled. 'So anyway, what did you and your mum get up to this morning? You'd better not have been shopping without me. Did you get the link to that bridesmaid's dress I sent you?'

'Yes, it's beautiful. I've already ordered it.'

'Great! I thought you'd love it. So how's your mum? What did I miss?'

'She's fine. We spent all morning writing the invites, so you didn't exactly miss much.'

'Fair enough. I'm not sure you'd have got me out of bed for that one.' She paused. 'Hey, speaking of invites, what are you wearing to the uni ball?'

'The what?' Lizzie vaguely recalled seeing an envelope from the alumni association a few weeks ago, but she'd assumed they were asking for money and chucked it in the recycling bin.

'They're having a big summer reunion for the old students. Remember how much fun we had in the first year, with the fancy dress?' As young freshers, Megan and Lizzie had already maxed out their student loan by ball week, so they'd simply stripped off their bedsheets and transformed them into Grecian togas. Lizzie felt a little self-conscious until she'd consumed several cocktails, but Megan pulled off the look perfectly and went home with a strapping gladiator.

'I'm not really sure I want to wear my bedding in public again, ta.'

'Don't worry – this time it's going to be black tie, so we can get all glammed up. Come round to mine and we'll raid Lily's closet.'

'When is it?'

'Next weekend. We are going to go, right?'

Lizzie's face fell. She hated to disappoint her best friend, but she really didn't feel like trying to rekindle their university days right now, especially with so much left to sort out. 'I'm just not sure I'm going to have time for something like that, Meg, with the wedding only two months away,' she said softly.

There was a long pause on the other end of the line.

'Look, Lizzie,' said Megan eventually. 'I know you're really busy and everything, but it would mean a lot if you'd come to this with me.'

'Why are you so keen to go?'

'I just think it'll be fun. We can get all dressed up and dance the night away like old times. It'll be one last girlie night out before the wedding.'

'Er, isn't that what my hen do's for?'

'That doesn't count. You'll be so drunk you're not going to remember that one.'

'Actually, I don't think I'm going to be that—'

'Oh come on, Lizzie, do it for me! Pleeeeeaaase?'

Lizzie was torn. Megan had been her best friend for years – always ready to pick her up with wine, wisecracks and *Sex And The City* reruns – so it seemed selfish to refuse her now. On the other hand, she was in no mood to take another trip down memory lane, especially when she was trying so hard to forget about . . .

Alex.

Did he get an invite, too?

'Oh, I don't know, Meg. What if Alex turned up or something? I don't think I could face running into him.'

'Alex? At a ball? Hardly his thing, is it? He didn't even go to them when we were at uni.'

That was true, Lizzie had to admit. Alex liked his gigs. He liked his festivals. But he definitely wasn't one for getting dressed up in a stuffy dinner suit.

'What if you're wrong?'

'Look, they've hired some stately home for the night, so it's going to be massive. On the off-chance Alex did turn up, you wouldn't have to go anywhere near him – you probably wouldn't even see him. But he won't bother with something like that, Lizzie. Trust me.'

'Oh . . . well . . .'

'Is that a yes?' Megan on a mission was impossible to resist.

'Alright, yes.'

'Yay, you're the best!' Lizzie heard what sounded like clapping down the phone. 'Honestly, this is going to be so much fun. You're not going to regret it.'

Hmmm, groaned Lizzie inwardly. *I wouldn't bet on that.*

10

6 October 2003

'What are you up to?' asked Lizzie, itching to remove the blindfold Megan had put on her in the car around 8pm.

'Sorry, I'm under strict orders not to say. Alex made me promise. You'll find out soon enough.'

Lizzie knew that they were on the beach, because she could feel the sand seeping into her pumps and hear the gentle lapping of the waves. What she didn't know was why – or how – Alex had managed to rope Megan into his plan.

'Do we really need the blindfold? It's dark out already.' She was shuffling along at a snail's pace, trying to keep her balance as the soft grains shifted beneath her feet. Every so often, she felt Megan's hand on her arm, navigating her around a potential pitfall. It was like being on some sort of bizarre team-building challenge.

'Look, that's what he said, so that's what I've done. It's all his idea.'

'Alright.' The salty tang of the sea air was intense as

Lizzie breathed it in through her mouth and nostrils. It wasn't a particularly cold evening, but she was glad she was wearing her denim jacket. 'Are we nearly there yet?'

'What are you, like, five? I'll tell you when we're there.'

'This isn't some kind of weird sex game, is it?' joked Lizzie.

'Damn, how did you guess? No, it's not some weird sex game. Or at least not the part that Alex told me about. What the two of you get up to afterwards is entirely your own business.'

'So why didn't Alex just come and get me himself?' She was growing more intrigued by the second.

'What's with all the questions? It'll make sense in a minute. Oh, hold on – sandcastle to your right.' Megan grabbed Lizzie with both hands and steered her out of the way. 'Hey, that's quite a good one, actually. Shame you can't see it.'

'Thanks.'

Just then Lizzie heard Alex in the distance: 'Ladies, over here.'

'Roger that,' said Megan, in a throaty cop-show voice. 'This is grey squirrel delivering moonlit badger. I think my work here is done.'

'Thanks, Meg,' said Alex. 'I owe you one. Are you alright getting home by yourself?'

'Er, let me see. I've managed to get Lizzie all the way down here – blindfolded, no less – without spoiling your surprise, but walking two minutes back to the car park could prove problematic.'

'I take it that's a yes. But send us a text when you get back.'

'Will do. Have fun, you two.' Lizzie felt Megan squeeze her arm and make a noise that sounded like an air kiss. Then everything was quiet, apart from the rhythmic swoosh of the ocean.

'Alex? Can I lose the blindfold? I'm starting to feel like I'm in some sort of bad crime drama.'

'Just give me a few more seconds.' She could feel the warmth of his body as he moved in closely behind her. 'Alright, you can take it off now.'

She removed the blindfold, and for a split second her eyes had to adjust from the darkness to the softly lit scene laid out before her. The night sky was dotted with Chinese lanterns, floating up into the heavens like tiny fireflies beneath the spotlight of the moon. Their gentle glow illuminated the cream picnic blanket spread out on the sand, which was weighed down by a wicker basket bulging with goodies in the top corner. There was even an ice bucket containing a bottle of Sancerre, which she loved but could only occasionally stretch to on her tight student budget.

'Happy anniversary,' he murmured in her ear. 'It's exactly one year ago that we had our first date here. Or sort of here. I didn't want to tempt fate by going back to that restaurant.'

Lizzie spun round to face him. 'You remembered?'

'Of course. Didn't you?'

'Yes! I just didn't figure you to be the . . .'

'The what?'

'You know, the anniversary-celebrating type. You never mentioned it.'

'I wanted to surprise you.'

'Well, you've certainly done that. This is amazing.' She wrapped her arms around his waist. 'I feel bad I didn't get you something now.'

'Don't worry about that,' he replied, pulling her close for a kiss. 'Just sit with me and let's crack open this bottle.' He crouched down on the blanket and she sat beside him, gazing at his silhouette as he pulled a penknife from his jeans pocket, uncorked the wine and poured it into two glasses. He handed one to her and raised the other in a toast. 'To us,' he said simply.

'To us,' she said, taking a sip of the chilled Sancerre. 'Alright then, don't keep a girl in suspense. What other goodies have you got in there?'

'Let's see . . .' He folded the knife away. 'There's some French bread and some of that brie you like, and some posh crisps—'

'What flavour?'

'Sea salt and vinegar.'

'Excellent choice. My favourite.'

'Yes, I do pay attention, believe it or not. And then for dessert I've got fresh strawberries and some chocolate brownies.'

Lizzie's mouth was watering just thinking about it.

'You're officially the best boyfriend in the world, you know that?'

'Well, I try.' Alex lay down on the picnic blanket, his dark hair flopping lazily across his right eye.

'I can't believe we've been together a year already,' said Lizzie, opening a bag of crisps and munching two hungrily. 'It's gone so fast.'

'Yeah, I guess it has.'

She leaned over and kissed him softly, leaving the tiniest trace of sea salt on his lips. 'I love you, you know. Though I'm not sure how you're going to top a private picnic on the beach next year.'

'At least I've got 12 months to work on it.' He reached up and pinched one of her crisps. 'Actually, these are really good.'

'Told you.' She looked out over the shore, where some of the lanterns – now tiny specks in the distance – were starting to extinguish themselves like dying stars. 'They're beautiful, aren't they?'

'You're beautiful.'

She smiled. 'Yeah well, flattery *and* food really will get you everywhere.'

'That's my cunning plan.'

She lay down beside him and rested her head on his jumper. 'I wonder what we'll be doing this time next year?' she said thoughtfully.

'What do you mean?'

'Well, you know, I guess me and Megan will be stuck

here for our fourth year, but your course will be done by then. Do you think you'll go full-time at the bar for a bit?'

He was quiet for a moment, and she could hear the sound of a siren in the distance. 'I don't know,' he said eventually. 'Connor and I had talked about maybe going travelling again after I finished my degree, but we'll have to see.'

Lizzie sat up straight, feeling like she'd just been punched in the gut. *You did what?* She couldn't conceal the shock that flashed across her face. 'Where were you thinking about going?'

'Asia, probably – India, maybe Vietnam, Thailand . . . We already did Australia, so we thought we'd try a different part of the world next time.'

She shovelled some more crisps into her mouth to avoid saying something she'd regret, but one went down the wrong way, causing her to cough and splutter.

'Lizzie, are you OK?'

'Uh-huh.' She took a large gulp of wine, trying to clear her throat. The errant crisp dislodged itself and she managed to catch her breath.

'You sure?' he said, frowning with concern. 'You scared me for a second there. Especially after last year . . .'

'I'm fine,' she said, not quite meeting his gaze. 'I should probably just eat slower, that's all.'

Alex reached for her hand. 'Are you mad about me mentioning the whole travelling thing, by any chance?'

'No. Course not.' She tried to keep her tone light, but she'd always been a terrible liar.

'Lizzie . . .' He looked at her with those big eyes and she caved.

'Alright, maybe I am a bit surprised that you're planning to go off and you've never even mentioned it,' she blurted. 'I wouldn't stop you, if that's what you're worried about. But I just figured you might have . . . you know, said *something*. How long would you be gone?'

'I'm not sure.' His face was almost touching hers now. 'Look, the reason I never brought it up is because I still haven't decided what I'm going to do next year. Yes, Connor and I had discussed maybe going away again, but that was before I fell in love with this gorgeous girl I met.'

Lizzie tried to crack a smile, though her stomach was churning wildly. 'Does she know about me?'

'No, I'm keeping you a secret.' He leaned in and kissed her fervently. 'I can't tell you what we'll be doing this time next year, Lizzie. But I can promise you this: whatever happens, we're going to find a way to make it work.'

She gnawed her lower lip nervously. 'How do you know?'

'I just do,' he said, silencing her with another kiss. 'It's a done deal.'

'Should we shake on it?' she teased, trying to hide the hurt in her voice.

Alex stood and took her right hand, pulling her up to her feet. 'We can go one better than that,' he said, leading her towards the tall cliff face behind them, which almost seemed to be glowing in the moonlight. He retrieved his penknife from his jeans again, flicking up the small blade, and began to carve their initials into the chalky rock: faintly at first, then deeper; the white dust crumbling away and trickling down to mingle with the sand.

'See? Now it's officially set in stone.'

Lizzie ran her fingers over the letters, the craggy surface cold beneath her skin. 'I'm holding you to this,' she said softly, feeling a sudden rush of love.

'I hope so,' said Alex, flipping the knife down and tucking it into his back pocket. He wrapped one strong arm across her shoulders. 'You don't have anything to worry about, you know.'

'I know.' She tried to ignore any lingering doubts as they strolled back towards the blanket. She belonged with Alex. And he belonged with her. *That's all that matters, isn't it? Even if we have to do the long-distance thing for a while.*

She glanced back at the towering rock behind her; so solid, so steadfast. Then the half-moon disappeared behind a cloud, plunging it into the shadows.

It'll be fine, she tried to reassure herself.

It has to be fine.

11

8 weeks to go . . .

Lizzie stood in front of the bedroom mirror, carefully applying lashings of mascara to set off her smoky eyeshadow. The last time she'd attempted to master this trend, she'd ended up looking like she'd been dealt two black eyes, but fortunately tonight's efforts had been more successful.

She scrutinised her reflection. The willowy gold ball-gown, borrowed from Megan's cousin, was not a bad fit – a little snug around the chest perhaps, but the length was almost perfect, and the elegant halterneck subtly showed off her slim build. Her hair, which she was growing for the wedding, was loosely curled, pinned slightly back with a delicate diamanté clip that matched the twinkling bracelet on her right hand. Her eyes were still the right side of smouldering, but she'd kept her lips simple, opting for a pale pink gloss. 'OK, you'll do,' she muttered to herself. 'Time to go.'

High heels in hand, she walked slowly down the stairs and into the lounge, where Josh was stretched out on the sofa, munching popcorn and watching the match. As soon as he saw her, he put down his bowl and let out a low wolf-whistle. Lizzie smiled. 'Yeah, yeah, I've trained you well.' She stepped into the pretty shoes, her freshly painted toes peeking out in a striking shade of scarlet.

'I'm serious. Do you know how sexy you look right now?' He got up from the couch and went to kiss her, planting his lips on her cheek as she turned her face slightly to avoid smearing her lipgloss.

'Sorry, but I don't have time to redo my make-up, given that Megan's meant to be here in . . .' – she glanced at the clock on the DVD player – 'about three and a half minutes.'

'I could show you a good time in three and a half minutes.'

She grinned. 'I don't doubt it. You sure you don't want to come with us?'

'I do now, with you all dressed up like that.' Josh pulled a sad face, which made him look even cuter. 'But like I said, I promised the kids we'd squeeze in an extra practice tomorrow. They've got a tough match coming up.'

'I understand,' she said. His devotion to the school football team was admirable, even if they didn't seem to win much.

'You would if you saw them last week,' he said. 'They only scored twice – and one of those was an own goal.'

Lizzie laughed. 'It's fine. You should stay.'

'Well, it's not like I'd really know many people, so I'm

sure you'll have a better night without me. Just make sure you fend off all those male admirers.'

'Seriously, I've seen what Megan wears to these things. It won't be me they'll be ogling.'

'Nah, you'll be the most gorgeous girl at the ball. But I hope you both have a great time.'

'Thanks. I guess it'll be fun to catch up with everyone again,' she smiled. 'And in two months you're going to be stuck with me for good, so one little evening apart won't hurt.'

'Well, when you put it like that . . .' Josh wrapped his arms around her waist and began to slowly kiss her neck. The warmth of his mouth made her skin tingle. 'This is OK, isn't it? Not going to ruin your make-up?'

'Yes, that's most definitely OK,' she said, suddenly wishing that she could cancel everything and whisk him upstairs instead.

Just then the sound of a horn beeped outside. 'That's Meg. I've got to go.' They moved into the hallway, and she gave him a big hug, letting her head linger on his shoulder. 'I love you.'

'Love you too. You really do look stunning.'

'Thanks. You're not so bad yourself.' She opened the door and waved at Megan, who was sitting behind the wheel of a convertible black Mercedes.

'Since when did she get a new car?' asked Josh, not even attempting to hide the envy in his voice.

'I've no idea,' said Lizzie. 'I've never seen it before in my life. I'll have to get all the goss.' She wrapped her arms tightly around his neck for a final hug. 'Right, I've really got to make a move now. I'll see you tomorrow.'

'Enjoy the ball, Cinderella.'

'I will.' She picked up the overnight bag she'd left by the door earlier and gave him a quick kiss. 'Bye, then.'

She could still feel his eyes lingering on her as she walked down the driveway, stuck her bag in the car boot and settled into the passenger seat. Megan gave a quick toot of the horn as the car purred to life and a waving Josh disappeared into the distance.

'Guess you're my hot date for this evening,' Megan joked. 'That dress looks incredible on you. I'll ask Lily if you can keep it. She's got so many she won't care.'

'Oh no, don't do that,' said Lizzie. 'It's nice of her just to lend it to me. And I love what you're wearing, too.' Megan was clad in a slinky topaz number, her tiny waist accentuated by a slim yellow belt that complemented her blonde corkscrew curls. She looked like she'd just stepped out of the fashion section of the website she worked for, a cross between a young Carrie Bradshaw and a fairytale princess.

'Thanks. I borrowed it from a stylist friend, so you can't let me spill anything down it, alright?'

'Er, OK. What about the new Mercedes? Don't tell me you "borrowed" that from the company car park?'

'Very funny. I did borrow it, if you must know – but only from my stepdad. He's still feeling guilty because he forgot my birthday. Worked out pretty well.'

'What's wrong with your car?'

'Nothing, I've left it at home. We haven't seen some of these people for years, Lizzie, so I thought we should turn up in style. Make a good impression.'

'Ah, so we're pretending it's yours . . .'

'No, we're not doing anything of the sort. But if people automatically assume it's my car then I'm not going to waste time correcting them.'

'I see.' Lizzie suppressed a smile. 'So how many people do you think we'll actually know at this thing?'

'A fair few,' replied Megan, checking her hair in the rear-view mirror. 'I sent an email to some of the old Cliffstowe crowd to see if they were going.'

'Like who?'

'Well, Louise said that she'll be there, with Helen and Joy.'

'Anyone else?' She did not name names, but Megan was sharp enough to pick up on the subtext.

'Oh, yeah, you'll be pleased to know that Alex is a no-show,' she said smugly.

Oh. Good. The mere mention of him always made Lizzie feel flustered. 'How do you know?'

'My old coursemate Ruby is married to his friend Dev. You remember Dev. Really tall. Great hair. Anyway, they're the ones who told me he was back in the first place.'

The names vaguely rang a distant bell. 'So? What makes them think he's not going?'

'I asked her to suss it out.'

'You did *what?*' Lizzie was horrified.

'No, don't worry, I was very discreet. But she said they'd already asked Alex if he wanted to go with them and he said – and I quote – "I'd rather jab a guitar pick in my eye."'

Ha. Lizzie gave a tight-lipped grin. 'Sounds about right. Like you said, it's not exactly his scene.'

'Told you. So now you can chill out. But Gareth's coming, by the way. Haven't seen him for ages!'

'Me either. It'll be good to catch up with him. And the girls.' She twiddled with her engagement ring. 'Do you think we should invite them to my hen do?'

Megan shrugged her shoulders. 'Up to you.'

'But what do you think?'

'Maybe play it by ear. See how this evening goes and then decide.'

'Good thinking. So are we heading straight to the ball now or swinging by the hotel?'

'Well, we're not going to be able to stop for long, but I thought we could dump our bags and then drive over to the venue. They've got parking there, so we can get a cab back to the hotel later and collect the car in the morning.'

'You're impressively organised today.'

'I'm always organised.'

Lizzie was tempted to remind her of the time she ran out of petrol on their trip to Devon, or the weekend they went to that music festival and Megan forgot where she'd pitched the tent, but decided to keep quiet. It had been a while since they'd enjoyed a girlie break and she didn't want anything to spoil it.

As they drove down the motorway, singing along to an old compilation CD of their favourite student anthems, Lizzie felt a wave of nostalgia wash over her. For most of her four years there, uni had been the happiest time of her life, but the final few months had cast a shadow over her previously sunny memories. *I'd forgotten how much I used to love all of this,* she thought, as Megan shamelessly murdered a Girls Aloud track alongside her. *I'm gutted I missed the graduation ball, but tonight things will be different. I'll get the chance to do it right.*

As the song came to an end, she hit the pause button on the stereo. 'You know, I probably don't say this enough, but thank you.'

'For what?'

'For everything. Not just tonight, with the dress and the driving, but all of it. I literally don't know where I'd be if it wasn't for you.'

Megan sniffed, and for a second Lizzie thought that her eyes looked a little watery. Then she shook her head, her curls bouncing around as if on springs. 'Stop it – you'll make me cry and then you'll mess up my mascara.'

'OK, sorry.'

'This wedding's turned you soft, you know. We only left Josh behind 30 minutes ago, and already you're getting soppy with me.'

'What can I say? I love both of you.'

Megan changed gear and smiled. 'Yeah, I'm pretty fond of you too, missus,' she said. 'Now stick my CD back on so that we can get to the Steps medley.'

Ninety minutes and one brief stop later, Megan turned the Mercedes on to a sweeping driveway leading up to a gravelly car park, her headlights illuminating the spectacular venue ahead of them. The stately home was huge, like something out of a Jane Austen novel, with imposing columns guarding the entrance and ivy creeping tastefully up the walls. The front lawn was beautifully manicured, its central walkway illuminated by cream candles in large glass lanterns, and fairy lights twinkled in the surrounding trees. 'It looks like a film set,' Lizzie marvelled, as they got out of the car. 'Don't you think, Meg?'

'Yeah, it's something to look at alright. Bet it's a bugger to clean, though.' She locked the car and threw the keys in her oversized clutch. Lizzie had forgotten to bring an evening bag, but Megan's was so big that it could take both their wallets and still hold enough make-up to launch a cosmetics counter.

'If I lived somewhere like this, I'd sit around writing novels all day long.'

'You'd have to write a hell of a lot of novels to fund this place. Maybe if you were the next J.K. Rowling.'

'A girl can dream, can't she?'

'Can she dream at the bar?' replied Megan, a smile spreading across her glossy lips.

The two of them linked arms and made their way towards the heavy double doors, where a doorman checked their tickets and ushered them down a long, red-carpeted corridor. Megan squealed with delight as the sound of the Backstreet Boys beckoned them towards the ballroom. 'I feel like a teenager again!' she shrieked.

When they reached a marble staircase stretching down to the dance floor, Lizzie looked around in awe. A magnificent chandelier dominated the centre of the ceiling, refracting the light from the DJ's booth like a grand glitterball. The left-hand wall was lined with a long row of tables, clad in pristine white cloths, all piled high with a tantalising array of party food. Glamorous guests were mingling by the bar on the right: the women so elegant in their eveningwear, the men a dashing army of Bond-alikes in their uniform dinner suits. It was amazing what a bit of black tie could do for even the average looker.

Lizzie made her way slowly down the staircase, tentatively raising the delicate hem of her dress to avoid catching her high heels. *Please don't let me trip*. Megan – who was more adept at walking in vertiginous footwear – strutted on ahead like a supermodel on a catwalk.

By the time Lizzie finally reached the bottom, Megan was already in the queue for the bar. 'What are you drinking?' she mouthed over the pumping music. 'Wine?'

'Yes, please,' Lizzie mouthed back. 'White. Large.' She was in need of a drink now, craving a little Dutch courage before she attempted to make small talk with people she hadn't seen for several years. She surveyed the room, scanning the sea of former students for familiar faces. It was a little like watching one of those celebrity TV shows, packed with people she half-recognised but couldn't quite place.

Suddenly a hand tapped her from behind.

'Lizzie?' squeaked a high-pitched voice. 'Is that you?'

She spun around to face Chrissie, a sweet but chatty girl who'd been in her dorm in freshers' year. Her once long red hair was now a fiery crop, and there were some faint wrinkles around her eyes, but apart from that she'd barely changed.

'Chrissie, hi! Good to see you.'

'What a gorgeous dress!'

'Thanks. You look great. How have you been?'

'Oh, can't complain. I'm working in recruitment now, after I was made redundant from my old job, so things are looking up.'

'That's good.'

Chrissie wasn't finished. 'And I ended up marrying my high-school boyfriend, of all people, and now we have two adorable little boys. Isaac is one and Danny is three.' She paused only for breath. 'You married?'

'Actually, the wedding's booked for this summer.'

'Oh, congratulations! Anyone I know? Not that guy you were dating at uni?'

'No,' she said, a little more abruptly than she intended. *I wish Megan would hurry up with those drinks.* 'His name's Josh. He's a PE teacher.'

120

'Sporty, huh? That's nice. So do you still see anyone from uni? What about that blonde girl you moved in with?'

'Megan? Sure, she's here somewhere. We just drove down together.'

As if on cue, Megan appeared with a tray of drinks and promptly handed over two glasses of wine to Lizzie. 'Are you trying to get me hammered?' she asked.

'Hey, you saw the wait for the bar. I'm not hanging around all night to get served. Thought we'd stock up.' She nodded at the new arrival. 'Hi, I remember you – Chrissie, right?'

'Yes, that's right. Long time no see.'

'I know. It's enough to make a girl feel old.' Megan shuddered.

'So how's life treating you?'

'Fabulous, thanks. You?'

'Yes, good. I'm married now, two kids. Have you got any little ones?'

'Me?! Noooooo.' Megan almost choked on her Chardonnay. 'Er, could you two excuse me for a second? I've just seen one of my old classmates. Be right back.' She scurried off as fast as her stilettos could carry her, waving at a leggy brunette in a neon pink dress. Baby talk tended to have that effect on her.

Trying to keep a straight face, Lizzie held out her spare wine glass to Chrissie. 'Here, do you want one of these?'

'Thanks, that's kind of you. So, are you working at the moment?'

'Yes, I work in London now, for a publishing firm.'

'That's exciting. I remember you always said you wanted to be a writer.'

'Yes.' A tiny ripple of regret ran through her, and she made a mental note to keep working on her exit strategy. 'I'm actually more on the PR side, but I do get to work with some great authors.'

'Well, that sounds interesting.' Chrissie took a sip of her wine before continuing to waffle on. 'So what do you make of all this? Seen many people you know yet?'

'No, apart from you I haven't seen anyone else I . . .'

Before Lizzie could finish the sentence, she realised she had spoken too soon. She heard the sound of the wine glass break before she even felt it slip from her fingers.

There was no mistaking the figure standing at the top of the stairway.

'Lizzie, are you OK? It's Megan.' She banged on the toilet door. 'I know you're in there. Let me in.'

Lizzie sat down on the loo seat, burying her face in her hands. Her forehead felt like it was burning up.

'Go away, Megan. I'm not coming out.'

'What on earth's the matter? Chrissie said you just dropped your drink and ran off, like you'd seen a ghost.'

The words caught in her throat. 'Alex is here.'

'What? Like here, here?'

'Yes. As in standing-at-the-top-of-the-stairs here.'

Megan wasn't convinced. 'That's impossible!'

'I'm telling you, I saw him . . .' He had swapped his casual clothes for a tux, and his once dishevelled hair was now surprisingly short, but the jolt of recognition had been as instant as it was painful.

'Are you sure? Because I just went up to some fit guy I thought was a friend of Gareth's, and turns out it wasn't him at all.'

'I'm positive.' Her chest felt like it was being clamped in a vice. She was afraid she was having a panic attack. Maybe even a heart attack.

'Lizzie, please let me in.' Megan's voice was soft, sympathetic. 'I can't help you if I'm stuck out here.'

'I'm not coming out. I don't want to see him.'

'Pleeeeasse? He's not going to come into the ladies.'

'No. Leave me alone.' Lizzie reached for a piece of loo roll and blew her nose loudly. *This whole night was a terrible idea.*

Megan changed tack. 'Lizzie Sparkes, you open that door right now. I've had enough of this crap.' She sounded remarkably authoritative, like a bossy teacher. Lizzie hadn't seen this side of her for years. Stunned and a little scared, she stood up and did as she was told.

'Good, that's better.' Megan gave her friend a long hug, then stepped back and peered at her in horror. 'Eek! We're going to have to get you fixed up before you go back out there. You've got eye make-up smeared everywhere.'

'I don't care. I don't want to go back out there.'

'Trust me, you will care. You look like a perturbed

panda.' She reached into her roomy clutch and whipped out a pack of pocket wipes. 'Here, let me help.' She gently dabbed at Lizzie's face, cleaning away the smudged traces of her misery. 'There, that's better. I've got my mascara in here if you want some?'

'No thanks,' sniffed Lizzie. 'I want to go back to the hotel.'

'But we only just got here!'

'You can stay if you like. I'll catch you later.'

'Now hold on a second,' said Megan, switching back to her stern voice. 'Remember what happened at our gradu-ation ball?'

'No. You know I didn't go.'

'Precisely. Are you really going to let Alex ruin it for you all over again?'

It was a point well made, and they both knew it.

'Look Meg, I see where you're coming from, but I'm not in the mood for the girl power lecture. I can't face dealing with him tonight.'

'So don't,' said Megan. 'Don't give him the time of day! Look, you've moved on, you're engaged to a great guy . . . why let Alex get to you? Just hold your head up high, stick with me and have some fun with your friends.' She paused. 'You know that's what they'd do on *Sex And The City*. Probably while ordering more cocktails.'

Damn, thought Lizzie. *I hate it when she's right.*

'OK,' she said reluctantly. 'I'll stay for a little while. But I mean it, Megan, make sure he keeps away from me.'

'Look, if he comes anywhere near you, I'll kill him myself. With my bare hands.' Lizzie wasn't sure she was joking. 'Shall we get you another drink and start over?'

'Alright.'

'Same again?'

I don't think that's going to cut it.

'Actually, I think I'll have a shot of tequila,' she said defiantly. 'And get yourself one while you're at it.'

A couple of hours and more than a couple of drinks later, Lizzie was having a surprisingly good time. She and Megan had hit the dance floor hard, partying away to lots of their favourite student songs, which were getting increasingly cheesier as the night wore on. Alex was nowhere to be seen among the jostling crowd, but they had bumped into a number of old friends who seemed genuinely glad to catch up with them. They'd even run into their ex-house-mate Gareth, who'd lost about two stone but none of his cheeky Welsh charm.

'I don't remember him looking like Justin Timberlake at uni,' Megan whispered to Lizzie when his back was turned. 'Do you?'

'No. He's definitely improved with age.' The dance floor started to sway ever so slightly in front of her, and she made a mental promise to cut down on her alcohol consumption for the rest of the evening. 'Wonder if he still puts the Tom Jones tunes on when he's getting down to business?' she giggled.

Megan winked. 'Well, if he plays his cards right, maybe I'll let you know!'

'Gross, I absolutely do *not* want to know,' laughed Lizzie. 'It'd feel like you slept with my brother.'

'You don't have a brother!'

'You know what I mean . . .' She felt the floor start to wobble again, and put a hand on Megan's shoulder to steady herself. 'I'm jussht saying it'd be kind of weird.'

'Whoa,' said Megan. 'You need to pace yourself. Here, have some of my water.' She grabbed her glass from a nearby table and handed it over. 'Although I have to say, I do prefer drunk Lizzie to crying-in-the-loo Lizzie.'

'Ha ha.' She took a quick sip, trying to cool herself down. *Is it me or is it getting like an oven in here?* 'Actually, I think maybe I could use some fresh air.'

'Good idea. I'll come with you.'

'No, don't worry. You stay here and chat up Gareth Trousersnake.'

'I wasn't chatting him up,' protested Megan. She grinned. 'Technically, he was chatting me up.'

'Either way, I'm sure three's a crowd,' said Lizzie. The DJ began playing some song she didn't know. 'I'll be back in five minutes. I'm just going to clear my head.'

'You sure you're OK?'

'Yes! I'm going for a walk, not a drive.' She raised the glass in her hand. 'I'll take this with me.'

'Alright,' said Megan. 'You know where I am if you need me. Don't be long or I'll have to send out a search party.'

'OK, Mum.' Lizzie took another swig of water as she tried to make her way out of the elaborate building. Spotting a door marked 'Fire Exit', she pushed the bar and prayed that she wasn't about to set off some noisy alarm. The door swung outwards. No sirens began blaring. She left it open and began to walk around the sprawling grounds, admiring the criss-crossed canopy of stars in the midnight sky.

'Impressive, huh?' said a low voice from the shadows, causing her to nearly jump out of her heels.

'Wow, you scared me,' she said, her hand flying up to her chest. 'I didn't realise anyone else was out here.'

'Sorry, Lizzie.'

She jumped again, a shiver running down her spine. The second he spoke her name, she knew that it was Alex. His voice was as recognisable as the one inside her head telling her to *run*.

Her feet refused to co-operate. 'What are *you* doing here?' she spluttered, her heart thumping so hard she thought she might shatter a rib. 'You hate this sort of thing!'

He stepped out of the darkness into her line of vision, all scrubbed up in a jet-black tuxedo and crisp white shirt. 'You're right,' he said, with a shrug. 'But then Dev mentioned that you were going, so I came to try to talk to you. I couldn't think how else to see you.'

He was about ten feet away now, getting closer with each step. Lizzie had to stop herself from pinching him to check that he was real. He was still disarmingly handsome, with those intense eyes and that same smattering of stubble. But he was less broad than before, with more pronounced cheekbones, and a haircut so short he looked as if he'd just returned from a tour of duty.

'Did it ever occur to you that maybe I don't want to see you?' she shouted, her blood starting to simmer. 'That I've spent years getting used to not seeing you?'

'Lizzie, listen, I need . . .'

'No, *you* listen – you can't seriously think that you can just show up out of the blue and expect me to fall at your feet!'

'I didn't. I don't. Look, maybe if you just cooled down a little . . .'

'YOU cool down!' And with that she threw the remnants of her drink in his face. Frankly, he was lucky she didn't throw the glass as well. She set it down on the low wall before she could change her mind.

The water hit him square in the jaw, dripping down on to his dinner jacket and pristine shirt, which swiftly became slightly see-through. 'Well,' he said, after a lengthy pause, wiping his hand across his chin. 'This kind of reminds me of the night we met.'

For a split second, Lizzie almost smiled in spite of her fury. *Don't you dare let him make you laugh*, she scolded herself. *He does not get to make you laugh ever again.*

'I wish we'd never met,' she shot back, her body trembling

as the rage returned. 'But if you've come here now out of some sense of guilt, to see what became of poor little me, you can leave with a clear conscience. You didn't break me. I'm fine. You fucked off on your travels, and I stayed here and moved on.'

'You think that's why I left?' he said, his eyes widening. 'To go travelling?'

'Isn't it?' she snapped. 'I know you blamed me for holding you back when you wanted to see the world.'

'I didn't think that. Believe me, the last thing I wanted to do was leave you.'

'Yeah, right. Admit it, you were itching to get away all along.'

'That's not true. Do you know how much I missed you?'

'What, so much that you didn't bother to get in touch for the past decade?' She pressed her fingernails into her palm, fighting the urge to slap him. 'I emailed you every day when you left. For a month!'

'I'm sorry. I was . . .'

She cut him off. 'Why didn't you reply, Alex? Not even once?'

A frown darkened his forehead. 'You have to realise, I wasn't myself back then. After that Christmas—' He loosened the grip of the black bow tie clamping his neck. 'You remember. I was a total mess.'

'Of course I remember. But all I ever tried to do was help you!'

'I know. But Lizzie, I felt like something was eating me

alive from the inside out. It's hard to . . .' He shook his head. 'I can't explain what it was like.'

Oh no? How do you think I felt when you left?

'Anyway, after we broke up I couldn't take any more. I woke up one morning and I just knew that if I didn't get out of there, I probably wasn't going to make it through to the next week.'

'But why leave without even telling me?' she said. 'We had one stupid row, Alex. Maybe we could have worked things out if you hadn't moved halfway round the world!'

'I couldn't stay, Lizzie – not after everything that happened. I needed a new start.'

'You could have at least talked to me, told me how you were feeling. I might have been able to go with you.'

'Lizzie, I couldn't ask you to give up everything to come with me. You had your exams to do, and I know how much you hate flying! Plus I could hardly take care of myself back then . . . let alone treat you the way you deserved.'

'So you just went? Without even saying goodbye?'

'Don't you get it? It would have killed me to stand there and say goodbye to you.'

'Oh, you decided it was better to love me and leave me instead?'

'No! I made a mistake. But I left you because I loved you.'

What? Lizzie's head was spinning now, and not just because of her alcohol intake. 'You're not making any sense.'

'I needed to sort myself out. I'd already let my family down. I couldn't drag you under with me.'

He sounded so sad that she felt herself thawing. 'Alex, you didn't let your family down. They love you.'

'But I did.' His eyes welled up, and for a second she was worried he might cry. 'I should have been there!'

'You couldn't have known what was going to happen . . .'

'But I keep thinking, maybe I could have—'

Her voice softened a notch. 'Alex, there was nothing you could have done. It wasn't your fault.' Instinctively, she reached out and took his right hand, her fingers pale beside his tanned ones.

He looked down, noticing the engagement ring pressed against his skin.

'So . . . this is new,' he said eventually.

Is he jealous?

'Yes,' Lizzie said. 'A lot has happened in the past decade, you know.'

'Tell me about it.' She could feel his eyes on her, as if absorbing the small but cumulative changes of the years.

'What did you expect? That I'd just sit at home and wait for you forever?'

'No, of course not.'

She dared herself to ask the question that had been keeping her awake at night. 'So then why did you come back, after all this time?'

'It's complicated. I . . . um . . . there's something I should tell you.'

'What?' Their eyes met, and she realised she was holding her breath.

'Er, I . . . the truth is, I've been . . .' He hesitated and placed his other hand on top of hers, cupping it gently. 'I've been an idiot,' he said finally, breaking her gaze. 'I guess I just wanted to tell you how sorry I am for the way I handled everything. And to see you again.'

'Well, now you've seen me.'

The corners of his lips curled up into a wistful smile. 'If it helps, you look even more beautiful than you did before.'

Lizzie blushed. *Why does he still make me feel so nervous?* They were quiet for a moment, and she realised she could hear the sounds of the party inside floating out on to the evening air. The DJ had obviously moved on to the slow-dance section of the evening, playing Adele's *Make You Feel My Love*.

'Dance with me,' said Alex softly.

'Are you drunk? You don't dance.'

'I'll make an exception,' he said. He lifted up her hand and placed it around his neck, pulling her in closely. The top of his shirt collar was still damp, but his body radiated heat.

The strength of the spark crackling between them caught her by surprise. Confused and a little light-headed, Lizzie felt like she'd been transported back to 2002, and for a fleeting second it was as if all the hurt of the years that followed had been swept away.

Where did we go so wrong?

His breath was warm against her ear, and she wondered if he could feel her heart pounding against his chest. Just as she began to give in to the moment, a flash of diamond winked at her in the moonlight. *Josh.* The butterflies in her stomach crashed guiltily against her insides. *What the hell am I doing?*

She knew what needed to be said:

Alex, this is a mistake.

Alex, I'm getting married.

Alex, I can't do this.

She pulled her head back to look him in the eye. 'Alex, I . . .'

He moved his face slowly towards hers until the tips of their noses were touching. His lips were so dangerously close that she could almost taste them. They stood like that for a second, and she wanted and hated him in equal measure.

'Lizzie!'

The shrill voice cut through the summer air with a sharpness that surprised her. She had been so lost in her thoughts that she hadn't noticed Megan emerging from the fire exit. 'I think it's time we were getting back to our hotel, don't you?' she snapped, pointedly ignoring Alex.

Lizzie jumped back from him, and as she broke contact all the electricity escaped into the ether. She did not say another word, but turned and fled in Megan's direction, leaving him behind. There would be no romantic reunion now; no stolen kisses tonight or any other night.

Fate had spoken, and she knew better than to tempt fate twice.

12

3 April 2004

'How long's it been now?' asked Connor, stubbing out his second cigarette. He rolled his eyes at Andi. 'I can't believe he didn't put us on the guest list.'

'You know he hates that kind of stuff,' said Lizzie. 'He thinks it's pretentious.' She squinted down at the watch she'd bought at the market last month, but it was hard to see the hands in the dark. If anything, they seemed to be going backwards. 'I think we've been here about 20 minutes.' She peered towards the front of the line. There were eight people still ahead of them. 'It's not normally this busy. Guess everyone's out for the end of term.'

'What's the point of having a brother who works in a bar if he won't get you VIP entry?' he grumbled, as they shuffled forward two paces.

'Never thought I'd say this, but for once I'm with Connor,' smiled Andi. 'You need to sort him out, Lizzie.'

They moved forward again, nearing the gatekeeper with the rope: a stocky man with a squished nose that had probably stepped into one brawl too many. He was clad in a white shirt and black suit, like he was guarding President Bartlet from *The West Wing* instead of the door at Ignition, though his trousers were slightly too short, revealing skull-covered socks. He let the group in front through and held up his hand.

'Hang on a second,' he said. His voice was softer than Lizzie was expecting, with a slight lisp. She noticed he was wearing metal braces, like the ones she'd had to wear in year ten. That stuck-up Penelope what's-her-face used to tease her endlessly about them, until her parents caught her smoking pot and shipped her off to private school. 'ID, please.'

Lizzie pulled out her NUS card and flashed it at him, cringing as usual at the sight of the unflattering photo, while Connor showed his driver's licence and traipsed in behind her. Andi gave the bouncer a big smile and he waved her straight through, his eyes lingering on her V-neck top. *Funny,* Lizzie thought with a grin. *When you're a DD, no one cares much about ID.*

As they made their way inside, the long-haired DJ in the corner launched into Britney Spears's *Toxic*, his head nodding up and down in time to the beat. 'Choon! I love this one,' cried Andi.

Connor groaned and pretended to cover his ears with his hands. 'It's not going to be pop chicks and boy bands all night, is it?'

'I hope so,' said Lizzie.

'Me too,' smiled Andi, linking her arm through Lizzie's.

'If you two start dancing round your handbags, I'm off,' said Connor. 'I'm definitely going to need a drink.'

They made their way to the bar in search of Alex, squeezing past a group of girls who were hugging each other and generally getting in everyone's way. He was mixing an order down the far end, flipping a silver cocktail shaker with impressive precision before pouring out its contents. He smiled when he saw Lizzie, and her insides flipped a little too. Watching him do his thing was a turn on, even if she couldn't get her hands on him until after midnight.

'Oi, barman!' shouted Connor. The tall brunette beside him thought he was being serious and tutted. 'It's alright – he's my boyfriend,' he deadpanned. The girl didn't reply and buried her nose in the cocktail list.

'Hey,' said Alex, coming over. 'I thought you guys were never going to get here.'

'We've been standing outside for ages,' complained Andi. 'These new heels are killing me. And I didn't bring a coat.'

'Yeah, what's that about?' asked Connor. 'Why can't you get us VIP entry?'

'I don't agree with that crap,' said Alex. 'It should be first-come, first-served. When I get my own bar there'll be no VIP treatment.'

'Do us very unimportant people have to pour our own drinks as well?'

'*You* might. Lizzie, you want a passionfruit mojito?'

'Yes, please.'

'Andi?'

'Cosmo, ta.'

'Could you two possibly order more girlie drinks?' said Connor. 'Why not get a sex on the beach? Throw in a strawberry daiquiri while you're at it?'

'We can have what we like, can't we, Lizzie?' said Andi.

'Yeah. Anyway, what are you having that's so manly?' Lizzie laughed.

'Easy. Pint of the usual.'

'Sure you don't want a strawberry daiquiri?' teased Alex. 'I'll do you 2-for-1 . . .'

'You could give me 10-for-1 and I still wouldn't do it.'

Alex went off to make the drinks, returning a minute later. He set three plastic cups down on the bar.

'What's with those? Where's the big boy glasses?' asked Connor.

'We don't use them any more. They kept getting smashed.' He grinned at Lizzie, and she blushed. Alex held out his hand. 'With the family discount, that'll be a fiver,' he said to Connor, with a wink. 'Call it 3-for-1.'

'Cheers, bro.'

They picked up their drinks and scanned the room for a seat, heading for an empty table near the back. The surface was sticky, swimming with beer and a couple of soggy coasters, and the ashtray didn't look like it had been emptied for a week. But at least they could hear themselves speak, away from the DJ who had now launched into a Busted track, much to the delight of the excitable girls still blocking the bar.

'I feel like I've been here before, when Alex first moved down,' said Connor. 'Did it used to be called something else?'

'Yeah, I think it was The Station. They changed it a while back. Caused a lot of confusion with freshers trying to find the actual train station.'

Connor laughed. 'That's so dumb. Sounds like something you'd do, Andi.'

His sister made a winding gesture and cranked up her middle finger. Then she caught sight of the slot machine by the wall. 'Ooh, I like that one! Back in a mo.' She hurried off in the direction of the flashing lights, rummaging around in her black clutch for some change.

'We've lost her now,' said Connor.

'What? She just said she'll be back in a minute.'

'You wait. She'll be on that thing half the night. Andi's the queen of the fruities.'

Lizzie was intrigued. 'Is she any good?'

'Not bad, actually. Most of the time she walks away up. You should see her play pool, though. Proper little hustler.'

'No way? Really?'

'Really. I've had to stop playing her. It's well embarrassing to get thrashed by your baby sister.'

Just then Alex came over and pulled up a chair. 'How's it going?'

'Alright,' said Connor. 'I'm not sure about some of this music, though. Someone needs to have a quiet word with the DJ.'

'I'm with you on that. But I think Lizzie might object.'

He squeezed her arm affectionately. 'You look gorgeous.'

'Why, thank you,' said Connor, and they all laughed. Lizzie was glad she'd made an effort tonight. She'd tried on several outfits before settling for a strappy pale pink dress, paired with some silver sandals she'd borrowed from Megan's wardrobe while she was away for the Easter break.

'What time are you done here?' she asked Alex.

'I'll have to see,' he said. 'Joe might need a hand clearing up. It's a big crowd tonight.'

'At least we get to see you a bit,' she said.

'Yeah, but I'd rather be this side of the bar with you guys.' The four of them had already spent a great afternoon chilling out and having an impromptu spring BBQ at the cottage. It had taken a while to get the cheap disposable kit going, and the first two sausages had made a bid for freedom by rolling off the end, but the rest had actually tasted alright once they got the hang of it.

It was rare to find a weekend they were all free these days, what with Connor's frequently-shifting gym rota and Andi's new job at the salon. Saturdays together were few and far between. But that was the great thing about brothers and sisters, Lizzie was beginning to realise. Even if you didn't see them for a while, you just picked up right where you left off.

'So what's the plan for tomorrow?' asked Alex.

'Dunno. I was thinking maybe we could try out that karting track after lunch?' suggested Connor.

'Sounds good to me,' said Lizzie. 'We could race boys vs. girls?'

'Now that sounds like fighting talk,' replied Alex, playfully wrapping his arm around her neck. 'But I'm up for it if you are.'

'Me too,' said Connor. 'I've seen Andi's driving . . .' He glanced in his sister's direction, just in time to witness the fruit machine start spitting out pound coins. 'Looks like she's on another winning streak.'

'Already?' said Alex. 'She cleaned us out last time.' He looked at his watch and stood up. 'Anyway, I'd better get back to it. Do you guys want another drink?'

'Same again, please,' said Lizzie. 'And a strawberry daiquiri for Connor.'

'Oh, she's all chat tonight,' said Connor, nudging her with his elbow. 'But can she back it up in a kart? That's what I want to know.'

'It's a good job none of you are at all competitive,' said Alex. 'But I'll grab you another round of drinks.'

'On you?' Connor pushed his luck.

'Alright, I'll get this one.'

'Thanks. If Andi's quids in on the fruity she can get the rest . . .'

Alex made his way back to the bar, collecting empty cups from the surrounding tables as he went. The DJ turned the cheese up to full fondue and started playing Peter Andre's *Mysterious Girl*. 'I bet you like this, don't you?' said Connor, lighting up a cigarette. 'I've got you pegged as a Peter Andre fan.'

'Actually, I did used to have a poster of him in my

bedroom,' smiled Lizzie. 'And I voted for him in the jungle.'

'Get out of here,' he teased, pushing her chair away. 'I can't sit with you now.'

'So what are you into?' asked Lizzie. 'Trance? Rock? Enya?'

'Anything that's not pop,' he said, blowing smoke across the table.

'You sound like Alex,' she replied. 'But I know the truth. He's got an S Club single at home and everything.'

Connor shook his head. 'He's been hanging out with you too much. I need to tell him—'

He broke off as Andi gave a sudden shout. 'Hey, back off, arsehole,' she warned a tall guy with a scruffy goatee and wandering hands. 'I'm playing here!'

'You're alright, daaarlin',' he slurred loudly. 'I'm just trying to help you.'

'What, by groping my bum? No thanks.'

Connor slowly stubbed out his cigarette, scraped back his chair and got up. Lizzie frowned. *I hope this doesn't kick off.* She watched him march over to where his sister was standing.

'Everything alright here?' he asked.

'Yeah,' said the bloke. He looked agitated, like a wild animal about to bite. 'We're just making convershashion.'

'Yeah, well, go make it someplace else,' said Connor, clenching his fists. The tattoos on his arm seemed to bulge angrily. 'She doesn't want to talk to you.'

'It's OK, Connor,' said Andi, holding up her right palm. 'I've got this.'

'What are you, like, her boyfriend?' sneered the guy.

'No,' said Connor.

'Well, then, wassit to you?'

'I'm her brother,' said Connor, looking like he might explode at any second. 'And you need to get out of here. Now.'

Lizzie rose and looked around the bar. Alex was nowhere to be seen. *Just walk away*, she willed the drunk. *Say you're sorry and move on.*

But he didn't.

'I'm not going anywhere,' he shouted. 'Piss off and mind your own.'

Connor was livid now, she could tell. 'What did you say?'

'I said piss off!' He shoved Connor hard. Any hope of the night ending peacefully made an exit through the fire escape. Word of the commotion began to ripple around the bar, as people backed off and gave the two men room.

Connor was almost red with rage. He let loose with a right hook to the guy's jaw, causing him to stumble. For a second the bloke looked stunned, then he hurled himself at Connor and the two of them began to fight it out.

'Connor, stop!' screamed Andi. 'He's not worth it!'

Without thinking, Lizzie tried to intervene, grabbing hold of the drunk's arm. He lashed out blindly, clocking her in the face so hard she lost her balance. She staggered back, her leg catching on one of the chairs, and went sprawling to the ground, her front tooth cutting into her lower lip as she crashed down. The coppery taste of blood began to build up in her mouth.

The two men were still locked in battle, knocking over chairs and drinks and anything in their path. Connor landed a clean punch and his opponent backed off momentarily, then surged forwards with so much force that the pair of them smashed through a wooden table.

'Connor!' cried Andi. 'Don't all stand there – someone get the bouncer!'

Connor picked himself up first. He had a cut above his head that was bleeding into his right eye, and his lower shirt buttons were ripped. He looked pumped as he surveyed the carnage around them.

His back was still turned when the guy jumped up, brandishing a broken table leg like a weapon.

'Connor, watch it!' Lizzie screamed. She had barely got the words out before a figure suddenly appeared out of nowhere and rugby tackled the lout to the ground.

Alex?

Before she could even blink, he'd disarmed the assailant and pinned him down, knocking the table leg out of reach. The man swore and struggled, his head banging against the sticky, wet floor, but Alex pressed his knee firmly into his back and refused to budge. Seconds later, the stocky bouncer muscled in and hauled the guy to his feet.

'Right, you, out – now,' he said, dragging him towards the exit. 'You're barred. If I see you round here again I'll be calling the police.' He turned his head and nodded at

Connor. 'And don't you go nowhere, neither. I'll be having a word with you.'

Connor dusted himself down, his mask of bravado firmly painted back on to his face. 'Can you believe that?' he said to Alex. 'That beardy prick's lucky I didn't kill him.' He patted him on the shoulder. 'Nice one, bro.' But Alex wasn't paying attention. He looked down at Lizzie, still dazed on the floor. Her mouth was beginning to throb.

'Are you alright?' he asked, helping her to her feet. He brushed her hair back from her face so he could take a closer look, wiping the blood off with a napkin.

'She's OK,' said Connor. 'Aren't you, Lizzie?'

'Well, I'll live,' she said, nursing her jaw. *No thanks to you.* Some blood had splashed down her dress, and she noticed that one of her straps had broken. 'But I'm going to have a nice fat lip. And I'm pretty sure this dress is ruined.'

'Yeah, you got a bit caught in the crossfire there. Sorry.'

Alex rounded on him, his eyes flashing. 'You should be, you know that? It's not funny. Someone could've got seriously hurt.'

Connor looked surprised. 'The guy was hassling Andi. What was I supposed to do? Just sit back and watch?'

'I could have handled him,' Andi mumbled, looking embarrassed. 'I wasn't exactly in danger.'

'Oh, so now I'm the dick?' said Connor, miffed.

'No one's saying that,' said Alex. 'But you can't get into a fight with every drunk you don't like in a bar. One of these days you'll wind up in hospital. Or jail.'

'But—'

'No buts. Remember that biker in Sydney? I can't always watch your back.'

'I don't need you watching my back,' shouted Connor. 'I can take care of myself.'

'You need to take care of your temper,' said Alex.

'Back off, Alex. I don't need another mum. You used to be on my side.'

'I'm still on your side. I'm just looking out for you.'

Connor softened slightly. 'Alright,' he said gruffly. 'But I was only doing the same thing for Andi.' His right eye was already beginning to swell. It was bound to be a nasty shiner by the time he went to work on Monday. 'Look, I think I'm going to bail. I'll see you back at home.'

'I'll come with you,' said Andi, grabbing her bag from the top of the fruit machine.

'Do you want me to stay?' Lizzie asked Alex. 'I could help you clear up.'

'I'll be OK. How's your face?'

'A bit sore,' she admitted. 'But it'll be fine.'

'Maybe you should head back with those guys, get some ice on it,' he said. 'Hopefully they can make it home without getting into any more trouble.'

'Alright,' agreed Lizzie. 'I'll see you back there.'

He kissed her forehead tenderly, avoiding her swollen lip.

'How bad is it?' she asked. 'On a scale of one to five?'

'Don't worry, you're definitely still a ten.'

The One

She smiled, which made her mouth hurt again. 'Love you,' she said. 'See you in bed later?'

He smiled back. 'That's definitely the best news I've had all night . . .'

13

7 weeks to go . . .

Lizzie leaned back, closing her eyes as he ran his hands gently through her hair. The touch of his fingertips did little to ease the pounding guilt inside her head.

'So, darling,' said Lloyd, her achingly cool hairdresser, 'what kind of wedding look are we going for?'

How about shameless flirt? she wanted to say. *Or maybe scarlet woman?* She fidgeted in the leather chair. The irony of being surrounded by salon mirrors wasn't lost on her, given that all week she'd barely been able to face her own reflection since her run-in with Alex. She had been tempted to cancel the appointment, but the prospect of trying to do her own hair for the wedding was almost as alarming as the rest of the thoughts currently running through her mind.

I didn't kiss him, she tried to console herself.

But part of me wanted to.

'Would you rather wear it up?' Lloyd scraped her hair back and plonked it high on top of her head to demonstrate. 'Or relaxed and loose? What feels more like you?'

Hmmm, I definitely don't feel relaxed. Though I have been a bit loose.

'I think I'll try it up, please.'

'Good shout. Go glam or go home, that's what I always think.' Lizzie hadn't met Lloyd properly before, but he was the bridal expert at her local salon and she felt confident that she was in safe hands. He was impeccably groomed, with a 50s-style quiff that looked both trendy and timeless, and a gleaming set of perfectly straight teeth. 'What's your wedding dress like?'

'It's white.' She attempted a smile for the first time that morning.

'Touché. And . . .?'

'It's full-length, one-shouldered, with little beads. Kind of a Grecian look.'

'Got any pics?' Lloyd was positively glowing with excitement. Bridal hair was clearly more stimulating than a boring old cut and blow-dry.

'I can show you on my phone.' She clicked on the boutique's website, scrolling through a selection of gowns until she found her own. 'See, it's this one,' she said, waving her mobile in front of his face.

He zoomed in on the image. 'Well, that's just stunning. And when I'm finished here, you're going to look like a Greek goddess.'

'You think?'

'Definitely. Let's go for something timeless, but very stylish.'

His enthusiasm was infectious, and Lizzie found herself perking up a little. 'Like what?'

Lloyd began playing with her hair again, this time twisting it around his fingers. 'Well, if your strap is on the left, I think we should sweep your hair ever so slightly to the right to really show it off,' he said. 'I could loosely curl it, then pin it up but leave a few tendrils hanging down for a romantic effect.'

'OK, let's give it a go.'

'That's the spirit!' He reached for a pair of hot tongs. 'Honestly, I don't know why brides bother to come in for these hair trials if they just want the same old look. It's your big day, so why not make a statement?'

Lizzie knew that if Megan were here, she'd agree with him wholeheartedly. 'Better to be anything than bland,' she often said. In her mind, the occasional fashion faux pas could be overlooked, but not making an effort was unforgivable. *Yes, she would definitely approve of Lloyd.* The only problem was, she didn't particularly approve of Lizzie right now.

After the ball, Megan had bundled her into a taxi so fast that they'd almost bumped heads. 'What was all that about?' she hissed, as they slid into the back seat. 'I thought you never wanted to see Alex again?'

'I didn't . . . I don't. It's just that he showed up and we got talking and then . . .' Her voice trailed off as she tried to explain the inexplicable. *I don't even know what happened myself.* Her whole body still felt in a state of shock. She'd never even come close to cheating on Josh before, but something about Alex and the music and the moonlight had caused her to momentarily waver.

'Did you kiss him?' Megan asked.

'No!' said Lizzie, noticing the driver glance at her in the mirror while trying to pretend he wasn't listening. She shot Megan an I-don't-want-to-talk-about-it-here look. 'Fine,' said Megan huffily, folding her arms over her chest for the rest of the short journey back to the hotel. She kept them crossed until the driver pulled up and stopped the meter, at which point she removed Lizzie's purse from her clutch and used it to pay the full fare.

By the time they got up to their room, Lizzie couldn't take it any longer. 'Alright, I'm sorry,' she muttered, kicking off her shoes. 'I know that looked bad, but it's not what you think.'

'Bad?' said Megan incredulously. 'Are you out of your mind?' She didn't shout, but whispered it quietly, which was somehow infinitely worse.

'I told you, nothing happened.' Lizzie tried to brazen it out, but the guilt began to spread rapidly across her body, infecting every cell.

'Oh yeah, it totally looked like nothing was happening.'

'We were just talking . . .'

'What, with your lips pressed together?'

'No!' Lizzie felt sick. 'You've got it wrong.'

'Really? Because the two of you sure seemed pretty close

to me.' Megan shook her head in disapproval, her curls flinging about in all directions.

'No! I mean, I guess there was a bit of a weird moment for a second there, but I had the situation under control . . .'

'What were you *thinking*?' Megan clearly wasn't going to let her off the hook that lightly. 'It took you years to get over him!'

'I wasn't thinking, OK? But it's not going to happen again, so you can spare me the lecture.'

'Maybe you need a lecture. You're supposed to be getting married soon, in case you'd completely forgotten. What about Josh?'

Something about Megan's indignation began to piss Lizzie off. 'What about Josh? I'd be at home with him right now if you hadn't forced me to come in the first place.'

'Oh, I see, so this is my fault!'

'I'm just saying, it wasn't me who wanted to go tonight.'

'Well, you certainly looked like you were having a good time with Alex.'

'Stop it!' Lizzie sat down on the end of the bed, the combination of shame and alcohol curdling in her stomach. 'I already feel terrible. You don't have to make me feel worse.'

'Are you still in love with him?'

'Who?'

'David Hasselhoff. Who do you think? Alex.'

Am I? 'No, definitely not.' She shook her head. 'I don't think so.'

'You don't think so?' Megan threw her arms in the air. 'Really, Lizzie, are we going to go through all this again?' She paused for breath, her face softening. 'I saw the way you looked at him tonight. I just don't want you to get hurt.'

'No one's going to get hurt,' she said firmly. She wasn't entirely sure who she was trying to convince, herself or Megan. 'It was a mistake, that's all. I got a bit carried away for a minute. But Alex and I are ancient history.'

'Well, I'd be careful if I were you,' said Megan, slipping out of her dress and into her satin nightie. 'Because history has a weird way of repeating itself.'

The following day, they drove back in painful silence, bar a stilted conversation about whether or not to stop at the services for a McDonald's. The only thing worse than falling out with her best friend had been seeing Josh's trusting face when she arrived home, as he bombarded her with enthusiastic questions about how the ball had gone. The encounter with Alex weighed heavily on her mind, crushing her conscience. She gave Josh an edited rundown of the evening then retired upstairs for a nap, citing the late night as an excuse.

Since then, she had felt unsettled every time they were together, as though he might see inside her troubled mind. But if Josh had noticed that something was amiss, he wasn't letting on. He'd probably put it down to last-minute Bridezilla brain.

Ouch!

A hairpin jabbing sharply into her scalp snapped Lizzie out of her guilt-fest. 'Oh, did I catch you with that one?' asked Lloyd. 'Sorry. I'm almost done, though. Just a couple more grips and . . . voilà!'

He spun the rotating chair 360 degrees with excessive enthusiasm, causing her to feel momentarily disorientated. As it slowed to a halt, Lizzie was finally able to catch sight of herself in the brightly lit mirror. She had not worn her hair up for years, but now it was piled high on her head in a way that was effortless yet elegant, with a few soft strands gently brushing against her cheek. It was faultless, but somehow not quite what she'd imagined.

'So, what do you think?' asked Lloyd, evidently pleased with his own handiwork. He held up a smaller mirror behind her so she could examine the back. 'If you get some sparkly pins, we could add those in too, for a bit of extra oomph.'

'You've done a brilliant job,' she replied politely, still trying to figure out if she liked it. 'It's beautiful . . .'

'I'm sensing a "but" coming . . .'

'No, it's lovely. It's just different to what I'm used to, I guess.'

'I think it really suits you,' he said encouragingly. 'You should have something special for your wedding. Now you look like a proper bride.'

The One

Yes, I suppose I do, thought Lizzie, turning her head to view it from both sides.

So why do I feel like such a fraud?

14

15 May 2004

Lizzie pulled on the rubber gloves and reluctantly lifted the loo seat, trying not to gag. *Eeeew. When was this last cleaned?* She was starting to suspect that Megan and Gareth were not actually sticking to their share of the rota, but just waiting for her to do it every third week. Grabbing the bottle of bleach, she squirted a generous amount around the rim. *This isn't exactly the way I'd imagined spending my birthday. They'd better have got me a bloody good present.*

She reached for the cheap plastic toilet brush, still wanting to retch, and was getting stuck in when she heard the door-chime go, a clunky version of *Greensleeves* that sounded like it had been knocked up on a child's keyboard. *Who's that? Megan's got her keys.* It played again. *We need a new doorbell.* Their landlady had tragic taste.

'Just a minute,' yelled Lizzie, throwing the loo brush back in its holder and peeling off the yellow gloves. 'I'm coming!' She bounded down the stairs, taking them two at a time, and turned the stiff latch.

The One

To her surprise, Andi and Connor were standing on the doorstep. She was carrying a bunch of tulips that were looking slightly battered, and he had a 12-pack tucked under his right arm. Confused, Lizzie glanced at the clock in the hallway: 12.45pm. *They're well early.* She hadn't been expecting anyone to turn up for at least another six hours.

'Surprise!' yelled Andi, grabbing her in an enthusiastic bear hug and bashing the flowers a bit more. Two of the petals fell off and floated into the hall. 'Happy birthday! Can I use your bathroom? I'm bursting.'

'Sure, it's up there,' replied Lizzie, glad now that she'd cleaned it. Andi rushed past her and ran straight up the stairs, her chunky heels causing the floorboards to creak loudly as she went. Connor ambled into the hall behind her, a roguish grin on his face.

'Hey there, birthday girl,' he said, bending down to give her a peck on the cheek. He was freshly shaven today, which made him look younger, and dressed casually in jeans and a Green Day T-shirt. 'These are for you,' he said, gesturing to the beer. 'Well, not all for you, obviously, or you'll be in a right mess. But for the party later.'

Megan had insisted on throwing a bash for Lizzie's 21st – 'a house party with a capital P' was how she'd put it – and invited pretty much everyone they knew over to theirs. Lizzie still wasn't sure how they were all going to fit inside, but Megan wasn't letting anything as minor as logistics get to her.

157

'Thanks, that's kind of you,' she said, showing him through to the kitchen. 'I didn't know you two were coming this early, though, or I'd have got something decent in for lunch.'

'Yeah, sorry. I just managed to swap my shift yesterday so we thought we'd come down a bit earlier and hang out with you and Alex. There wasn't any answer at his place so we figured you guys must be here.' He glanced around the empty room. 'Unless he's off getting his hair and nails done for tonight?'

Lizzie smiled. 'No, actually, he's working at the moment. He won't get here till about seven.'

'What, so you're all alone on your birthday? That's not right.'

'I'm not alone. Meg and Gareth will be back in a minute. They've just gone down to Asda to do a food and booze run.'

'Then what's your plan?'

'Nothing much. I was going to give the place a tidy up before later . . .'

Connor set the drinks down on the table and pulled a face. 'No way. You can't be doing that on your birthday.'

'Well, it just needs a quick . . .'

'Grab your jacket,' he insisted. 'We'll go out for lunch.'

'Where?'

'I don't know,' he shrugged. 'Wherever the road takes us.'

'Oh, well, I haven't got a car. And Meg's taken hers to the supermarket.'

'Never mind. I borrowed Mum's for the weekend. We're parked just outside.'

'What, no bike?'

'Nope, not with Andi. I'm missing it already, though. Mum's car is, like, the saddest thing ever. The embarrassment alone could kill you.'

'What could kill you?' asked Andi, readjusting herself as she clomped down the stairs. 'Your bad driving?'

'Funny. I was talking about Mum's lame car.'

'You know, you two are really selling this,' Lizzie joked.

'We're going out for lunch,' explained Connor. 'Otherwise Lizzie's going to spend her birthday cleaning.'

'Cool,' said Andi. 'I'm starving.'

Lizzie grabbed an old envelope out of the recycling bin and scribbled a quick note for her housemates on the back. *It won't kill them to do some housework for once.* Then she picked up her keys and nodded at Connor. 'After you two,' she said, gesturing to the door.

'Alright then, birthday girl. Let's go.'

Half an hour later, they were all sitting in a red leather booth at a cheerful coastal diner, working their way through generous portions of fish and chips. Connor was recounting some of the scrapes he and Alex had got into as kids, including the time they'd attempted to free the school gerbil, only for it to end up wriggling off at high speed and re-emerging three days later in the lost-property bin.

'Whose bright idea was that one?' Lizzie grinned.

Andi rolled her eyes and took a long slurp of her strawberry milkshake.

'Alex's,' he said. 'He was the brains – I was just supposed to be the brawn. Make sure Mrs McGuigan didn't walk in mid-rescue.'

'And did she?'

'No! So I kept up my end of the bargain, right?' Connor took another bite of his fish, his tattoos catching her eye under the neon restaurant lighting as he raised his fork.

'I like these,' she said, gesturing to his arm. 'Where'd you get them done?'

'Different places,' he said. 'Got the first when we were in Oz a few years back. Then I did another when I was in Dublin with the lads. And the last time was down here, actually, while I was visiting Alex. See?' He stretched out his arm and showed her the intricate design. 'I think that's my favourite.'

'What does it mean?' asked Lizzie.

'One life, one chance,' he said proudly.

'Yeah, right,' scoffed Andi. 'It probably says "I'm a total loser" or something.'

'I did do some research, believe it or not.' He picked up a chip with his fingers and dunked it into his ketchup, before polishing it off whole. 'I'm guessing you don't have any, then?' he asked Lizzie.

'No,' she said. 'But I've always secretly fancied a small one, somewhere subtle. Like maybe the inside of my wrist.'

Connor and Andi looked at one another like they were trying not to laugh.

'What? What's so funny?'

'I don't know,' Connor smirked. 'I'm just not sure I can quite picture you getting a tattoo.'

'Why? I could totally get one!'

'Really . . .' He crunched another chip.

'Yes, really,' she said defensively.

'So why don't you?' asked Andi.

'What?' Lizzie took a swig of her cola. 'I was talking hypothetically, that's all.'

'But what's stopping you?' Connor pressed.

'Well, I imagine it'd hurt, for one thing.'

'It doesn't hurt that much,' he said. 'Especially if it's small.'

'Like your brain,' Andi quipped.

'Or the opposite of your gob,' he fired back.

Lizzie looked down at her bare wrist. 'Anyway, my mum would go ballistic if she saw it. She hates tattoos.'

'I'm sorry, what birthday are you celebrating today – five?' asked Connor. 'You're old enough to do what you want. You don't need a note from your mum.'

Maybe he's right. She was tired of people assuming she was sensible and predictable. Why shouldn't she take a risk, do something spontaneous for once?

'It's your call,' continued Connor. 'But if you're serious, I'll come down and get a new one with you.'

'Me too,' said Andi. 'I mean, I won't get one, but I'll definitely tag along and watch.'

'You would? Now?'

'Sure,' said Connor. 'I'll even treat you for your birthday.' He leaned back in the booth, teasing her with his dark eyes. 'You know, sometimes you've got to live dangerously.'

A surge of adrenaline mixed with birthday boldness swept through her. 'OK. Let's do it!'

'Are you sure?'

'Not really,' she smiled. 'But let's do it anyway.'

An hour later, she was sat in what looked like a dentist's chair, trying hard not to hyperventilate. 'First timer, eh?' said the tattooist, a middle-aged woman by the name of Donna, who looked more like a librarian. 'Don't worry, hon – it's not as painful as you think.'

'Uh-huh,' said Lizzie nervously, glancing over at Connor for support. He wasn't paying any attention, admiring the designs plastered all over the walls of the small studio. 'How long is this going to take?'

'For that? In black? I'd say 15-30 minutes tops. You need to relax a bit, though, otherwise you're gonna tense up. Try taking some deep breaths.'

Lizzie breathed in and out noisily, feeling anything but relaxed. *Why the hell did I agree to this?* 'Maybe my friend can go first,' she said, gesturing to Connor.

'Nah, you're better off going first,' said Donna. 'Get it out of the way. It'll be fine. I've done this before, you know!'

Lizzie gave her a weak smile, but her legs were turning to jelly. 'How'd you feel?' asked a beaming Andi. She looked like she was finding the whole thing highly entertaining, like a sadistic version of those reality TV shows she was always watching.

'Alright,' Lizzie lied. 'I think I'm ready.'

'Bricking yourself, huh?' said Connor, tearing himself away from the artwork and coming to stand beside her. 'I get it. The first's the worst. After that it's easier.'

'Oh, this is definitely going to be a one-off.'

'That's what they all say to start with,' chipped in Donna. She pulled on a pair of gloves. 'Arm, please.'

Lizzie grudgingly held out her left arm, which Donna cleaned with a special solution. It smelled like the antiseptic wipes her mum kept in the first-aid kit, and she tried not to imagine the expletives her mum would use if she could see her now. Then Donna placed the stencil in position and unveiled the imprint of the transfer Lizzie had chosen: two small interlocking hearts that made her think of Alex. *I wonder what he'll say when he sees it?*

'Last chance to back out,' teased Donna.

But she wasn't going to back out now. No way. Partly because she wanted to prove to herself that she could do it, and partly because she didn't want Connor and Andi telling everyone that she'd been a total wuss. She looked over at Donna, who was whistling as she loaded the needle into the machine.

Damn, that looks big . . .

'You're going to use *that?*' asked Andi incredulously, clearly thinking the same thing. Lizzie willed her to shut up before she chickened out.

'Go for it,' said Connor, patting her on the shoulder. 'No regrets.'

Ask me in an hour and we'll see.

'You might feel a bit of a scratching sensation,' warned Donna. 'Are you ready?'

'Ready,' she replied defiantly.

Her voice was drowned out as the device was switched on. It whirred loudly, sounding like a cross between an electric razor and a power tool. She squeezed her eyes tightly shut as Donna swooped in for the drill.

If my arm drops off before the party tonight, I'm totally blaming Connor.

'Urrrrgggggghhhhh.' Lizzie didn't know which seemed more fuzzy, her brain or her teeth. The left side of her face was practically welded to the pillow. *What time is it?* she tried to say, but her lips were so dry and stuck together that it came out more like 'Worteyesit?' Her head felt like it was stuffed with sawdust.

'If you're asking about the time, it's just gone eleven,' a disembodied male voice proclaimed. Lizzie forced her right eye open and was nearly blinded by the sunlight streaming in through a small gap in the curtains. She quickly closed it again. Her vision was admittedly a little hazy this morning, but she was pretty sure there was no one else in the room. 'Dad?' she called out, croakily.

The voice laughed. 'No, you weirdo, it's me.'

'Alex?' This conversation wasn't making any sense. 'Where are you?' She peeled her head off the pillow and tried to spot him, thinking that would be a lot easier if the room stopped spinning around.

'I'm down here.'

Lizzie rolled over and finally saw him on the floor, lying on a makeshift bed made out of cushions and her gym towel. He was still fully clothed and wearing a bemused smile.

'Why you down there?' She did not have the energy for complete sentences yet.

'Well, it might have been easier to sleep next to you if you hadn't been throwing up quite so much.' Suddenly Lizzie remembered how she'd ended up in this state: the party. Or, to be more precise, Megan's free-pouring punch-making efforts.

'Meg OK?' she groaned.

'I'm not sure OK is the word, but she's alive,' he said. 'I heard her getting up a little while ago, but she only got as far as the bathroom before she was sick too.' He screwed up his nose. 'The walls in this place are pretty thin.'

'Everyone else?' asked Lizzie.

'Doing better than you, I'd imagine. Most folk went home around midnight when we ran out of beer. Andi took a cab back to mine and Connor crashed on your couch. Gareth's still locked in his room with some girl. No idea what they were up to, though – they kept me awake half the night playing some Tom Jones track.'

'*Sex Bomb?*'

'Yes! Could you hear it too?'

'No. Lucky guess.'

Lizzie lay back on the pillow and shut her eyes. The events of last night were starting to return to her brain now in fragmented bits and pieces. There had been blaring music, four types of pizza, Gareth's special brownies (the recipe was a closely guarded secret, and possibly a class C offence) and, last but definitely not least harmful, Megan's home-made punch.

'Are you sure you're meant to put that much alcohol in?' Lizzie had asked suspiciously, after Megan decanted a generous helping of vodka into a bowl that was already swimming with rum.

'Of course!' Megan had said confidently. 'Once you add the fruit juice and ice, the alcohol gets diluted right down anyway, so you don't want to start off with it too weak.' Lizzie wasn't convinced. The concoction looked strong enough to take on 12 rounds with Lennox Lewis.

'Here, try some,' Megan insisted, filling a plastic white cup and thrusting her hand out. Curious, Lizzie took a sip. It tasted different – kind of zesty and tangy with a weird aftertaste – but it wasn't unpleasant. 'Are you sure it's meant to have that strange kick to it?' she asked suspiciously.

'Yes, that's how it's supposed to be,' sighed Megan, giving the mixture an exasperated stir. 'This is going to go down a treat, trust me.'

As it turned out, the punch had gone down rather well. The trouble was, it came up even more easily.

'Bleeeeeuuuurrgh,' Lizzie groaned, clamping her hand across her mouth as the sharp taste of sick rose in her throat yet again. She swung her legs out of bed and took an uneasy step towards the bathroom.

'No, Lizzie, Megan's still in there!' shouted Alex. Her stomach heaved, and she knew she wasn't going to be able to hold it long enough to get to the garden. 'Use the bucket – the bucket!'

What bucket?

As if to answer her question, Alex sat upright and thrust a plastic orange bucket under her chin. Judging by the stench emanating from it, she could tell it wasn't the first time he'd had to suffer through this rigmarole in the past few hours. If she hadn't felt nauseous already, the smell alone would have tipped her over the edge – but, as it turned out, the contents of her guts didn't need any prompting. She threw up all over the bucket and – to her horror – a bit on Alex's hand as well. He grimaced, and Lizzie died a little inside. *I am never getting pissed with Megan ever again*, she promised herself. *That's if my liver manages to survive this bender.*

'Sorry,' she muttered, collapsing back onto the bed as he put the bucket down on the floor. 'So gross.'

'Well, it's not your finest hour, I'll give you that,' he said.

She reached across to her bedside table to pass him a tissue, but as she did so she caught a blurry glimpse of a mark on the inside of her left wrist. She was about to rub it off when another burst of memory rebooted in her brain. *Bloody hell, I forgot about the tattoo!* She stared at it again. It was raised and slightly red this morning, like she'd been lying out in the sun for too long. Her head was still too scrambled to decide whether or not she liked it.

'Ah, the new tattoo,' said Alex. 'Was that your idea or Connor's?'

'Mine,' she replied slowly. *I think.* 'Did I already show you?'

'It was kind of hard to miss. Especially when you stood on the sofa and made a special announcement about it to everyone.'

'What?! When?'

'Right before you suggested we do those shots of tequila.'

'Noooooo.' She wanted to yank the duvet over her face to hide her embarrassment, but she was lying on top of it and couldn't face the idea of moving again just yet.

'Why don't you rest here for a while? I'll go down to the kitchen and maybe make me and Connor some breakfast.' He rested his right hand gently on her leg. 'Do you think you could eat something? It might do you good.'

Lizzie shook her head. The only thing that was going to do her any good now was lying perfectly still in a dark, quiet room. Preferably with the bucket close to hand.

'Rest,' she murmured, her eyelids feeling heavy in their sockets. The sound of silence greeted her, and she was glad.

Thirty minutes or so later, she found herself stirring again, her senses awoken by the aroma of bacon wafting up the stairs, which was infinitely preferable to the smell of vomit wafting from her bedside. Though she hadn't felt the slightest bit hungry when Alex had asked, all of a sudden she was ravenous. Her head had also stopped spinning to the point that movement now seemed like a vague possibility. She got up slowly, taking baby steps across the carpet, and reached for the fluffy white robe hanging on the door. *You can do this*, she told herself. A bacon sarnie would be her reward.

She tackled the stairs gingerly, one at a time, not wanting to lose her balance and go sprawling to the floor. Her body had already been through enough for one weekend. As she was about halfway down, she heard male voices coming from the kitchen. It sounded like Alex and Connor were in the middle of a heated debate, their loud voices grating on her brain like nails down a blackboard. Part of her was tempted to retreat back upstairs to the library-like peace of her bedroom. But another part, the nosy one, made her stop in her tracks and listen.

'So that's it?' said Connor angrily. 'You're just going to forget everything we'd planned now? To do what – stay down here and play house?'

'It wasn't set in stone,' said Alex. 'It's not like we booked anything.'

'But we'd discussed all this. You said that once you'd got your degree, we'd go travelling again. I thought we'd decided.'

'That was ages ago. Look, you know I'd love to go, but I just don't think another year abroad is the right move for me at the moment.'

'Alright, what if we went for six months?'

'I can't, Connor. I'm sorry.'

'*You're* sorry? Do you know how hard I've been saving up for this trip? How long I've been counting down the months in that crappy job, because we were supposed to be getting out of here this summer?'

'I didn't realise things were that bad.' Alex sounded despondent. 'Look, what if we went away for a holiday instead? Two weeks, maybe three . . .'

Lizzie heard the sound of something – possibly Connor's fist – banging against the kitchen table. 'I don't want to go out there on some sort of package deal, Alex! I want to do it properly, off the beaten track. The way we talked about it.'

'I can't do that any more. Things have changed.'

'So this is about *her*.' Lizzie assumed that she must be the 'her' in question and felt strangely guilty, even though she wasn't aware that she'd actually done anything wrong.

'Don't bring her into this . . .'

'But I'm right, aren't I? Now it makes sense. You're bailing on your own brother for a girl.'

Alex's voice grew louder. 'I thought you liked her? Yesterday you were the tattoo twins, remember?'

'I do like her. But I didn't take you for one of those blokes who ends up completely under the thumb. Girlfriend says he can't come out and play . . .'

'It's not like that, alright? She didn't stop me from going, because I didn't ask her permission in the first place.'

A momentary hush descended over the house. Lizzie crouched down and leaned closer to the banister.

'I don't understand.' Connor sounded puzzled. 'Why don't you just talk to her about it? I'm telling you, she'll be cool. And she could always come out and meet us for a bit, maybe over the Christmas holidays or something.'

'No, that won't work. She hates flying.'

'It's only 11 hours!'

'No, you don't get it – she really hates it. She's got a phobia.' Alex paused. 'So I can't ask her to do that.'

'Well, then, you call one another, and you email. If it's meant to be, I'm sure she'll still be here when we get back.'

'Connor, you're not listening. It's my decision. I don't want to go away for a year.'

'Why? You're 22, Alex. You've got the rest of your life to settle down. I know you think that things are serious with Lizzie now, but—'

'You just don't get it, do you?' interrupted Alex crossly. 'This isn't like one of your flings. I'm going to ask her to marry me after she graduates.'

Whaaat? Lizzie's heart began beating so loudly she was sure both boys would hear it. The only other person who seemed more surprised than her was Connor.

'Are you serious? When did you decide all this?'

'I've been thinking about it for a while. But I was sure last night.'

'At the party?'

'Sort of. When she threw up in her room.'

Connor had nothing.

Alex tried to elaborate. 'I mean, I know that sounds . . . it wasn't like . . . I just realised I don't want to leave her. Ever.'

It wasn't an elegant explanation, but to Lizzie it was the most romantic thing she'd ever heard. Ever since that night on the beach, she couldn't shake off the niggling dread that he might decide to go travelling. She'd tried to broach the subject several times, but had always clammed up: too scared of what he might say or what she might ask of him. Now, not only had he decided to stay, he was also planning to propose! The excitement even managed to trump her hangover.

'So let me get this straight – you're blowing off the trip of a lifetime because your missus can't hold her booze?'

Ouch. That one hurt. She might have overdone it a bit

last night, but she wasn't exactly an alcoholic. Also, she wished he hadn't mentioned booze. Her insides were still feeling delicate.

'Don't push it, Connor. I said I'm sorry. But I can't give up everything and jet halfway round the world with you right now.'

'So what, you're just going to stay here? Keeping working some dead-end job at that bar of yours?'

'I'll stay for a bit, yeah. Lizzie can finish her course and then we'll decide what we're doing together.'

'And what am I supposed to do in the meantime? Take off by myself?'

'That's up to you, I guess.'

'Well, don't think I'm not going just because you've changed your mind. Jeff's still out in Thailand. I can always stay with him.'

'Fine.'

'Fine!' Connor was really angry now. 'I'm telling you, in six months you'll regret this. Be begging to come out and see me.'

'Of course I'll still come and see you. You're my brother.'

'Whatever. Don't do me any favours.' Lizzie heard a set of keys being jangled. 'Well, I'm going to get on my way. No point hanging around here.'

'Don't you want to finish your breakfast?'

'No. I've lost my appetite.'

The sound of footsteps grew louder, and Lizzie realised she needed to move quickly before she was caught eavesdropping. She tried to head back up the stairs, but a floorboard creaked and gave her away.

'Is someone there?' called out Alex.

Busted. She turned around and plodded back down the stairs, more loudly this time, in the hope that they would think she'd just woken up. 'It's only me,' she said. 'Maybe I'll have some of that bacon after all.'

'Here Lizzie, you can have my seat,' Connor said awkwardly. 'I was just going to fetch Andi and get on the road.'

'Are you sure you can't stay a while?' she said, trying to play peacekeeper. She knew how close Alex was to his brother, and she wanted them to work this thing out before it came between them. *Before I come between them*, she suddenly realised.

'No, I can't today, I'm afraid. Stuff to do,' he said, not quite looking at her. 'I'd better head off.'

She caught sight of Alex's crestfallen face out of the corner of her eye, but there was nothing more they could do this morning.

Connor will get over it. He just needs a few days to cool off.

'Alright,' she said. 'Thanks for everything yesterday. We'll see you again soon.'

'Yeah,' he said, mumbling to himself as he headed for the front door and pulled it shut behind him. She couldn't quite make out his reply, especially with her woolly head. 'What did he say?' she asked Alex.

'Nothing,' he said.

She knew that wasn't the truth. To her, it almost sounded like, 'Don't count on it.'

15

6 weeks to go . . .

Delving around in the back of her desk drawer, Lizzie pulled out a dried highlighter with no lid and a half-eaten chocolate bar. *Yuk.* She aimed for Naomi's bin, basketball style, and quietly punched the air as both items went in. There was no one else around to witness her good shot apart from Serious Will the accountant, but she knew better than to distract him. He wouldn't be impressed.

After all the drama of the past few weeks, Lizzie was determined that this one was going to be stress-free – and though Thursday mornings didn't exactly fill her with joy, at least she wasn't filled with dread. She'd been in the office since 8am and had already finished a report that wasn't due on Ella's desk until tomorrow. Right now she was alert, organised and in control.

At work, anyway. If only it would rub off on the rest of my life.

It had been 12 days since the ball – not that she was counting – and she still couldn't shake it from her mind. Thoughts of Alex stalked her at strange, random moments:

in the shower, in the office, in her dreams. At least Megan was just about speaking to her again, which was a big relief. She wasn't sure how she'd have explained to Josh that their sole bridesmaid had gone on strike.

She was still feeling flashes of guilt around him, too, but she'd thrown herself into the wedding prep by way of penance, and they were finally starting to make some progress on that front. This week they'd managed to sort out their table plan, which had been easier than she'd thought. OK, so they'd have to keep Auntie Carole well away from Uncle Ken, and Megan wanted to be strategically seated next to Gareth, but apart from that all the other guests had fallen into natural groups: her family, Josh's family, work colleagues, friends from school and uni, plus a few sub-human specimens from his football team, whom she'd purposefully placed as far back from the top table as possible.

For extra conscience-cleansing, she'd also volunteered to take the afternoon off work yesterday to help out with his school sports day. It had been so sweet watching him with the kids: showing them how to take part in the various races, and consoling the wailing young boy whose egg simply wouldn't stay on his spoon. Whether he was cheering on the children or running in the teachers' relay, Josh seemed to have a limitless supply of energy and enthusiasm. It was clear that the pupils adored him – some even more than others.

'Are you Mr Cooper's secretary?' one little girl in pigtails had asked curiously. She couldn't have been more than about seven.

'What makes you think that?' asked Lizzie, amused.

'My daddy has a secretary who helps him. She's nice, too. Once she took me for ice cream.'

'Ah, I see,' smiled Lizzie. 'No, I'm not his secretary. I'm actually his fiancée.'

The little girl had scrunched up her face. 'What's a fear-say?'

'It means we're going to get married.'

'Oh.' She nodded approvingly. 'I'm going to marry him when I grow up, too.'

Lizzie managed to keep a straight face, but she couldn't stop giggling when she told Josh on the drive home. 'You're quite the heartbreaker,' she teased. 'Do you have any other fiancées at this school I should know about?'

'I think you're quite enough for me,' said Josh, overtaking a cyclist. 'I can barely afford one wedding as it is.'

'I know,' she said. 'It's wiping me out, too. But I promise I'll make it up to you on the wedding night . . .' She'd splashed out on a gorgeous basque and suspender set, which had set her back the best part of £100. At least Josh could save some cash there. He'd probably wear his lucky boxers.

'I can't wait,' he said. 'That's really the only reason I proposed.'

She laughed. Ever since they first met five years ago – on the night bus, of all places – he had a knack for making her smile. Admittedly, it wasn't a conventional tale of love at first sight: she'd been glaring at him for chatting too loudly on his mobile, while he got the wrong end of the stick and thought she was giving him the eye. But within a few minutes of him introducing himself, there was something about his warm, unassuming demeanour that made her let her guard down. With him, it had been different: no drama, no tears. He had detangled her messy life, and she'd have to be mad to let this recent hitch with Alex tie her up in knots again.

Since Josh was clearly in a good mood, Lizzie decided it might be the perfect opportunity to bring up her new career plan.

'So, I was thinking about after the wedding,' she said, trying to sound casual. 'And I thought that maybe this would be a good year for me to have a go at my book.'

'What book?'

'You know, the novel I've always wanted to write.' She took a deep breath. 'It just feels like this might be the right time.'

'OK. Sounds fun.' Everything was fun to Josh. She could have told him she was writing about depressed serial killers and he'd have sounded no less cheery. 'But won't you be knackered?'

'What do you mean?'

'Well, that's a lot to take on round a busy job.'

'Actually, that's what I'm trying to tell you. I was thinking about going freelance for a while instead. That way, I could still pay the rent but have more time to write. Plus I'd be working from home, so I'd get to see more of you. No more late nights at the office.'

'What?'

It wasn't going as smoothly as she'd hoped. She tried again. 'I know it would be a change, but I've thought it through and I'm pretty excited about the whole thing. I can't see any real reason not to give it a shot. Can you?'

He stopped at the traffic lights. 'Lizzie, I think it's cute that you want to have a go at this. Really, I do. But I can't support us both on my salary. And do you seriously think now's the best time to be leaving a good job?'

'Actually, I thought after the honeymoon would be better. I'll be feeling all refreshed and I'll be able to come up with lots of ideas and . . .'

He didn't wait for her to finish. 'But then we'll be starting our family, won't we? So that's something we need to consider.'

'Whoa, go back. We're doing what?'

'You know, having kids.'

Lizzie was stunned. She'd known for ages that Josh was keen to have children, and she'd always envisaged that in their future as well. She just didn't realise he was expecting her to start popping them out the minute their plane touched down at Heathrow.

'Look, you know I love kids, and you're going to be an incredible dad,' she said delicately. 'But I was thinking we could enjoy married life a bit first?'

'I dunno, Lizzie. I mean, the clock's ticking . . .'

Whaaat? He sounded just like Auntie Carole. 'Excuse me?'

Josh tried to hop out of the hole he'd landed in. 'That came out wrong. Obviously I'm not saying you're old or anything . . .' The lights changed and he pulled away. 'But we're not in our 20s any more. I don't want to be one of those ancient dads who can't kick a ball about.'

'I get that, but don't you have things you want to do first?'

'Sure. I'd love to be playing up front for Chelsea. But it's not going to happen now, is it?'

'So that's what you think my plan is? Some silly pipe dream?'

'I didn't say that. But just think for a minute how many people want to write books. What are the odds of you actually making it?'

'I don't know.' *But I was hoping for a chance to find out.* Lizzie fell silent as he turned into their road, trying to hide the disappointment on her face. Josh parked on the drive and switched off the engine.

'Look, let's just take one thing at a time for now,' he said gently. 'See how we both feel after the wedding.'

'OK.' Her throat suddenly felt dry. She unlocked the front door and headed straight for the kitchen, opening the fridge and pouring herself a glass of orange juice. The cold tanginess made her teeth tingle.

'Hey, Lizzie . . .' Josh called out from the hallway.

'Yes?' she said softly.

'Could you grab me a beer while you're in there?'

She was still dwelling on their conversation when her telephone rang.

'Hello, Lizzie Sparkes speaking,' she said in her most professional voice, just in case it was Ella calling to check up on her.

'Hey, Lizzie Sparkes.' Despite the slight static, it was a voice she knew all too well. *How did Alex get my work line?* She tried to say something clever, but it came out closer to frosty. 'Funny, I don't remember giving you this number.'

'You didn't. I just called the front switchboard and asked to be put through.'

Damn that new receptionist, with her cheerful demeanour and extensive phone directory. Was she really allowed to connect you to your past, just like that, without so much as a warning?

'You shouldn't be calling here,' said Lizzie firmly, glancing around to make sure none of her other colleagues had arrived. 'I'm glad we were able to finally clear the air a bit. Really, I am. But please don't contact me again.'

There was an uneasy hush on the other end of the line. 'Lizzie, I know you're engaged so I've been trying to give you some space, but I can't just leave things like this. I wasn't completely honest the other night. There's still some stuff I need to tell you . . .'

'Like what?' She pressed the handset to her ear.

'I can't really go into it over the phone.'

'Fine, don't,' she sighed. 'Let's not go into it at all.'

Right then Phoebe appeared and made the universal gesture for coffee. Lizzie gave her a thumbs-up and lowered her voice. 'Look, Alex, I can't sit and chat all morning. I've got to go. Have a nice life.'

'Lizzie, wait!' There was an urgency to his voice that she'd never heard before, and she found it strangely unsettling. 'I really do need to talk to you. Then, if you still don't want to speak to me after you've heard everything I've got to say, I promise I'll leave you in peace. For good.'

She hesitated. 'You swear?'

'Scout's honour.'

'You weren't in the Scouts.'

'True. But will you meet me? Please?'

She took a deep breath while she agonised over his proposal. Part of her was tempted to meet him, she had to confess, if only out of curiosity. She hadn't exactly given him much chance to talk at the ball, and she wanted to have the one thing that was still missing from her life: closure. *If I hear him out now, then I can shut that door for good and start married life with a clean slate.*

On the other hand, she knew that if Josh – or possibly worse, Megan – ever found out, she was going to have some serious explaining to do. 'I'm not sure . . .' she said reluctantly. 'Your timing couldn't be worse, you know.'

'What do you mean?'

'What do you mean, what do I mean? I'm getting married in six weeks, Alex. And I've still got a million things to do. I don't have time to drop everything and meet up.'

'I understand,' he said. 'I could come to you?'

'No!' she shrieked, slinking down into her chair as more people began to file into the office. 'That's definitely not an option.'

Even over the phone, Alex could read her like a book. 'Don't worry, Lizzie. I meant come up to town, not to your house. I don't exactly want to bump into your fiancé, either.'

'It's not that . . .' she protested feebly, though they both knew she was fibbing.

'Look, I understand. Believe it or not, Lizzie, I didn't come back to ruin your life. But I think we need to talk while we've got the chance.' *Sounds like he's going back soon, then.* She felt a twinge of regret. Or was it relief? She wasn't quite sure.

'So can we meet?' he pushed. 'Please?'

She knew that the sensible answer was no. She knew that if she asked Megan, or her mum, or that nice agony aunt in the Sunday paper, they would all advise her to turn him down. She felt like she was trapped in one of those after-school specials: Just. Say. No.

'Oh . . . alright then.'

'Thanks, Lizzie.'

'It'll have to be this Saturday afternoon, mind.' Josh was

going to the match with Freddie then, so she could slip away without anyone noticing.

'Fine. Where do you want to meet?'

'I'm not sure.' A dull headache was beginning to build in her temples. First Alex had caught her by surprise, and now she was paranoid Ella was about to spring up at any second. 'Um, let me think.'

'Somewhere public or private?'

'Public, obviously,' she coughed. 'But, you know, not *too* public.' If she was heading for her own funeral, she didn't need it attended by anyone she knew.

'OK, so somewhere privately public . . .' He had some nerve, mocking her. 'How about Richmond Park?'

'Too busy. Hold on a sec.' Phoebe returned with a cup of strong coffee and Lizzie gave her a grateful smile, gesturing to the phone. 'Journos, eh?' she mouthed, and Phoebe wandered off. 'Alright, I'm back. Where were we?'

'You were trying to think of somewhere besides Richmond.'

'Yeah, OK. I was thinking a bit more like . . .' She tried to rack her brains for somewhere low-key. 'Like Ravenhall House. Do you know it?'

'No, but I can look it up.'

'Just give me your number and I'll text you the address.' She keyed it into her mobile and hit the save button, anxious to wrap up this conversation before Ella appeared. 'When you get there, there's an old bandstand just past the main house. I'll meet you there.'

'Alright. How about three o'clock?'

'Make it five. I've got some wedding jobs to do first. But if you're late, Alex, I'm not hanging around. I mean it.'

'I'll be there,' he promised.

She put down the phone, trying to get her head around what had just happened. *Is this a terrible idea?* She still wasn't sure, but at least this time she would be the one calling the shots. And if Alex wasn't there on time, she certainly wasn't going to give him another chance.

I wasted too much of my life waiting around for him, she thought. *And I'm certainly not going to wait any more.*

Lizzie reversed into a parking bay, locked the car door and walked up the narrow street towards Ravenhall House. It was a beautiful Georgian building, white and well preserved, with landscaped gardens open to the public at weekends. When she'd first moved to west London, it was one of her favourite spots to visit for some peace and quiet, a little oasis amid the buzzing metropolis of the city. *I forgot how much I loved this place*, she realised, admiring the elegant architecture. *I really must remember to bring Josh here after the wedding.*

As she stepped past the wrought iron gates, which were already open, she noticed that the sprawling grounds were fairly empty. A young father kicked a ball to an overenthusiastic toddler, who tottered unsteadily after it in delight, his blond hair bouncing in the breeze; an elderly couple sat beneath the big oak tree, reading in relaxed silence, and two teenage girls stretched out on the grass, their vests rolled up to expose their tanned midriffs, trying to soak up the final few rays of sun before it set for the evening. None of them even glanced in her direction as she made her way down towards the walled gardens. *Good*, she thought. *I'm not going to run into anyone I know here. Well, except for the obvious. If he even shows.*

She looked at her watch. It was just before five. *I'll give it ten minutes*, she reasoned. *If he's not turned up by then, I'm off.*

As the outline of the bandstand became discernible in the distance, Lizzie was surprised to spot Alex already sitting at the top of the steps. He was dressed in grey jeans and a white linen shirt with the sleeves rolled up, clutching a single white rose. Her stomach gave a sudden lurch.

It'll be fine. You don't have to stay long. Just hear whatever he's got to say and then you can put all of this behind you.

When he saw her approaching, Alex stood up, holding the flower out in front of him. The gesture totally threw her. *Should I greet him with a kiss, a hug or a handshake?* In the end, she hung back awkwardly and did nothing, fiddling with the pockets on her skirt.

'Alex, you didn't need to do that,' she said softly. She couldn't quite bring herself to look at him up close, like trying not to stare at direct sunlight. 'This isn't a date.'

'I know,' he said. 'Think of it as a peace offering. I owe you one of those, at least. And an apology.' He held out the rose again and she took it instinctively, its petals even paler than her sunlight-starved hands.

'So what, no sky lanterns this time?'

'Nope. I've gone off them. Apparently they're not so great for the environment.' He gestured to the concrete steps. 'Do you want to sit down? Best seat in the house.'

Lizzie shook her head. 'I don't think so. I've got loads to do this weekend. I can only stay for a few minutes.'

'Don't worry, I promise I won't bite.'

She let out a long breath. 'I'm just really busy at the moment.'

'I forgot what a different pace of life it is back here,' he said slowly. 'Everyone's always rushing around. Makes people uptight.'

His words stung, and she flinched. Even though she had no intention of ever seeing him again, she did not want his final impression of her to be someone with a stick wedged up her arse.

'That's not fair,' she said defensively. 'I'm not normally this wound up. It's just that things have been complicated since you came back.'

'Look, the last thing I want to do is make you uncomfortable,' he said, shaking his head. 'Why don't we start over?' He held out his hand. 'I'm Alex. Alex Jackson.'

He caught her off-guard, and she gave a small smile. 'Lizzie. Lizzie Sparkes. Uptight is my middle name.' His palm seemed surprisingly cold to the touch, or perhaps she was just feeling flushed. It was hard to tell.

'Well, Lizzie Sparkes, do you want to go for a walk or something?'

She nodded. A quick trip round the grounds would do her good. She was starting to feel a little faint, perhaps because of her stuffy car, or the fact that her nerves had sabotaged any attempts at eating lunch.

They made their way along the footpath, the sweet scent of summer jasmine filling the air. 'So did you find this place OK?' she asked, grasping for words. She'd spent years imagining all the clever remarks she'd make to Alex if he ever tried to get in touch, but now that he was beside her, she suddenly didn't know what to say.

'Yes,' he said. 'It's a great spot. I can see why you like it.'

'I used to come here all the time after I left uni,' she told him. *After you left me, remember?* 'But I haven't been back for a while. It kind of looks the same.'

'I guess some things don't really change,' he said, giving her a sideways glance. She looked away and fixed her eyes firmly on the track in front, stepping over a broken branch that was lying in wait.

'Most things do,' she muttered, not sure where all of this was going. She stared down at the rose in her left hand. *What's he up to?* It didn't make sense. OK, so there were moments when she still felt a flicker of something between them, but he couldn't seriously think that she'd just upend her new life for him now, could he?

'So,' he said, as if reading her mind, 'you're probably wondering why we're here.'

'Yes, I am actually. You haven't even told me why you're back in the country. Is it for work?'

He stopped and turned to face her, running a hand over his shaved head. 'No, I'm taking a break,' he said. 'I had some things I needed to sort out . . . and I really wanted to talk to you.'

'What, you couldn't use Skype?'

'I needed to talk to you in person.' His slate eyes, usually so seductive, now looked sad and tired. 'I want to say that I'm sorry for the way things ended between us—'

'Well, it would have been pretty hard to keep it going with you 6,000 miles away.'

'Can you please hear me out for a minute?' She noticed his hand was shaking, and she bit her lip. 'I'm trying to apologise here, Lizzie. I made a big mistake, and it's one I've had to live with every day since. But that doesn't mean I ever . . .' He paused, staring at the ground. 'That I ever stopped caring.'

Lizzie's heart began to beat wildly. *Why is he telling me this now?* For a second she felt glued to the spot, but then she forced her feet to resume walking. Alex followed, striding alongside her.

'If you cared that much, why didn't you ever – oh, I don't know – maybe email or pick up the phone?' she snapped.

'I've been asking myself the same question,' he said. 'I wanted to . . . loads of times. But the longer I left it, the harder it got. It took me ages to properly sort myself out.'

'OK, so why not contact me then?'

'I was going to, about four years ago. I found you on Facebook, and I thought I'd sign up and send you a message. See if you wanted to talk to me.'

Huh? 'I don't get it. What changed your mind?'

'You did,' he replied quietly. 'You'd posted these photos of you with some other guy. It was pretty obvious he was your new boyfriend.' He winced. 'You looked so happy. I figured you must have moved on and wouldn't want me messing up your life again.' He gestured to the sparkling engagement ring on her finger. 'Anyway, I can see I was right about that.'

Lizzie spun round abruptly. 'How could you say that to me, Alex? I spent years waiting to hear from you. Years! Every time my phone rang and it was a blocked number, I nearly had a heart attack. But how long did you think I could keep hanging around? My whole life?'

He stiffened, looking shocked. For a second, it felt as though the whole garden had been switched to silent, until a noisy magpie swooped past.

Alex took a deep breath. 'I've really screwed things up, haven't I?' he said sadly. 'I'm sorry.' He tried to take her hands, but she snatched them away, dropping the rose in her haste. 'I'm sorry I was such a mess. I'm sorry I didn't call. And mostly I'm just sorry I ever left you in the first place.'

Hot tears pricked at her eyes. 'I still don't get it. If you felt that way, why didn't you just come home?'

'I don't know.' He bent his head. 'It crossed my mind a lot, but I guess I couldn't stand the thought of . . . of having you hate me.'

'I didn't hate you!' she exploded. 'I was completely in love with you, you idiot! But you can't just abandon somebody like that when you've been planning your whole life together and not even say goodbye . . .' She trailed off, afraid she might cry as years of hurt came tumbling out.

'Oh, Lizzie . . .' Alex's eyes welled up too. 'I've missed you so much. Tell me how to make it up to you.'

'You can't,' she shouted. 'You're too late! It's not something you can just fix with flowers.'

'I get that.'

'Clearly you don't, or we wouldn't be here . . .' Frustration mixed with anger and regret rushed through her. Her legs suddenly felt like they might give way at any moment, and she took a shaky step back.

'Whoa,' said Alex, reaching out to steady her. 'You OK?'

'I'm fine,' she lied, feeling hot and dizzy. 'I didn't have much lunch, that's all.'

'Let's sit down for a sec.' He steered her gently to a nearby bench, wrapping one arm protectively around her shoulders before she could tell him to stop. The nearness of him was unnervingly intimate yet comfortingly familiar. He still smelled the same as the first night she'd met him, like his old leather jacket, but without the coconut.

She sat on the warm wood, trying to catch her breath.

Her heartbeat was racing like she'd just put in an hour at the gym.

'Try lowering your head between your knees,' said Alex, settling down beside her.

'I'm alright.' She checked her watch. 'I need to get going soon.'

'This was a bad idea,' he sighed, leaning forwards. 'I didn't come here to upset you. That's the last thing I want.'

'So why did you come?'

'To talk.' He seemed pained now, rubbing his forehead. 'I was hoping for a chance to make things right between us, Lizzie.'

'Why now? Did someone tell you I was getting married?'

'What? No!' He seemed so surprised that she believed him. 'I didn't even know you were engaged until I saw you wearing a ring at the ball.'

'So what, then? After all this time, you suddenly woke up one morning and decided you want to be friends?'

'Would that be so terrible?' He swatted away a large fly that dared to descend onto his leg.

'No, I guess not . . .' she stuttered, though she wondered what Josh might have to say about it. 'But honestly, what's the point? My life's here and you'll be leaving again soon, anyway.'

Alex's head jerked up. 'I'm not going back to Thailand. Not for a while, at least. Maybe never.'

'What? Why?' Her confusion came back with a vengeance. 'Has something happened?'

Alex looked uneasy. 'Maybe we should talk about this some other time. When we're both less emotional.'

'No! Let's talk about it now,' Lizzie pushed. 'I can't keep walking around with all these questions in my head, Alex. What's going on that you had to fly halfway round the world to tell me?'

He let out a long sigh.

'Lizzie, I've got cancer,' he said.

16

23 July 2004

Lizzie squeezed into the foyer, scanning the packed room for the rest of the Jackson clan. It was hard to find anyone when all the graduates were dressed alike, a moving black wall in their gowns and mortarboards, surrounded by beaming parents. *This will be me and Megan next year*, she thought with a smile. *Mum and Dad are going to be so excited.*

But today was Alex's day, and she couldn't wait to watch him collect his degree, a 2:1 he'd worked so hard for. The only problem was that Mrs Jackson had the tickets, and now Lizzie couldn't find the family anywhere. She reached into her clutch and pulled out her mobile to ring Andi. The call went straight to voicemail.

Just then everything went dark, as a pair of large hands covered her eyes. 'Guess who?' said a familiar deep voice.

'Hmmm . . . Ryan Gosling?'

'Who?'

'That guy from *The Notebook*.'

'Nope. Haven't seen it. Try again.'

'Brad Pitt?'

Alex laughed. 'Don't get your hopes up.' He lowered his hands and spun her round into a tight hug, the folds of his gown almost enveloping her. She stepped back to get a proper look at him.

'Check you out!' she said, thinking she must have the hottest boyfriend there. The long, flowing robe matched his wavy hair, and he'd shaved for the occasion. She brushed her fingers lightly along his smooth jaw. 'How come everyone else looks like a penguin and you look like a superhero?'

'Really? I feel kind of stupid.'

'No, you look great!'

'So do you,' he replied, admiring the burgundy wrap dress she'd bought with her birthday money and been saving specially for today. It felt good to finally get a chance to show it off; plus Megan would be happy it had now made its debut, seeing as she'd spent the past month trying to swipe it. He pulled her back towards him and bent down for a kiss, which was harder with the headgear. His normally stubbled chin felt soft against her skin.

'Hey, you two, get a freakin' room!' squealed a voice from behind. They broke apart and saw Andi running over, throwing her arms around them both. 'Go on then, let's have a peek at the graduate . . .'

'Don't be soft,' said Alex, embarrassed.

Andi ignored him, surveying his outfit. 'You look well posh,' she declared. 'But you sort of pull it off.'

Seconds later, his parents filed in, looking smart and a bit out of breath. 'Oh Alex, I'm so sorry . . .' puffed his mum, smoothing down her polka-dot dress. 'I wanted to be here half an hour ago, but the hairdresser took ages.' She patted her heavily lacquered do, which must have been as hard as a mortarboard. *I hope there are no open flames at this ceremony*, thought Lizzie.

Alex leaned over to give his mum a kiss. 'Don't you look handsome?' she said proudly. 'We need to get lots of pictures later.' She turned to Lizzie and pecked her on the cheek, the powerful rose notes of her perfume wafting through the air. 'And how are you, sweetheart? I hope you weren't waiting long.'

'No, I'd only just got here myself,' said Lizzie. She moved round to give his dad a hug. 'Hi, how are you?'

'Fine, thanks,' bellowed Mr Jackson before she could extricate her eardrums to safety. He greeted Alex too, then undid his grey suit jacket. 'Warm in here, isn't it?'

'I think it's cos we've been rushing, Dad,' said Andi. 'But I saw a vending machine by the entrance if you want to grab a drink.'

'Yes, I might,' he shouted. 'Anyone else want one? No? Back in a minute.'

Alex looked around the room, squinting. 'Where's Connor?' he said eventually.

'What? Oh, he's outside, having a smoke,' said his mum. 'I keep nagging him to stop, but you know Connor. He never listens.'

'What's going on with you two, anyway?' piped up Andi. Alex's face fell. 'Why, what's he said?'

'Nothing, but I can tell something's up. He's been acting strange for weeks. And he said he didn't want a leaving party before he goes away. When did Connor ever turn down a party?'

'Andi . . .' said her mum, silencing her with a dart of the eyes.

'What? You said yourself you thought it was weird!'

'Today's not the day.'

Andi closed her mouth just as Connor strode into view, looking awkward in a navy blazer over dark jeans. It was about as dressed up as Lizzie had ever seen him, though he hadn't bothered to shave.

'Were your ears burning?' asked Andi. 'We were just talking about—' She broke off as Mrs Jackson administered a discreet kick to the ankle.

'What?' he said.

'Nothing. We were just wondering where you'd got to,' said his mum, reaching out to straighten his lapel.

Connor flinched. 'Mum, it's fine. Stop fussing.' He nodded in their direction. 'Alright?'

'Yes, thanks,' said Alex. 'It's good to see you. I'm glad you came.'

'Yeah, well, I don't really think Mum would let any of us miss it.' He forced a hollow laugh, but his eyes were flat.

'Hi, Connor,' said Lizzie. 'How's things?'

'Busy. Got a lot to get ready before I go away.'

'Where are you flying to first?' said Alex.

'Malaysia, then Cambodia, then over to see Jeff in Thailand. It's going to be wild.' He glared at his twin. 'Shame you'll miss all the fun.'

Just then Mr Jackson returned, clutching a bottle of water. 'One pound fifty!' he barked. 'One fifty! For water . . .'

'Ssshh, Frank, keep your voice down,' said Mrs Jackson. 'People will hear you.'

'I hope they do hear me!' he said. 'Someone ought to say something.'

'Not now.' She placed one hand gently on his arm and all the hot air seemed to drain out of him, like she was deflating a rubber ring.

'Alright, everyone!' shouted a lady in a pink suit who Lizzie didn't recognise. Half the room continued to chatter away, so she dinged a glass with a pen and tried again. 'Excuse me. EXCUSE ME!' An expectant hush rippled through the crowd. 'Right, the ceremony is going to start in ten minutes, so please can all our guests start taking your seats now? The graduates will need to come with me.'

'Here we go, then,' said Alex. 'I'd better follow this lot.'

'Alright son, good luck,' said his dad, suddenly looking a bit misty-eyed.

'Break a leg!' added his mum, straightening his cap.

'I think that's in the theatre, Mum,' he said with a smile. 'But I'll do my best.'

'Have you been perfecting your walk-and-wave technique?' teased Lizzie.

'Yeah, for weeks,' he laughed, planting a kiss on her cheek. 'I'm nearly at royal level now.'

The pink-suited woman was flapping her arms nearby, shepherding the remaining graduates into line. 'Right, I'd better go,' said Alex. 'Catch you all afterwards.' He turned and followed the stream of students, disappearing into the throng.

'OK, then, I think we're this way,' said Mrs Jackson, fumbling around in her handbag for the tickets. 'Now I know I packed them this morning . . . ah, yes, here you go.' She pulled them out and handed them one each. 'Shall we get up to our seats?'

'Fine,' sighed Connor.

What's his problem? wondered Lizzie, as they climbed the stairs. *Surely he's not still sulking about the whole travelling thing?* She'd hoped he would have calmed down by now, but if anything he seemed more moody. *He needs to get over it.*

When they reached the top, she deliberately slowed her pace, allowing him to file into his seat after his sister and parents as she perched on the end. It would be harder for him to ignore her if they were seated together.

'So,' she said brightly, turning to face him, 'what's new with you?'

'Not much.'

'Still working at the gym?'

'For now.'

'When do you go on your trip?'

'Soon,' he said, staring straight ahead. 'About six weeks.'

'You must be excited . . .'

'Yeah.' He looked about as excited as her dad putting out the bins. *This is going to be tougher than I thought.*

'How long are you away for?'

'I don't know. Till I run out of money, I guess.' He reached inside his pocket and pulled out a bag of Maltesers, opened the top and offered them to his parents. Then he tipped a few into his hand, twisted the wrapper and slipped it back into his blazer.

She decided to change tack. 'Look, Connor, if I've done something to offend you, then let's talk about it. But if you're blanking me because Alex isn't going travelling, you need to know that was all his decision. It had nothing to do with me.'

Connor was quiet for a second, crunching a chocolate between his teeth. 'You might not have chained him to the sink,' he muttered eventually, 'but trust me, it has *everything* to do with you.'

His words needled her, but even as she tried to refute them, the grain of truth in there lodged in her throat. Alex would be going away if it wasn't for her, and all three of them knew it.

What do I do now?

Before Lizzie could say anything else, the university band struck up and the audience erupted into applause.

There was no escaping for at least two hours now. She was well and truly stuck: trapped with a guy who hated her guts and a head full of questions she couldn't answer.

As the sun began to dip, the class of 2004 were still having photos taken in the courtyard outside, throwing their mortarboards into the air and grinning wildly. Alex was laughing with his coursemates, looking happy and carefree; his future stretched out before him like an open road. Lizzie felt as though she was watching a beautiful butterfly prepare to take off, unaware that a glass jar was descending overhead.

We really need to talk about this trip.

She knew today wasn't the right time, but she would have to speak to him soon. Her stomach tightened anxiously. She didn't know what she was afraid of more: that they might grow apart if he left, or that he might resent her if he stayed. She knew she didn't want to be *that* girl, the one who stood in his way, and yet the thought of not seeing him for a year made her feel physically sick.

'I'm not sure about those hats,' said Andi, nodding at the students. 'Seems a bit strange to me that on the one day you're having a million pictures taken, you wear something that totally squishes your hair.'

'I guess so,' said Lizzie absent-mindedly.

'You OK? You seem a bit quiet.'

'I'm alright,' she sighed. 'I've just got a bit of a headache. It was pretty stuffy in there.'

'Oh, I thought maybe Connor had said something to upset you,' Andi replied. 'I was just going to say don't pay any attention to him. He's been grumpy for weeks.'

Lizzie looked at her uneasily. 'Do you think it's because Alex isn't going travelling?'

'Maybe.' Andi shrugged. 'He doesn't exactly get all deep and meaningful with me. But I wouldn't worry about it too much. He'll come round.'

'You reckon?'

'Yeah. He sulked for, like, the entire summer when Alex said he was going away to uni. I think it's the whole twin thing.' *Oh, great.* 'But, you know, I'm sure some time apart will do them good. They've got to cut the cord eventually, right?'

Lizzie knew that she was only trying to help, but every word that came out of Andi's mouth just made her feel worse. She nodded half-heartedly and waved at Alex, who was now jogging towards them, his dark cloak billowing in the summer breeze.

'So how are my favourite girls doing?' he said playfully, taking off his headgear and letting his sister try it on.

'I'm kind of hungry,' replied Andi. 'Dad's promised to take us to that nice steak place in town. Are you nearly done here?'

'Sure – food sounds good. Lizzie, you in?'

The thought of spending the night cooped up round a table with Connor annihilated her appetite. 'Actually, I'm not feeling so hot,' she said. 'I think I should head back. But you guys should definitely go out and enjoy yourselves.'

'You sure?' said Andi.

'Yeah. Thanks anyway. Have a great night.'

'OK. Hope you feel better soon.' She wrapped Lizzie in a warm hug. 'I'll go and find the folks, tell them the plan.'

'Alright,' said Alex. 'Can you put my cap in the boot, carefully? It's got to go back to the hire place.' He waited until she'd gone, then fixed his eyes on Lizzie. 'Are you OK? You seemed fine when I left you earlier.'

'Yeah, I know. I just got a headache all of a sudden.' It was sort of true. *A big Connor-shaped headache.*

'Did something happen?' He looked concerned.

'No, nothing.' Alex wasn't buying it, she could tell. A lifetime of being a twin had given him heightened powers of intuition.

'Something's going on. It's Connor, isn't it?'

She felt like a murder suspect being grilled down at the station. 'It's nothing. Everything's fine.'

'You can tell me.' He put his hands gently on her shoulders. 'What exactly did he do?'

'He didn't do anything,' she whispered, not wanting to spark another row between the brothers. 'We were just talking about his trip, and it made me realise that . . .' She paused, choosing her words cautiously. 'That I've never asked how you feel about not going with him.'

'And you want to ask me now?' Alex lowered his arms, looking puzzled.

'No, not here. Not like this. I'm just saying I think we need to have that conversation. Maybe I could come over tomorrow, after your family's gone back?'

'What's to discuss? I already told Connor I'm not going.'

'I know,' she said, suddenly remembering she wasn't meant to have overheard that conversation after her birthday. 'Er, I mean . . . I figured. But I don't want you to look back one day and think that you missed out.'

'On what? There'll be other trips.'

'Maybe. But maybe not like this.' She paused. 'Look, I wish I could tell you that we'll go off round the world together when I graduate, but the truth is I don't think I can. Not unless you want to sedate me every time we get on a plane.'

'I'm not with you for your air miles,' he said, his eyes shining. 'I'm with you because I love you. Even when you're not making any sense.'

'I know. But I don't want you to end up resenting me because you think I held you back.'

'That's not going to happen,' he said, tilting his head quizzically. 'But I don't get what's going on here. When I told you about all this last year you seemed really upset. Now you're suddenly shipping me off?'

'I was upset,' she admitted, slipping her arms around his waist. 'I don't want to be apart for a year. I'd totally hate it. But I don't want you to stay purely for me.'

'I'm not staying for you,' he said quietly. 'I'm staying for *us*. Because I think we've got a real shot at something here,

Lizzie – and that's way more exciting to me than another stamp in my passport.'

Her heartbeat began to quicken. She looked up at him, his breath cool against her face. 'Are you sure? Because I'm trying to say that if you really want to go, there'll still be an us. You don't have to choose between me and Connor.'

Alex frowned. 'What brought this on? Did he say that to you?'

'He didn't have to,' she sighed. 'It's pretty obvious he's not my biggest fan at the moment.'

'Well, then, that's his problem, not ours.' Alex kissed the top of her head. 'Look Lizzie, there's no point us having this conversation now. Six months ago, maybe – but I can't go at this short notice. I'd need more money, plus I already told Joe I'll stay on at the bar until your course finishes.'

'So that's it? Decision made?' She felt bad about the relief that washed over her.

'That's it. And I'm fine with it.'

'What about Connor?'

'Connor will just have to deal with it.'

'Deal with what?' said a loud voice behind Alex, causing them to break apart. Lizzie took a step back. She had been so caught up in their discussion she hadn't spotted Connor coming towards them.

'Nothing,' said Alex. 'What's up?'

'Mum sent me to get you. She's only got another ten minutes on the meter.'

'OK. I'll be there in a second.'

'What, so you can talk about me some more?' Connor grumbled. 'Why don't we save some time and you can say whatever it is to my face?'

'I'm not doing this now,' said Alex. 'Let's just get in the car and we can talk about it later.'

'Oh, are you coming with me or waiting for her?' asked Connor drily.

'Leave Lizzie out of it,' said Alex. 'If you're pissed off at me that's one thing, but stop taking it out on her. I know you've been saying stuff.'

She felt Connor glare at her like she was some kind of snitch. *Thanks a lot, Alex. Like that'll help.* Then he turned back to his brother.

'I'm not pissed at you,' he snapped. 'I feel sorry for you. You used to be a laugh, but these days you might as well be middle-aged. You're basically becoming Dad.'

Alex bristled. 'What, and your life's so great? Sleeping with a different girl every weekend and trying to remember her name in the morning?'

'I only forgot once . . .'

'Yeah, and who gave you the money to call her a cab?'

'This isn't about money, Alex. This is about you bailing on me. Who ditches their own brother?'

'I'm not ditching you,' said Alex. 'I'm just not coming on one trip with you, that's all. We'll do something together when you get back.'

'What, you, me and Lizzie on a cosy camping break? Or maybe we could all go for a nice spa day?'

'Hey,' said Lizzie. 'Stop being a jerk. I'm right here, you know.'

'I know,' said Connor. 'That's my point. You're always here.'

'That's enough!' yelled Alex, rounding on his brother. 'Just shut up! I'm sick of feeling caught in the middle between you two. This is supposed to be my graduation day, and you're ruining it.'

'I didn't even want to come,' muttered Connor. 'The whole thing was boring.'

'Well, in that case, sod off to the pub while the rest of us get something to eat. I can't keep having this argument with you.'

'You sod off,' sulked Connor, his nostrils flaring. He skulked back off to the car like a sullen teenager, his hands shoved firmly in his pockets.

Lizzie turned her attention back to Alex. A reddish tinge had swept across his features, as if an extension of the summer sky.

'I'm sorry,' she said softly, reaching for his hand. 'I didn't mean for things to kick off, and I really didn't mean to spoil your day. You know how proud I am.'

'I'm sorry, too. I shouldn't let him get to me like that.' He leaned down for a kiss. 'Are you sure I can't tempt you out for dinner? It's a really good restaurant.'

'No, it's OK,' she replied. 'You should go and celebrate with your family tonight. Let's give Connor a bit of space.'

'Alright.' Alex's forehead was creased with frustration. 'I just wish he'd calm down about this whole thing.'

'He will.'

'What, when hell freezes over?'

'Maybe not as fast as that,' she smiled. 'But I'm sure it'll happen eventually.'

17

5 weeks to go . . .

Lizzie stood on the pool edge, staring over the side of the deep end. Her reflection fragmented with each ripple of the water, a fragile replica bobbing along on an ever-shifting surface. *I know how you feel*, she told the floating doppelganger. Suddenly a stocky boy with red shorts and an even redder face ran up alongside her and divebombed in with a splash, causing the mirror image to shatter.

'Stop that!' shouted the lifeguard, blowing his whistle zealously. The boy emerged laughing, not paying any attention. His dark hair was splayed out across the top of his head like a drowning spider.

Lizzie waited for the swell to settle. Then she raised her arms and plunged into the pool, the cool water engulfing her as she broke the surface and settled into a steady front crawl. She didn't come swimming as much as she used to, what with work and all the wedding prep, but whenever she managed to fit in a session she always felt at home. *Alex was right. I guess some things don't change.*

Except, of course, that everything *had* changed for Alex. And she couldn't stop thinking about the bombshell he'd dropped in the park.

When he told her that he had a brain tumour, she didn't know what to say. The first thought that crossed her mind was that it might be a twisted joke, but that didn't make any sense and, besides, he wasn't laughing. She wanted to say something meaningful, something that would fill the silence to offer comfort, support and compassion.

'Fuuuuuck' was all that came out.

He tried to smile. 'Well, that's the best reaction I've had so far. Most people either cry or pretend everything's going to be OK.'

'Oh, Alex . . .' Lizzie's insides went into freefall. 'How bad is it?'

'It's not great. They say it's low-grade at the moment, but it's an awkward shape. So we're just watching and waiting for now.'

What does that mean? Her mind was throwing up questions so fast she couldn't think straight. 'Why don't they operate, take it out? There's got to be something they can do, right? Lots of people recover from cancer these days.'

'They will operate if it grows any bigger, but they're not going to be able to get it all. It's too embedded.'

'Are they sure? Maybe you should see another specialist, get a second opinion . . .'

Alex stared at his shoes. 'I've been to see two specialists here, Lizzie. They only confirmed what I'd already been told in Thailand. They can buy me more time, but they can't cure it.'

She exhaled loudly, the sound of her breath echoing in her ears.

'How long?' she asked slowly.

'Hard to say. Could be two years, could be twenty. Or I could get hit by a bus tomorrow. No one really knows how long they've got, do they?'

Lizzie's eyes brimmed with tears. 'Surely there's got to be something you could try? Doctors are coming up with new cutting-edge stuff all the time.'

He slid his arm around the back of the bench, squeezing her shoulder. 'I don't think that's going to come fast enough for me,' he said gently. 'And I don't want to spend whatever time I have left going in and out of hospital. I want to spend it with . . .' He stopped and took a deep breath. 'With my family, and the people who matter. That's all. I'm not here to make any trouble for you.'

She wiped her eyes, feeling awful that he was the one consoling her and not the other way around. 'So you've told the family, then?'

'Yes,' he sighed. 'That wasn't a good day.'

'They must be distraught.'

'Yeah. When I flew back they figured I had an announcement to make, but I guess they assumed I was getting engaged or something. They sure as hell weren't expecting that one.'

'I'm so sorry,' she stuttered, still reeling with shock. 'And there was me being a total bitch to you when you got back. I feel terrible.'

'Don't,' he said. 'I don't want you to feel terrible. And I don't want you to feel sorry for me, either.' He hesitated. 'I just wanted to see if we could start over, as friends?'

'Sure,' she said quietly, looking up through her wet lashes. 'I think we could manage that.'

Lizzie stepped out of the leisure centre into the sunlight, thoughts of Alex still swimming in her head. Her hair hung loosely around her shoulders and she shook it slightly, hoping the fresh air would remove the faint smell of chlorine that her shampoo couldn't quite erase. It was a beautiful July day: a bright blue sky dotted with a few wispy clouds. She pulled out her mobile and sent Alex a quick text.

How r u 2day? Thinking of u. Lizzie

Then she deleted it and typed the whole thing again in proper sentences. Megan always mocked her for not using text speak, but she couldn't bring herself to do it. It felt like a betrayal of writers everywhere.

Three seconds later, Alex called her.

'Hey,' she said. 'I was just wondering how you were getting on. What are you up to this weekend?'

'I'm in London, not too far from you,' he said, his voice echoing slightly.

'Oh, that's cool,' she said, straightening the strap on her top. 'Anywhere nice?'

'Actually, I'm in A&E.'

'What?'

'It's nothing,' he said quickly. 'I was up in town yesterday for my hospital appointment, so I thought I'd stay over with my friend Sam for the evening.'

Lizzie didn't know Sam. *Is that a boy or a girl?* she wondered before she could stop herself. 'Right . . .'

'Anyway, I was walking back to the Tube this morning when I had a bit of a seizure, and by the time I came round this nice lady had called an ambulance so they took me to the hospital to get checked over.'

'Are you OK?' She tightened her grip on the phone. 'That sounds serious.'

'I'll be fine. It happens from time to time. But I hit my head on the way down, so the doctor says I shouldn't be alone today.' The line went silent for a second. 'I hate to ask, but I don't suppose there's any chance you could come and hang out with me for a while, is there? I know you're probably busy, but Sam's at work and I didn't know who else round here to call.'

'Er, OK. Now? At the hospital?'

'Well, we can move on someplace else,' he laughed. 'Maybe grab a bite? Sam says he can fetch me after six when his shift ends, then I can stay there another night.'

She checked the time on her phone. It was 1.45pm. 'Alright. I've got the car so I'll get there as quick as I can. Can you text me the postcode for the sat nav?'

'No probs, I'll do that now.' He cleared his throat.

'Thanks for doing this, Lizzie. Otherwise they might ring my mum and I'm worried she'll drive up in a right state.'

'No, there's no need to do that,' she said quickly, knowing poor Pamela would panic. She threw her swimming kit in the boot and shut it. 'I'm already on my way.'

Lizzie pulled into the hospital car park, balking at the exorbitant short-stay prices. She shoved the sat nav in the glove box then fumbled around for the bag of coins she stashed in there. *I hope Josh hasn't been spending it all at the McDonald's drive-thru again.*

She found the change, and to her relief there was enough for a few hours. She slipped it into the meter and popped the ticket on the dashboard, then grabbed her handbag and made her way inside the sprawling reception. The place was heaving, with doctors, nurses, patients and visitors all milling around in different directions. Finding Alex in here wasn't going to be easy.

She pulled out her phone and fired off another text: I'm here. Where are you? x

A few seconds later, his reply popped up: Meet you by the front in 2 mins. x

She hovered by the main door, stopping to use some of the antibac gel on the wall. The stuff smelled of pure alcohol. It took her back to last night, when Josh had rolled in after a late one with the boys and then clambered into bed, showering her with boozy kisses. He'd been sleeping off his hangover when she slipped out this morning, but she wondered if she should send him a quick text to let him know she wouldn't be home until later. Then she remembered he was planning to head to the pub to watch the Wimbledon match with Freddie. He probably wouldn't even notice she hadn't returned from the pool.

Seconds later the lift opened and Alex stepped out into the corridor, sporting butterfly stitches above his right eye. He waved and walked towards her.

'Ouch, that looks sore,' said Lizzie. 'Is it deep?'

'Nah, it's just a scratch. I must've landed a bit funny.' He handed her a leaflet on concussion with a list of scary-sounding symptoms in bold letters. 'The doc said I should give you this, though, just in case I take a weird turn later.'

'What, weirder than normal?' she grinned.

'Hey, you're not supposed to pick on the patient. What's a guy got to do for some TLC round here?'

'Would you settle for some tea? I saw a café round the corner on my way in. We could go get a drink and some lunch.' She caught sight of the large clock on the wall behind him. 'Late lunch.'

'Sounds good to me. I'm starving.'

They made their way out past the car park, taking a left at the end of the road and heading for the small parade of shops. The café looked like a bit of a greasy spoon, with a pillarbox-red door and walls the colour of eggyolk, but by this point Lizzie was so hungry she didn't care.

She turned the brass handle and stepped inside, causing

a bell to jingle overhead. The place was largely empty, apart from a man in a paint-splattered T-shirt tucking into a bacon sarnie and an elderly gentleman enjoying a plate of gammon and chips. Lizzie and Alex headed for a table in the far corner and plonked themselves down on two red plastic chairs, like the stackable ones Josh put out at school when the kids performed their Christmas play. She tucked her bag underneath the seat.

'I hope this is OK,' she said. 'It was either this or the hospital canteen.'

'This is fine,' said Alex. 'We've got food, we've got good company – what's not to like?'

'Great.' She picked up the plastic menu. The smell of grilled meat made her mouth water, and she reminded herself that she still had a wedding dress to get into in five weeks. Not that it looked like the kind of place where there were many slimline options.

The pregnant waitress waddled over, resting her pad on top of her baby bump. 'What can I get you?'

Lizzie summoned every last bit of willpower. 'I'll have a poached egg on toast, please,' she said. 'Wholemeal, if you've got it.'

'Is that all?' asked Alex. 'I'll have the all-day breakfast, with extra-crispy bacon.'

'You're so mean!' said Lizzie. 'Now I'll have food envy.'

'Well, there's still time to change your mind,' he said.

Ah, screw it. At least I went swimming. 'Go on, then,' she told the waitress. 'I'll have the same.'

The waitress nodded and crossed out the earlier order. 'Any drinks with that?'

'Tea, please – no sugar,' they both said at the same time, then smiled at each other in bemusement.

'Well, that's an easy order.' The waitress trundled back to the kitchen, her ponytail bobbing as she went.

Lizzie leaned in, resting her elbows on the table. 'So, how are you feeling now?'

'I'm OK. Better for getting out of the hospital. There's something about the smell of them I can't stand, like they're almost *too* clean.'

'I know what you mean. When do you have to go back?'

'Not for a couple of months, as long as I don't have any more seizures.'

'Is it painful?'

'The tumour? No, not really. It's not like I can feel it or anything. Half the time I forget it's there, but then . . .' His voice tailed off, and he fiddled with his paper napkin.

Lizzie wished she hadn't brought it up. 'I'm sorry about all the questions. We don't have to talk about it if you don't want to.'

'No, it's OK. Maybe it'll help.' He set his napkin down. 'Ask me anything.'

'Anything?'

'Yeah, go for it.'

'Alright.' She gestured to his crewcut. 'When did this happen?'

'About two months ago.'

'Did you have to do it for the scans?'

'No. But I figured it would have to go at some point, so I shaved it off for charity. I made, like, £800 in the end.'

'Wow, that's amazing. Do you miss it?' She had loved his thick hair, the way it used to feel between her fingers. Although she had to admit, he looked surprisingly good with it short.

'Not as much as I miss my driving licence. It's only hair.' He leaned back in his chair. 'What else do you want to know?'

'Who have you told?'

'Just the family, and then you, Dev and Sam. That's it.'

'Should I tell Megan?' Trying to keep something so momentous to herself all week had been torture, helped only by the fact that Megan was on holiday with Lily. The one time they'd tried to phone from Ibiza, Lizzie had ashamedly ducked the call.

'Can we leave it a couple more weeks?' he said. 'I'd like to see her at some point, but I don't think I'm ready for everyone to know just yet. I don't want people treating me differently.' He raised his brows ruefully. 'Besides, we both know Megan hates me.'

'She doesn't hate you,' lied Lizzie. 'She's just protective, that's all. But if you told her what you've told me, I know she'd want to see you. She still cares, deep down.'

Alex gave a thin smile. 'How is Megan, anyway?'

'She's brilliant. Kind of the same, really. I still see her a lot.'

'That's good. Did she find Mr Right or is she still, er, auditioning?'

'No, she's not seeing anyone at the moment. Strangely enough, though, we bumped into Gareth at the ball and she seems to have her eye on him now. I think they'd make a cute couple.'

'That's hilarious,' said Alex. 'Is he still into his Barry Manilow?'

'It wasn't Barry Manilow,' she laughed. 'It was Tom Jones. And if they ever hook up, I'm going to be afraid to ask her, because she *will* tell me in detail.'

'No, you've got to,' he said. 'That's so funny. Poor Gareth – she'll have him for breakfast.'

As if catching the perfect segue, their waitress suddenly reappeared with a tray carrying their drinks and fry-ups. The plates were piled high: fried eggs, fat sausages, well-done bacon, juicy tomatoes, fried mushrooms and fluffy hash browns, slathered with a generous helping of baked beans. The aroma was incredible. Lizzie wished she could bottle it and spritz it round her kitchen.

'Here, let me get that,' said Alex, jumping up to help.

'Thanks, darl,' said the waitress. She smiled at Lizzie. 'You've got a good 'un there.'

'Oh no, he's not . . .I mean . . .'

'She means we're just friends,' finished Alex with a grin. 'Friends in need of bacon. And maybe a little ketchup.'

'Ketchup's in there,' said the waitress, pointing to the bright red dispenser shaped like a giant tomato.

'Right. I probably should have noticed that. Thank you.'

She returned to the kitchen and Alex tucked into his fry-up, a dreamy smile on his face. 'Damn, that's *good*. It's been ages since I had a full English.'

'That's probably not the worst thing,' said Lizzie, not sure what to eat first. She took a sip of tea and prodded the food with her fork. 'This looks like a heart attack on toast.'

'Well, I'm a bit more relaxed these days,' said Alex amicably. 'I don't think it's the cholesterol that's going to get me.'

Lizzie's hand flew up to her mouth. 'Oh no, that was totally insensitive of me, wasn't it? I'm sorry.'

'Stop being sorry. I don't want you walking on eggshells.'

'Alright, sorry.' She caught it a second too late. 'Now I'm sorry for saying sorry.'

Alex laughed, lifting a large forkful of fried egg to his lips and washing it down with a mouthful of tea. 'Apology accepted. Anyway, enough about this. How's your writing going?'

She felt a flicker of embarrassment. 'Er, about as well as a decade ago,' she said, taking a bite of salty bacon.

'Really?' Alex seemed surprised. 'You shouldn't give up on it.' He looked at her expectantly. 'I want to be the first to buy your books someday – as long as you promise to sign them.'

'Don't hold your breath.' She gave a shrug. 'I'm hardly Emily Brontë.'

'Was she the *Jane Eyre* one or the *Wuthering Heights* one? I get those Brontë sisters mixed up.'

'*Wuthering Heights*. Did you know that was the only novel she ever wrote? But it's my favourite.' She cut her tomato in half, juice spilling across the plate. 'Who's your favourite author these days?'

'Well, I'm hoping it'll be you.' He smiled, and she blushed. 'You just need to keep going. That short story you let me read was brilliant.'

'You remember that?' Even she'd almost forgotten. It was probably long recycled by now, or languishing up in the loft somewhere.

'Of course. Great twist. Have you shown anything to the people you work with?'

'Not yet,' she admitted, cutting into her sausage. 'I was thinking about having another stab at it, but something always seems to get in the way.'

'Like what?'

'I don't know. Life. Work. The wedding.'

'Ah, yes. The wedding.' He chewed his bacon for what seemed like an eternity. 'So, what's his name, anyway? Is he a good guy?'

Lizzie sipped her drink, unsure of how much to tell him. 'You really want to talk about this?'

'Sure, why not?' His voice sounded light, but his eyes turned a shade darker.

'Alright.' She shuffled uncomfortably on her plastic seat. 'His name's Josh.' *He's different to you*, she almost added, but that sounded kind of rude, which wasn't the way she intended it. 'He's . . . nice.'

'What does he do?'

'He's a teacher.'

'I can sort of see you with a teacher,' said Alex slowly, pushing his mushrooms around his plate. 'I bet you sit there reading through the homework, spotting all the terrible spelling and grammar. Right?'

'Actually, you're wrong,' she said with a grin. 'He teaches PE. So most of the time he's outdoors with the kids.'

'Stop. I hate him already,' said Alex. 'Please tell me he at least wears a shell suit?'

'Only for special occasions . . .' She speared a single baked bean with her fork. 'What about you? Are you seeing anyone?' The café seemed eerily quiet as she waited for his reply. It felt strange talking to him about this sort of stuff, but if they were going to be friends she would have to at least try.

'No,' he said. 'I was seeing a girl in Thailand for a while, but I had to call it off.'

'Why?'

'Because one day she told me that she loved me, and I couldn't say it back.'

'Oh.' She finished the dregs of her tea, suddenly feeling calmer. 'That must have been tough.'

'Yeah, it wasn't great. She cried a lot.'

'Don't beat yourself up,' she said. 'I'm sure she'll be OK.'

'Like you, you mean?' He mopped up the last of the

beans with his hash brown. 'You seem like you've got everything sorted.'

'Hardly,' she winced, not quite sure what he was getting at. 'I can't even sort out my own wedding. It's turned into this huge big thing and I hate the best man and I didn't invite my boss and now I'm worried maybe I should have and . . .'

'Whoa,' said Alex. 'You're going to have to rewind a bit. Fill me in on everything.'

'Alright,' she said, screwing up her serviette. 'But we're going to need more tea.'

Lizzie slid inside her car and pulled the door shut, slinging her bag onto the passenger seat. She couldn't believe it was 6.30pm. The past few hours had flown by, as she and Alex traded amusing tales from their uni days in the way that you could only do with someone else who'd lived through them. She'd never heard the one about Connor throwing up in Alex's airing cupboard after drunkenly mistaking it for the bathroom. He didn't know that Megan had leant on a statue in the park, only to find she'd pushed over a mime artist. Neither of them noticed the time until Sam had called Alex to say he'd arrived at the hospital.

It had been fun hanging out again, chatting about nothing and everything, from the Thai weather to his mum's newfound interest in social media ('apparently once she even tweeted Clarence House to ask who does Camilla's hair,' he said). She'd forgotten how much she enjoyed his company; how easy he'd been to talk to before it all went wrong. Just because they weren't meant to be together didn't mean they couldn't still have a laugh together.

It did mean, though, that she would have to talk to Josh.

There was no point postponing the inevitable: if she wanted to keep seeing Alex, then she needed things to be out in the open. *Josh will understand*, she reassured herself. *He's not the jealous type.*

She started the engine, turning on the radio. The anthemic chorus of *Wonderwall* soared out through the speakers. *That's weird timing.* She hadn't been able to listen to the song again after she and Alex broke up, switching it off swiftly if ever it caught her unawares. But now, her hands resting on the steering wheel, she was able to let it play to the end, a small smile crossing her face. She felt sure that the two of them had finally turned a corner, and could forge a real friendship after all.

Turning the radio down, she pulled out of the car park and indicated left, joining the queue of traffic snaking out of London.

I'll talk to Josh tonight, she decided, *as long as Freddie's not around. I should have told him about Alex sooner, but better late than never.*

Megan's voice rang in her ears. *What he doesn't know won't hurt him.*

Lizzie turned the radio back up and tried to drown her out.

*   *   *

An hour later, Lizzie pulled into her drive and walked up to the house. The first thing she noticed was that all the blinds were drawn and the lights were off. *Is Josh still out?* She opened the front door and flicked the switch on the wall, but nothing happened. *Have we had a power cut?* That would be annoying; they had a large chicken in the freezer for tomorrow's roast.

She fished around in her bag for her mobile, using the screen to gently illuminate the hall. All of Josh's trainers had vanished. *Shit! Have we been burgled?* She held her mobile higher, trying to see up the stairs. Then she realised that the hall lightbulb had been removed.

What the hell? Surely even burglars aren't taking bulbs now?

'Josh,' she whispered, confused and a little alarmed. 'Are you there?'

There was no answer, so she set her bag down quietly on the console table and rummaged inside for the fiercest weapon she could find. The best she managed to come up with was her umbrella, so she held it upside down and extended the handle like a baton. Gripping it tightly, she nudged forward and gently pushed open the lounge door, noticing a strange glow coming through the crack. Her heart was trampolining into her throat.

She could hardly believe what she saw inside.

The living room was immaculate, with not so much as a beer can in sight. At the far end, beneath the beam of a tall candle, their small dining table was set for two. Josh was standing behind a chair, uncorking a bottle of wine. She noticed it was a decent bottle of Chablis, not that £4.99 crap he normally came back with.

'What's this for?' she said. She racked her brain, trying to remember if she'd forgotten some special occasion.

'It's for you,' he said simply. 'I know we've both had a lot on lately, and I suspect I might have overdone it last night. So I wanted to do something to spoil you.'

'Josh, this is amazing.' She was genuinely touched. 'You didn't have to do this.'

'I know, but I thought it might be nice. We haven't had a proper date for a while.' He caught sight of the upturned brolly in her hand. 'What's with the umbrella?'

'Oh, this.' Lizzie put it down on the sideboard and slipped off her shoes. 'Long story. Never mind.' She surveyed the room again, stepping forward to give him a big kiss. 'It looks great in here. This must have taken you ages.'

'Yeah, a while. I was feeling slightly fragile so I decided to watch the tennis at home instead. Then I thought I'd clean up and surprise you.' He looked at his watch. 'You were just starting to get me a bit worried, though. I suddenly had a horrible feeling that maybe I'd got the date of your hen do wrong, and then all my good work would have gone to waste.'

A shot of guilt jabbed at her again. 'Sorry – I thought you'd be down the pub, otherwise I'd have called. How long have you been sitting here in the dark?'

'Not long. I heard your car coming up the road. You've really got to get that exhaust fixed.'

'I know. What happened to the bulb in the hall?'

'Oh, that. I unscrewed it this afternoon for a bit of mood lighting,' he said, looking pleased with his ingenuity. 'Don't worry, I'll put it back later.' He pulled out a chair and gestured for her to sit down. 'You relax while I check on the dinner.'

'What are we having?'

'Homemade chilli con carne. I just need to get it off the hob. Back in a sec.'

She took a seat and poured herself a glass of Chablis, admiring Josh's handiwork. He'd managed to find the good cutlery – even if he had put out the teaspoons instead of the dessert spoons – and the wine was beautifully chilled.

If this is what married life's going to be like, bring it on.

Josh stepped back into the room, carrying a bowlful of chilli and a plate of boiled rice. Lizzie wasn't starving after her late fry-up, but she helped herself to a large spoonful of each and tucked in enthusiastically. She knew from experience that Josh would probably polish off the rest anyway.

'What a great idea,' she said, taking a sip of wine. 'I'm very impressed.'

'So I'm not in the doghouse after last night, then?' he said.

'No, it's fine, I'd already forgotten about it.' By now it felt like a week ago. 'It's been a busy day.'

'So what did you get up to?'

She set her glass down slowly as she debated how to answer that question, though Josh seemed oblivious to her hesitation. He shovelled a small mountain of food onto his fork and scoffed it happily, a bit of mince spilling down his Superdry T-shirt.

'I went to the pool for a swim,' she said, taking a bite of chilli and nervously chewing a kidney bean. 'Then I had lunch with a friend.' *Tell him now,* she urged herself. *The sooner you bring it up, the sooner you can stop stressing.*

'Is Megan back?'

'Oh, right. No, actually, I went to meet . . .' She paused as he sprang up from the table. 'You OK?'

'Yep, I just forgot the sour cream.' He bounded back out to the kitchen, returning moments later with it in his hand. 'Sorry, what were you saying?'

He looked down at her, his eyes wide and trusting like a giant puppy. She opened her mouth to speak, but the words refused to budge.

I can't do it.

She didn't want to risk even the slightest chance of an argument tonight, not after he'd gone to all this trouble. She didn't think for one second that Megan was right about not telling him at all; in fact, now that Alex was back on the radar, she knew it was inevitable. But she definitely didn't want Josh worrying before the wedding.

Maybe I should just hold off a little longer.

Perhaps it would be kinder to do it after the event, once

there could be no doubt in his mind that she was 100 per cent committed to their relationship. And besides, that was only a few short weeks away.

'Nothing, doesn't matter. How was your night out with the lads?'

'Yeah, it was pretty funny. Freddie stole Big Phil's phone and sent some hilarious texts.' He sat back down. 'Phil sends his love. I think he's got a soft spot for you.'

'Are they all coming to the wedding?' asked Lizzie. 'I haven't had any RSVPs from that lot yet.'

'Oh yeah, they'll be there for sure.' He spooned some more chilli onto his plate. 'And I've told them they've all got to be on their best behaviour.'

Like that's ever stopped them.

'Alright.' She emptied her wine glass and reached for a refill. 'I can't believe it's only five weeks away, can you?'

'No,' he said. 'But it seems like we're on the home straight now, right?'

'I think so. Everything's booked, so there's not much more to do for about a month.' The wedding planning had taken over so much of her life lately that it felt weird to have this brief window of respite.

'The calm before the storm, eh?' he joked.

'Something like that,' she smiled.

'You know what you're forgetting, don't you?'

'What?' she said quickly, her heartbeat speeding up a gear. *I hope it's not something important . . .*

He wiggled his eyebrows. 'Stag and hen dos, baby!'

'Oh, yeah,' she said, relieved. 'Those.' She'd left Megan in charge of planning hers with only one rule: no nudity. That went for both her and for any gyrating beefcakes. She still had no idea what she was letting herself in for.

'Do you want ice-cream?'

'For the hen do?'

'No, now! I got your favourite. Mint choc chip.'

'Ooh, yes please.' She pursed her lips and blew him a kiss. 'Someone's in the good books tonight.'

'Well, you know what they say,' he grinned. 'Happy wife, happy life.'

She watched him get up again, whistling to himself as he passed. A comforting warmth came over her. They were good together, she knew that. And in just five short weeks, it would be official.

She raised her glass in a silent toast: *To happily ever after.*

18

26 December 2004

'Hey you,' said Lizzie, slipping into Alex's airbed and planting a kiss on his cheek. 'Any room for me?'

Despite the fact that she and Alex had been dating for more than two years, her mum still stubbornly refused to swap the ancient single bed in Lizzie's old room for a double, and as a result Alex was forced to sleep on an inflatable on the floor. He swore he didn't mind, but Lizzie wanted him to feel relaxed in her family home, and she wasn't convinced a blow-up bed was entirely welcoming.

'I'm not sure,' he said, half-opening his eyes. 'If I eat much more of your mum's cooking, I'm barely going to fit in here myself.'

'Yeah, I know what you mean,' she said, pressing herself against his bare chest. 'I feel about two sizes bigger after all that turkey, but it's compulsory to put on a few pounds over Christmas, isn't it?'

He slid his hands beneath her oversized T-shirt. 'You still feel in good shape to me . . .'

'Is that so?'

'Yes.' He lifted her top higher and pretended to scrutinise her closely. 'Where are you putting it all?'

'That's for you to find out,' Lizzie smiled, running her fingertips over his pecs. She hesitated as she reached the jagged edge of his scar. 'I don't think you ever told me how you got this?' she said curiously.

'Oh, that. Shark bite. On my gap year in Australia.'

Her eyes widened. 'Are you serious?'

There was a second's silence before he burst out laughing. 'Nope. I was having a bike race with Connor when we were kids, and I came flying off. Went straight into the neighbour's fence.'

'Ouch. Sounds painful.'

'The fence came off worse. Though I did have to spend the night in casualty.'

'Poor Alex.' She kissed her fingers and lightly pressed them to his chest.

'Don't worry, I'm back to full strength now.' He shifted his weight so that she was beneath him and started kissing her midriff under the duvet.

'Oh, really?' she sighed, sinking slightly into the inflatable bed. His lips felt soft against her skin. She was just drifting into a state of deep bliss when she was interrupted by the sound of her mother's voice floating shrilly up the stairs. 'Elizabeth! Alex! Your breakfast is ready . . .'

'Alright!' she shouted, silently cursing her mum's terrible timing.

'Do you want me to stop?' whispered Alex.

'Not really, but I can't relax now. If we don't go downstairs soon, she'll be up in a minute. And trust me, you don't want that.'

'I believe you.' He rolled back onto his side of the airbed. 'Another time.'

'It's a promise.' She kissed him on the cheek and slid out of the sheets, grabbing her dressing gown from her old wardrobe. 'Do I look decent?'

'Yeah, unfortunately,' said Alex. He stood up and stretched, throwing a navy sweater over his six-pack and retrieving his jeans from the floor. Lizzie watched as he wriggled into them, never bored by the sight of his body. She still fancied him as much as the day they met, and she wondered if she would always find him so irresistible, or whether that would slowly fade over time, like the weathered denim he was wearing.

'Elizabeth,' her mum shouted again.

'Alright!' She smiled at Alex. 'See?'

Together they joined her parents in the kitchen, taking their seats at the large wooden table. Lizzie reached for the orange juice and poured out two glasses, passing one over to Alex. Her mother hovered expectantly by the stove.

'Right, you two, we've got eggs, bacon, beans, sausages and toast. Do you want a bit of everything?'

'Yes, please,' said Alex. 'I'm powerless to resist your cooking.'

'Me too,' said Lizzie. 'You've got to stop with the fry-ups, though. We'll never fit into our clothes by the end of the week.'

'Nonsense,' she replied. 'I think you could both use a bit of fattening up. Goodness knows what rubbish you're eating when you're left to your own devices. Don't they feed you at that university?'

'I eat just fine on campus. And Alex doesn't even go there any more, remember? I showed you those pics from his graduation!'

'Potatoes po-ta-toes,' she huffed. 'You both still look thinner every time I see you. Don't they, Harry?'

'What's that?' said her dad, not paying attention.

'I was just saying the kids could use feeding up a bit, don't you think?'

'Maybe,' he replied, his mind obviously elsewhere.

'Dad, are you alright?' asked Lizzie.

'Oh yes, love, I'm fine. I was just thinking about those poor people on the news.'

'What news?' As was quite often the way, Lizzie didn't have a clue what he was on about.

'You know, all that flooding. Such a tragedy.'

'What flooding? Where?'

'Loads of places, by the look of it. It's all over the telly.'

Curious, Lizzie rose from her chair and went into the living room, as Alex followed closely behind. She fumbled with the remote control to turn the TV back on.

'BREAKING NEWS: EARTHQUAKE TRIGGERS

TSUNAMI' screamed the caption across the screen in bold letters.

Lizzie's jaw dropped in horror. She wasn't quite sure what a tsunami was, but the grainy videos flashing before her were terrifying, as giant walls of water appeared out of nowhere and swept away everything in their path. She turned to stare at Alex, who was losing colour by the second, as though pints of blood were being sucked from his body. Then she remembered.

Connor.

Her stomach started to churn. For a second, she wondered if perhaps she was still asleep, locked inside a nightmare she would shortly wake up from.

'Has it hit Thailand?' said Alex, shaking his head in disbelief. The fear on his face was so real that Lizzie knew she couldn't possibly be dreaming.

She scanned a list of affected places scrolling across the bottom of the screen: Indonesia, India, Sri Lanka, Somalia, the Maldives . . .

. . . Thailand.

Alex's legs buckled and he stumbled backwards, dropping down onto the couch. Lizzie sat beside him and threw an arm around his hunched shoulders. 'Alex . . . Alex, listen to me. I'm sure that Connor's fine. Chances are he wasn't anywhere near the coast. The best thing you can do right now is to keep calm and think. Where was he travelling this week?'

'I'm not sure,' he replied, his whole body trembling. 'He

didn't exactly tell me much about his itinerary after I bailed on him.'

'But he's in touch with your parents, right? They must know where he's staying.'

'Possibly. He might have tried them yesterday, to wish them a happy Christmas. Although he didn't try to contact me.' A flicker of hurt flashed across his face, before he leapt back up to his feet. 'He should have his mobile with him. I need to call that, check he's OK.'

'Of course,' said Lizzie, grabbing the cordless handset from the coffee table. 'Here, use this.' She watched as he punched in the numbers with excessive force. A few seconds later, he hung up in frustration.

'What happened?' she asked.

'It's not connecting!' he said angrily. 'Why can't I get through to him?'

Lizzie tried to act calmer than she felt. 'The phone lines have probably been damaged by the water. The whole system could be down. I'm sure Connor's somewhere safe but he's just not been able to contact you yet.'

'I don't know what to do,' said Alex, looking like a little boy lost. Lizzie had never seen him like this before: so helpless, so afraid.

'You said your parents might have spoken to him yesterday, right? You could try giving them a ring, see if anyone knows where he is.'

Alex nodded. 'OK,' he said numbly, reaching for the

handset again. He was in the middle of dialling when Lizzie heard a shout from the kitchen.

'Elizabeth! What's going on?' yelled her mum. 'Your breakfast's getting cold.'

'This is urgent,' she yelled back.

It wasn't the most detailed of explanations, but it was enough to make her mum leave the cooker and poke her head around the lounge door. 'What's happened?' she whispered, spotting Alex's pained face as he waited for someone to pick up.

'His twin's in Asia,' said Lizzie. 'We don't know if he's caught up in all this. We need to make some calls. Forget about breakfast.'

Her mum stared at Alex in shock, looking like she was about to cry. 'That's awful,' she said eventually, her words barely audible. 'His poor family. They must be so worried.' She cleared her throat. 'Tell him to make as many calls as he wants. Your father and I will be next door if either of you needs anything.'

'Thanks, Mum.' Lizzie turned her attention back to Alex and hovered anxiously beside him. She wanted to say something – do something – that would help him in some way, but her brain was scrambling to think straight. All she could do was place her palm gently on his back to let him know that she was there. She felt him tense up as someone answered the phone.

'Hi Mum,' he said, his voice sounding small and strangled. 'It's Alex. Where are you?'

Lizzie tried to hear the response, but she couldn't make out anything.

'So the others are still in bed?' *They haven't seen the TV yet.* Lizzie felt sick as the realisation sank in. She tried to keep her composure, if only for Alex's sake, but it was getting harder by the second. She could feel the stress emanating from his body.

'Look, Mum, did you speak to Connor yesterday by any chance?' he asked, a tiny note of hope buried beneath his breaking voice. Lizzie couldn't hear the reply, but the crushed look on Alex's face told her it was negative.

'Well, have you had any texts or emails from him lately? Did he say where he was staying?' His mum murmured something inaudible, and Alex's hand tightened around the handset until his knuckles went white. 'I'm asking because there's been a disaster in Asia,' he said quietly. 'It's all over the news. I'm not saying he's caught up in it – we don't know much at the moment – but it's really important that we find out where he is, OK?'

Even Lizzie could hear the primal shriek that echoed down the line. She wondered if Mr Jackson had heard it, or whether his deafness had afforded him a few final moments of undisturbed slumber.

'Mum? Mum! I need you to hold it together,' said Alex, clearly distraught at being the bearer of such unspeakable news. 'Do you have any idea where he might be?' There was a pause. 'Well, if he sent you an email on Christmas Eve, you need to get on the computer and see if it says where he is.' Lizzie could detect a note of impatience creeping into his voice. 'I'll stay on the line while you do it. Go now, Mum, *please!*'

After what seemed like the world's longest three minutes, his mother returned with an update. 'Uh-huh,' said Alex. 'And does it say where, exactly? Near Khao Lak? OK, that's helpful. At least we've got a starting point now.' He stopped. 'Mum, please don't cry. We're going to find him. He'll be alright. He *has* to be alright.'

Lizzie wished more than anything in the world that would turn out to be true. The images on the TV were getting scarier by the second. 'Biggest quake in 40 years' read one caption. 'Thousands feared dead' scrolled another.

'Mum, I need you to stay calm and wake up the others, in case any of them have heard from him. Everyone should check their phones and emails now, OK? I'm going to come straight over to yours and we'll deal with this together.' His voice sounded strong, but Lizzie could see his hands were still shaking. 'Yes, alright. I'll be with you in a bit.' And with that he hung up and dropped the phone on the couch.

Lizzie reached for his arm. 'So you know where he is now – that's a start, right?'

Alex began to pace around the living room. 'I need to get on the internet. Do your parents have a computer here?'

'My dad's got a laptop for work, but I think he left it at the office over the break,' she said. 'Do you want me to see if he can fetch it? I'm not sure they're open on Boxing Day.'

'Shit!' Alex was beyond frustrated now. His previously pale face was turning a blotchy red. 'I have to get out of here and find out what's happening.' He rushed up the stairs two at a time, with Lizzie trailing closely behind him, and stomped into the bedroom.

'Is there anything I can do?' she said, desperately wanting to make herself more useful than she felt.

'Not right now,' he said, grabbing his clothes out of her wardrobe and stuffing them into his holdall. 'I need to get to my family, see if we can track him down.'

'How are you going to do that?'

'I don't know,' he said, grabbing his car keys off the bedside table. 'But I can't just sit around here doing nothing. I have to go home.'

Lizzie didn't like the thought of him going anywhere by himself in that agitated state, let alone driving on the motorway. 'Look, you're clearly upset—'

'You think?' he snapped. 'For fuck's sake, Lizzie, I've got to get on the road. I haven't got time for this right now.'

She felt as though she'd been slapped across the face. He had never spoken to her like that before. *He's upset, that's all.* She took a deep breath and tried again.

'I just don't think you should be driving alone when you're all worked up like this. Give me two minutes to throw on some clothes and grab some stuff, then I'll come with you, OK?'

She reached under the bed to look for her case, but he was already halfway out of the door. 'Alex!' she called.

'Hold on!' She ran to the top of the stairs. 'Why can't you wait for me?'

He turned to face her. 'I'm sorry,' he said. 'I've got to go. You should stay here with your family.'

She opened her mouth to tell him to be careful, to remind him that she loved him, but he was halfway down the drive before the words could make their way out.

The last thing she heard was the screech of his tyres as the car raced away down the road.

19

4 weeks to go . . .

Lizzie got off the Tube at Camden Town, making her way up the High Street – or was it down? It had been a while since she'd gone out this far north of the river, and she struggled to get her bearings, trying not to bump into the pedestrians pounding the pavement in both directions. In the end she pulled over against a wall and checked the map on her mobile. *Yes, this is right.* She didn't remember the place being so gentrified, with its Waitrose and its coffee chains and its mobile phone shops, and she wondered what Alex would think about it all.

She was looking forward to seeing him tonight. Admittedly she hadn't expected them to meet up again quite so soon, but she didn't have much else on and was secretly glad of a break from all the wedding build-up. He'd sent her a text on Monday to say thanks for meeting him at the hospital (or 'Alex-sitting', as he'd put it), so she'd called him back on her lunch break to see how he was doing.

'I'm good,' he said. 'No concussion. I'm sure that bacon helped.'

'Well, it couldn't hurt,' she agreed, as she strolled to the little café by her office. 'It's making me hungry just thinking about it.'

'Me too.' His voice was warm, relaxed. 'What are you up to this week?'

'Nothing, really. I think it's the first week in months we haven't had a million jobs to do. You?'

'Not much. But I'm coming up on Thursday to check out a gig in Camden with Sam. There's this great band playing.' The line went quiet for a second. 'You know what, you should come with us. Bring your fiancé. I'm going to have to meet the guy sometime, right?'

'Right,' mumbled Lizzie, her shoulders tensing. 'I guess so. What night did you say it was?'

'Thursday.'

'Oh, Josh can't do Thursdays. He's got his five-a-side thing.'

'With the kids?'

'No, with his mates.' It wasn't often that his football team proved useful, but she was grateful for small mercies. The more she thought about it, the more she was convinced that it would be better to introduce the two of them after the wedding. 'Another time, though.'

'Well, why don't you come?' said Alex. 'If Josh is out anyway there's no point you staying home all by yourself. Plus you can meet Sam properly.'

She mulled over his offer. *Why not?* It had been ages since she'd been to a proper gig, and it might be fun to have a change of scene. 'It's not like that awful death metal band Connor made us watch, is it?' she asked.

'No, it's a new indie rock group. They're going to be huge.' His enthusiasm was catching, even down the phone. 'You have to branch out from Take That one day, you know.'

'Hey, leave Take That out of this,' she laughed. 'But you've twisted my arm. Count me in.'

'Great, I'll send you the details. Meet us there around 8.30pm?'

'OK. See you then.'

By the time Lizzie reached the bar, she could see a long queue snaking out of the front door and around the side. *Is Alex already here?* She walked to the front and couldn't spot him, so she slowly made her way back down the disorderly line, trying to squint at people without looking like she was staring.

She hadn't got far when a hand suddenly shot out and grabbed her by the wrist, pulling her into the melee. She jumped a mile, and was hugely relieved when she looked up and saw Alex's smiling face. His butterfly stitches from last week had been removed, but he still had a scrape above his eye.

'Oh good, you're here,' she said. 'You must have been in the queue a while?'

'Yeah, we were,' he said. 'We wanted to try to get a table.' He was still holding her arm, though he'd loosened his grip. His fingers felt familiar against her skin. 'Did you find it OK?'

'Just about. It's been a while since I came to Camden.'

He released his grasp and introduced her to Sam, who she'd met fleetingly through his car window last weekend. Physically, he was almost the polar opposite of Alex, with dirty blond hair and a smattering of freckles. He was wearing a blue and pink checked shirt that seemed to have a grass stain on it, as if he'd taken it to Glastonbury and forgotten to wash it afterwards. But he had twinkly eyes and a gap-toothed grin that dominated the whole of his face. Lizzie liked him immediately.

'So how did you two meet?' she asked. 'At a gig or something?'

'No, we first met out in Australia,' said Sam. 'This guy taught me how to play the guitar.' He slapped Alex jovially on the back. 'We lost contact for years, but then he got back in touch.'

'That's cool.' She smiled. 'Do both of you still play?'

'Now and again,' said Alex. 'I'm a bit rusty, mind.'

'I do,' said Sam. 'Maybe we should get our guitars out sometime?'

'Is that a euphemism?' joked Lizzie. 'Hey, if it goes well you could start your own boy band . . .'

'You wish,' grinned Alex. They all moved a few steps forwards. 'I think we're about 20 years too old to be in a boy band, I'm afraid. But nice try.'

'Do you play anything?' asked Sam.

'Nope, not even the triangle,' she replied. 'I'm not exactly musically gifted, unless you count my one and only karaoke performance. Sadly, never to be repeated.'

'Well, I thought you were sensational,' said Alex. 'I'd pay good money to see that again.'

'Sorry, not gonna happen. Don't get me wrong, I love music – but it's purely a spectator sport for me.'

'Fair enough,' said Sam. 'You should come with us next month, though. We're going to see this awesome band in Hammersmith.'

'I'd love to, but I can't,' she said. They edged forward again. 'Maybe another time.'

Alex turned to Sam. 'Lizzie's getting married soon, so she'll be away on her honeymoon.'

'Oh, really?' said Sam, giving Alex a puzzled glance before switching his focus back to Lizzie. 'Where are you going?'

'We're off to Italy,' she replied. She and Josh had finally booked it in the week, which was a weight off her mind. The hotel looked amazing.

'I see.' Sam dialled his smile back up. 'Exciting times.'

The three of them reached the front of the queue and handed over their tickets. The doorman took a quick look inside Lizzie's bag before waving them through. She was secretly disappointed he didn't ask her for ID. Back at uni she used to hate getting carded, but now she'd have taken it as a massive compliment. Lucky Megan had been stopped at the supermarket last month while trying to buy a bottle of Bacardi. *Must be those anti-ageing creams she's always being sent.*

Inside the dark bar, the anticipation was building, with fans already pushing their way towards the stage for a front-row spot while the support act played an acoustic set. Lizzie took out her wallet, checked the rest of her bag into the cloakroom, then followed the boys to a wooden table by the side. The chairs seemed so old that they could almost have been classed as antiques.

'Right, who wants what?' said Alex, resting his left elbow on the table. The whole thing wobbled so hard it almost tipped over. He picked up a beer mat, folded it in half twice and jammed it under the offending leg.

'I'll take a pint of Foster's, mate,' said Sam.

'Ah, you can take the lad out of Australia . . .' joked Alex. 'Lizzie? Please don't make me ask for a passionfruit mojito.'

'Er, I might try a Foster's myself,' she said. It didn't look like the sort of place that was going to have a cocktail list.

'Really?' said Alex, his eyes glinting. 'Since when did you start drinking lager?'

Since now, she thought, but she wasn't about to tell him that. 'There's still some things you don't know about me, Alex Jackson.'

'Is that so? Alright, back in a sec.' He stood up and walked to the bar, looking as relaxed as his loose-fit jeans. He seemed at home here among the other musos, like he'd been released back into his natural habitat. She realised she was still watching him as she heard Sam speaking to her.

'This should be good,' he said. 'I'm glad you could make it. I've heard a lot about the famous Lizzie Sparkes.'

'Really?' She felt her face flush a little. *I wonder what Alex said?*

'Don't think he told me how you met, though. Was it at school or university?'

'Uni,' she said. 'Actually, it was in a place sort of like this. I spilled about five drinks down him.'

'That's a novel icebreaker,' he said. 'Maybe I should try that one tonight.'

'So you're single?' She tried to work out what Megan would make of him. He was attractive in a quirky kind of way, though he wasn't groomed to within an inch of his life like most of the blokes she went out with.

'Yeah, nearly six months now. I caught my last girlfriend messing around with our gardener. Such a cliché.'

'I'm sorry,' she said sympathetically. 'That sucks.'

'I know,' he said. 'It took me ages to find a good gardener.'

Lizzie smiled. 'Obviously she wasn't The One.'

'Guess not,' he said. 'Still, I don't think I'll meet many women hanging out with Alex, will I? He gets all the attention. Look.' He gestured to the bar where a raven-haired glamazon in wet-look leggings was pawing at Alex's arm, throwing her head back with laughter.

'I . . . I don't think she's his type,' Lizzie stuttered, suddenly realising she didn't know what his type was any more. She looked down at her favourite black jeans and lace-trimmed T-shirt and wondered if she might be under-dressed.

'She'd definitely be my type,' said Sam. 'I'm not sure how he does it. Must be the whole hard-to-get thing. You know, some days I'd almost hate him if he wasn't such a damn nice guy. Which is incredible given everything he's . . .' He changed the subject abruptly as Alex made his way back to the table, clutching two pints and a water. 'Hey Alex, aren't you going to ask your new friend to join us?'

Lizzie decided she was starting to go off him.

'Who, her? No. Nice girl, but she's got to be younger than my sister.'

'I don't have any sisters,' said Sam with a wink.

'Go for it,' replied Alex. 'Lizzie and I can watch you in action.'

Sam looked at the girl, then back at the table. 'Maybe later,' he said, his face turning almost as pink as his shirt. 'I'll have my pint first.'

'Are you not drinking?' asked Lizzie, nodding to Alex's water.

'No, I'm taking it easy at the moment. The doc says too much alcohol might interfere with my meds.'

'Oh, OK, sure.' She kept forgetting he was on medication. He looked so well at the moment. 'How are you feeling tonight?'

'I feel pretty good,' he said. 'How's that Foster's working out?'

Lizzie lifted it to her mouth, the froth tickling her lips. She took a sip, then a bigger one, the lager cold and crisp against her tongue. 'Yeah, I like it.'

'Well, pace yourself,' he teased. 'I don't want you throwing up on me again.'

'Ooh, low blow, Jackson.' She flicked his shoulder.

'What's that?' asked Sam, curious.

Lizzie set her glass down on the table. 'Right, I had a *tiny* bit too much to drink at my 21st birthday . . .'

'If, when she says tiny, she means like a small off-licence.'

'You're such a liar! Anyway, we were having a bit of a party and—'

Before she could finish the story, the spotlights at the front of the room fired up and the headliners spilled out on to the stage. The crowd cheered loudly, with the hard-core fans leaping up and down as though they'd all acquired pogo sticks. It was an atmosphere unlike any she'd experienced before, and she could sense the excitement in the air. It spread to every inch of the room, intense and infectious.

Her eyes fell on Alex, and she noticed the way he seemed to come alive with the music, his face lit up with an energy she hadn't seen for years. It reminded her of their first date: how he'd seemed so unstoppable, ready to take on the world before the world had taken everything from him. Seeing him smile like that made her happy, and yet somehow she felt a twinge of sadness, thinking about their sorry past and his uncertain future.

He caught her looking at him, and she quickly turned away, standing to watch the show. *Now's not the time to get sentimental.*

She took another swig of her pint, and let the loud song drown out her rambling mind until all that was left was the beat of the music.

Nearly 90 minutes later, Lizzie was having one of the best nights out she'd had in months. Alex had been right: the band were brilliant and she decided she was going to download their album tomorrow.

Less brilliant was the air conditioning – or lack of it – in the bar. By now the place was sweltering and she could feel a bead of sweat starting to run down her neck. Sam had gone off to get his round about ten minutes ago and still not returned. She wondered if he was having any luck with the flirty brunette.

'I'm really hot,' she said to Alex between songs.

'And modest too . . .' He smiled.

'No, I mean I'm boiling over here.' She waved her hand in front of her face. 'Aren't you?'

'Yeah, it is pretty warm.' He undid another button on his short-sleeved black shirt, revealing a glimpse of his chest. Lizzie kept her eyes on the stage, trying not to think about all the times she'd undone his shirt in the past. 'But you know what we have to do now, right?'

'What?'

'Get to the front.'

'Er, how's that going to cool us down?'

'It won't. At all. But it'll be worth it.' He cupped his hand around his mouth like a megaphone as the next song started up. 'Come on!'

'Alright,' she shouted. She followed him towards the pack of writhing bodies, all moving to the music with mixed degrees of rhythm.

Alex forged his way forward and she stayed right behind him, not wanting to get lost in the frenzied crowd. It was harder than trying to navigate the Christmas sales with Megan. A flying elbow jabbed her in the ribs and she stumbled slightly, her hand pressing up against Alex's back. She could feel the heat emanating from him, or perhaps it was coming from her. They were so close now it was hard to tell.

Before they could reach the stage, Alex ran into the girl from the bar again, her hair swinging seductively. She beckoned him closer and purred something in his ear, her feline eyes narrowing. Lizzie couldn't hear a thing over the music. She knew it wasn't any of her business, but something about the brazen move bothered her.

For all she knows, me and Alex could be an item.

He bent down and said something with an apologetic smile, gesturing to Lizzie behind him. The girl looked put out but slinked off in the opposite direction, wiggling sexily past him as she went. Lizzie wanted to ask what all that had been about, but they were almost at the front now, the booming tune sweeping her along with its hypnotic hooks.

Finally they broke through the last human barrier, where there was nothing but soundwaves between them and the band. Alex immersed himself in the moment, his arms in the air and a contented smile on his lips as he sang along to the catchy track. Lizzie threw her hands up too, jumping along beside him while the music reverberated through her, the bassline pumping as hard as her pulse. It was a freedom she hadn't felt for as long as she could remember.

As the spotlights soared, circling the band like a white halo, she suddenly saw a flash of the life they might have had; of how different things could have been.

What happened to us?

She closed her eyes, straining to see the picture play out in her mind, but it had already evaporated before the song came to an end.

The band took a bow to rapturous applause, and the house lights slowly came on. The gig, like the moment, was over.

As the crowd began to file out into the street, Alex offered to walk Lizzie to the taxi rank round the corner. She'd never got a cab all the way back to Surrey from town before, but he insisted on paying for one and in the end it was easier to give in. She had to admit it was nice not to have to rush for the last train.

'Say bye to Sam for me,' she said. 'I'm sure he'll be out in a minute.' By the time they'd found their way back to the table, he was snogging a petite blonde in a David Bowie t-shirt, deaf to the pleas of the poor bouncer who was ushering everyone towards the exit.

'I will.' They strolled slowly along the pavement, the cool night air a refreshing change from the sweltering bar. 'I'm really glad you could come along tonight. You look like you enjoyed it.'

'Yeah, I had a great time,' she agreed. 'We'll have to do it again after the wedding.'

'Sure.' He pressed his lips together. 'Tell your fiancé I'm sorry for keeping you out late. Especially on a school night . . .'

'OK,' she said awkwardly. There was an uneasy silence, interrupted only by a bus going past.

Alex raised his brows. 'You didn't tell him you were coming out with me tonight, did you?'

How does he do it? Even after all those years apart, Lizzie sometimes couldn't shake the feeling that he knew her too well.

'No. No, I didn't,' she admitted. 'I haven't actually told him about you being back yet. I'm going to do it soon – honestly – but I need to pick my moment. Right before the wedding probably isn't the best time.'

'I didn't realise.' Alex frowned. 'You should have said. I don't want you to have to lie to see me.'

'I didn't lie! I told him I was going to a gig with some friends – I just didn't specify which ones. It's not the same thing.'

'You still should have told me if I was making life difficult for you.'

'You're not. It's not a big deal, OK? I'm going to tell Josh, and he'll be fine with it. But I just want to hang on a few more weeks until everything else quietens down. That's all.'

'Are you sure?'

'Yes.' She stopped as they reached the rank. There was only one other couple in the queue. 'Don't be mad at me. I had such a fun night.'

He gave her a slow smile. 'You're very hard to be mad at, you know. And I had fun too.' A taxi arrived, and the pair in front climbed in. 'Text me when you get home, won't you? Just to say you're back alright.'

'I will,' she promised. 'And I'll see you soon. But I'm on my hen do next weekend, so it might not be for a bit now.'

'Alright.' His face was hard to read in the semi-darkness. 'Have a great hen do.'

'I'll try. I'll text you before then, anyway.'

Another cab came round the corner, pulling up just past them. Alex leaned over to hug her goodbye, holding her a fraction tighter than she was expecting. She hugged him back, her arms instinctively wrapping around his shoulders the way they had so many times before. For a second she thought she felt him stroke her hair, but then he let her go and she wondered if it had merely been the wind. A breeze skimmed the back of her neck, making her shiver.

'Right,' she said, composing herself. 'I guess I'd better go.'

He opened the car door for her. 'OK. Catch you later, Andi.'

'Lizzie,' she corrected, sliding inside the back seat.

'What?'

'You called me Andi.'

'Did I?' Alex looked confused. 'I don't think so. Maybe you heard me wrong.'

'Possibly.' Her ears were still buzzing slightly from that final number. 'Anyway, thanks again for tonight.'

'No problem.' He handed some cash to the driver and slammed the door of the cab shut. 'Have a safe journey.'

The car pulled away from the kerb, and she watched him out of the back window until he was just a small dot in the distance.

Lizzie nudged the front door open and switched on the hall light, turning it down to dim. She went into the kitchen and rummaged through the fridge, hoping to find a late-night snack. There was nothing left but a tub of coleslaw, some pickled onions and a random lemon. *That's not much use to me*. She made a mental note to grab more supplies on the way home from work tomorrow.

She threw a slice of bread in the toaster instead and waited for it to brown. Grabbing her mobile, she sent Alex a quick text to thank him for the cab and let him know she'd got back alright. He didn't reply straight away, and she hoped that he'd found Sam and got home safely himself. Ever since she'd picked him up from the hospital the other week, she found herself worrying about him a lot, thinking about him when her mind should be on other things. Like the wedding. Or, in this case, like bed.

She looked at her phone: 1.02am. *Urgh.* She had to be up for work in less than six hours. It was going to be a long Friday, but at least it had been worth it. She'd been surprised by how much she'd enjoyed tonight, just relaxing and drinking and dancing. *Hopefully my hen do's going to be a bit like that.* Though with Megan at the helm, she suspected there would be less relaxing and more drinking.

Her toast popped up and she wolfed it down, not even bothering with butter. It wasn't exactly fine dining, but at least it took the edge off her hunger. She'd been so busy having fun that she'd forgotten to stop and eat.

She picked up the phone and checked it again to see if there was anything from Alex, but he still hadn't replied. She sent one more message: Off to bed now. Are you OK? x Then she went back into the hall and climbed the stairs slowly, not wanting to bang around and wake up Josh, even though he'd done it to her enough times over the years.

She undressed quietly in the bathroom, set the alarm on her mobile, then moved next door and slipped into bed beside him. Josh was snoring softly under the duvet, and she planted a gentle kiss on his cheek. *This is a bit of a role reversal*, she smiled. *It's not often I get in after you.*

She rolled over and tried to nod off, still wondering what had happened to Alex. Just then her phone beeped.

'Wassthat?' murmured Josh, stirring.

'Nothing,' she whispered. 'It's only me.'

'You're late,' he said, half-opening one eye. 'How was the gig?'

'Good, thanks,' she breathed. 'I didn't mean to wake you. Go back to sleep.'

He rolled over, and she waited in the darkness for his snoring to start up again. Then she slid out an arm and checked her phone. It was Alex.

Sorry. Battery died but back home now. Sleep tight. x

She set it down and lay her head back on the pillow, relieved. Her eyes were heavy now and she let them close, her breathing slowing as she gave in to the tiredness. For the first time in weeks, she managed to drift off easily, dreaming of other lives she might have led if fate had danced her down a different path.

20

18 February 2005

Lizzie stood outside the church, waiting for the hearse to arrive. Alex had wanted to travel in the funeral car with his mum, dad and Andi, which she completely understood. He hadn't asked her to ride with them, and she didn't want to intrude on their grief. Instead, she'd got a lift up the motorway with Megan and Gareth, who she'd now sent inside, out of the cold, to find a seat.

She didn't want to join them, though; not without at least seeing Alex first. She had been so worried about him lately. He had barely spoken to her for the past few weeks since word of Connor's fate reached home.

The wait for news had been agonising: all attempts to make contact by phone or email had failed, while scenes of devastation replayed endlessly on the TV, like a disaster movie stuck on repeat. As she watched the distressing footage, Lizzie knew deep down that the chances of him being found safe and well were diminishing with each day that passed. Still, Alex clung on to the hope that perhaps Connor had been prevented from getting to a phone somehow, be it through injury or the damage to the tele-coms infrastructure. He was so sure his brother was alive that he had booked a flight out there for the first week of January, determined to find him no matter how long it took. 'Connor's tough; he's a survivor,' he kept repeating, like a mantra. 'I'd know if something happened to him. You'll see.'

But even Connor's survival instinct could not save him from such a force of nature, and on New Year's Eve his bloated body was unearthed beneath a mountain of wreckage, just 100m inland from the beach. Both his legs had been crushed, but his intricate tattoos were just about recognisable. His friend Jeff – who had luckily been spending Christmas with his Thai girlfriend's family in Bangkok – felt confident enough to identify him, and subsequent DNA testing confirmed he was right. Alex's search was over before it had even begun.

Lizzie had not been at the Jacksons' house when the call came, and for that she was guiltily grateful. Seeing that pain on Alex's face would be something she could never erase; even now, it hurt her to watch him struggling. *Does he blame me for not being there with Connor?* She was scared to ask that question. Alex's decision to stay had almost certainly saved his life, and yet she sensed the regret was slowly killing him.

It had taken a further five weeks for arrangements to be made in order to repatriate Connor's body, which had to be returned in a closed casket. Lizzie tried hard not to think about what lay beneath the coffin lid, or whether he had felt any fear in his final moments. But the thoughts she tried to avoid by day snuck up on her in her sleep, and she watched helplessly night after night as Connor drifted away to a watery grave.

If Lizzie was struggling to come to terms with the tragedy, though, Alex's grief was off the scale. Moving back in with his parents for a while, he avoided leaving the house unless he absolutely had to, and while he tolerated Lizzie's frequent visits, he made little effort to move from the couch or get dressed beyond his boxers and greying T-shirt.

The other night, when she woke up at 3am to go to the bathroom, she heard a strangled howl that made her blood run cold. At first she thought it was Jagger or foxes outside, but then she realised the noise was coming from Alex's room. When she tried to push open the door, she discovered she'd been locked out, in every sense. She wondered if she should talk to his parents about him, but they both looked utterly broken too and she couldn't bear to add to their stress.

Besides, they had to have noticed he was in a bad way. He'd stopped taking any care over his appearance, to the point where he resembled a walking ghost. He didn't shave, he didn't exercise; she didn't want to guess when he'd last had a shower. Lizzie worried he might be suffering from depression, but Alex stubbornly refused to see a doctor. 'What's the point?' he'd snapped when Lizzie tried to broach the subject. 'It's not like a bunch of pills is going to bring Connor back, is it?'

As the date of the funeral drew closer, the fuse on his temper shortened further, until even the tiniest thing sent him flying off the handle. Lizzie was hugely sympathetic, but walking on eggshells the whole time was tough, and she hoped that today's service might be the first step towards him finally finding some closure.

While she stood there consumed by her thoughts, the hearse and a black Jaguar pulled up in front of the gothic chapel, and one by one the members of the Jackson family slowly filed out. Frank was first, looking sombre in his smartest black suit, his eyes never leaving the tarmac path in front of him; next came Pamela, the wide rim of her hat casting a shadow across her face. Behind them was Andi, her face all red and puffy, tears streaming down both sides of her nose and dripping on to the front of her blouse.

Finally, she saw Alex. He was dressed entirely in black, from his shirt down to his socks, and his hair was blowing wildly in the cold wind. His eyes seemed much darker than usual, as though they had absorbed the blackness of his outfit. He had shaved off his increasingly unruly beard – possibly at his mum's insistence, as he'd totally ignored Lizzie when she suggested it – and she could see his jawline at last, angrily jutting away from his neck. Everything about him looked uncomfortable. She wanted to rush towards him, to wrap him in her arms and hold him tight, but he moved into position with five other pallbearers and waited, his eyes never finding Lizzie's face.

As the coffin was slowly lifted out of the car, she noticed a display of flowers shaped like a motorbike on top, and felt the tears slide down her cheek before she realised she was crying. *How could this happen?* she wondered, as she had done so many times these past few weeks. The universe did not have an answer, though; or, if it did, it certainly wasn't planning to share it with her. She and Alex would have to figure this out for themselves, and find a way to move forwards.

The pallbearers were on the march now, walking together with one stride. Alex was at the front, his vacant eyes staring straight ahead. He didn't glance in Lizzie's direction, but she hoped he might be able to sense her presence somehow, and know that she was sending him all the love in her heart.

The coffin floated towards her, then slowly past, and instinctively she bowed her head. *Goodbye, Connor*, she mouthed silently, her breath foggy against the winter air. *I'm sorry.* By the time she looked up, the pallbearers were passing through the double doors leading into the church, and all she could glimpse of Alex was the back of his head.

As his family followed the coffin inside, Lizzie caught his sister's gaze, and Andi gave her a grateful half-smile through her tears. Her eyes were all bloodshot, as though she hadn't stopped sobbing since Boxing Day, and her nose was beginning to run. She looked like she might dissolve into a puddle at any second.

At least she's not bottling it up, Lizzie thought. *Unlike someone else I know.*

Shuffling along behind them through the front doors, she was struck by how packed the place was, with stunned mourners jammed tightly into pews along both sides. She had always figured that Connor was a popular guy, but seeing all these people whose lives he had touched made his loss seem even greater. She imagined how chuffed he would have been to witness that kind of turnout. 'Told you people couldn't resist this charm,' she almost heard him whisper in her ear.

The colossal congregation, though, presented her with a dilemma. *Will there be space for me with the family down the front? Or should I stay here at the back?* She could not see as far as the front pew, and had no idea whether Alex would have thought to save her a seat in his current state. She looked around for Megan and Gareth, but it was impossible to spot them among the sea of black.

Lizzie nearly decided to loiter near the door with the latecomers, but one thought propelled her forwards: *What if Alex needs me and I'm not there?* It was a risk she wasn't prepared to take, so she scuttled quickly down the aisle behind Andi, praying that there would be room for one more.

But as she neared the altar, she realised that the front pew was smaller than the others, and clearly intended for immediate family only. *Now where do I go?* Just as she was contemplating an awkward walk back, a kind lady in the second row took her hand and gestured for the couple beside her to scoot over. Lizzie slid into the space gratefully and breathed a sigh of relief, nodding her head in unspoken thanks.

As the priest asked for everyone to be seated, Lizzie found herself faced with the back of Alex's head for the second time that morning. *What are you thinking in there?* She wished he would talk to her, or cry with her, or do anything to let her know how he was really feeling.

I'm here for you, Alex. All you have to do is let me in.

Instinctively, she reached out and placed her right hand gently on his shoulder. His body was so rigid it was as if rigor mortis had set in. He did not turn to look at her, but gave a small shrug, as if brushing off an insect. Stung, Lizzie withdrew her hand and tried to stop her fingers from trembling.

He is as lost to me right now as Connor is to him, she realised. She just had to hope that someday, given enough time, Alex might come back to life.

21

3 weeks to go . . .

Lizzie surveyed the bar, amused by the varying degrees of effort her friends had gone to on the fancy-dress front. After much deliberation of potential hen themes, Megan had decreed an 80s dress code, which left plenty of scope for imagination – or in some cases, lack thereof.

Louise and Helen from uni had both turned up as Madonna, a safe bet requiring little outlay other than a pair of lace gloves, a ra-ra skirt and some fishnet tights. Naomi had come as Cyndi Lauper, wearing an outfit that looked strikingly similar to the uni girls, but with the addition of a spiky punk wig that actually really suited her. Her girlfriend Mel – currently back in the good books – was dressed as a dancer from *Fame*, while Phoebe, who had almost burst with excitement upon being invited, had gone to the trouble of buying a She-Ra outfit. However, best costume of the night arguably had to go to leggy Lily, who had somehow managed to get hold of a Miss Piggy mask. It had gone down a storm with the blokes in the bar, who kept trying to swipe it from her head.

'Right, sexy ladies,' said Megan, dressed in a tight *Top Gun* jumpsuit set off with a pair of Aviator sunglasses. 'You're still a bit sober for my liking. Time for a shot of tequila.' She beckoned to the hostess behind her, who placed a tray of drinks on the table.

'Good shout on the tequila,' said Lizzie's cousin Caz, whose Princess Leia attire the jury was still out on. 'I don't want to be spilling red wine down my white costume.'

'I meant to say, you *do* know that the original *Star Wars* was the 70s, don't you?' said Megan, clearly put out that someone had dared to deviate from her specific sartorial instructions.

'So?' replied Caz. 'I could be Princess Leia from *Return of the Jedi*.'

'Well, in that case, I'd have been inclined to go with the bikini,' said Megan. 'But I suppose it'll do.'

Lizzie flashed her cousin an apologetic smile. 'I think you look great,' she said.

'You too,' said Caz. 'I'm loving the suit.'

Despite Lizzie's protestations, the girls had forced her to wear a full-on *Ghostbusters* outfit, complete with Proton Pack. 'It's good for exorcising demons,' Megan said with a wink. Lizzie would have zapped her on the spot if the kit wasn't made from plastic. She didn't even want to imagine what Megan might have made her wear if she'd known Lizzie had been hanging out with Alex.

'Right, let's get this tequila down us and then we'll crack on with truth or dare,' said Megan. 'One, two, three . . .

go!' She necked her drink then slammed her shot glass on the table with a satisfied thud, looking round to make sure the rest of the group had done the same. 'Good. Now, hen rules state that the bride goes first . . .'

'I thought hen rules meant the bride has to do every other go,' chipped in Naomi.

'Actually, that's better. We'll alternate turns with Lizzie.'

'In that case, I'm going to need *way* more tequila,' said Lizzie.

'Not a problem,' replied Megan cheerily. 'I've told the waitress to keep 'em coming. Alright then, truth or dare?'

'Dare.'

'Interesting . . . OK, I dare you to go and flash the barman.'

'No way! I'm not that drunk.'

'Alright then. Go into the gents and make yourself a veil out of loo roll.'

Lizzie figured that was probably about as tame as it was going to get. She set off in the direction of the toilet, and had a surreptitious check round to make sure no bouncers were watching. With the coast clear, she slipped into the men's loos and began hunting around for some toilet paper. She guessed she wasn't going to find any by the urinal, which smelled like a stale litter tray, so she nipped into one of the cubicles and grabbed hold of what she really hoped was a fresh roll. Tearing off an extra long piece, she wrapped it around her head twice, then let it trail down her back in what was as close to a veil effect as she could get. *That'll do*, she thought, anxious to make a quick exit. As she made her way back towards the door, a six-foot guy wearing a rugby shirt walked in and did a double take.

'Er, am I in the wrong one?' he asked, looking confused.

'No, you're fine,' she said. 'Ghostbusting emergency. But the coast's all clear now.'

She walked back out into the bar to the sound of her friends clapping. 'Well played,' said Naomi. 'Bet that bloke got a shock when he found you in there.'

'Yeah. Not every day you see a girl dressed as a Ghostbuster in the gents.' She turned to face Megan. 'I believe that means it's your turn. Truth or dare?'

'Dare,' said Megan confidently.

'OK, go over there and snog the bouncer.'

'I can't do that. He's nearly twice as tall as me. And he's wearing a wedding ring.'

'No, not the bald one! The other one by the bar.'

'Oh, OK. Consider it done.'

She got up, sashayed across the room in her flightsuit, and made a beeline for the sexy bouncer before the poor guy knew what hit him. Lizzie's jaw fell as Megan then dropped to one knee and broke into a loud rendition of *You've Lost That Lovin' Feelin'*, causing half the bar to put down their drinks and promptly sing along. At the end she stood up with a flourish and kissed the bouncer full on the lips, while the crowd erupted into spontaneous applause.

'She hasn't changed much,' said Helen, shaking her head incredulously. 'If anything, she gets worse.'

'Yeah, good luck following that,' laughed Naomi.

Megan made her way back to the table, a triumphant grin lingering on her lips. The bouncer's eyes followed her all the way over. 'Hey, can we get another round of tequila, please?' she asked their hostess. 'Anyway, back to the bride – truth or dare?'

'Truth.'

'Best shag ever?' asked Louise. 'Excluding Josh, of course.'

Megan looked miffed. 'I'm sure we can come up with something better than that.'

'No,' said Lily. 'You can't change the question once it's asked. 'Fess up, Lizzie.'

Lizzie paused for a minute, pretending she had to think about it. 'Well, I guess I'd say Alex,' she said finally.

'I knew it!' said Louise. 'He looked like he'd be good.'

'Who's Alex?' asked Phoebe.

Megan swiftly changed the subject. 'Well, if you're so chatty, Lou, maybe you should go next. Truth or dare?'

'Truth.' But before anyone could pose a suitably nosy question, a tall guy with an old-school stereo in his hand sauntered over to the group. 'Excuse me ladies, but I'm after Lizzie Sparkes?'

Lizzie felt that last shot of tequila slosh around in her stomach. *Megan, what have you done now?*

'She's over here,' said Megan with a grin.

'Well, that's good. Seems one of you ladies put in a call

for a little assistance from *The A-Team*.' He pressed play on the machine and the iconic theme tune blared from the speakers. Suddenly a hulk of a guy decked out in gold chains, a denim waistcoat and a rather distinctive haircut made his way towards the group, and began rhythmically rubbing oil over his muscles.

'Oh no you didn't . . .' Lizzie mouthed to Megan.

'Hey, I pity da girl who wants a tame hen night,' she replied.

'But I specifically said no strippers!'

'Don't worry, I only booked a lookalike to show us a few moves . . .'

22

4 March 2005

Lizzie rolled over and jabbed at her mobile, her camisole stretching across her chest as she tried to knock off the alarm. No matter how many times she heard that beep, it never grew any less annoying. This morning it felt even worse than normal, as she'd only just managed to drift off after another night of disturbed sleep. She wondered how new mums managed to do it without wanting to punch everything in their path.

It was the first time she and Alex had returned to the cottage since the funeral. She had hoped that being back in his own space might be good for him, away from the constant reminders of Connor's absence that haunted every inch of his family home. But something had shifted here, too: the familiar surroundings only amplifying the fact that everything else had changed. There might have been less physical traces of his twin, but ghosts weren't bound by geography.

Alex had barely slept at all last night, thrashing around in the darkness and frightening the crap out of her at

273

random intervals. Once, he lashed out so much he nearly whacked her on the chin. She had tried her best to calm him down: holding him close, stroking his hair, wishing she could wipe away all the pain inside his head. She whispered over and over that he was going to be alright.

But was he?

He needed help, she knew that much. The bigger problem was getting Alex to admit it. He'd practically snapped her head off when she suggested he consider seeing a counsellor. Lizzie was trying to be patient, but she was out of her depth and the stress was starting to take its toll. By day she was permanently exhausted and by night she was practically an insomniac.

She hated to admit it, but their relationship was feeling the strain. It wasn't that she loved him any less – if anything, seeing him so fragile made her love him even more – but she had no idea how to help him out of such a dark hole if he wasn't willing to help himself. Plus there was also the matter of her final exams, which were only a few weeks away. With everything that had been going on, she hadn't exactly been doing her best revision, but she needed to get her head down or else she was facing an epic fail. It was enough to keep her awake at night – if she wasn't already.

At least exams were one thing Alex didn't have to deal with. His boss at the bar had been sympathetic, promising to keep his job open until he felt ready to return. Still, she wondered how much further Joe's patience would stretch given Alex's current condition. *Maybe going back to work would do him good? At least it would get him out of the house, give him something to get up for?* Then again, it might be a terrible idea. He didn't exactly scream happy hour.

The snooze function on her phone interrupted her thoughts, and Lizzie had an overwhelming urge to throw it out of the window. The last thing she felt like doing now was dragging herself off to a tutorial, but she couldn't afford to miss any more at this crucial point in the term.

OK, OK. She reached over again and switched it off. *One more minute.*

She cuddled up next to Alex and planted a gentle kiss on his cheek, her lips brushing his rough stubble. 'Alex, I've got to get to class,' she whispered. 'Are you going to go in and have a chat with Joe today? I could swing by the bar and meet you for lunch if you like.'

He stared blankly at the wall. 'No, I'm alright,' he mumbled.

He didn't look alright. 'Are you sure?' she said, running her fingers gently down his bare arm. 'Maybe you could just swing by for a bit and then we could walk home together? I know Joe would love to see you.'

'I'm not going to the bar,' he said gruffly.

'OK then. Maybe next week.'

'No.' He rolled onto his side. 'I'm not working there any more.'

Lizzie sat upright. 'What? Did something happen?' She shook her head. 'We should go down there right now and speak to Joe. You've obviously been through a lot and they need to give you some more—'

'Nothing happened,' he interrupted. 'I just don't feel like going in there.'

'So you're quitting?' She couldn't hide her surprise.

'I already did. Three days ago.'

What?

She tried to reason with the stranger beside her. 'Alex, if you want a new job then I'm behind you, 100 per cent. But maybe you shouldn't make any drastic decisions while you're . . .' Her voice trailed off awkwardly.

'I don't want another job,' he sighed, his back still to her.

'So what are you going to do?'

'I'll manage,' he said. 'I've got some savings I can live off for a while.'

'But then what?' He was really scaring her now. 'How are you going to afford, like, food?'

'I don't care.'

'Well, I care. I can't just sit here and watch you throw your life away!'

'It's my life!'

'I know, but I'm really concerned about you. Connor wouldn't have wanted to see you like this . . .'

He sat bolt upright, his eyes flashing. She immediately regretted bringing up the C word, but it was too late.

'How do you know what Connor would have wanted?'

She held up her hands defensively. 'I know, I'm sorry. I didn't mean—'

'The only thing Connor wanted was for me to go travelling with him,' he spat out. 'But I didn't do that, did I? Because I wanted to stay here with you.'

His words pierced like a knife. 'How long are you going to keep holding that against me?' she cried. 'I didn't force you to stay. It's like you think this is all my fault . . .'

'No, it's *my* fault,' he roared, his chest shaking. 'I should have been there for him. And I wasn't. He was so angry when I told him I wasn't going . . . and I can't . . . I didn't . . .' In frustration, he smashed his fist into the wall, causing the plaster to splinter into tiny cracks. Then he curled up into a ball and began to cry.

For a second, Lizzie felt as though the world had stopped. 'Sshhh,' she whispered, holding him tightly, not knowing what else to say or do. 'I'm right here.'

They sat like that for a full two minutes, until Alex finally lifted his head and wiped his red, puffy eyes. A trickle of blood ran down his swollen right hand and splashed onto the duvet. 'What am I going to do?' he asked quietly.

'Look, we're going to get through this,' said Lizzie, with as much conviction as she could muster. 'But you need help, Alex. I really think you should go and see the doctor. I'll come with you.'

He shook his head. 'No, I don't want to.'

'Why? You've been through a really tough time.'

'I need to deal with this in my own way, Lizzie.'

She took a deep breath. 'Alex, please listen to me. I'm worried about you. I'm worried about . . . us.'

He flinched ever so slightly, and she knew her words had struck a nerve. 'I know,' he said eventually. 'I can't have been easy to be with lately. I'm sorry.'

'You don't have to be sorry,' she said, stroking his back. 'We can get through this together. All I'm asking you to do is try. Please. For me?'

'Try what?' She felt his muscles tense up. 'Try to pretend like nothing's happened? I can't do that, Lizzie.'

'That's not what I meant. I just thought—'

'Thought what? That I should be over it by now? Poor pathetic Alex, moping around like some sort of loser . . .'

'No!' she said, wishing he'd stop shovelling words in her mouth. 'I'm just trying to be supportive, that's all.'

'You're not supporting me, you're smothering me,' he shouted. 'Connor was right – you're always here. And it makes me feel like I can't breathe.'

His outburst completely stunned her. *What's got into him?* She shot out of bed, grabbing her jeans from the floor and wriggling into them furiously. 'You're out of order,' she said, her voice cracking. 'And you can't keep blaming me for the fact you didn't go to Thailand. I gave you that chance!'

'What, just before he left? You knew I couldn't go then!'

'Did it ever occur to you that if you had gone, maybe

you'd be dead too?' She bit her lip, but it was too late to hit pause. The words left a nasty aftertaste on her tongue.

He looked at her angrily. 'You think that makes me feel better? Because it doesn't. You don't know what might have happened if I'd been there to look out for him.'

'Alex, you can't keep tormenting yourself like this.' She took a deep breath and tried again. 'Let me get you some help . . .'

'No,' he snapped. 'Just leave me alone.'

'Fine!' she shouted, throwing her jumper on over her cami before realising it was inside out. She picked up her bag and reached for the bedroom door. 'I'm going. I can't be with you when you're like this.' She needed to get out of the cottage, to walk along the beach and vent into the salty air.

'I can't be with you either,' he said quietly. 'It's too hard.' *What?*

She spun round to face him, her heart racing so fast she thought she might go into cardiac arrest. *Is he breaking up with me?* She couldn't believe it, didn't want to believe it, and yet it was hard to know what this person who had replaced her boyfriend might be capable of.

'What's that supposed to mean, Alex?'

He looked down at the duvet.

'I don't think we should do this any more. I'm sorry.'

'So that's it?' she whispered, every word scraping her tight throat. 'We're done?'

He didn't reply. She stormed out of the room and the

cottage without looking back, slamming the front door so hard his windows shook. Then she ran down the steps and along the beach, angry tears tumbling down her cheeks and burying themselves in the sand.

There was a faint knock on the bedroom door. 'Lizzie, can I come in?' asked Megan. She pushed the door ajar and peered round the corner. 'Gareth and I thought you might like some chicken soup for lunch?'

You thought wrong, Lizzie wanted to say, but she didn't like to be mean to Megan. Especially since she'd finally managed to knock. 'Thanks,' she mumbled, not bothering to move. She'd spent the last two hours just stretched out on top of the duvet. 'Can you put it on the desk over there?'

'Will do,' said Megan, looking her up and down. 'So, I see you're still modelling pret-a-pyjamas?'

Lizzie nodded glumly. She really didn't feel like getting dressed, or anything else that required much effort. Feeling miserable was sapping all her energy.

'I'm revising,' she lied, lifting up her textbook and burying her nose in the tear-stained pages. The words swam blurrily before her tired eyes.

'It's upside down,' said Megan helpfully.

'Oh.' Lizzie chucked it on the bed and hauled herself into a sitting position, hugging her legs up to her chest. 'Have you been here all morning? Did anyone call?'

'Only your mum. Twice. You need to ring her back.'

Megan went over to the window and opened Lizzie's curtains. 'We've got to get you out of the house soon. Being cooped up in here isn't going to do you any good.'

Lizzie didn't care. The one person she had cared about more than anything had decided he didn't want to be with her. From now on she was going to stay locked in her room, with only her books and PJs for company.

'This is ridiculous, you know,' Megan continued. 'It's been ten days. One of you needs to pick up the phone.'

'Why does it have to be me?'

'Because you can't both be stubborn sods!' Megan gave an exasperated sigh and sat down on the bed beside her. 'Look, you know you're my best friend, and I'm not trying to defend Alex or pretend he's not been an idiot.' She paused, and rested one hand on Lizzie's shoulder. 'But he's been through a horrible, horrible time, Lizzie. He's just hurt right now, that's all. I know he doesn't mean it.'

'You think?' The faintest flicker of hope stirred inside her.

'I'm positive. Like, 110 per cent.'

'That's not a real thing. You can't have more than 100 per cent.'

'Whatever. It's blatantly obvious you two are supposed to be together. You just need to stop this stupid argument.'

Maybe she's right. With every day that ticked by, Lizzie's misery was multiplying. *What if Alex feels the same and he's just too proud to say so?* They had both traded blows in the heat of the fight, but it was nothing they couldn't get up from.

'Do you think I should call him now?'

'Yeah, totally! Or, even better, go round there and then you can have make-up sex. That's the best.'

Actually, perhaps it would be better to talk to him face to face. She leaned over and gave Megan a large hug. 'Alright, I'll go over there this afternoon.'

'Great. Just one more thing before you go . . .'

'What?'

'You might want to take a quick shower first. I think those PJs have gone off.'

Lizzie sat on the bus, looking past the white splodge of bird poo and out to the people on the pavements, all walking around casually with their heads full of work or their plans for the weekend. She slid open the top section of the window, breathing in a mix of sea air and car fumes as the number 6 trundled along its regular route, never stopping for a spontaneous scenic detour of Cliffstowe.

She had been feeling optimistic when she left Megan, but now – sat by herself on the scratchy blue seat – the doubts were beginning to creep back in. She tried to think what she would say to Alex when she saw him. What he might say to her. She was suddenly afraid that he really didn't love her any more; that he blamed her for driving a wedge between him and Connor. *He can't believe that was all my fault, can he?* Maybe it didn't matter. Maybe just the sight of her was a permanent reminder of why he'd stayed behind.

The bus dawdled along the coast towards the cottage, slowing down as it trailed behind a queue of traffic. *Oh, come on! I could walk faster than this!* Actually, that wasn't a bad idea. Out of luck – and totally out of patience – she asked the driver to pull over.

'I can't stop here,' he said. 'You'll have to wait till the next one.'

'Fine,' she said impatiently, pressing the 'stop' button twice for good measure. She was starting to feel slightly travel sick. Or was it lovesick?

'Are you alright?' The driver eyed her suspiciously, probably worried that she was some hungover student about to spew all over his bus.

'Yes . . . no . . . I don't know.' She was too flustered to lie. 'I just need to get off.'

The driver pulled into the bus stop as swiftly as he could and released the doors. She set off in the direction of Alex's place, slowly at first then almost running, her patent pumps nearly slipping off her feet. The cool breeze sent her hair billowing out behind her, and stung against her exposed cheeks.

As she rounded the corner to the cottage, Lizzie struggled to catch her breath, each mouthful of air feeling like sandpaper against her throat. But she could not slow down, not until he held her and admitted that he hadn't really meant to break up with her after all. *He loves me. I know he loves me.* She had always been sure of that before. *So why do I feel so scared?*

She could see his front door now, and she flung herself upon it, knocking hard with her right fist until it hurt. 'Alex! It's me. I need to see you.'

He didn't answer. *Is he ignoring me?* She peered through the windows at the front of the cottage, noticing that the downstairs lights were off. She could just about glimpse the outline of his living room furniture, and the giant tower of CDs standing in the corner, but there was no sign of Alex. She wondered if he was still in bed or whether he'd actually managed to leave the house.

After another minute and still no response, she reached for her mobile and rang him. It went straight through to voicemail, the message telling her to leave a number after the beep. 'Alex, it's me,' she said quietly. 'I've come over to see you because I think we need to talk. Please call me when you get this. I miss you.'

She hung up and knocked on the door again, trying to work out where he might be. *Maybe he's gone to see the doctor after all?* She wanted to believe that, but she knew she wasn't going to feel at ease until she saw him with her own eyes. She would have to wait here until he came home.

A sudden gust of wind made her shudder, and she realised too late that she'd left her denim jacket on the bus. *Damn! That's my favourite as well.* Annoyed and chilly, she decided to go round to the side of the cottage and see if

The One

Alex had left his spare key under his gran's old garden gnome. *He won't mind me waiting inside, will he? I don't want to seem like a stalker.* She decided to chance it. Everyone had warned Alex not to keep a key outside, but if he was going to keep doing it anyway, she might as well wait in the warm.

As she approached the other entrance, she looked for the colourful figure and caught sight of something unusual. His cheery face was blocked by what appeared to be a piece of paper. *That's weird.* She bent down and realised it was an envelope – and that it was addressed to her.

Oh Alex . . . what have you done?

With a shaking hand, she tore it open, and slowly removed the note inside. Alex's distinctive handwriting leapt off the page:

Dear Lizzie,

If you've found this letter, you're probably wondering where I am. Truth is, by the time you read it, I'll be halfway round the world, missing you more than I know how to say.

I never thought that we'd break up, but maybe it's for the best. I'm going to Thailand to help with the relief effort and I don't know when I'll be back. I wish things were different and you could come with me, but that would be wrong when you've got your exams and whole future ahead of you. You have made my life better in so many ways, but one day you will wake up and realise you deserve more than me, so I think it's kinder on both of us if we just admit that now.

I promise I'll never forget you, but you should forget about me.

Alex xxx

Lizzie let the piece of paper fall from her fingers and flutter to the floor. She felt numb, like someone had sucked all the emotion out of her with a giant vacuum. *So he's gone? Just like that?* Her brain struggled to process this information. She and Alex were meant to move in together, to start a family together, to grow old together. *Surely this is some kind of mistake?*

The gnome looked up at her pityingly with his big unblinking eyes. 'Screw you!' she snapped suddenly, throwing him against the cottage wall and smashing him into a hundred pieces as her heart shattered into thousands more.

She began to cry then, harder than she ever had before. She cried for all the broken dreams and promises; for the wedding that would never take place. She cried for herself; for the parents who'd abandoned her; for the family of her own she might not ever have. She cried for Connor. And most of all she cried for Alex, poor mixed-up Alex, who hated his life so much he'd left it all behind.

23

2 weeks to go . . .

*N*ot long now . . .

Lizzie was walking back from the station, her blazer strewn over her arm. It had been a scorcher of a day, which would have been perfect if she was relaxing by a pool with a good book on honeymoon, but was way less fun when she was stuck in that sauna of an office. She couldn't wait for a fortnight in Sorrento with Josh, scoffing seafood and sipping limoncello and exploring the stunning Amalfi coast, with its pretty candy-coloured houses set into dramatic cliffs. *I might never want to leave.*

As she crossed the road by the off-licence, her phone began to beep. She fished it out and realised it was a text from Alex.

Can you talk? x

Is he OK? If he was messaging on a Friday evening it might be important. She pulled over under the shade of the empty bus stop and called him back.

'Hey.' He sounded flat and distant. She immediately began to worry.

'What's happened? Are you at the hospital again?'

'No, I'm at home, just sitting in my old room.' She wondered if his parents had redecorated, or if it still had the same dark blue walls. She tried to picture him in there now and couldn't.

'OK. What's up?'

'Are you free tomorrow?'

'As in tomorrow, tomorrow?'

'What other kind is there?' He couldn't resist teasing her.

'No . . . I get it . . . I just wasn't expecting you to say that.' A bus pulled into the stop and the driver let a woman with a pushchair get off. He waited for Lizzie to board, then looked baffled as she waved him on.

'I know it's short notice,' said Alex. 'But I've got to go in for a few more tests, so I don't think I'll get another chance to see you until after your honeymoon.'

Disappointment poked her in the ribs. *That's over a month away.* But now that she actually thought about it, she wasn't going to get much free time before then. She and Josh had the hired suits to collect and the Euros to order and the honeymoon packing to do. She was lucky if she was even going to make it to the wedding on time. Still, she did want to see Alex before his next round of tests.

'OK,' she said, trying to figure out how she was going to fit everything in. 'Josh is off to Dublin for his stag do tomorrow, so I was going to drive him over to Gatwick first thing in the morning. Then I've got to come back and pick up my wedding dress while he's away. And then after lunch I'm supposed to be having some sort of seaweed facial.' She stopped, anticipating more teasing. 'Don't laugh. Megan booked it for me as a present.'

'I wasn't going to laugh,' he said, though she couldn't read him as easily over the phone. 'It sounds busy. I don't want to get in the way of all that seaweed and shuttling.'

'Well, maybe we could do something in the evening instead, give me something to look forward to?' She briefly considered inviting him over to the house, but something about that felt slightly inappropriate. 'I could meet you at Waterloo, grab a bite down by the South Bank?'

'Look, it sounds like you're going to be rushing around all day, so why don't I come over to you?' he offered. 'We could meet at those gardens you like. I'll bring us some dinner if you don't mind crisps and sandwiches.'

She had a flash of déjà vu to the amazing picnic he'd laid on for their first anniversary. It seemed like another century. *At least we're still able to be friends,* she thought. *It's better than not being in touch at all.*

'Sure, sandwiches and crisps sound perfect. I'll be ready for that.'

'OK. Just don't eat all the seaweed and spoil your appetite.'

'I won't.' She smiled. 'See you tomorrow.'

When she arrived home, she found Josh upstairs in their bedroom, his overnight bag open on top of the quilted throw. He held out two shirts for her inspection.

'Do you like the blue shirt or the checked one?' he asked.

'Doesn't matter,' said Lizzie. 'Ten minutes after you arrive they're going to dress you up in some silly costume and you'll just have to wear what you're given. Look what happened to me.'

'Yeah, I guess you're right. I may as well just take the blue one.' He stuffed it into his bag. 'So, what are you going to do tomorrow while I'm away?'

For a split second, she reconsidered whether she should tell him about Alex before the wedding after all. *Josh trusts me. He'll understand.*

'Um, actually—'

'Do you think I should take shoes or trainers?' he interrupted.

'What? Oh, er . . . shoes. Some bars are funny about trainers.'

'OK. I'll grab them.' He shot out of the room, and she could hear the sound of his size 11s pounding down the stairs. 'Hey, where'd the black pair go?' he yelled.

'They were in the kitchen last time I saw them,' she called out. *Why, I'll never know.*

Moments later, he was back in the bedroom, shoes in hand. 'Got them. Thanks. What were you saying about your weekend?'

She bottled it and opted for a safer version of events. 'Oh, not much. After I drop you at the airport I'm going to a spa for a facial. Nothing as exciting as you.' She didn't like to think what kind of lewd activities the lads had planned for Josh. As long as he came back with both his eyebrows and no broken bones, she'd try not to think about it.

'That sounds like a good idea,' he said. 'You have seemed kind of distracted lately. Maybe you should take this weekend to chill out.'

'Yeah, that's what I thought.' She peered down at her bare feet, noticing the chips in her nail varnish.

'Are you going with Megan or your mum?'

'What?'

'To the spa?'

'Oh, neither. I'm just going by myself. Megan's got some family wedding and Mum's getting her highlights done before ours.'

'Won't you be bored on your own?' asked Josh. 'I'm sure my mum would love to go if you want some company. She could drive down and stay over.'

'No!' Lizzie shouted, a little more forcefully than she'd intended to. 'Er, I mean, these things get really booked up on a Saturday, and they could only just squeeze me in. I doubt they'll have any slots left for your mum.' She hated herself for not being completely honest, but a visit from Celia Cooper was anything but relaxing. Plus it would definitely put paid to her picnic with Alex.

'Alright, I can take a hint,' laughed Josh. 'It was only a suggestion. Go by yourself if that's what you want.'

I wish I knew what I did want, she thought. *Because some days, I don't have a clue.*

*   *   *

Lizzie pulled into the car park outside Ravenhall House and slowly made her way to the gardens. Alex had texted her instructions to meet at the bandstand at 8pm, and unless her watch had stopped she was ten minutes early. She was glad she didn't have to rush: it was another hot and humid evening, the air thick and sultry against her bare arms. As she stepped through the gate, she noticed the grounds were largely empty by now; she guessed most visitors had gone home for a cold beer or a cool shower. Her strappy sundress clung tightly to her warm skin.

When she approached the bandstand, she noticed Alex had beaten her to it yet again; this time, he had decked it out with a red and white blanket, and was just unpacking some plastic cups and paper plates.

'I thought I was early,' she said. 'What time did you get here?'

'A little while ago,' he replied. 'I wanted to get it ready for you. Here, have a seat.'

She sat on the blanket and stretched out her legs, feeling a light breeze on her face. 'How was the seaweed thing?' asked Alex.

'Erm, interesting. Do I look slightly green to you?'

'No, you look great.'

She watched him pour two lemonades, wondering what else was in the cool bag. All that rushing around had left her famished. 'What have we got?'

'Well, I didn't go mad because I don't have the car this

time, but we've got some sandwiches and some crisps and
a pack of chocolate brownies for dessert. Do you want the
chicken sarnie or the LBT?'

'You mean BLT?'

'Yeah.' He fished it out for her inspection.

'Ooh, I'll have that please.' She peeled off the wrapper
and sank her teeth into the soft bread and juicy tomato.
'Mmmm . . . so good. I've been looking forward to this.'
She devoured the first one ravenously. 'I don't know what
it is, but sandwiches always taste so much better outside.'
She looked over at Alex, who was picking at his chicken.
'Are you OK with that? I'll swap the other half of the pack
if you want.'

'No, it's fine,' he said. 'I've just lost my appetite a bit
lately.'

'That's not like you,' she said, thinking about that afternoon at the café. She bit into her second sandwich and
glanced at him again. He did look slightly tired tonight. *I
knew I should have met him somewhere nearer the station.*
'You alright? Can I do anything?'

He didn't reply, but gave her a thin smile and changed
the subject. 'So, did you manage to pick up your dress this
morning?'

'Yeah, just about. It might look all light and floaty, but
that thing weighs a ton. I had a right job getting it up to
the loft.' She finished the last bite of her BLT. 'Still, at least
it's out of the way now before Josh gets back. If he sees it
that's meant to be really unlucky.'

'He seems pretty lucky to me,' said Alex. Lizzie didn't know how to respond to that. He was in a strange mood this evening.

'Do you want some crisps? Or maybe a brownie?' she said, leaning over him to the cool bag. 'I'll get them.'

'No, wait . . .' he said, but he didn't move fast enough to stop her. She reached her hand into the bag and pulled out what she thought was a box of treats. Instead, she realised it was a parcel, wrapped up neatly in silver paper.

'What's this?' she asked.

He let out a long breath. 'It's your wedding present,' he said eventually. 'I was going to give it to you later, but I guess you can have it now.'

'Alex, you didn't need to get us anything,' she said quietly. It felt odd to be getting a wedding gift from the man she once thought she'd be marrying.

'Well, it's really more for you.'

'Should I open it now or later?' She could feel his eyes on her, watching her closely.

'You can open it now, if you want.'

'Are you sure?' The suspense was starting to get to her.

'Yes.'

Lizzie prised away the shiny paper, letting it fall on the blanket to reveal a smart blue case. She opened it slowly and blinked hard. Inside was an antique copy of *Wuthering Heights*, in near perfect condition.

'It's not a first edition or anything, but it is a collector's item,' he said. 'I thought maybe it would inspire you to get going again.'

She ran a finger over the beautiful cloth cover, her heartbeat accelerating. 'Alex, I can't keep this. It must have cost a fortune.'

'Of course you can. It's up to me what I want to get you. And anyway, it's rude to give back a wedding present.'

'Not when it costs the price of a car, it's not.' This was not the kind of present you casually gave to an old friend. It was a gift that had been sourced with care; a gift that really meant something. She knew suddenly, shockingly, that his feelings for her ran deeper than she'd realised – and worse, much worse, that she was surely falling back in love with him.

No, no, no . . . The thought was as ludicrous as it was obvious. She had moved on, met Josh, made promises to him that she couldn't possibly break. And yet . . .

This can't be happening now.

She placed the book gently back in its case, her hands trembling, and returned it carefully to the cool bag. 'It's unbelievably generous of you, but I can't take that,' she whispered, staring down at the blanket. 'I hope you understand.'

'You have to take it.' His voice was firm, insistent.

'Really, I can't . . .'

'You can,' he said, his jaw set. 'It's important to me. I want you to have something to remind you.'

'Remind me what?'

'Of me.'

'What are you talking about?' she said, her emotions swirling. 'Has something happened?'

'No,' he said uneasily, hauling himself up and striding to the edge of the bandstand. 'Forget I said anything.'

'Alex, what's wrong?' She jumped to her feet and followed him. The sun was just starting to set now, turning the sky a dramatic shade of red. 'Please, talk to me.'

He rested a hand on one of the pillars and tilted his head towards her. 'I wasn't going to tell you this before the wedding, but I've been having a few problems . . . head-aches, mainly, and sometimes with my words.' He inhaled sharply. 'Then I had a pretty bad seizure at home last week. The doctors did another MRI scan and they've decided they want to operate soon.'

'How soon?'

'Probably while you're away.'

'But that's a good thing, right?' She was struggling to keep up. 'Doesn't that mean they'll remove most of the tumour?'

'It means that it's growing,' he said bluntly. 'They'll take out what they can and then I'll have some radiotherapy, but I don't know how long it's going to buy me.'

What? Lizzie was aghast. 'That doesn't make . . . you seemed to be doing so—' Tears began to pour down her face as the magnitude of what he was saying sank in. 'What if we researched more treatments, or raised money? There must be something we can do to help you?'

'I wish there was,' he said, sweeping her into a hug. 'But I need to be realistic about this, Lizzie. It's not just going to go away.' He was crying as well now, his salty tears mingling with hers until she couldn't tell whose were whose. 'I wish things had turned out differently.'

'Me too.' They stood like that for a while, just clinging on to one another, like they might drown if either one let go. She could feel his chest rising and falling, his breathing as ragged as her own.

He lifted his hand gently to her wet face, softly wiping her cheeks. 'You're beautiful even when you cry, you know that?' he said eventually.

'No, I'm not,' she sniffed. 'Megan says I look like a panda.'

Alex attempted a smile. 'Pandas mate for life, apparently.'

'No, they don't. You made that up.'

He took her hand and squeezed it softly. 'Well, they should. Maybe they're just searching for their soulmate.'

She locked her eyes on his, and in that moment she could see only the old Alex, the one she'd been so sure of before everything fell apart around them. Still holding her hand, he leaned in and gently brought his lips down to hers, the urgency building as she surrendered and kissed him back with a passion that surprised her. She hadn't felt that way for years, not even with—

Josh.

What am I doing?

'Wait . . .'

She thought it was the voice in her head, but in fact it was Alex, pulling away. 'I don't want us to do something you might regret.'

Confusion rained down on her like a cold shower. 'I've no idea what I'm doing any more,' she confessed.

'Me either.' He backed up and gave her some space. 'What's going on with us, Lizzie? Really?'

'I don't know,' she said, her heart hammering. 'I'm still trying to figure it out. There's so much to think about right now.'

'Actually, I'm not sure there is,' he said softly. 'I shouldn't have let it go this far.' A frown crossed his face. 'I've been selfish, wanting to keep meeting up when I knew you were getting married. I just enjoyed being with you again so much. But we need to face the facts, and stop this now before things get even more complicated.'

Her blood froze. 'But what if I want to be with you, too?'

'You don't really want that,' he sighed. 'There's no future for us, Lizzie. You could have 50 years with Josh . . . I don't even know what's going to happen next week.' He cleared his throat. 'It wouldn't work out. You should go home and be with him.'

Lizzie realised that everything Alex was saying was true, but she still felt ready to be sick all over the bandstand. 'So where does that leave us?'

He looked out over the gardens, his voice almost lost in the summer air. 'I guess it means we have to go our separate ways. For good, this time.'

'But we could have another go at being friends, right? I want to be there to support you after your operation. Maybe I could visit you after I . . .'

'We can't be friends, Lizzie,' he cried. 'Don't you get it? I'm in love with you! Every time I see you, I want to be with you so much I feel like I'm going to explode. You can't imagine what that's like.'

I can, actually.

'And I can't ask you to risk everything for me – not when we might only have a few months together.'

His logic made perfect sense, but it still didn't stop Lizzie from feeling torn right down the middle. 'So what exactly are you saying, Alex?'

'I'm saying what I should have said in the first place.' He cupped her face in his hands and kissed her like it was his last 60 seconds on earth. 'I love you, Lizzie Sparkes. I always will. But now I think we need to say goodbye.'

24

1 week to go . . .

Lizzie climbed the rickety ladder up to the small loft, realising she could see the stars through the skylight. Her wedding dress hung portentiously in the corner, hovering like a sequinned ghost in the semi-darkness. She quickly switched on the light and began to rummage around the motley assortment of boxes and crates.

It's got to be here somewhere.

She had spent hours this week hunting high and low for a jewellery box she'd inherited from her great-aunt June, inside which was a beautiful vintage brooch that was meant to be her 'something old'. Unfortunately, it was proving more elusive than she'd anticipated. It wasn't in her wardrobe or beneath her bed; it wasn't in her bottom drawer or the crate under the stairs. She knew she had carefully squirrelled it away for safekeeping several years ago. Trouble was, she'd hidden it so well that now she couldn't find it.

She lifted the lid off one box, only to discover the remnants of her old CD collection. She didn't really need the discs these days – hadn't played them for years, in fact – but she couldn't quite bring herself to give the lot to the charity shop. She picked up a few of the cases and flicked through them: Sugababes, S Club 7, Westlife. 'Best left in the loft,' she muttered, though she knew she'd never part with them.

The next box was crammed with glowing school reports; another was stuffed with Josh's old sports gear. She was tempted to chuck that one out, knowing he'd never notice, but reluctantly popped it back in the corner. The fourth one she opened looked more promising: inside she found a number of important items, including her degree certificate, her adoption certificate and her old passport, which she really should have hidden better given her terrible teenage haircut.

Removing the pile of documents, Lizzie spotted the antique wooden jewellery box, a little chipped on the front left corner but otherwise in mint condition. She opened it up to see a small velvet pouch, feeling a moment of relief as she slipped her fingers inside and retrieved the delicate brooch. It was every bit as lovely as she remembered: a sparkling circle of crystals surrounding a single pearl in the centre. The perfect 'something old' indeed – if only she could stop obsessing over her old boyfriend.

She wondered what her wise great-aunt would have made of her recent behaviour. June had met Alex several times and taken a real shine to him, but Lizzie was sure she would not approve of her meeting him behind Josh's back. *Funny business*, she used to call it. Good girls didn't carry on like that. Especially not when they were about to get married.

And yet she couldn't stop thinking about Alex, and everything he'd told her last week in the park. If the doctors were right and his cancer was terminal, then their relationship literally had no future. She would be throwing away a lifetime with Josh and all that went with it – children, grandchildren, growing old together – for a few more moments with her first love. But, still, the thought of a world without Alex made her feel like she might break in half, causing her heart to fall out of her chest and sink into the ground forever.

For the first time, Lizzie began to comprehend the depth of Alex's despair after Connor was killed. *I didn't understand when you left, but it's starting to make sense now.* She realised that losing someone you loved wasn't something you would ever get over, or find closure from; it was something you had to learn to live with, like a scar, and carry to the end. Connor was still part of Alex, the way Alex would always be part of her.

She closed her eyes and traced the outline of her lips with her finger, trying to fix every moment of their final kiss in her mind. She wished she could package up the memory and stash it in one of these boxes, to lie quietly next to her old passport, and be dusted off and revisited from time to time.

How long will I be able to remember the outline of his face, or the exact shade of his eyes? What if I start to forget the little details, like when you wake up and that dream just slips away right in front of you?

For what felt like the millionth time that week, the tears threatened to fall. She had already broken down in front of Megan on Tuesday, too distraught to keep secrets any longer. She needed to talk to someone before she silently crumbled, the worry gnawing away at her, piece by piece.

'I can't believe it,' said Megan, her own eyes filling up. 'I mean, I know I said some horrible things about Alex in the past, but . . . that poor guy.' Lizzie knew that despite all the verbal abuse her best friend had given Alex in absentia, she'd never want anything bad to actually happen to him. 'And there's really nothing they can do to remove the tumour completely?'

'That's what he says,' wept Lizzie. 'And it's crushing me that I can't do anything to help because . . . because . . . I still have all these feelings for him.'

'Does Josh know?' she said softly.

'No! You're the only person who knows, besides Alex.' Lizzie wiped her nose with her wrist. 'But you can't say anything, to anyone.'

'I won't,' Megan promised. 'But Lizzie, what are you going to do about the wedding?'

'I'm not sure,' she sobbed. 'I mean, it's not like I've suddenly stopped loving Josh. I know we could be happy together. But lately I keep finding myself thinking about Alex, wishing that I could be there for him . . .' She struggled to breathe through her tears. 'What am I going to do, Megan? You have to tell me what to do!'

Megan wrapped one arm around her, pulling her in for a hug.

'I wish I could, but I can't help you with this one,' she said gently. 'This is a choice you've got to figure out on your own.'

Desperately trying to keep it together, Lizzie took a deep breath and continued to rifle through the jewellery box, as though the dazzling trinkets might somehow distract from her dilemma. She wished that June was here now to dispense some sage advice, or even just to hug her and make everything better, like she used to when Lizzie was a child.

She was about to close the lid when she caught sight of a small, dark box that looked vaguely familiar. With trembling hands, she lifted it out and slowly opened the gold-embossed top. Inside lay Alex's silver pendant, shining up like a miniature searchlight, as beautiful as the day he'd given it to her. *So that's where it went.* She must have stashed it there after the break-up, too traumatised to look at it, yet unable to throw it away.

Turning it over, she ran a finger over the tiny engraved letters.

Forever.

The wave of emotion struck with a force she could not have seen coming. She dropped the necklace and angrily swiped away the jewellery box, its contents spilling across the floor as the tears tumbled down her cheeks. She cried softly at first and then harder, louder, until her whole body started to shake. Her chest ached so much she could barely catch her breath.

Alex, what am I going to do without you? She knew for sure that there was a part of her that still loved him, that would always love him, and that would disappear with him. She wanted to be there to support him, to be by his side whenever the end came.

But Alex did not want her there as a friend, and she could not give him her whole heart while she was engaged to Josh. Laid-back, lovable Josh, who had never dumped her or deserted her or driven her to distraction. *OK, so it's different to what you had with Alex, but Josh is a great guy,* she reminded herself. *You've spent the past five years building a life together. How could you even think about letting him down so badly now?*

She dared to imagine, just for a moment, what would happen if she called off the wedding. Her dad would lose all the money he'd so generously paid for the reception. Her mum would never be able to face the ladies from her badminton group again. And Josh's mum . . . well, Celia would probably beat her to death with the bridal bouquet.

But all of that paled into insignificance at the thought of telling Josh. She would break his heart, the way hers had been broken all those years ago. He would never forgive her. All the promises they'd made, all the happy times they'd shared, would be destroyed in a heartbeat.

And for what?

Though she couldn't hide the fact she still cared for Alex, it was clear that their story would not have a happy ending. But with Josh, the future was unscripted: fresh chapters they could fill together. If she picked him, life would be straightforward; she knew that he would make a devoted husband, a doting father. He could give her all the things she'd never have with Alex. Time. Security. A family of her own.

I can't throw all that away, right?

I just need to calm down and concentrate on next week.

Wiping her eyes, Lizzie began to scoop up the jewellery she'd sent flying, gently placing each item back in the box. She was still so absorbed in her thoughts that she almost didn't see the folded piece of paper on the floor, its edges crinkled and discoloured. *What else have I hidden in there?*

Confused, she opened it carefully.

Then she realised it wasn't her who had hidden it after all.

14 February, 1946

My darling June,

I hope you will forgive me for this letter, but I don't think I could forgive myself if I didn't send it.

Since the first time I saw you on that bicycle, my every thought has returned to you – the curl of your hair, the blush of your cheeks, the warmth of your hand slipped into mine. Even in my darkest moments, when I couldn't picture any way out, I never stopped picturing your lovely face. You were my angel, my anchor, my path home.

I didn't ask you to wait for me, not because I didn't care for you, but because I couldn't promise that I would make it back. I should have known then that you would have other admirers, that someone else would say the words I dared not. Perhaps it was foolish of me to think that you could hold me in the same regard as I have come to hold you.

I realise I am likely too late to reclaim your affection, but if there is any chance that I am not, I need to tell you this now. I love you, June. I never stopped. So the question is, have you?

I'll be waiting for your answer, and am sending this brooch as a token of my feelings. If I see you wearing it at the dance tomorrow, I'll know there's still some hope for us. If not, then I must say farewell, and wish you a lifetime of happiness with him.

Happy Valentine's day, my darling.

Love always, Henry

Lizzie's mind began to whirr. She had no idea who Henry was, but she knew one thing for sure: he certainly wasn't June's husband.

Did she love someone else once, too?

Lizzie would never get the chance to ask, but she felt strangely comforted to know that June might have sympathised with her situation after all. She wondered what had happened to the one that got away, or if great-uncle Alfred had ever found out that he had competition. June and Alfred were married for more than 50 years, with two children and five grandchildren, and they had always seemed like the perfect pairing.

Reading the letter again, Lizzie tried to imagine June with this other man, but couldn't. *How differently might her life have turned out if she'd worn Henry's brooch?* It was impossible to say. Whatever the truth, June had made a choice and committed to it.

Like I need to do.

Folding the note back into a neat square, Lizzie replaced it inside the jewellery box and gently closed the lid.

I've made up my mind, she told herself.

It's time to grow up and get married.

25

4 days to go . . .

Lizzie sat on the bed and wriggled out of a pair of stockings, trying not to snag them in the process. She had bought two shades for the wedding – 'nude' and 'natural' – but now she'd tried them both on they looked almost identical. Slipping back into her jeans, she decided to go with 'nude' and keep the other pair in case she got a ladder. No one besides Josh was going to see them under the dress anyway, and she doubted he'd be able to tell the difference.

Next this evening, she needed to email Peggy Bloom to confirm access arrangements for Saturday. *Where's my mobile?* Looking around, she realised she must have left it in the lounge. 'Josh!' she yelled. 'Is my phone down there?'

He didn't reply.

She went downstairs and opened the door to the lounge. 'Hey, Josh, did you hear me? I was asking if . . .' She stopped as she noticed him sitting on the sofa with the TV turned off. He had a pained look on his face and her mobile beside him.

'Who's Alex?' he said quietly.

Lizzie felt sick to her stomach. *Say something. Anything.* 'What are you doing with my phone?' was all she could manage. Her voice came out small and strained, her indignation strangled by shame.

'Answer the question,' he said, looking her straight in the eye. She couldn't hold his gaze and stared down at the faded cream carpet, wishing it would open up and swallow her. 'Is he your ex-boyfriend?'

So she was right – Josh had heard the name whispered somewhere before. But if it bothered him, he had never let on until now.

'Well?' he pressed.

Tell the truth. You owe him that much.

The guilt that had been weighing on her since the ball suddenly became unbearable. If she didn't come clean now, their whole marriage was going to start off under the shadow of a lie.

'Yes,' she said finally. 'But it's not—'

Josh picked up the remote control and hurled it against the wall, the batteries flying out as it hit the ground with a crack. His eyes flashed with anger.

'Josh, don't!' She had never seen him so upset. 'I can explain . . .'

'I don't want to hear it,' he said furiously. 'I trusted you. I asked you to marry me! And now I find out you've been sneaking off to see your ex behind my back?'

'It's not like that!'

'Oh, so you haven't been meeting him, then?'

'No, I did, but . . .'

'I'm out of here.' Josh stood up and stomped towards the lounge door, and Lizzie tried to block him with her outstretched arms.

'Will you just listen to me for a minute, please? It's complicated.' She took a deep breath. 'Alex is sick, really sick. Cancer. That's why he got back in touch.'

'What?' Josh looked stunned, unsure. Of all the possible scenarios racing through his mind, this clearly wasn't one he'd anticipated. 'What did you say?'

'He's dying, OK? He's got a brain tumour.' She could feel her body tensing up, the words jamming in her throat. 'I only found out recently. I just wanted to spend a little time with him, while he was still . . .' Her voice began to break and she pressed her palms to her face, trying to stem the tears that threatened to spill out yet again.

'OK, OK.' Josh's scowl softened a little and he retreated to the sofa. 'Let's sit down and go back a bit.'

'Alright.' She moved slowly, cautiously, her knees feeling weak as she sank into the centre cushion. Josh perched warily on the arm, as though he couldn't quite bring himself to sit next to her just yet. His body was rigid, like a statue. 'Where do you want to start?'

'You tell me.' He clenched his jaw. 'How long has this been going on?'

'Not long. A few weeks, maybe. I hadn't heard from him for years before that, honestly.' She looked up, willing Josh to believe her. 'He moved abroad after we broke up, and I didn't think I was ever going to see him again.'

'So what changed?'

'He came back. He kept saying we needed to talk, that it was important.' She chewed on her lower lip. 'I didn't want to see him at first, but in the end I felt like I should hear him out, I guess.'

'Why didn't you want to see him before?'

'Because . . .' There was no good way to finish that sentence. *Because there was too much history. Because he broke my heart. Because if he hadn't left town, I'd probably be married to him now, instead of sitting here with you.* 'Because things didn't end well between us.'

Josh didn't push the point further, and she was grateful – until he came out with an even trickier question. 'If that's all true, why didn't you just tell me you were meeting up with him?'

'I don't know.' She flinched, and he shook his head. 'I came close a couple of times, but then I got a bit nervous about how you'd react, so I thought I'd wait till after the wedding. I didn't want you getting stressed before.'

He raised his brows. 'You think finding out like this isn't stressful?'

'I'm sorry,' she said sheepishly. 'I should've told you. I was just all upset and confused and I was worried you might—'

'Confused about what?'

She stared at him blankly. 'Sorry?'

'You just said you were confused. About what?'

Lizzie didn't know what to say. 'I . . . er . . . that came out wrong,' she stammered.

Josh was back on his feet now, pacing around in front of the widescreen TV. 'Are you still in love with this guy or something? Is that what you're telling me?'

'I didn't say that!' cried Lizzie, jumping up. 'I love you, Josh. I'm marrying you.' She stood directly in front of him, forcing him to look at her. 'Listen to me: the reason I agreed to meet Alex in the first place was because I wanted a clean slate for our wedding. And then he dropped this huge bombshell on me and I feel terrible for him, OK? But that doesn't change things between me and you. I just need you to trust me, and talk to me, instead of going through my phone while I'm upstairs.'

Now it was Josh's turn to look guilty. 'I've never done that before, Lizzie – but you've just seemed so distant these past few weeks and I couldn't figure it out. I was afraid you might be having an affair.'

Realising how much she'd hurt him made Lizzie feel awful. She wished that she could go back to that day in the bridal shop and do everything differently.

I should never have kept secrets from Josh in the first place. I'm a terrible, horrible person.

'No, I'm not having an affair. I was hoping that maybe Alex and I could be friends, but . . .' She tried to choose her words carefully. 'I'm not sure that's going to happen.' Even just saying the sentence out loud made it seem more final, and she tried to ignore the cold grip of sadness squeezing her heart.

'I'm sorry he's sick,' said Josh. 'Is he in hospital?'

'Not at the moment, but it's not looking good.'

'Now I know why you've seemed so sad lately.' His voice was calming down a notch. 'But I still wish you'd told me sooner.'

'Me too.' She reached for his hand. 'I promise I won't keep anything from you when we're married.'

'So you still want to marry me?' He looked vulnerable, unsure.

'Yes, of course.' For a second, all she could feel was relief. But Josh couldn't quite let it lie.

'And absolutely nothing happened between you and this other guy?'

'No ... well ...' The word escaped from her mouth before she could catch it, and she immediately wished she could stuff it back in. But it was too late.

'What do you mean, well?' asked Josh, pulling away. 'Well, what?'

'Look, it ... it was nothing. I don't want you to get the wrong idea.'

'About what? Lizzie, what's going on? Have you been sleeping with him?'

'No! Of course not.'

'Did you kiss him?'

She couldn't lie now. 'Yes. But nothing else happened, I swear! We were both very emotional and it just sort of ...'

Lizzie cut herself off as his face began to turn a peculiar shade of purple. 'I should have told you, and I'm sorry. Really sorry. You have to believe me.'

'I don't have to do anything!' yelled Josh. 'How can I believe a word you say now? We're supposed to be getting married this week and you've been messing around with some other guy!'

'Josh, please! I know you're mad at me, but let's sit back down and talk about this,' she urged. 'I made a mistake, and I'm trying to apologise.'

'A mistake? A *mistake*? A mistake is like forgetting to buy a birthday card. It's not forgetting you've got a fiancé while your tongue's wedged down some guy's throat!'

'It was a kiss, Josh! That's all.' She was almost hyperventilating now. 'It's not going to happen again.'

'It shouldn't have happened at all!'

'I know that!' Her eyes blurred with guilty tears. 'But didn't you ever do something and then wished you could take it back?'

Josh thought for a second before he spoke. 'Yeah,' he said bitterly. 'I bought you an engagement ring.'

'Don't say that,' she whispered. 'We can still get past this.'

'I don't think so.' He screwed up his forehead. 'I need to get out of here.' He stomped into the hallway, swiping his wallet and keys from the console table. Lizzie followed him, her legs unsteady.

'Where are you going?' she cried. 'What about the wedding?'

Josh began to laugh hysterically. 'Are you off your head? There's not going to be any wedding now. How can I marry you after this?'

His words took the wind right out of her. 'You don't mean that . . .'

'Yeah, I do,' he said, snatching the jacket he'd left strewn over the banister. 'Don't you get it? It's over. The wedding. Us. All of it!'

This can't be happening.

She placed a hand on his arm, but he shook her off coldly and reached for the latch. 'Get out of the way.'

Her heart froze. 'Please don't, Josh. You can't just leave like this . . .'

'Watch me,' he said loudly as he stormed out into the darkness, slamming the door behind him.

26

3 days to go . . .

Lizzie lay on the couch eating Frosties out of the packet with her fingers, a few falling from her grasp and clinging stickily to the duvet. She had been lying there for most of the night, after giving up her futile attempts to sleep and crawling back down the stairs to numb her mind with TV repeats. Since then, she had only moved three times: twice to shuffle to the bathroom, and once to fetch the cereal. She wondered how long someone could survive on Frosties alone if they were stranded in space with nothing else to sustain them.

She tried to turn her focus to the telly, where an old episode of *Friends* was playing. Ross and Rachel were having one of their famous arguments about being on a break. *Is that what Josh and I are doing? Or are we broken up for good?*

He was fuming with her when he'd marched out yesterday, that much was certain. Not that she blamed him. She had been so caught up in her feelings for Alex that she'd never really stopped to consider Josh's.

She glanced down at her phone for the hundredth time that morning. Still nothing. *Where are you?* Lizzie didn't know what to do or who to call. She couldn't try reaching him at the school because of the summer break. If she phoned his mum and he wasn't there, Celia was going to fly into a tizz and assume he'd been run over or kidnapped. Then she'd have to try to explain the situation, and she didn't really want to confess that they'd had a blazing row over her ex-boyfriend.

She briefly considered calling her own mum, but the thought of having to tell her that the wedding was off filled her with dread. *Can't deal with that yet.* The most obvious person to call was Megan, but it had only been three short days since she'd told her the wedding was definitely on. Plus she'd come straight over and ask 20 questions and make Lizzie do things like change out of her pyjamas. *Not ready for that, either.*

In the five years that she and Josh had been dating, she had never seen him as angry as yesterday. And he'd never stayed out all night before without at least telling her where he was going. *Did he head to Freddie's? To a bar? Home with some other girl?* The thought made her feel nauseous. *He wouldn't do that, would he?* She wasn't sure any more. Maybe he wanted to hurt her the way that she'd hurt him.

What if it was even worse? What if he really was hurt? Anything could have happened to him in that state. *What if he'd got into a fight? Or had an accident?* She was starting to sound like his mother now. Not good. She tried to snap herself out of it, but those two scary words refused to budge from her brain: *what if, what if, what if?*

Loneliness wrapped itself around her like a dark veil. The first boy she had ever loved was dying, and she couldn't imagine a world without him in it. The second guy she had fallen for was hurting, and she didn't know how to fix it. There was no fairy godmother to offer advice on how to deal with this kind of situation. She felt like her heart had been sliced in two before both sides were fed through a shredder.

So much for happily ever after.

She flicked channels absent-mindedly, desperate for something to distract her from the miserable thoughts racing round her head. A screechy singer murdered a Michael Jackson track on a US talent show. She hit the button again. This time a badger poked its head out of a hole on a nature documentary, then swiftly retreated back into its sett. Lizzie didn't blame him. Right now she wanted to burrow underground and hide for at least the next 12 months.

What am I supposed to tell everyone about the wedding? Her parents were going to go ballistic. Guests would have sorted hotels now. And outfits. And presents. Then there were all the suppliers to cancel: the venue, Peggy, the photo-cab firm, the DJ. It had taken more than a year to plan the whole thing; now she was going to have to unpick it in less than a week. She lay back on the sofa, threw the duvet over her head and wished again that she was a badger.

Will Josh ever forgive me? She didn't know. *Is anyone going to speak to me after this?* Hopefully. Her parents would calm down eventually. Megan would think she was mad, but she'd always had her back. The girls at work wouldn't treat her any differently after the initial gossip had subsided. It might seem awful now, but it wasn't as though her whole life would literally end.

Not like Alex.

She thought again about what he must be going through, but couldn't even begin to wrap her head around it. *How do you cope with something like that?* She wished that she could do more to help him. There was something about Alex – always had been something about Alex – that seemed so alive. The thought that he might die young was incomprehensible.

Even now, there was part of her that felt connected to him in some way. That feeling had never really gone away, even when they were on different sides of the planet. It was like an invisible string had been wrapped round her heart and was tugged on from time to time – only now it felt like it was being yanked so hard her heart might fall out altogether. She knew that if Alex hadn't come back, she wouldn't be in this mess with Josh. But she also knew that if she'd cut all ties completely, she would never have had the chance to say goodbye.

Whatever happens, I can't regret that.

Besides, it wasn't really Alex's fault that she'd screwed things up royally with Josh. If she'd just told the truth from

the beginning, then he might have been more under-
standing about it. Sure, he could be a little immature at
times, but he wasn't mean. He'd probably even have invited
Alex over to watch the football.

I've made a total hash of this, haven't I?

The house felt empty without Josh. She missed his laugh,
and the way he bounced out of bed in the morning, filling
each room with noise and energy. She'd got used to his
little quirks – like the weird way he loaded the dishwasher
– and sharing her life with someone again. She was even
just about used to him leaving his shoes all over the place.
Her eye fell on one lone trainer sticking out from under
the armchair, looking lost without its other half.

Lizzie pulled the duvet back down and glanced at her
phone: 11.20am and still no word. She debated whether to
call Josh again, but decided not to. If he hadn't got back
to her four previous voicemails, a fifth wasn't likely to make
much difference. Feeling miserable, she shovelled another
handful of dry Frosties into her mouth. Maybe she'd just
lie here for days and comfort-eat, surrounded by wedding
memorabilia, like a hungry Miss Havisham.

Just then, she heard the key turn in the lock, followed
by heavy footsteps in the hallway. 'Josh?' she croaked.

He stuck his head around the living room door. He
looked rough, with bloodshot eyes and tufts of hair sticking
out at weird angles, but the sight of him filled her with
hope. He squinted, like he was trying to adjust to the light
after a deep sleep. Not that he looked like he'd had much.

'Why'd you kip in here?' he asked.

'I didn't. I couldn't.' Her voice wobbled. 'I just kept thinking about how I screwed everything up. But I wasn't having some sordid affair, I promise. I just didn't handle the situation well. I'm sorry.'

'I'm sorry, too,' he said finally.

'You are?' He came into the lounge and she could see that he was holding a bouquet of flowers from the local petrol station.

'These are for you,' he said sheepishly. He'd forgotten to take off the yellow £4.99 sticker, but to her they seemed priceless.

'I thought you were furious with me?'

'I was,' he admitted. 'I'm still not thrilled about it. But then I tried to put myself in your position and imagine how I'd feel if one of my ex-girlfriends turned up and said they were dying. I'd want to see them, I guess. I just like to think I'd have told you.'

'You're right, I should totally have told you.' She sat up and swung her legs round, making room for him on the couch. 'I did think about it, more than once, but then it all just got so . . . so complicated.'

He came and sat beside her, on top of the duvet. He smelled like he'd been drinking. 'Is it still complicated?'

'What do you mean?'

'Are you in love with him?'

He looked at her with his tired red eyes, and she gave the best answer she could. 'I love *you*, Josh.' That much she knew was true. As for Alex, she would have to let her feelings for him go, filed under another lifetime.

'And you're never going to keep stuff from me again, right?' Relief softened his features.

'Never. I promise.'

He leaned across and kissed her deeply, hugging her so tightly she could barely move. His mouth smelled of morning breath, but she didn't care. He was home, she was forgiven – and this time next week they'd be Mr and Mrs.

She pulled back a little, her nose still pressed to his. 'So we're still on for the weekend, then?'

'What's happening at the weekend?' he smiled.

'I thought we had something to go to . . .'

'Is that right?' His eyes twinkled mischievously. 'I'd better check my save-the-date card.'

'You do that,' she said, beaming back at him. 'Because this is going to be one wedding you definitely don't want to miss.'

27

1 day to go . . .

Josh and Freddie were already waiting outside the church doors by the time Lizzie, her parents and Megan arrived for the wedding rehearsal. Lizzie had shipped Josh off to his best man's last night so that she could get all her bridal gear ready without him seeing it. 'It's bad luck otherwise,' she warned him. 'You don't want to jinx things, do you?' Earlier this afternoon, her parents and Megan had dropped everything round to their hotel before getting dressed for the run through. After changing her mind a couple of times, Lizzie had finally settled on a cornflower blue shift dress, topped with a white mohair shrug. She was already starting to regret the latter, which was moulting little hairs all over her, but it was too late to turn back now.

Josh had clearly made an effort as well, looking smart in a grey blazer and what she knew were his best black trousers. 'Hey, handsome,' she called out as she walked up towards the chapel. 'Someone scrubs up well.'

He tapped his watch. 'Someone's ten minutes late.'

'Yeah,' said Freddie. 'We've been here ages.'

She ignored him and kissed Josh on the cheek. 'Sorry, bride's prerogative. We got to the hotel a bit later than planned. Turns out Mum's the slowest driver in the world.'

'I can hear you,' said Mrs Sparkes huffily.

'I know,' said Lizzie.

'Well, I've never loved driving in town, Elizabeth – especially not when it's busy. I was hoping your dad would do it but . . .' She leaned in and lowered her voice. 'He's been *drinking*.'

'What?' Her dad had never been a big drinker. 'Since when?'

'Since he got nervous about tomorrow and helped himself to two large glasses of whisky. Straight after breakfast!'

'Oh.'

'Exactly.' She moved past Lizzie and gave Josh a welcoming hug. 'Hello, son. Can I call you son, yet? Not long to go now!'

'Call me whatever you like, Lynda,' said Josh. 'I must say you're looking lovely this afternoon.'

'Oh, this old thing?' Her mum beamed. Both she and Lizzie knew that she'd spent two hours getting ready. 'You don't need perfect hair and make-up today,' Lizzie had tried to explain. 'It's only the rehearsal.'

'But it's the first time I've met the priest!'

'So? I very much doubt he's an expert on women's cosmetics.'

'That's not the point, Elizabeth.' Her mum shook her

head like she was explaining something to a four-year-old. 'You never get a second chance to make a first impression.'

'Well, you're not going to make a very good impression if we're half an hour late, are you?' Lizzie had pointed out, before her mum finally got a move on and started shepherding everyone down to the car.

As the group stood greeting one another outside the church, the wooden doors swung open and Father Brenner emerged. He was a small man with a friendly demeanour, the fine lines around his eyes creasing when he smiled. Lizzie and Josh had tried to work out his age once, but it had been impossible to guess; he had one of those timeless faces that could have been 55 or 75. He also had a very thick Irish accent that made him sound like he'd stepped straight out of *Father Ted*.

'Hullo there,' he said, shaking hands with everyone. 'It's good to see you all. Shall we come through?'

Josh offered Lizzie his arm. 'Shall we?'

She smiled. 'I think my dad's supposed to walk me down the aisle.'

'I didn't realise I was marrying such a stickler for the rules.' He put his arm around her shoulder. 'You look lovely, by the way. I can't wait to see what you wear tomorrow.' Lizzie hugged him tight and stared down the long aisle as the group gathered in the back of the church.

'Alright you two, save it for the honeymoon,' groaned Megan. 'Some of us are trying to rehearse here.'

'There's not actually that much to rehearse,' chipped in

know-it-all Freddie. 'It's pretty straightforward when you think about it.'

Megan caught Lizzie's eye as if to say, 'Who is this guy?' Lizzie knew she would be disappointed that the best man looked more like a ferret than a Hollywood heartthrob. Even though she was hoping to hook up with Gareth at the reception, Freddie was still going to be escorting her back down the aisle in front of everyone, and he wasn't exactly Megan's idea of arm candy.

'Sorry,' Lizzie mouthed. Megan poked out her tongue in silent protest.

'Right then,' said Father Brenner, clapping his hands. 'If I could just have your attention for a moment. I don't think this'll take terribly long, but if we have a little run through now, then everything should go smoothly tomorrow. The good news is it's all very simple.'

'Told you,' said Freddie triumphantly. Lizzie suppressed the urge to whack him. She wondered how long Megan would show the same restraint.

'OK, so most people will already be in position by the time the bride arrives. Not too late, I hope!' He winked in her direction. 'So the groom and the best man will be at t'front of the aisle, and the bride's mother can take a seat in the first pew.' He gestured with his hands for people to take their places, like a choreographer staging his latest spectacular.

'OK, good. Now then, Elizabeth, do you want your bridesmaid to come in before you or after you?'

'After, please,' she said. 'I might need some help with my dress.'

'Very well. In that case, once everyone is in place, you and your father will start to walk down the aisle, and your bridesmaid will follow behind you. Do you want to have a practice?'

'Yes, please,' said her dad, nervously.

Lizzie smiled. 'I think he was talking to me, Dad. But sure, we can have a go now.'

'OK.' She wrapped her arm through his, and could feel him shaking ever so slightly. 'Don't worry, Dad, all you've got to do is stick one leg in front of the other.'

'Alright,' said the priest. 'So the music will start playing, and then you two will come down the aisle. When you reach the end, Mr Sparkes, you'll give your daughter to Josh and take a seat next to Mrs Sparkes on t'front there. Let's give it a try, shall we?'

The two of them set off slowly, trying to walk in time. 'Step, together. Step, together. Step, together,' she heard her dad muttering under his breath.

'Relax,' she whispered, her arm still gripping his. 'You're walking me down the aisle, not trying to win *Strictly Come Dancing*.'

'I'm just trying to keep count,' he mumbled.

'OK. But could you count inside your head, please?'

'I'll try.' They got halfway down the aisle and he began to loosen up a little.

'You're doing great, see?'

He nodded. 'I just want everything to go well tomorrow.'

'It will, Dad. Everything will be perfect.'

As they neared the front of the aisle, she looked into Josh's beaming face and her stomach gave a little flutter. She smiled back at him as her father gave her a proud peck on the cheek and took a seat next to her mum.

'Good, good,' said Father Brenner. 'Then I'll say a little introduction, and we'll have a hymn followed by your readings. It's best if your readers sit on the end of a pew so it's easier for them to get out.'

Lizzie nodded, trying to concentrate. She was starting to feel a little hot and bothered in the church, probably because there wasn't much air circulating. *I hope it's not this stuffy tomorrow.* She took a deep breath and tried to loosen her shrug a little.

'Then there'll be another hymn, and the best man will need to make sure he has the rings ready,' the priest continued. Freddie patted his pocket smugly. 'I'll do my address, and check that no one has any objections to the marriage, and then we'll proceed to the vows. You two should be facing one another throughout this part,' he said to Josh and Lizzie.

She turned towards her future husband and looked up into his brown eyes, which were sparkling with happiness, or perhaps just reflecting the glow of the candles on the altar. Suddenly the enormity of the occasion hit home, and she could feel a prickling warmth rising from her chest and spreading up her neck. She hastily took off her shrug and draped it over the nearest pew.

'Are you alright?' whispered Josh.

'I'm fine,' she said. 'Just a bit warm.'

'So this will be the main bit: for better, for worse and so on, till death us do part, etc, etc.'

Till death us do part. For a split second the thought of Alex flashed across her mind, and she squeezed her eyes shut, trying to force the image out.

'Are you alright, Elizabeth?' Father Brenner asked, leaning closer.

'Yes, yes, I'm fine,' she mumbled. 'Please carry on.'

'Then we'll do the giving and receiving of the rings, and I'll pronounce you husband and wife, at which point, Josh, you can kiss the bride.'

Before she could react, Josh caught her off-guard, bending down and pressing his lips gently to hers. It was the perfect wedding kiss: soft, tender, filled with warmth and hope and love. *Wow.* Her parents, Megan and Freddie all burst into spontaneous applause.

'I didn't mean right now,' laughed Father Brenner. 'But clearly these young lovebirds can't help themselves. Go ahead, have all the practice you need!'

Lizzie tried to look as though she was listening, but her thoughts were running wild. *I've been so busy trying not to think about Alex that I forgot about Josh.* She wanted to kick herself with her new Zara heels. *How could I have come so close to throwing this away?*

Josh looked down at his neatly polished shoes, clearly a little embarrassed at having jumped the gun. 'Sorry

Father, I thought we were rehearsing the lot,' he grinned sheepishly. The tiniest blush flickered across his cheek, making him look even more adorable.

'Well, that is an important bit,' joked the priest. 'You don't want to mess that up in front of everyone.' He chuckled so hard he began to cough. 'Now, where were we? Ah yes, after that we need to go to the vestry so you can sign the register. So that will be you two, your witnesses and your parents.' He turned to Josh. 'Will your parents be . . . er . . . with us on the day?' he asked delicately.

'Oh yes,' said Josh cheerfully. 'They're just driving down now. They'll both be here later this evening.'

'OK, good,' said Father Brenner. 'In that case, they'll follow you all into the vestry and we'll get everything signed. Any other questions?'

'I don't think so,' said Lizzie.

'Me either,' said Josh. 'Thanks, Father.'

'In that case, I'll bid you good evening,' the priest replied, as they all began to file back down the aisle towards the exit. 'Such a lovely couple, aren't they?' he said to Mrs Sparkes, while Lizzie was still in earshot. 'I'm sure it's going to be a wonderful wedding.'

'Oh yes, Father,' gushed Mrs Sparkes, as she shook his hand. She was beaming so hard her cheeks must have hurt. 'See you back here tomorrow.'

Megan bounced through the wooden doors, throwing her arms around Lizzie's waist. 'Right then, bride-to-be, you're coming with me. Don't worry, Josh, I won't let her get up to anything I wouldn't do.'

Josh raised a playful eyebrow. 'Does that rule out much?'

'Probably not.'

'In that case, do you mind if I take a minute to say goodnight to my future wife?' He took Lizzie's right hand and led her a few paces away from the rest of the group. 'I can't believe we're finally getting married,' he said, an excited grin on his face.

'Me either! Seems grown-up, doesn't it?'

'Ah, it's not that serious. It's only, like, forever.' He slipped his arms around her waist. 'I'll see you back here tomorrow, then?'

'OK. I'll be the one in the white dress.'

'Damn! That's what I was planning to wear. I'd better rethink my outfit.'

She laughed. 'I'd stick with the sexy suit.'

'Alright. Anything to keep the old ball and chain happy.'

She ran her fingers through his freshly trimmed hair and pulled him towards her for a long kiss. 'I can't wait to marry you, you know that?' he whispered.

'Me too,' she said. She meant it. Josh was handsome and sweet and loyal, not the kind of guy you let go.

'I hope so,' he said. 'I know the other day was a total nightmare, but it feels like I've finally got my old Lizzie back.'

Once more, a sharp pang of guilt stabbed at her. *I came so close to wrecking this.* She made a mental promise that she would totally make it up to Josh on their honeymoon. She'd bought some more lingerie – the posh stuff from Agent Provocateur – that would come in handy.

'Let's not dwell on that any more,' she said softly. 'We should just look forward to tomorrow.'

'You're right,' he nodded. 'I love you.'

'I love you too,' she said, tilting her head back for another kiss.

'Hey, you two, normally I'd say get a room, but you can't tonight because it's bad luck,' Megan shouted.

'Alright,' grinned Lizzie. She turned back to Josh. 'See you down the other end of the aisle?'

He smiled. 'If you're lucky.'

28

5 hours to go . . .

Lizzie looked at her alarm clock for the 11th time that morning: 7.56am. *Only four more minutes and the bloody thing will go off, which means we can finally get up.* She had not slept a wink last night, overcome with a mix of excitement and nerves. It would have been nice to have some soothing words of encouragement from Megan, but she had been snoring away loudly like an asthmatic narcoleptic, blissfully unaware of Lizzie's restlessness. *Enjoy it while you can*, she thought. *You'll be waking up any minute.*

Lizzie looked around the elegant hotel room, with its rich burgundy wallpaper and velvet chaise lounge, over which her wedding dress was draped. *I wonder if Josh got any sleep last night, or if he's as wired as I am?* She doubted it. Aside from the other day, Josh didn't tend to get worked up much. It was quietly comforting in a way, like when you hit a patch of turbulence on a plane and the air hostesses keep calmly passing out sandwiches.

BEEP! BEEP! BEEP! The alarm clock did its thing, and

334

Megan began to stir from her near-coma. 'Urrrrrrrgh,' she groaned. 'Pleeeeeeasemakeitstop . . .'

'Alright,' said Lizzie, 'but we'd better start getting up soon.' She reached for the clock at a deliberately slow pace, allowing a few more beeps to sound for good measure.

'Switchitorrrrrf!'

'I'm doing it now.' She set the snooze button for ten minutes later, just in case Megan was tempted to doze back off.

'What time is it?' Megan rubbed her eyes.

'It's 8am. Time we got up and started getting ready.'

'Have you ordered breakfast?'

'No, I'm not hungry. But you can get some if you like.'

'Lizzie, you've got to eat something. You can't go rushing around all morning on an empty stomach. Let's order room service.'

Lizzie knew she had a point. 'OK, but nothing too stodgy for me. I still need to fit into that gown.'

'Croissant?'

'Oui, merci.'

Megan picked up the phone and dialled the internal number. 'Hello, I'd like to order some room service for suite 205 please. Please could we have a full English breakfast with all the trimmings—'

Lizzie threw her pillow on her friend's bed. 'What? That one's for me,' mouthed Megan, returning to the phone, 'and a couple of croissants please. Yes, we would like orange juice.' She glanced again at Lizzie. 'And perhaps some strong coffee as well. Yes, that's all.' She hung up. 'They'll be here in 15 minutes. So, how are you feeling?'

'Excited. Jittery. Both, I guess.'

'Well, that's pretty normal. I think everyone feels a bit like that beforehand.'

'Really?'

'Yeah, my boss was exactly the same when she got married. Probably worse than you. But once she got to the groom, she was fine.'

'Do you think Josh is nervous, too?'

'Josh? Nah, he's just excited about marrying you. He told me so last night.'

'He did?'

'Yes. And he asked me to give you this.' Megan reached under the bed and pulled out an expensive-looking box tied with silver ribbon. Surprised, Lizzie opened it up to reveal a delicate white gold watch with a small gift tag attached to it. She turned it over and read the neatly inscribed message: *Time to get married! xxx*

'This is gorgeous,' she declared. 'Who knew he had such good taste in accessories?'

'He might have had a bit of help there,' smiled Megan. 'But it was all his idea, to be fair.'

Lizzie clambered out of her own bed and onto Megan's, giving her a big hug. 'We've been through a lot together, haven't we, you and me?'

'Look, if you're going to start hitting on me now, it's probably not the best day . . .'

'Ha. Actually, I was just going to say that I'm very lucky to have you. You're like the sister I always wanted, even if I have given you some headaches lately. So I'm trying to say thanks, I guess.'

'You're welcome,' said Megan quietly. 'I must admit you had me worried for a while there. Last week, I even thought you might call the whole thing off.' She laughed nervously. 'Clearly I've been watching too much telly.'

'No, it's been difficult,' sighed Lizzie. 'But I think I've got my head straight now. I just want to focus on the wedding today.'

'And you're 100 per cent sure about Josh.'

Is that a statement or a question? 'What?'

'Are you sure you want to get married?'

'Who are you, the priest?'

'I'm serious, Lizzie.' Megan sat up straight. 'I know we haven't seen eye to eye over everything lately, but you're still my best friend and I want you to be happy. But only you know whether that's with Josh or . . . whether it's not. So if you've got anything you want to tell me – anything at all – now's the time to 'fess up or . . .'

'Or what? Forever hold my peace?'

'Something like that.'

'Alright, now you mention it, I do have something to tell you,' said Lizzie.

'I'm listening.'

'After breakfast, I'm bagging the shower first.'

Megan looked her in the eye. 'So we're good here?'

'All good.'

'Phew!' She pretended to wipe her forehead. 'Then let's get you married!'

Three hours later, Lizzie was sitting in a white robe in front of the large dressing table mirror, while Lloyd was busy working his magic with the curling tongs. 'Nearly time now,' he said. 'A couple more hours and you'll be a married woman.'

'Yes,' she said, her pulse quickening every time someone brought that up, which seemed to be about every five minutes. 'Not long at all.'

'Have you spoken to the groom this morning?'

'Isn't that meant to be bad luck?'

'Oh, I thought that was just if you saw him. But now you mention it, I'm not sure.' He winked. 'Maybe stay out of his way altogether, just to be on the safe side.'

'Yeah, I think he'll cope without me for one morning.'

'Exactly. And we've still got plenty to do here.' He pinned up a curl with a hair grip, accidentally poking her in the scalp. She flinched enough for him to notice. 'Sorry. That one got away from me. But it's looking fan-tas-tic.' He stressed each syllable like it was a separate word. 'Don't you think, Meg?' The two of them had only met that morning, but were already hitting it off famously.

'Huh?' Megan was rolling around on the bed in her

underwear, trying to pull on a pair of sheer tights. 'Sorry Lloyd, I'm a bit half-dressed here.'

'So I see. You carry on. I was just telling Lizzie that her hair looks gorgeous.'

'Indeed it does.' Suddenly there was a loud ripping noise. 'Damn! That's the second pair I've laddered this morning. Lizzie, please tell me you've got some spare tights around here? Preferably ones that aren't going to snag the minute I touch them.'

'Yes, in my suitcase. Be careful with those ones, though – I don't have any more I can give you.'

'OK, thanks.' Megan rummaged around in the case until she found what she was looking for. 'Your hair really does look amazing, by the way. You're a star, Lloyd.'

'Thanks, hon. I'll be doing you next.'

'Ooh-er,' joked Megan, and all three of them laughed.

Their banter was interrupted by the ringing of the hotel phone. 'I'll get it,' said Megan, leaping into action. 'Hello, this is Ms Sparkes' assistant,' she said, putting on a silly voice. 'How may I be of service?' There was a pause. 'Oh, hi, Mrs S,' she said. 'No, it's only me. How's it going?'

Lizzie strained to hear the conversation on the other end of the line, but couldn't make it out.

'Uh-huh,' Megan nodded. 'She's right here. I'll ask her.' She put one hand over the mouthpiece and whispered, 'It's your mother. She's wondering if you want her to come up now and lend a hand?'

Lizzie looked around the room, which was strewn with clothes and underwear and lotions and hair gear and all kinds of shoes she didn't recognise but assumed must be Megan's. The make-up artist would be here any minute too, and the last thing she needed was more people trying to squeeze into the confined space.

She shook her head.

'Keep still!' hissed Lloyd, narrowly missing her ear with the tongs.

'Actually, Mrs S, I think we're alright at the moment. There's quite a lot going on, what with hair and make-up and stuff, so you might be more comfortable getting changed in your own room and then coming over to ours after.' There was a pause. 'Yes, she's fine. Just having her hair done right now. We'll see you in a little bit.' There was another pause, then she laughed. 'Yes, I did sneak in some champers – you know me so well. Let's have a glass in an hour or so. Bye then.'

She put down the phone. 'Bloody hell, your mum sounds more jittery than you. What's with the Sparkes women this morning?'

'Well, you should know by now that we're a high-main-tenance bunch.'

'Too right. I might need that bottle of bubbly to myself at this rate.'

'Hey, don't forget me,' said Lloyd.

'I won't,' promised Megan. 'As long as you help me keep an eye on Lizzie's mum. Last thing we want is a tipsy mother-of-the-bride before we even get to the ceremony. The woman can't handle her booze.'

'Megan!' scolded Lizzie, but she knew that it was true. Two glasses of fizz and her mum would be singing *Chapel of Love* all the way to the church.

Just then, there was a knock at the door. 'That'll be Cemile,' said Megan, grabbing her dressing gown and throwing it on. She had personally recommended the make-up artist, who was someone she knew through work. Flinging the door wide open, she kissed the petite brunette waiting outside on both cheeks.

'Cemile, hi! Come in. You've met Lizzie – aka The Bride – and this is Lloyd, hairdresser extraordinaire.'

'I'm nearly finished here,' he said, popping the final grip in place. 'But then I've got to start work on Megan.'

'Not a problem,' said Cemile. 'I can set up over by the bed, then I can do Lizzie's make-up while you carry on there.'

Lloyd began spritzing so much hairspray over Lizzie's head that she nearly began to choke. 'Hang in there,' he said cheerfully. 'It'll be gone in a second, but we need that do to stay in place.' He wafted away some of the mist with his hand. 'All done!' he declared, holding up an oval mirror behind her head. 'What do you think?'

Lizzie peered into the glass, her eyes stinging slightly from the spray. But the result was worth it. Her hair was swept into loose, elegant curls, like something out of a romantic drama, and at the back he had dotted in some crystal pins for added sparkle. It was a red-carpet-worthy hairstyle for her moment in the spotlight.

'I love it!' she said.

'Well, thank goodness for that,' replied Lloyd. 'I think I'd have lopped it all off if you hadn't!'

She smiled, smoothing down the bottom of her robe as she stood up. 'Megan, you're next.'

'OK,' said Megan, who had finally managed to pull on a pair of tights without destroying them. 'But be gentle with me, Lloyd.'

'I will, hon. I will.'

Fifty minutes later, Lizzie and Megan were alone, with their hair and make-up almost perfected. Cemile had gone downstairs to grab herself a coffee, while Lloyd had popped outside for a quick cigarette break.

'Don't worry, ladies, I won't be long,' he'd said.

'Be as long as you like,' said Lizzie. 'Everything looks great. There's not a lot more you can do here.'

'Listen, I'm not going to relax until you're all dressed up and ready to walk out that door,' he replied. 'You wouldn't believe how many brides can fuck up putting on a frock. I'll hang around just in case.'

'Good idea,' said Megan. 'But you're fine to go out for a while. We need to get our gowns on, anyway.' Closing the door behind him, she turned to Lizzie. 'Right, it's probably time we started getting you into that incredible dress, don't you think?'

'I guess so.' Lizzie really didn't know where the morning had gone. One second she was scoffing croissants in bed, the next she was about to put on her wedding gown.

'We stop?' asked Megan, disrupting her train of thought.

'Stop what?' said Lizzie.

'No, I meant have you been for a wee? You'd be better off going now, you know – not once you've got all this gear on.'

'Oh, OK. Fair enough.' Suddenly Lizzie's mobile phone rang. She picked it up from the bedside table and noticed the caller was phoning from a withheld number. *Who would be calling me now, of all days? Nearly everyone I know is getting ready. Unless . . .* Her hand began to shake. *Unless it's news about Alex.*

She toyed with not answering it, but the need to know was overwhelming. There was a silence on the other end of the line.

'Hello. Anyone there?' she said hesitantly.

'Ah, hello, is that Miss Sparkes?'

'Yes. Who is this?'

'My name's Doug, and I'm calling to see what I can do to help you. How much are you currently paying for your mobile phone package?'

'Aaaargh! Never. Call. Me. Again,' yelled Lizzie, hanging up and throwing the phone down on the bed.

Megan looked startled. 'Who was that?'

'Just some random cold-caller.'

'Oh, thank goodness. I thought for a . . .' She cut herself off and pulled her bridesmaid's dress out of the cupboard. 'Anyway, no harm done, right? Let's get ready.'

'You thought what?' said Lizzie.

'Huh?' Megan played dumb. She slipped the long, coral maxi dress over her head and adjusted it around her boobs.

'You said, "I thought for a second . . ." and then you changed the subject. What did you think?'

'It doesn't matter. We've got more important things to do now, in case you'd forgotten.'

'It matters to me,' said Lizzie quietly. 'Who did you think it was?'

'Oh, alright. I was worried that maybe it was something to do with Alex,' Megan confessed. 'But it wasn't, so let's just forget I said anything.'

'I thought it might be something to do with Alex, too,' Lizzie admitted. 'Does that make me a terrible bride? I shouldn't be thinking about him today, right?'

'No, Lizzie, it doesn't make you a bad bride,' said Megan sympathetically. 'You're bound to think about him under the circumstances. I've been thinking about him a lot myself lately.'

'So do you think one of us should call him? Just to see how he's doing?'

'Whoa, hang on a minute! No, I don't think we should call him. That would be, like, the worst idea ever. Why would you even suggest it?'

Lizzie's heart sank. 'I get what you're saying. But I'm just about to go off on honeymoon for two weeks. What if something were to happen to him while we were away, and I hadn't at least tried to call? I know we agreed not to see each other again, but I don't want him to think that I don't care.'

'Lizzie, he'll know that you care,' said Megan. 'But he's not going to expect you to phone him on your wedding day. And anyway, what would you say? "Well, I can't chat for long, I'm just about to go off and marry someone else . . ." That's hardly going to cheer him up, is it? Promise me you won't call.'

'But . . .' said Lizzie.

'No buts,' said Megan firmly. 'Unless it's "But I need to go for a quick wee before I put on my dress."'

'Fine.' Lizzie knew when she was defeated. 'I'll just be a minute.'

As she sat down on the toilet, she twiddled her thumbs nervously. The tiny mark on the inside of her wrist caught her eye. Even after all the laser treatment, she could still make out the faint outline of that tattoo. She wished she'd left it alone now, but at the time she had desperately wanted to erase every painful reminder of Alex and his family from her life.

Her thoughts were interrupted by a knock at the door. 'It's the fashion police!' yelled a male voice outside.

'Hey Lloyd, could you just give us a few more minutes?' said Megan. 'We're still getting dressed. Maybe you could go and grab a coffee with Cemile?'

'No problem,' he replied. 'I might go on a little recce of the hotel. I just overheard one of the porters saying they'd seen Ant and Dec in the restaurant.'

'Alright then. Enjoy! See you in a bit.'

Lizzie flushed the loo, washed her hands and stepped out of the en-suite bathroom. 'Well, I suppose we'd better get this show on the road,' she said with a smile.

'Yes, we had. Are you ready for your dress now?'

'Ready and waiting!'

Megan went over to the chaise longue, unzipped the protective dust cover and carefully lifted out the dress. 'I love this so much, Lizzie – I really do. I'm tempted to run off with it right now.'

'Hmmm, unfortunately you can't, otherwise I'd have to turn up at the church in my knickers.' Lizzie untied the belt of her robe and let it fall to the floor, revealing her bridal lingerie: a beautiful ivory satin basque and French briefs, plus a delicate suspender belt and nude stockings.

'Yeah, I'm not sure the priest would be entirely cool with that. Nice gear, though.'

'Thanks.' Lizzie moved in front of the mirrored wardrobe, and Megan fanned out the dress in front of her feet. 'Right, so the lady in the shop said you're supposed to step into it – that way you won't spoil your hairdo.'

'OK, here goes.' Lizzie stepped into the gown, closing her eyes while Megan pulled it up and adjusted it around her. 'I'm not going to look until it's on.'

'I'm nearly there,' said Megan. 'Here, just lift your left arm up a little. Alright, breathe in for a minute while I do the zip . . .'

'What are you saying? It looks tight?'

'No, don't be stupid! I just don't want to get any skin caught in the zipper . . . blood would be a nightmare to get out of a white gown, you know.'

'Grim! You're supposed to be keeping me calm, in case you'd forgotten.'

'Quit your moaning. I'll be done in about . . . hang on . . . three more seconds.' Lizzie heard the sound of a zip being done up.

'Fine. Can I look yet?'

'Any second . . . now!'

Lizzie opened her eyes and looked at the bride staring back at her. The dress was every bit as beautiful as she remembered, if not more so, cinching in perfectly at the waist before flowing all the way down to the floor. The delicate beading shimmered under the artificial hotel lights, like a dusting of snowflakes on a freshly frosted morning. If it was possible to fall in love with a frock, Lizzie was head over heels.

'Well, what do you think?' said Megan. 'It's amazing, right?'

'It's perfect,' said Lizzie. 'I love it so much I'm almost scared to wear it outside.'

'Here, let me get your other bits so we can see how it all looks together.' Megan moved over to Lizzie's case, and returned with June's vintage brooch, a pair of silver peep-toe heels and a sparkling diamanté clutch. 'There you go.'

'Thanks.' Lizzie slipped her feet into the dainty shoes and took another long look in the mirror. It all seemed so surreal, she could barely recognise herself. 'This doesn't feel like it's really happening to me, if that makes any sense?' she said, pinning the brooch in place. 'I feel like I'm watching a film or something.'

'Yeah, I know what you mean. It's a lot to get your head around. Like, we're standing here and you're still Lizzie Sparkes, but by this afternoon you'll be Mrs Cooper.' A grin spread across her pretty face. 'Who knows, maybe this time next year, there might even be a mini Cooper?'

Lizzie began to giggle. 'It's a shame you can't be our best man, you know. You're way funnier than Freddie.'

'I'm just so happy for you, that's all. You've got a gorgeous dress and a gorgeous man waiting for you at the church. This is going to be the best day of your life.'

Exactly. What's not to love?

'Shall we hug it out?' said Megan. The two girls embraced, and Lizzie clung on to her friend for a split second longer than usual. 'Thank you,' she whispered.

Just then, there was a loud knock at the door and a chorus of multiple greetings from outside. 'Sounds like the rest of the wedding party's arrived,' said Megan.

'Or Lloyd's found Ant and Dec,' grinned Lizzie.

The One

'Are you ready for everyone to come in yet? I think the photographer should be here by now as well.'

'Yes,' said Lizzie, taking one last glance at her reflection. 'I'm ready.'

29

30 minutes to go . . .

Lizzie glanced around the hotel room, wondering how on earth they'd managed to squeeze everybody inside. Her mum was in full-on Liz Taylor mode, resplendent in a bold emerald two-piece complete with a massive hat, holding court and sipping away at a glass of champagne. 'I'm keeping an eye on her,' Megan had promised, but she didn't seem to be doing a particularly good job. Her dad kept taking a folded piece of paper from his pocket and peering at it nervously; she suspected that it was his speech for later, which her mum said he'd been fretting about all week. Lloyd was having a good gossip with Cemile in the corner, springing up every now and again if a strand of hair threatened to fall out of place, and the photographer had arrived and was trying to take spontaneous snaps of everyone – which, of course, immediately meant they all started posing awkwardly.

'The wedding cars will be here in five minutes,' said Megan, co-ordinating everything from her mobile. 'Should we start moving the first group downstairs?'

'Yes, I suppose we should,' agreed Lizzie.

'How are you feeling?'

'Nervous as hell.' The butterflies in her belly were doing a fandango. 'I'm not sure those croissants were such a good idea.'

'Try taking some deep breaths.'

Lizzie did as she was told, but it only made her feel more light-headed. 'I'm not sure that's helping. I'll be OK.'

'Are you sure? I can ask the drivers to give us another five minutes if you like. Everyone expects the bride to turn up late anyway. It's practically obligatory.'

'No, I'll be fine. Dad will be with me. You should go down soon and start getting people into the car.'

'Alright. But call me if you need anything.' Megan clapped her hands loudly. 'OK folks, the first wedding car is here, so we need to start heading downstairs now. Mrs S, we're going in that one. Mr S, you wait here with Lizzie and the photographer for the second car. Lloyd and Cemile, I'm going to get you to do all my weddings. You've been brilliant.'

'Yes, you really have,' added Lizzie. 'Thank you both so much.'

'You're welcome,' said Lloyd. 'Let's have one more look at that hairdo.' She twirled around slowly while he stood admiring his handiwork. 'Yes, you look perfect.' He kissed her on both cheeks, before doing the same to Megan. 'Right then, Cemile, our work here is done.' They waved goodbye to the group as they stepped out into the corridor. 'Break a leg, everyone.'

'Remind me again why that's lucky?' Lizzie whispered to Megan.

'I've no idea,' she replied. 'Please don't break anything. That would be awful.'

'You don't say.'

'Right then, Mrs S, we'd better bust a move,' said Megan, as Mrs Sparkes polished off the remnants of her champagne.

'Buster what?'

'Never mind. We need to get going.'

'Oh. Alright, love.' She adjusted her large hat once more in front of the full-length mirror. 'Well, Elizabeth, my precious girl . . . this is it.' She looked teary as she kissed her daughter on the cheek, taking care not to leave a lipstick mark. 'I'll see you in there. Best of luck.'

'I love you, Mum,' said Lizzie sincerely.

'I love you too. Look at you, all elegant.' Her lip began to quiver. 'And to think, I still remember the day we brought you home like it was yesterday . . .'

Megan moved swiftly, aware that any emotional outburst now might set them back precious minutes. 'Alright, Mrs S, the driver's waiting outside for us. Let's go.' She ushered the older woman out of the door and took Lizzie's hand. 'You look incredible, Lizzie, really you do. I'll see you outside the church. Love you.' And with a swish of her silk chiffon gown, she was gone.

'Looks like it's just you and me then, kid,' said her dad, still fiddling with his folded paper as though he was taking a course in origami. The photographer carried on snapping away in the background, no doubt used to being totally ignored by members of the bridal party.

'Actually, Dad, could you just give me a moment?' said Lizzie. 'There's something I need to do. You know, on my own.' She knew she wouldn't need to tell him twice; he never asked questions where there was even a hint of a chance it might involve any kind of 'women's problems'.

He looked at his watch. 'Will it take long? We're meant to be downstairs in five.'

'No, it'll only take a minute,' she said.

'OK then, I suppose I could pop back to our room and pick up a spare memory card for the camera.' He gave her a wink. 'Just don't go anywhere. Your mother will *kill* me if I lose you.'

'I'll be right here.'

'Alright then, I'll be back soon.'

'Would you like me to wait outside?' said the photographer, the camera never leaving her face.

Lizzie gave her a grateful smile. 'Yes, please. Just for a couple of minutes.'

With the room finally empty, she sat down on the bed, her hands tingling. *Here I am, a nearly married woman . . . and I still feel like a naughty schoolkid. But if I'm going to do this, I need to do it now. I won't get another chance until after the honeymoon.* She picked up her mobile phone from the bedside table and quickly entered the passcode. *I promised Megan I wouldn't call him,* she reassured herself. *But I never said I wouldn't send a quick text.*

Dear Alex, she typed. I just want to say I'm thinking of you. Please don't give up hope. I know it's hard for us to stay friends after everything we've been through, but it doesn't mean I'll ever stop caring. Love Lizzie xx

Her thumb hovered momentarily over the send button, but she knew there wasn't much time to lose. *Get on with it.* She pressed the screen, and her phone emitted a small ping to confirm that the deed had been done.

She did not expect it to start ringing a few seconds later.

It was Alex.

What I am supposed to do now? Should I leave it? Her brain was whirring so fast she felt dizzy. *But what if it's important? How bad would I feel if it's the last time he calls me and I send him straight to voicemail?*

She gave in and answered it. There was silence on the other end of the line. 'Alex?'

Suddenly she heard a loud sob, and what sounded like a female voice. 'Lizzie, is that you?'

'Yes, who's this?' Every inch of her wedding dress suddenly felt as though it was constricting around her. 'Where . . . where's Alex?'

'It's Andi,' she said, her voice breaking. 'I just saw your message and I didn't know what to do. I didn't realise you and Alex were still close.'

'We . . . um . . . kind of made our peace recently,' she

said, all the heat draining out of her body. *Will you please just tell me what's going on?*

'That's good,' sniffed Andi. 'He really loved you, you know. We always thought maybe you two might get back together some day.' She began to wail again.

Lizzie's heart went on strike.

No . . . he can't have.

'Andi, what's happened?'

Is he dead?

'He collapsed yesterday,' she cried. 'We called an ambulance, but he was in a bad way and he was transferred to a specialist unit in London. They've operated on him, but the doctors don't know if . . . if he's going to pull through.'

Lizzie began to tremble all over. 'Andi, that's terrible. I don't know what to say.'

'I think they'll let you see him if you can get to the hospital? I can text you the postcode. It's supposed to be family only, but I'm sure they'd make an exception under the circumstances.'

A swell of nausea began to rise from her stomach to her throat. 'Actually, Andi, I'm getting married,' she said softly.

'Oh . . . I see,' she sniffed. 'When's the wedding?'

'No, I mean I'm getting married today!'

'You're *what*?'

'I'm getting married now. Well, in about 15 minutes. But then we leave straight for the airport. I won't be back for a fortnight.'

'Oh, Lizzie, I had no idea!' said Andi. 'I'd never have

called you if I'd known it was your wedding day. Now I feel awful.' She began to cry even louder.

'No, please don't. You're absolutely right to tell me. Please send over the address. I'm going to come and see him the second I get back.'

'Well, of course you'll be welcome to see him, if he's still . . . you know . . .' Andi was clearly having the most uncomfortable conversation of her life.

There was a loud knock at the door.

'Andi, I think we're about to leave. I'm so incredibly sorry. But I'll call you this afternoon, as soon as I can, OK? Please give my love to Alex.'

As she hung up the phone and tried to stand, Lizzie felt like the room was swimming. The knock on the door came again. 'Just a second,' she shouted, shakily pouring herself a glass of water and gulping it down. 'I'm coming.'

'Elizabeth, our car will be here any minute,' said her father. 'I think it's time we went.'

'OK, Dad.' She took a deep breath and tried to compose herself. *You can do this. Everyone's at the church, waiting for you.* She picked up her diamanté clutch and opened the door.

'Are you feeling alright?' asked her dad. 'You've gone white as a sheet. Did you eat breakfast?'

'Yes, I had a croissant,' was the last thing Lizzie remembered saying before she hit the floor.

When she came to, the first thing she saw was her father's anxious face, fanning her with his now-unfolded speech.

356

'What should we do?' he was asking the photographer in a panic. 'Should we get her to a hospital? She's supposed to be at the church in ten minutes!'

'I'm not sure,' said the photographer, who was at least not attempting to capture the latest turn of events for posterity. 'Is there someone we could call?'

'What, like my wife?'

'I was thinking more like the hotel doctor.'

Lizzie sat upwards, her head spinning.

What am I going to do about Alex?

'Oh, thank goodness,' said her dad, still wafting his paper in front of her in an exaggerated motion. 'Are you alright? Does anything hurt? You really had me worried there.'

She was feeling more than a little worried herself. *Do I delay the wedding, go over to the hospital? Or do I get married first, then go afterwards?*

'Earth to Lizzie!' he said nervously. 'Here, sit on the bed for a second.' She obliged, and he poured her another glass of water. 'Get this down you.'

She took a small sip. 'What's the time?' she asked, still feeling shaky.

'It's ten to one,' said the photographer, pointing to the clock on the back wall. 'We're due to be there in a minute.'

'Well, they'll just have to hang on,' said her dad. 'Until I'm sure she's alright, we're not going anywhere.'

Lizzie checked herself up and down. Nothing seemed too badly bruised, and by some miracle the dress was still in one piece. Then she spotted a crushed crystal pin lying tragically on the floor, and her hand flew up to her head.

'Did I ruin my hair?' she asked in a daze.

The photographer took a closer look. 'No, I think we can salvage it,' she said. 'He's sprayed it in place pretty well.' She reached for her camera bag and pulled out a packet of hair grips. 'A couple of the curls have fallen down, but I can pin them back up with these.'

'You keep hair grips with your cameras?' asked Mr Sparkes. He looked quietly impressed.

'Let's just say that this isn't my first wedding. Over the years I've become quite good at hair and beauty touch-ups. I've seen all kinds of things mess up a bride's look – rain, wind, pigeons . . .'

'Pigeons?'

How can they be talking about birds at a time like this?

'Don't ask. The key thing is just to fix it, fast.' She moved behind Lizzie and pinned a grip into place. 'Think you're the first bride that's ever fainted on me, though.'

'I'm sorry.'

'Please. It's hardly your fault.'

Hmmm. If I'd listened to Megan and not sent that text, then none of this would have happened. She swallowed guiltily. *But if I hadn't done that, I wouldn't have known that Alex was in the hospital, would I?*

'Hold extra still for a second,' said the photographer. 'I've just got one more to pop in . . . There. How does that look?'

Lizzie spun around in front of the mirror. 'It's great,' she said slowly, her mind a million miles away. 'You're a lifesaver.'

Am I really going to do this while Alex might be dying?

'Well, if everything's alright here now, don't the three of us have a wedding to get to?' said her father. 'Poor Josh is going to think you're not coming!'

'Yes, we should go,' said the photographer, handing Lizzie her bag and her bouquet, and ushering her out of the door.

'Right, then, love.' Her dad pressed the switch on the wall, causing the spotlights to dim. 'Let's get you hitched without any more hitches.'

30

Here comes the bride . . .

It was possible to hear a pin drop in the back of the bridal car. Lizzie had already asked her dad not to make any emotional speeches en route to the church, just in case he made her cry and ruined all her make-up. The photographer sat quietly, too, observing the unspoken code of silence like an obedient visitor at the library. But with no casual chatter to keep everyone occupied, Lizzie's thoughts began to run away with themselves, screaming in her head until she thought it would burst.

What are you doing?

She tried to distract herself by counting the seconds on her father's watch.

Why aren't you going to the hospital?

'Nearly there, Miss,' said the driver cheerily. 'I've just got to go round the one-way system.'

'Uh-huh,' Lizzie mumbled.

When you close your eyes, who do you see yourself with? Josh or Alex? Josh or Alex? JOSH OR ALEX?

'I don't know!' she blurted out.

'Don't know what?' asked her father, looking concerned.

'I don't know . . . what everyone's going to think about me turning up so late,' she fibbed.

'Well, you'll certainly have them wondering,' he said, removing his paper from his pocket yet again. 'You know, I should probably add a little joke about you fainting in my speech. Do you think that would be alright?' He checked himself before she could object. 'Maybe I should run it past your mother first. She warned me not to improvise.'

'We're here!' said the driver, pulling over to the kerb. Lizzie could see Megan standing outside, flashing her cosmetically whitened teeth with the brightest of smiles. The driver came round to the rear door and helped her out of the vehicle.

'Thank you,' said Lizzie. 'I suppose we'll see you soon.'

'I can't park here, Miss,' he said. 'I'm just going to pull in round the corner and wait until you come out. Have a wonderful wedding.'

'Right, Lizzie, we'd better get inside,' said her dad, extending out his elbow. 'Shall we?'

'OK,' said Lizzie, suddenly feeling like she was having an out-of-body experience as she floated towards the church. 'I guess we should.'

With everyone finally in position, the organist struck up the opening chords of the processional. Twenty rows of guests all stood and swivelled around to face the back.

Lizzie could spot Naomi and Mel, Auntie Carole and Caz, Gareth and her other friends from uni, all craning to get a better look at the bride.

She did not let her gaze linger on any of them, but stared straight ahead to Josh, so handsome in his smart grey suit. Then she glanced up at her dad, and remembered the words her mum had once told her.

When I saw your father standing at the other end of the aisle, I just knew that there was no one else I'd rather marry . . .

When Lizzie looked down the end of the aisle, she wished she was marrying Alex.

'I can't do this,' she whispered to her dad. 'Something doesn't feel right.'

'You don't feel right? Where you hit your head?' The look on his face was one of pure concern.

'No, *this* – the wedding – doesn't feel right.'

Now her dad looked as if he were the one who might faint. 'What are you talking about?' he said. 'Now's not the time for jokes.'

She ignored him and spun round to face her best friend. 'Megan,' she hissed. 'I need to talk to you.'

'What, *now*?'

'Yes, now. Can we go outside?'

They did an about turn, a curious chatter rippling through the pews. The organist stopped playing as the two of them stepped through the large wooden doors.

'What's the matter?'

'I . . . um . . . I . . .' Lizzie was breathing so fast she thought she might hyperventilate. 'I don't think I can go through with this.'

Megan put a hand on her shoulder. 'Because of Alex?' she asked gently.

'Yes. I'm in love with him.'

'I knew it,' Megan sighed. 'Though it would have been a lot better if *you'd* known before now.' She gestured towards the packed church. 'What are you going to do about all this?'

Lizzie felt like she might pass out again. 'I've no idea,' she said, her voice wobbling. 'I'm going to have to talk to Josh. Can you stall?'

'Shit, when you said you wanted me to help co-ordinate stuff, I thought I'd be handing out confetti and things. I didn't realise you were going to get me to call it all off.'

'Oh Megan, what am I going to do?' She leaned forwards and gasped for air, dropping her bouquet to the ground. Her body was starting to feel like it was made of paper, slowly crumpling under the tension.

'Alright, don't panic,' said Megan, rubbing her shoulders. 'I'll deal with it. Just stand up and try to breathe.'

Just then Josh burst out of the church, his forehead lined with worry. 'What's going on?' he said quietly. 'Are you OK?'

Megan looked uncomfortable. 'You two should talk. I'll just wait . . . inside.' She picked up Lizzie's lilies and hurried back into the church.

'I don't understand,' he said, looking nervous. 'Is there something you want to tell me?'

Lizzie felt so awful she wished the pavement would split in half and swallow her. There was no wedding guide for what she was about to do.

'I don't think I can marry you,' she whispered, her heart lodged in her throat.

Josh looked gobsmacked. 'Is it Alex?'

'Yes.' A tear slid down her cheek. 'I told you everything, honestly I did. And I really thought I could do this, but I just found out today that he's in the hospital and it's made me realise that—'

'You don't love me any more,' finished Josh.

'I do love you,' said Lizzie softly. 'I love you so much I almost married you.' She hesitated, both afraid and relieved to tell the truth. 'But I don't think that would be fair to either of us.'

Josh reached for her hands, cupping them in his. 'Please don't do this, Lizzie,' he pleaded. 'For all you know, Alex might not even be here next year, and then what? You'll be on your own.' He frowned. 'I think you're just confused at the moment, that's all. You don't mean it.'

'I do,' she confessed. 'I'm so sorry.'

'You're sorry? You're *sorry* . . .' He let go of her, looking like he might cry. 'So let me get this straight: you're breaking up with me on our wedding day?'

Lizzie stared down at the floor. *I'm the worst person who ever lived.*

'How can you humiliate me like this?' he continued. 'In front of our families? All our friends?'

'I feel terrible about it, believe me,' she cried. 'I never meant for things to turn out this way. You've got every right to be angry with me.'

Josh stared at her angst-ridden face.

'Angry?' he shouted. 'I'm past angry. I'm completely . . .' He began to choke up. 'I'm gutted.' He wiped his eye with the back of his hand. 'I thought we were going to spend our lives together.'

'So did I,' said Lizzie. 'But one day you're going to meet someone else – someone way better than me – and you'll realise it happened for a reason.' She twisted the diamond ring on her left hand until it slid over her knuckle. 'Here, you should have this,' she said gently, placing it in his palm. 'I hope that one day you'll be able to forgive me.'

'I doubt it,' he said.

She nodded sadly. 'I understand.'

'No,' he said finally. 'I doubt I'll meet someone better than you.' He bent down to kiss her softly on the cheek, the scent of his aftershave so achingly familiar. Then, without glancing back, he walked slowly around the corner and disappeared.

Megan stuck her head out of the double doors, waving for Lizzie to come closer. 'I can't stall much longer,' she said. 'Your dad's starting to go ballistic and I'm out of excuses.' She looked up and down the street, realising the groom had gone. 'What did you tell Josh?'

'The truth. That I couldn't marry him.'

Lizzie rubbed her eyes, still in shock at what she'd just done. In about 20 seconds, her parents were going to kill her. Literally. Not to mention Josh's. She had never felt so horrible in her entire life.

And yet, she couldn't deny the truth: the heaviness that had been crushing her was lifted. She knew now for certain that her heart belonged to Alex. And there was no way she could give it to anyone else while he was lying in the hospital.

'That poor guy. He must feel like Adam Sandler in *The Wedding Singer*.'

'Look, you can make me feel as bad as you like later, but right now I've got to go.'

'What? Go where?'

'Alex is in the hospital. It's an emergency, so I need to get there fast.'

'OK,' said Megan, rallying. 'I think your car's still round the corner. I can stay here and tell everyone that they won't need their confetti after all.'

'Thanks!' said Lizzie, hitching up the train of her dress and setting off up the street as fast as her silver heels could go. She sprinted around the corner, sparkly pins flying from her hair as she raced along the pavement. To her relief, the bridal car was still parked by the side of the road, the driver waiting patiently inside instead of heading off for a coffee. He looked visibly perplexed as she flung open the car door and hopped into the back seat.

'Have you forgotten something, Miss?'

'No.' She whipped out her mobile. 'I need you to take me to this address please, as fast as you can.'

The driver pulled himself together and turned on the engine. 'Of course, if that's what you want. It must be urgent?'

'It is,' said Lizzie, trying to catch her breath. 'It's a matter of life or death.'

Fifteen minutes later, they pulled into the hospital car park. Lizzie rummaged around in her clutch for some cash, only to realise all she had in there was a tissue, some lip gloss, her mobile and a couple of spare hair grips. 'I'm so sorry – I'd give you a tip but I don't have any money on me,' she told the driver.

'Please don't worry, miss,' he said politely. 'You look like you've got a lot on your plate. It's been my pleasure, really.'

'Thank you.' Wriggling out of the back seat, she ran across the car park towards the main entrance, her shimmering white train skimming over the dusty concrete. She burst through the automatic doors and grabbed the nearest nurse she could find. The woman looked at her like she'd just escaped from the psychiatric ward.

'Er, can I help you?'

'Yes, I'm trying to find Alex Jackson,' said Lizzie frantically. 'He was brought in here yesterday, and he just had a big operation, and I need to see him . . .'

'OK, take a breath,' said the nurse. 'Let me check with

our receptionist.' She went over to the main desk and a short, grey-haired lady typed something into the computer. Lizzie looked around the nearby waiting area, suddenly self-conscious of the fact that everyone was staring at her. A little girl with a cast on one arm tugged at her mother's jacket with the other. 'Look Mummy, a princess,' she said loudly, her mouth hanging open in awe.

Lizzie was relieved when the nurse came back. 'OK, I've found Mr Jackson. He's in the red wing, ward D, in one of the intensive care bays. Take the lift to the third floor, turn right and then just follow the signs.'

'Thanks,' said Lizzie. She raced over to the row of lifts and hit all the buttons pointing upwards. The one on the far right arrived first, though its occupants then seemed to take an eternity to get out, doing a double take as they spotted her. *Hasn't anyone ever seen a bride before?* Finally, she was able to get inside and select the third floor, her heart thumping as the metal doors slid shut.

Please be alive. Please be alive. Please be alive.

When the lift finally reached its destination, Lizzie shot out of the doors and turned right, almost knocking over a porter wheeling an empty bed.

'Hey,' he yelled. 'This is a hospital!'

'Sorry,' she called, without looking back or slowing down, her twinkling train still trailing behind her as she sprinted past wards A, B and C.

But as she got closer to D, she suddenly felt a strong dose of fear in her bones. *What if I'm too late? What if, when he needed me, I wasn't there?* Her questions hung heavily in the air, threatening to come crashing down around the eerily quiet ward.

Before she could have a total meltdown, one of the nurses approached her. 'Hello, are you lost?' she said, clocking Lizzie's attire but politely not commenting on it.

'No, hopefully I'm in the right place,' she replied. 'I'm looking for Alex, Alex Jackson.'

'Ah,' said the sister, pulling the kind of face that medics pulled on *Casualty* when they were about to deliver bad news. 'Are you a relative?'

'Not quite,' said Lizzie, her voice shaking. 'But I wouldn't be here if it wasn't urgent.' She gestured to her wedding dress, and the nurse nodded sympathetically.

'Look, why don't you take a seat for a moment?'

Lizzie burst into tears. 'No . . . oh, no . . . he's gone, isn't he? I didn't even get to say goodbye!' The sound of her loud wails echoed around the sterile corridor.

'No, he's not dead.' The nurse put a sympathetic arm around her and steered her towards some uncomfortable-looking plastic chairs. 'But he is very ill, and he's currently in a coma. We don't want him to be overcrowded, so we're limiting visitors, and it's usually close family only. I'll need to check with his parents first to see if they're willing to make an exception for . . .'

'For however long it takes!' she said adamantly.

'No, I meant for you. What's your name?'

'Oh. Lizzie. Lizzie Sparkes.'

'OK, Lizzie. I'm Jenny. You stay here for a minute while I have a word with his mum and dad, and I'll be right back.'

'Alright.' Lizzie nodded, retrieving the sole tissue from her sparkly clutch and blowing her nose loudly.

Jenny disappeared into a side room, and Lizzie surveyed the ward. There was row after row of curtains, giving each patient a modicum of privacy from the person next to them, and a number of high-tech machines lined up against one wall, ready to leap into action in an emergency. There was a small vending machine by the nurses' station providing some basic sustenance; no doubt the relatives of those in intensive care were too scared to make the long trek down to the main canteen, in case anything happened while they were off queuing for lunch. *Don't you die on me, Alex,* Lizzie willed him. *Don't even think about it.*

A nurse pushed an elderly man in a wheelchair along the corridor, heading for the communal toilets. 'Hello, Martha,' he said. 'You look beautiful, my love.'

'I'm sorry?' said Lizzie.

'I think you remind him of his late wife,' the nurse explained quietly. 'She looked a lot like you – especially dressed like that. He's been showing me photos of their wedding day.'

'I won't be long,' said the man. 'I'll see you at the church!'

'OK,' said Lizzie, and blew him a friendly kiss. *Some people do find their soulmate,* she thought. *I just always thought I'd grow old with mine.*

Just then, Alex's parents stepped out into the corridor. Though it had been little more than a decade since she last saw them, they looked about 20 years older; their faces worn with tragedy. But she recognised them instantly, as they did her.

'Oh, Lizzie, would you look at you,' said Mrs Jackson, her hands flying up to her cheeks. 'Andi told us you were getting married today, but we certainly weren't expecting you to rush straight over afterwards.' She looked down the corridor. 'Where's your husband?'

'I don't have one,' said Lizzie, wringing her hands. Mrs Jackson looked bewildered. 'I . . . well . . . I couldn't go through with the wedding. Not once I knew what was happening here.'

'Oh, I'm so sorry to hear that! I know Andi would never have bothered you today if she'd known.'

'No, I'm glad she called me. It made me realise I was making a mistake.'

'I see.' Mrs Jackson's eyes were red and puffy, but the kindness in them remained. 'Why don't you go in and see Alex? He's not awake at the moment, but the doctors think he might still be able to hear us, so it's good to keep talking to him. We'll sit out here for a bit so just call if you need us.'

'OK.' Lizzie stepped into the cubicle, afraid of what she would find when she drew back the curtain. Alex was always so spirited that she couldn't possibly picture him in a coma, and she knew it would destroy her to see him in any kind of pain. Her hand shook as she peeled back the flimsy fabric and saw him lying on the bed for the first time. But to her surprise he looked more peaceful than she was expecting, as though he was simply in a deep sleep.

'Hey there, stranger.'

Lizzie spun round in the direction of the voice and found herself facing Andi, who had got up from an armchair in the corner. She was paler and thinner, and her once blonde hair was now a mousy brown, but the family resemblance was still clear.

'Andi! I didn't see you. I'm so sorry to hear about Alex.'

'Why aren't you at your wedding?' Andi's face flushed bright red. 'Is it because of me? I shouldn't have called you.'

'No, I'm here because I was getting married to the wrong person,' she said. 'You did me a favour. Thank you.'

Andi's curiosity got the better of her. 'So are you, like, the runaway bride?'

'You could say that.'

'How did that go down with everyone?'

'I honestly don't know. They're still there and I'm here. I don't imagine they'll be best pleased, though. I'll probably have to spend the next 100 years paying my dad back for the reception.'

Andi gave her a hug. 'I bet Alex would like to hear about it. Why don't you talk to him for a bit while I grab something to eat? I could murder a Mars Bar.'

Lizzie suspected she wasn't hungry at all, but was just trying to give her some space. 'Sure, I can talk to him for a while,' she said. 'How did his surgery go?'

'Hard to tell,' she sighed. 'The doctors seemed to think it went well, under the circumstances. They managed to remove a large chunk of the tumour that was pressing on his brain. Not all of it, but enough that it should give him more time. Only now he's not waking up and no one seems to know why. It's almost like he just lost the will to live.'

Lizzie shook her head. 'Alex will pull through. He's a fighter.'

'Yeah, I used to think so,' said Andi quietly. 'But he's been different these past couple of weeks, you know. Distant. And sad.'

'He's been through so much,' said Lizzie. 'But he can't give up now. Who knows what new treatments might be around the corner?'

'I really hope you're right,' said Andi. 'Maybe you should tell him that while I go and check on the folks.' She bent down and kissed Alex gently on the forehead. 'Don't go anywhere, bro. I love you. I'll be right outside.'

As she left the room, closing the curtain behind her, Lizzie moved closer to Alex. His face was pale, but still handsome; his breathing shallow but audible. If it wasn't for the bandage wrapped tightly around his head, and the IV feeding into his arm, she could have sworn he was taking an afternoon nap.

'So it's just you and me now,' she whispered, holding

his right hand, which was cold to the touch. 'You need to wake up soon, because there's lots I need to tell you. I called off the wedding . . .' She hesitated, glancing at him to see if there was any reaction. There wasn't. 'Of course, that was after I'd already fainted in my hotel room. I think as far as wedding days go, this one was about as crap as it gets. Josh won't ever want to see me again, and I doubt my mum and dad are going to be speaking to me anytime soon, either. So you really need to get better, otherwise I'm not going to have anyone to talk to . . .'

Still he didn't move. 'I'm really sorry if I wasn't there for you enough after Connor died, and that I was so angry when you first came back. I've been thinking about it a lot lately, and I've realised how hard it must be to lose someone you love.' She swallowed. 'But I'm not ready to lose you yet, Alex, I'm really not. I don't know how much longer we've got, but I promise you we're going to spend that time together. I just need you to come back to me. Please. I love you so much.'

She was crying again now, fat teardrops rolling down her face and on to his hand. 'I'm not supposed to be making you soggy,' she said, grabbing a tissue from a box on the bedside table and dabbing his skin dry. She was just about to throw it in the bin when she thought she saw the tiniest flicker of movement in his index finger. *Is that a reflex? Or did he just respond?*

'Alex, it's me, Lizzie. Can you hear me? If you can, please try to move your finger again.' She looked down at his hand, but it was still. 'Alex, you can do this. I need you to wake up so we can be together, like we were meant to be.' This time, his finger twitched, causing her to jump up so fast she almost fell over the chair.

'Come quickly!' she shouted, rushing out into the corridor and waving at his family.

'What is it?' said Mr Jackson, leaping to his feet. 'What's happened?' Panic was written all over his face. 'Do we need the nurse?'

'I think he just moved,' said Lizzie. 'I was talking to him and holding his hand and he started to move his finger. I think he can hear me!'

All four of them piled back into the cubicle and looked at Alex expectantly. He lay there, still as a statue again, but Lizzie wasn't ready to give up that easily.

'Alex, it's Lizzie, and your family. I know you can hear me now.' She took his cold hand in hers. 'Can you squeeze my hand, please?' Nothing. 'Can you move your finger?' There was a long pause, and then suddenly his finger jerked. 'See! Did you see that?'

'Yes, I saw it!' shouted Mrs Jackson. 'Alex, darling, it's Mum. We're all waiting for you to give us a smile.' She gestured frantically at Lizzie on the other side of the bed. 'You try again, Lizzie. He seems to be responding to you.'

'Alex, we're all here for you when you're ready to wake up,' she said. 'Your family love you, and I love you, and I need you to open those eyes for me so I can tell you to your face.'

She perched on the edge of his bed, the bright white of her wedding dress merging with the sterile white of the hospital linen. Lowering her face down close to his, she whispered, 'Alex, will you marry me?'

There was a long silence, and then his eyelids fluttered and closed again, before they settled in a half-open state. He stared straight at Lizzie in all of her ethereal attire.

'Am I dead?' he said at last.

Lizzie didn't know whether to laugh or cry. 'No, you're not,' she said eventually, her voice cracking. 'You're very much alive, and you have to promise me you'll stay that way for as long as possible.'

'I'll try.' He looked at her outfit again. 'Am I too late?'

'Too late for what?'

His voice was thin and hoarse. 'To stop the wedding.'

'Yes,' she said. 'Yes, you are – because I already stopped the wedding.'

'Really?' The corners of his mouth crept up into a smile.

'Yes, really.' Lizzie leaned over and kissed him gently on the lips, as the Jacksons all hugged one another tightly. 'But you have to promise to hurry up and get out of this hospital, because I'm expecting my second wedding to be better.'

'OK. I will.'

'Actually, it's "I do",' she smiled. 'But we can work on that.'

Epilogue

Two years later

Lizzie lay on a lounger beneath a straw parasol, gazing out at the azure waves and the tall rock formations rising majestically from the water. *This place is incredible. I can see why he loved it here.* She had promised Alex that if anything happened to him, she would get a plane to Thailand and tell his friends there the news in person. 'You don't need to do that,' he'd said. 'Just call them. You'll hate the long flight.' But after everything they had been through, she was determined to do this one last thing for him. 'No, it's OK,' she said. 'I'm sick of being scared. I want to meet them for myself.' Alex had relented then, seeming pleased about that. 'Well, it's so beautiful there, I think the trip would do you good. You can't stay sad for long when you're staring out over the ocean.'

I won't be sad for ever, I swear, she promised silently, knowing that had been his biggest fear. *But it's hard right now. I just miss you so much.*

The flight had not been easy, with her stomach churning and her throat tightening at the slightest turbulence. But every time she felt afraid, she closed her eyes and could almost feel Alex placing a protective arm around her shoulders, the way he used to do whenever she felt frightened about the future. 'I can't imagine life without you,' she told him once, tearfully. 'Well, you'd better start imagining a great one,' he'd replied. 'Because you're going to have to live for both of us, so you can't screw it up.'

I'll try my best. It seemed more important than ever now to do something with her life, something that would have made her husband really proud. *Husband.* The word still sounded funny sometimes in her head. It had taken her a year to get used to calling him that, and then, just a few short months after she'd started getting the hang of it, she suddenly didn't need to any more. She was a wife without a husband, like a knife without a fork, or a night without day. It felt like the earth should have stopped, yet somehow it kept turning, whether or not she wanted to come along for the ride.

But she had no regrets about marrying him, not even for a second. *And I never will.* Their spring wedding had been perfect. They had both wanted to avoid a big bash – much to her dad's relief – and instead sealed the deal with a quiet register office ceremony in front of just their parents, Andi, Sam and Megan. Lizzie wore a pretty cream sundress from Reiss, and Alex wore a pale blue linen suit that brought out the colour of his eyes. 'I could be your something blue,' he'd joked when he tried it on.

After the ceremony, the nine of them celebrated at a

charming little inn on the coast, where they sat outdoors and enjoyed a three-course feast under the stars, washed down with plenty of bubbly. Alex wasn't meant to be drinking alcohol in case it interfered with his medication, but he insisted on having a couple of glasses anyway, which went straight to his shaved head. An hour later, he was chuckling away like a naughty schoolboy who'd spiked the punch at the disco.

'Are you drunk already?' asked Lizzie.

'No, my good wife, I am 100 per cent sober,' he replied, almost falling off his chair. 'Well, maybe 90 per cent. But who's counting?'

As she looked into his eyes, she saw nothing but happiness; there was no thought today of anything that might spoil the moment. He was here, he was alive, and he was hers.

'Should I make a toast?' said her dad, clinking on the side of his glass with his dessert spoon.

'Yay, speech! Speech!' cried Megan, who had quaffed even more champagne than usual and was in high spirits.

'Well, I'll keep this short . . .' he said.

'Thank goodness,' heckled Lizzie.

'I'll pretend I didn't hear that,' he said. 'Anyway, I'd just like to thank you all for being here today to see these two tie the knot. Now I'm sure it's no secret that this isn't the first time I've walked Elizabeth down the aisle—'

'Dad!' she yelped, mortified.

'—but it is the first time she's gone through with the

wedding. And seeing the love between her and Alex today, I think we all know that she made the right decision.'

'Does that mean I don't have to pay you back that ten grand?' Lizzie muttered. Once again, Mr Sparkes pretended not to hear.

'But a wedding is more than a union between two people – it's also a union between two families,' he continued. 'And nothing makes me happier than to welcome Frank and Pamela and Andi into ours. We are all joined together now, and I for one couldn't be more thrilled. So let's raise a glass' – to which the group dutifully obliged – 'to the bride and groom, and to family.'

'Here, here!'

'Cheers!'

'To family!'

It had been, hands down, the best day of Lizzie and Alex's life. But their marital bliss didn't stop there: over the next few months it grew and spread, at an even more accelerated rate than the cancer, squeezing every last bit of joy from the precious time they had left. They camped out at three different festivals, saw Alex's favourite band live at Wembley, and spent five glorious days shored up in a Devon bolthole on an unofficial 'mini-moon'. On their last evening, they'd even rocked up to the local open mic night, where Alex surprised her by playing an incredible acoustic version of Train's *Drops of Jupiter*. 'Well, I've seen you sing, remember?' he said. 'I think it's about time I returned the favour.'

The One

At moments like these, when he was so full of life, she came close to forgetting that he was staring death in the face. From time to time, she let herself imagine that a miracle might come their way: that the doctors would declare it had all been a mistake, or that they had discovered a pioneering new treatment that would turn out to be the cure they'd been waiting for.

But Alex's miracle must have made its way to someone else, because he died two months ago after going into a sudden decline, his organs shutting down in rapid succession. If Lizzie thought he had broken her heart once before, it was nothing compared to the pain when he left her permanently, his family all by his side. She was so shattered she couldn't even cry. It was as if his death had closed off even her most basic functions, and she could barely remember how to breathe, let alone weep. Everyone warned her not to make any big decisions while she was still grieving, but two weeks later she followed in Naomi's footsteps and finally quit her job. She wasn't sure what she was going to do next, but she knew that Alex believed she could do something special, and that was enough for now.

Start that book you always wanted to write, he sometimes said to her in her sleep. *Just put some words on pages.*

So here she was now, with a notebook in her hand, scribbling down ideas for her first novel. Some of them were dreadful, a couple had potential, but she knew that she would eventually find The One. In that sense, she thought, books were a little like love: you had to trust your instinct and go with your heart, even if you made mistakes along the way.

She wondered for a minute what Josh was up to now; whether some day he might speak to her again. She hadn't seen him since the wedding-that-wasn't: he'd made himself scarce when she went to fetch her belongings from the flat, and only left her a short note saying she owed him £900 for the final month's rent and bills. She had sent a letter with her cheque to say how much she regretted hurting him, but he didn't reply. *Not that I can blame him.* Still, she hoped he might change his mind someday and finally forgive her. She'd heard on the grapevine that he'd moved in with his new girlfriend, a sports reporter for the local paper. Wherever he was, and whatever he was up to, she just wanted him to be happy.

All of a sudden her phone beeped, piercing her thoughts. She sat up. It was a text from her mum: Hi love, how are you today?

Both her parents had been nervous about her travelling so far, especially in her fragile state, but they accepted that she wanted to meet the friends Alex had left behind. Breaking the news to his mates had been deeply upsetting: some hadn't even realised that he was ill, while others had known but – like her – found it impossible to believe that he was gone. But she was glad she had been able to tell them in person, and they in turn had gone out of their way to be welcoming and show her Alex's favourite hang-outs. That was both comforting and hard: sometimes she felt so close to him she almost expected him to walk through the door.

I'm OK, just chilling by the beach, she typed back. It was more than her life was worth not to respond within the hour; once she had forgotten to reply for a whole day and her mum was on the verge of buying a plane ticket to come out and find her.

Any idea when you'll be home? pinged the reply. Her mum made no secret of the fact that she was desperate for her daughter to return. 'Why do you have to go out there all alone?' she had asked more than once. 'Because, it's something I think I need to do by myself,' Lizzie tried to explain. 'And besides, it'll do me good to get away for a while.'

Not just yet, she typed. I'm going to stay a couple more weeks. But I'll be back soon, I promise. Love you. xx

We love you too, replied her mum, abandoning her attempts at nagging for another day. Take care. xx

Lizzie sighed with relief. She knew her mother meant well, as did everyone else, but what she really needed at the moment was space: space to think, space to grieve, space to get her head straight. Now more than ever, she understood why Alex had fled halfway around the world after Connor's death, and she wished that he was here so she was able to tell him so. 'I get it now,' she whispered, the words drifting from her lips and off over the Andaman Sea.

She sent a quick text to Megan while she had her phone out, just to check in and say hi. When she had announced that she was going to Thailand, Megan had immediately offered to take a sabbatical from her job and go with her. 'No, I can't expect you to drop everything,' said Lizzie. 'I'm OK to go by myself, really.'

'Work will understand,' said Megan. 'And if they don't – well, screw it, I'll quit and come anyway.'

'What about Lloyd?' Lizzie asked. 'I thought things were getting serious between you two?'

Much to everyone's surprise, Megan had been dating Lloyd since they ran into one another at a glamorous hair awards bash and he confessed he'd just split up from his partner. 'Oh, what was his name?' Megan had asked.

'Nicole.'

'Oh, I . . . I . . .'

'Let me guess, you thought I was gay?' he'd said, bemused. 'You can be a straight hairdresser, you know.'

'Yeah, you're right. I don't know why I assumed . . .' Suddenly her hand flew up to her mouth. 'Oh! And I was running around half-naked in front of you at Lizzie's wedding. Well, non-wedding. I'm officially embarrassed.'

'Don't be,' he'd said, grinning. 'With that figure, you've got nothing to be embarrassed about.' Three more champagnes and a cab ride later, he was back at her flat getting an action replay.

'Yeah, things are going great,' said Megan. 'But Lloyd knows what you've been through, Lizzie. He'd be supportive. And it's not like we'd be moving to Thailand . . .' she hesitated. 'Is it?'

'No! It's like an extended holiday.'

'Well, then, that's fine. He can manage without me for a month or so.'

'That's kind of you, Megan. Really it is. But it's not fair for you to put your whole life on hold, not for this. And besides . . .' she paused, 'I think I just need to get used to being by myself for a while.'

'Are you sure?'

'Yes.'

There was a hush on the other end of the line. 'OK,' she said eventually. 'But I want lots of texts and emails and postcards. Don't think you're going to get away from me that easily.'

'I won't.'

Sticking to her word, Lizzie sent a quick text. Hi Megan, hope all's good with you. It's beautiful here, and sunny too! Say hi to Lloyd for me. Miss you xxx

Thirty seconds later, she received one back: Hi gorgeous girl, glad you're OK. The weather here's crap. At least Lloyd's hot. Can't wait to catch up. xxx

Smiling, Lizzie put her phone away and turned her attention back to her notebook. But before she could write anything, a petite Thai waitress approached with an empty tray. 'Hello, Mrs Jackson,' she said, in perfect English. 'Can I get you a drink?'

'Yes, thanks,' said Lizzie. 'Just some bottled water please.'

'No problem,' nodded the waitress. 'How do you like the bar?'

'I love it.'

Lizzie surveyed the beachside venue just behind her, with its charming outdoor terrace, whitewashed walls and spacious, though currently empty, dance floor. She had stopped by there the previous night, when the place was packed with both locals and tourists, but it looked different during the day: calmer and cuter. She read the sign outside for the 17th time, just to check it said what she thought it said.

Lizzie's Bar.

Yes, it definitely still said that.

In the short but precious time that they had been married, Alex had never once let on about this place; she wasn't sure why, but she guessed he must have liked the idea of one more surprise. It was only when his will was produced by his solicitor that Lizzie even discovered its existence – a shock that was soon doubled when she learned he had left his share of it to her, along with the small profit he had made in the six years since he'd opened it. The first time she set foot in there, she could feel his presence everywhere, from the laid-back vibe to the photo of Connor hung lovingly on the wall behind a row of spirits. It was Alex to a T, and she drank it in, revelling in the dream he had realised without her even knowing. But it was the name on the door that meant the most: the knowledge that, even when they'd been 6,000 miles apart, his heart had still belonged with her.

Lizzie had never worked in a bar before, let alone owned

one, and she had no idea what on earth it entailed. Fortunately Alex's friend and business partner, who had done a great job overseeing the place in his absence, was only too keen to continue on a permanent basis. Lizzie would take on a more advisory role, keeping in touch via Skype to make sure that everything was running smoothly. With the modest income from the bar, and the money Alex had left her, she would have financial freedom to pursue her dream of being a writer.

I'll make you proud of me, she thought. *The way I'm so proud of you.*

Just then, the waitress returned with her drink, and Lizzie took a long swig of the cool, refreshing water.

Ooof.

She felt the fleeting kick deep inside her belly. 'Oh, you like that, huh?' she whispered to her bump, stroking it over her sundress. 'Someone's feeling thirsty.'

As she reclined on her lounger, Lizzie looked back out to the ocean, enjoying the warmth of the sun on her legs. Soon she would barely be able to see her toes, but she loved watching her body change, shifting to accommodate the tiny life inside her.

In a way it was Alex's final surprise, she thought with a smile, though she wished he could have lived long enough to share the good news, and to see their little one grow up. He'd have loved their child to the heavens and back, and now it was up to her to tell them all about their daddy.

Inspired, she picked up her pen and began to write.

Acknowledgements

A grateful thanks must go to the following:

My amazing agent Judith Murray, rights director Kate Rizzo and the rest of the team at Greene & Heaton for your faith and invaluable guidance.

The wonderful folk at HarperImpulse who have worked so hard on the UK edition, especially Charlotte Ledger and Kimberley Young.

Everyone I met through the Curtis Brown Creative novel-writing course, who made me believe this might just be possible – including Anna Davis, Paul Golden, James Hall, Michael Hines, Dan MacDonald, Fiona Perrin, Christina Pishiris, Sara-Mae Tuson, Christopher Wakling and Lisa Williamson.

Bella Pearson for your thoughtful insight.

The One

Paddy Wex, Jean MacPherson, Dan Hogan and all the teachers who encouraged my passion for writing.

British Red Cross and others who assisted in my research.

My mum and dad for your love, patience, lifts, generosity and good advice. You are the best parents a girl could wish for.

My brother Stephen, the bravest person I ever met. You are missed every day, but that smile will live on forever.

My sister Kathryn, for your positive vibes from the other side of the planet.

Geoff, Gerry, Amy and Tristan, who give in-laws a good name, and my nephew Harrison, who would much rather be reading about superheroes.

My colleagues past and present for your kind support, particularly Sue Peart and the talented team at *YOU Magazine*. A special shout out to Cath Sheargold and co (Emerson, Kirsty, Leo, Pippa, Alice and James) for appreciating the importance of both grammar and cake.

My best friends Jenny, Louise, Helen, Joy, Gem and Nick, for just being yourselves over the years (and not being too embarrassed to hang out with me).

And finally my husband Rob, The One for me, and our son Zac, The One who melts my heart. This one is for you.

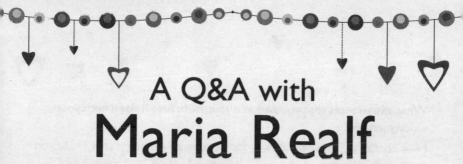

A Q&A with
Maria Realf

The One is such an emotional book — what prompted you to explore the themes in it that you do?

I think most people can relate to the idea of 'the one that got away' and wonder how they'd react if they ever crossed paths with their ex again — even if they'd really rather not! Originally I was planning to write more of a rom-com, but I know that life doesn't always deal the hand you expect, so I started adding twists and turns. In particular, cancer is something that has affected my own family and I found myself thinking a lot about life, love and loss. While Alex's story is fictional, it's a sad fact that brain tumours are now the biggest cancer killer of children and young adults under 40 in the UK.

Do you believe there is one soulmate for every person?

Ironically, given the title of my book, I'd have to say not necessarily — I'm sure some people enjoy more than one great romance during the course of their lives. That said, I knew within a few weeks of dating my husband that we would end up getting married...though it took him another ten years to propose!

Do you have a particular writing routine that you stick to? Or is every day different?

I've written everywhere from trains to coffee shops, libraries and beaches — you never know when inspiration is going to strike. I'd highly recommend joining (or forming) a writing group, too — for me that was invaluable, both in terms of feedback and motivation.

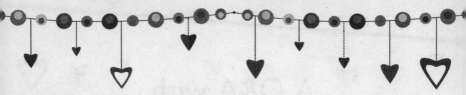

What experiences that you had as a journalist have helped with your writing a novel?

I was on staff at *Cosmopolitan Bride* for a couple of years, and later freelanced at *You & Your Wedding*, so that was a brilliant education in all things bridal! More generally, I think that working in the media helped me to edit my early drafts with a critical eye and taught me the discipline of sticking to deadlines.

Did you prefer working for newspapers or magazines? Why?

I've spent most of my career on magazines and have always enjoyed that environment – far from being like *The Devil Wears Prada*, the places I've worked have been friendly, fun and collaborative. There's something exciting about the way the whole team pulls together to produce a mag we can all be proud of.

Was *The One* inspired by any films or TV shows that you've seen?

Not directly, but I've always been partial to a good love triangle, from *Dawson's Creek* to *Bridget Jones's Diary*. Plus I'm a sucker for a will-they-won't-they wedding scene – I thought *Gavin & Stacey* did that brilliantly, as did *Friends*.

What is your favourite genre of book – do you write for the genre that you read?

Yes, I love contemporary romantic fiction and read a lot of books in that genre. I also enjoy the occasional dark, twisty thriller – I thought *Gone Girl* was a real game-changer.

What do you find helps you think through ideas when you're not sure how to develop a plot, or how to seal the fate of your characters?

For *The One*, I compiled a playlist of songs – some romantic, some sad, some from the era of Lizzie's uni days – to put me in the right mood for whatever chapter I was about to attempt. If I wasn't sure where a scene was heading, I found that writing longhand in my notebook really helped to get my creativity going...even if half of what I scribbled down was total gibberish.

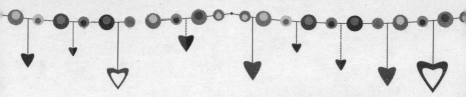

What is your favourite love story? (Film, theatre or novel?)

There are so many great romances out there I couldn't pick just one.
On the book front, *Me Before You*, *One Day*, *The Fault in our Stars* and
Great Expectations are a few of my favourites, and all share that theme of
enduring love prevailing over heartbreak. As for films, I never get tired of
The Notebook, *The English Patient*, *Dirty Dancing* and pretty much anything
by Richard Curtis. More recently, I loved *La La Land*, while the emotional
Manchester by the Sea had me bawling like a baby.

Did you know from the beginning how your story was going to end?

Once I'd decided against the traditional 'happy ever after', I knew how I
wanted my novel to start and finish. The first and last chapters came easily,
making the final edit with barely any tweaks, but the middle constantly
evolved as I went along. For example, I was originally going to have Lizzie
find out about Alex's illness just before the wedding, but that didn't give
them much time to reconnect, so I ended up revising the timeline.

What do you like about the creative process of writing, in comparison to your other experiences as a journalist in multiple different formats?

In journalism, accuracy is paramount, and you often have to stick to a
certain style and word count, whereas with a novel you're free to let your
imagination run wild. Also press deadlines are a lot tighter – you definitely
don't have the luxury of tinkering with pages for weeks on end!